UNDER A FALSE FLAG

UNDER A FALSE FLAG

Tom Gething

THE TACITURN PRESS
An Independent Publisher of Few Words

Published by The Taciturn Press

http://tomgething.wordpress.com

ISBN: 978-0-9854804-1-7

UAFF.CS.2014.05.15

Author's Note:
This is a work of fiction. It draws on the historical events surrounding
the 1973 coup d'état in Chile and its aftermath. A few real-life persons
associated with those events appear in this work as characters. However,
insofar as this work expresses any opinions or theories about the coup
or the persons involved, those opinions and theories are solely the
product of the author's imagination.

Cover Design: Elizabeth Gething

Cover Photo: © Marcelo Montecino
http://marcelomontecino.blogspot.com

Printed in the United States of America

For Janet

List of Acronyms

CODE Confederación de la Democracia (Confederation for Democracy, coalition of right and center opposition parties)

CWHD Chief, Western Hemisphere Division

DCI Director of Central Intelligence

DCOS Deputy Chief of Station

ECLA Economic Commission for Latin America (UN)

ITT International Telephone & Telegraph Corporation

MIR Movimiento del la Izquierda Revolucionaria (Movement of the Revolutionary Left, extreme left paramilitary organization)

MLN Movimiento de Liberación Nacional (National Liberation Movement, extreme left organization)

MUI Movimiento Universitario de la Izquierda (University Movement of the Left, sub-group of the MIR)

NOC Non-Official Cover

NSC National Security Council (US)

PDC Partido Demócrata Cristiano (Christian Democratic Party)

PyL Patria y Libertad (Fatherland and Liberty, extreme right paramilitary organization)

PN Partido Nacional (National Party, on the far right)

RMD Related Missions Directive

SDR Surveillance Detection Run

UP Unidad Popular (Popular Unity, coalition of Socialist, Marxist and Communist parties)

USG United States Government

Our actions are nothing but a patchwork…and we want to gain honor under false flags. Virtue will not be followed except for her own sake; and if we sometimes borrow her mask for some other purpose, she promptly snatches it from our face.

—Michel de Montaigne, Of the inconsistency of our actions

"If we give it to A and A gives it to B and C and D," the official said, "in a sense it's true that D got it but the question is—did we give it to A knowing that D would get it?" The official added that it's "awfully hard" to maintain control over local field operatives, particularly when large sums of cash were involved.

—Seymour M. Hersh, "C.I.A. Is Linked to Strikes In Chile That Beset Allende," *The New York Times*, Sept. 20, 1974.

PART ONE

Young Will

October 1972 – February 1973

IT IS FIRM AND CONTINUING POLICY THAT ALLENDE BE
OVERTHROWN BY A COUP... WE ARE TO CONTINUE TO
GENERATE MAXIMUM PRESSURE TOWARD THIS END UTI-
LIZING EVERY APPROPRIATE RESOURCE. IT IS IMPERA-
TIVE THAT THESE ACTIONS BE IMPLEMENTED CLANDES-
TINELY AND SECURELY SO THAT THE USG AND AMERI-
CAN HAND BE WELL HIDDEN...

> —Secret, eyes-only CIA cable from Langley headquar-
> ters to Santiago Station, Oct. 16, 1970, declassified
> and approved for release, July 2000.

1

Two immigration officers led Will Porter away from the noisy customs hall in the lower level of Santiago's Pudahuel Airport. They escorted him through a maze of vacant desks to a small windowless room with a flickering florescent light.

The jefe told him to sit. The eager subordinate—in his twenties, possibly even younger than Will—hastened to insert a cassette into a tape recorder.

"Dígame su nombre completo y nacionalidad," the jefe demanded as soon as the junior officer pressed record.

"Richard Henry Allen," Will said. "American."

The room was stuffy. The officers seemed unfazed by the late October heat that glued Will's clothes to his skin.

The jefe inspected the passport, rubbing his thumb over the embossed seal on the black-and-white photo as if to discover a forgery. It was a perfectly legal document. Of that Will was confident.

"And your company?"

"First Republic Insurance Group. We have an office here." Will took a business card from his wallet and pushed it across the table. Frigging FRIG, they'd joked in training.

The jefe didn't bother to look at the card. He leafed through the new passport until he came to the Mexican entry and exit stamps.

"You were in Mexico before coming here?"

"Yes. To meet a business colleague."

"And before that?"

"New York."

"Your Spanish is very good. Do you go to Mexico often?"

A compliment followed by a seemingly benign question—it was an old interrogation trick.

"No. I studied there for a semester, in college."

"But you came from Buenos Aires?"

"Yes. Braniff from New York to Mexico City. Aerolíneas Argentinas from Mexico to Buenos Aires. The same here."

"You must be very tired. Did you stop over in Buenos Aires?" Feigned commiseration—more guile.

"No."

But Will struggled to stay alert. He had been awake for thirty hours, traveling for twenty. His head pounded and he needed a cigarette. He shifted on the hard seat.

"And what is the purpose of your visit?" the officer persisted.

"To work. The visa is in my passport."

"Yes, I see."

"It's valid for three years. I got it from your consulate in New York."

"How long were you planning to stay in Chile?"

"My assignment is for two years."

The jefe nodded, a slow, hypnotic rocking of the head. The junior officer checked that the recorder was still working and inched the bulbous microphone closer to Will.

"So…then we come to the money."

"Like I told your associate," Will said, indicating the wide-eyed junior officer, "it's company money. I didn't realize I had to declare it."

"It's much money to conceal."

"The compartment is to protect against thieves."

"Of course. Thieves. Forty thousand dollars is much money."

"Yes, it is."

"It would be worth four, five times that on the black market."

"I wouldn't know."

The jefe tapped the spine of the passport against the table as if he were mincing Will's story into bits.

"Señor Allen, I would like to believe you. But businessmen don't typically hide large quantities of hundred-dollar bills inside secret compartments. Businessmen don't fail to declare the money they carry on their company's behalf." The tapping stopped. "Businessmen don't, but smugglers, agitators, they do."

"This is ridiculous." Summoning moral outrage like a professional actor. "I'm not a smuggler. I'm a businessman and an American citizen, and if you are going to detain me, I demand to speak with my embassy."

"We won't keep you much longer, Señor Allen. But we can't permit you to enter the country either. We are confiscating the money and sending you back to Buenos Aires."

"That's my company's money! Forty thousand dollars!" Adrenaline shot through Will like an electric current. His cheeks and ears burned. "You can't!"

"I assure you we can," the officer said. "We can also prosecute you. If this is only an unfortunate mistake, as you say, you may file an appeal from the United States. Or your company may do so from here."

"Then why can't you contact my office now? They will confirm everything I've said."

"Whether or not you are acting as a representative of your company is immaterial, Señor Allen. The issue is that you have attempted to bring undeclared foreign currency into the country. Tell me, if one were to attempt this in the United States, what do you think would happen?"

It was the worst possible scenario, a screw-up before his first assignment even began, a black mark beside his name in the agency files. What would his new boss say?

If this were Mexico he would offer a bribe, but the jefe, with his tape recorder and threat of prosecution, gave no indication that this was a shakedown. The suggestion might only make matters worse.

"Is there nothing we can do to resolve this now?" Will hinted anyway.

The jefe shook his head. "The law is quite specific. Our choice is to deny you entry or place you under arrest. Either way, the money will be confiscated."

For CIA Deputy Station Chief Ed Lipton, the day was not going well either. Mid-morning he received word that President Salvador Allende was reshuffling his cabinet again. The government, led by Allende's fractious coalition of Marxist and Socialist parties, Unidad Popular, had failed to settle a nationwide general strike now in its twentieth day.

What began with truck owners protesting government plans to set up a state-run transportation company quickly spread to taxi drivers, shopkeepers, doctors and nurses, accountants and engineers, students and teachers. Stinking garbage piled at curbsides, restaurants closed, theaters darkened, shops remained shuttered. As rationing lines lengthened, tempers flared and fights erupted. Someone was to blame.

Lipton skipped the elevator and jogged up the flight of stairs to the ninth floor where the Station Chief's large office was situated a few doors down from the ambassador's. He marched past Bill Bradshaw's secretary without breaking stride, without asking if Bill was busy, and closed the door behind him.

"Have you heard?"

Bill looked up from his reading and took the pipe from his mouth. "Good morning to you, too."

"The cabinet just resigned."

"Brother, here we go again!" Bill ran a hand through thinning reddish-gray hair. His wide brow creased.

Lipton had known his boss for over ten years, yet it was hard to tell if he was truly surprised. Bill's pale face always bore a wooden expression, an acquisition of age and experience.

Bill clenched the pipe between his teeth and leaned back in his padded chair to ponder the ceiling tiles. A puff of cherry tobacco. "So, who'll be left standing when the music stops this time?"

For the next thirty minutes the two men discussed the impact of the cabinet shakeup on operations. Would the general strike collapse now? Would the deepening power struggles between UP extremists and moderates fester into a coalition rupture? How would the trade unions react? The rank and file in the military?

As Lipton named each of the rumored new cabinet members, he and Bill traded one-line profiles: Staunch constitutionalist, Trotsky of the South, the Sycophant, Mr. Flip-flop, Yon Cassius. They weighed positions and posited scenarios until they were mutually assured they had a handle on the most likely outcomes.

"Well, I better go inform the ambassador," Bill said, tapping the bowl of his pipe into the ashtray. "Do me a favor and let Langley know ASAP."

Scarcely half an hour after Lipton sent the encrypted cable to CIA headquarters, Dave Phillips, head of the Western Hemisphere Division, telephoned. A call instead of a cable from headquarters, Lipton knew, was significant.

"Hello, Ed. Nice to hear your voice. Where's the big chief?"

"Still with the ambassador."

"I see. So, we weren't the only ones caught off guard by this."

Lipton detected the mild rebuke in Phillips' voice. It was true. They'd been caught with their pants down. Not one of their assets had predicted this turn of events.

"What's the real story?"

"We think Allende's struck a deal to end the strike. Rumor has it he's going to offer key cabinet posts to General Prats, Admiral Huerta and General Sepúlveda. It's a pretty smart move.

Bringing in the top brass placates the centrists and helps ensure that the troops stay loyal. It's hard to overthrow yourself."

"Hmm. So, good news or bad?"

"Depends on your point of view. Bill thinks a coup won't happen now. That we should focus on the mid-term elections."

"And you?"

Lipton quashed the impulse to speak his mind—loyalty to one's boss above all.

"I think Bill's right. A coup *is* less likely, and that's too damn bad because it will be tough to beat the UP in the elections. The sad truth is we were almost there, Dave. This place is right on the brink. If the military ever needed a pretext to intervene, this strike was it. But if Allende survives, and now it looks like he will, he'll be that much stronger and harder to take out later."

He had managed to insert his own point of view after all.

"I see...well...we'll take that into consideration. In fact, that's why I'm calling. The 40 Committee meets in an hour," Phillips said, referring to the White House's highest-level covert-action committee. "This news is only going to add fuel to the fire. I wouldn't be surprised if K gives us new marching orders. Can you and Bill stick around?"

An order politely posed as a request.

"Of course. We're not going anywhere," Lipton replied.

No sooner had he hung up than Bernie Hassam called from the airport.

"The new guy didn't show up."

It took Lipton a moment: the new guy, the rookie, Will P. "What do you mean?" He glanced at his watch—already twelve-thirty.

"I've been waiting for over an hour. The flight landed. The passengers cleared customs. No new guy."

"Did you check with the airline, make sure he was on the flight?"

"Yep. He was."

"Shit."

"Yep. Know anybody at Immigration?"

"No way. He knows the drill. He gets himself out of it."

"Okay, then what do you want me to do?"

"Wait a while longer. If he isn't out in half an hour, he probably isn't coming out."

"Christ! Not to make this personal, Ed, but my wife will be pissed if we're stuck here another bunch of months just 'cause some dipstick screwed up."

Always whining. "Not now, Bernie," Lipton cautioned.

Will waited in the windowless room alone, hands folded on the table. Garbled flight announcements sounded over a faulty PA system. The junior immigration officer stood outside the open door chatting with several peers, keeping casual guard while the jefe documented and safeguarded the contraband.

The flight to Buenos Aires was not for another half hour, but there was little Will could do to remedy his situation. He felt like crap. Sleep deprived, angry at being caught, angrier still at failing to talk his way out of it.

He had done everything by the book. It wasn't his fault the Chilean diplomat didn't show up for the flight from Mexico City. Will got the money from his Mexican colleague, Juan Lemantour. His seat beside the diplomat was arranged. Then the guy doesn't show. What was he supposed to do? Leave the cash in a locker in Buenos Aires?

On arrival in Santiago, to highlight his own businesslike appearance, he purposely fell in line behind a long-haired backpacker and breezed through passport control. After retrieving his suitcase, he proceeded to customs, careful not to rush or look as if he didn't know where he was going. He was forewarned of the newly implemented inspection process. Russian roulette, they called it. He watched the passengers ahead of him press a button to see if the light turned green or red. Green. Green. Green. Green for the hippie backpacker. He would have been through except for the damn red light.

"Open your bags, please."

If only he'd gone ahead of the backpacker.

"Your briefcase as well, Señor."

Did he somehow give himself away? He felt his cheeks flush—a curse since childhood whenever caught in a lie.

The young officer removed the First Republic product brochures, the spiral notebook, and the paperback copy of *Slaughterhouse Five* from Will's briefcase. He rifled through the loose pens, the packs of chewing gum and open carton of Marlboros. Almost through, then more bad luck. Having trouble closing the lid, the hinge catching on the lining, the officer accidentally pulled away the vinyl fabric to expose the compartment underneath.

He glanced at Will then bent closer to study the compartment panel.

"Here, let me," volunteered Will as if nothing were wrong. Exposing two sealed manila envelopes. "Is there a problem?"

The officer slit one envelope with a penknife and peered at the cash inside. In an excited voice he called over his supervisor.

The secretaries stopped working after lunch to decorate the desks, hallways and office doors with construction paper cutouts of jack-o'-lanterns, half moons and witches' hats. It was Halloween, and at three-thirty the local staff's children were due to arrive at the embassy to trick or treat.

Lipton shut his door to the noisy distraction and concentrated on the afternoon cables, but his mind kept wandering to the 40 Committee meeting taking place in Washington. The phone's ring startled him.

"So, after two hours and still no sign of the guy, I went over to Immigration and asked what the hell was going on." Bernie again. "Wouldn't tell me squat. 'Señor Allen has been detained,' was all... Now what?"

"Nothing. Go home." And before Bernie started to complain, Lipton added, "Have you heard the news?"

"About the cabinet? Yeah, it's all over the radio. The cat's used up another life is how I see it. So, what do you think happened to the new guy?"

"No idea. He was coming from BA, right? I'll let them know in case he shows up unannounced."

Lipton tuned his clock radio to Radio Agricultura. Bernie was right. The news about the cabinet was out. He began to write the cable about Will P but paused when the broadcaster interviewed Leon Vilarín, leader of the syndicate that initiated the truckers' strike.

"The head of the Socialist Party, Carlos Altamirano, calls you a traitor and blames your strike for the cabinet's resignation. He accuses you of trying to bring about the collapse of the government. How do you respond to these charges?"

"That's a good one! I was a Socialist long before he was," Vilarín said. "Besides, what have we done but defend our rights as workers? If the government will rescind its initiative to nationalize the transportation sector and guarantee not to destroy our jobs, we will gladly end our strike. But it's in their hands. I trust the president's sincerity, but we must wait to see what kind of offer his new interior minister brings to the table."

What Vilarín didn't mention was the heavy toll the strike was exacting on the truckers. Twenty days without income, despite CIA subsidies, commitment was waning. From Vilarín's conciliatory tone Lipton sensed a deal was already in the works.

"Trick or treat!" Bill Bradshaw entered without knocking. Proud of being one-sixteenth Chippewa, he liked to steal up on colleagues and tap them on the opposite shoulder as if counting coup. "Hot off the press." He handed a classified file to Lipton containing a single-page cable from Dave Phillips.

IMMEDIATE SANTIAGO (EYES ONLY) / CLASSIFIED / SECRET:
YOUR ANALYSIS OF CABINET SHAKEUP BECAME THE TOPIC OF
MUCH DISCUSSION TODAY. DUE TO THE LOW PROBABILITY YOU

HAVE ASSIGNED TO THE LIKELIHOOD OF A COUP, THE 40 COM-
MITTEE HAS APPROVED ANOTHER $1.43 MILLION FOR BLACK OPS.
FUNDS ARE TO BE DIRECTED TO OPPOSITION PARTIES AND ME-
DIA. K WAS EMPHATIC: A FAVORABLE OUTCOME TO THE MARCH
ELECTIONS IS EXPECTED. POSITION OF USG TOWARD GOVERN-
MENT OF CHILE REMAINS UNCHANGED. YOUR PLAN OF ACTION IS
REQUIRED IN 48 HOURS. INCLUDE KEY TARGETS, OBJECTIVES,
TACTICS AND RESOURCES NEEDED TO GET THE JOB DONE.

"Jesus!"

"Yessiree," Bill said. "Looks like we have our work cut out
for us."

Typical understatement. They had until March 4—four mea-
sly months—to shift the momentum of Chilean politics and deliver an electoral defeat to Salvador Allende.

Around the time the costumed trick-or-treaters were parading
through the eighth-floor hallway of the embassy in Santiago, Will
arrived in Buenos Aires for the second time in twelve hours.

He needed to get to the embassy, call Bernie Hassam or Ed
Lipton from a safe phone and explain what had happened. How
to explain the seizure of forty thousand bucks? Why they wanted
him to deliver a bribe on his way in was beyond him. Was it a
test? Some stupid fraternal rite of initiation? In the humiliation of
his failure he questioned everything.

At passport control the Argentine immigration officer granted him a transit visa good for 48 hours. Will went through the
green lane and cleared customs without a hitch.

He was heading toward the exit when he saw a row of domestic flight desks and noticed a blinking departure for Mendoza.
He put down his heavy suitcase and brushed a lock of hair from
his eyes. The green light blinked like a beacon. Mendoza was on
the eastern slope of the Andes with a highway going over the
pass into Chile. Will took out his wallet and counted ninety-four
dollars, plus fifty dollars' worth of Chilean escudos. In his briefcase were another five hundred dollars in traveler's checks. He
approached the counter and purchased a one-way ticket.

Two hours later he landed in the desert scrublands of Mendoza. He took a taxi to the bus terminal and bought a ticket on the 8:00 p.m. bus to Santiago.

"How long is it?" he asked.

"Ten hours without delays," said the ticket agent.

"And with the strike?"

The agent shrugged. "Fewer trucks, fewer delays."

As soon as the crowded bus left the terminal Will's tired eyes closed. He woke with a start in darkness, a dim red bulb overhead the only light. He felt the curve of the road in the sway of his body and leaned into the aisle to peer ahead, but all he could see through the bug-spattered windshield were a few meters of yellow dividing line illuminated by the headlights. The clutch lugged as the driver shifted to a lower gear. The bus was climbing.

A fragrant burst of orange filled the air around him, making his mouth water. The middle-aged man next to him nudged his arm and offered him a quarter of the orange.

"Thanks. Where are we?"

"About a half hour from the border," the man said, tossing the peel onto the floor. "Norteamericano?"

"Yes. And you, Chilean?" The bittersweet juice tingled in Will's mouth.

"Yes. But I live in Mendoza now."

"Are you glad to be going home?"

"Of course. 'How can I live so far away from what I loved, from what I love?' That's what Pablo Neruda wrote from exile."

"Are you an exile?"

The man's face was hard to make out in the semi-darkness but Will sensed that he smiled. "No, Communists like Neruda, they were once the outlaws and exiles. I'm just a salesman. But the way I see it, what's good for Communists and poets isn't so good for businessmen like me."

Will would have asked more questions but the man pushed his seat back, crossed his arms and closed his eyes.

At the border crossing on the continental divide, the passengers were ordered from the bus and told to bring their documents and personal belongings. A Chilean immigration officer directed the file of passengers into a concrete building wedged between the hillside and the road.

The shadowy slopes of the pass were awash in blue-gray moonlight. Patches of snow glowed at higher elevations and the breeze carried their chill. Will could trace the outline of glacier-cloaked peaks against the starry sky. It was beautiful—haunting, mysterious and thrilling. He inhaled the thin air with a renewed sense of confidence. Someday he might get to tell someone, a girlfriend or a colleague, how he entered Chile for his first assignment in the most romantic way, not by commercial jet, but over a high pass in the Andes by night.

The driver pulled the empty bus forward into a large shed and began unloading the luggage from the cargo hold. Will waited in line and shivered. Worried that the entry and exit stamps from the day before might raise questions, he prepared a story about a business emergency in Buenos Aires. But the incurious officer, who wore a heavy alpaca sweater over his uniform and woolen gloves with the fingertips cut off, merely confirmed that Will was the person in the passport photo and that the visa was valid. Like a somnambulist, he stamped the passport and pointed Will to the customs line.

"Nothing to declare," Will said to the customs officer. This time it was true. The officer waved him through. Will lugged his bags back to the bus.

Near dawn on Wednesday, November 1, 1972—All Saints' Day, a holiday in Chile—the bus pulled into the terminal in downtown Santiago. After traveling forty-two hours, Will arrived, nineteen hours later than anticipated and minus forty grand.

2

*F*rom the air, Santiago was a smoggy, sprawling, dun-colored city pushing against the foothills of the Andes. From the bus, the terrain looked like Arizona, a land of arroyos and parched hills. Except for the vast cordillera to the east, Will might have been approaching Phoenix. In his imagination he had pictured the elegance of a capital city, with monuments and boulevards and grand colonial buildings. Instead, as the bus entered the city from the north, and later in the taxi from the bus station to his hotel, he caught glimpses of concrete anarchy—crowded, dirty, dusty—like TV images of Beirut or rundown sections of Los Angeles.

But from his corner room in the massive art deco Hotel Carrera, Will saw why the cab driver had said "Qué rico!" when he stated his destination. Before him was a commanding view of Plaza de la Constitución, with the tall office building housing the American Embassy to his left and the block-long colonial façade of the presidential palace, La Moneda, to his right. It was like having a room overlooking the White House.

He showered and shaved and resisted the urge to sleep. He smoked a cigarette and watched the bustling pedestrian traffic on the bright plaza. Four sentries in white bandoliers and gleaming white helmets stood at attention in the tall arched entrance to La Moneda. Will exhaled a soothing stream of smoke as the realization struck him—he was now an active field operative in country.

The significance of the fact was just sinking in when a dizzying wave of exhaustion hit him. He stubbed out his cigarette, closed the drapes and undressed.

The ringing telephone woke him from a deep dreamless sleep. Groggy and disoriented, he groped for the receiver.

"Bueno?" he answered.

"Is this Richard Allen?" the voice asked in American English.

"Yes."

"Your Uncle Bill sends his congratulations."

It was his new boss. Will sat up and clicked on the bedside lamp. He glanced at his watch and tried to collect himself.

"Sorry. I was asleep." He needed to present his bona fides but momentarily couldn't recollect the countersign.

"Sorry to disturb you. Your Uncle Bill sends his congratulations," the gruff voice repeated.

"Thank you, but my birthday was last month."

"Welcome to Santiago," Lipton said, modulating to a softer tone now that Will had delivered the countersign. "I understand you had a little trouble at the airport."

"Yes, I'll tell you about it later." Dreading the thought. "But I'm here."

"Good, take a few days to get settled. Bernie will show you the ropes. Then call me at this number Monday morning. Got something to write with?"

"Yes." Will jotted the number in stacked pairs on the inside back cover of *Slaughterhouse Five*, then summed the numbers to make it look like a scribbled bit of arithmetic.

"Got it?"

Will repeated it.

"Good. Get some rest. I'll talk to you Monday."

* * *

In a mutually beneficial arrangement, First Republic Insurance Group provided cover to CIA officers in various parts of the world. The insurance company gained personnel willing to monitor troubled markets for its corporate clients, and the CIA gained a convenient cover for officers placed outside the protective walls of the embassy. For the case officers involved, the arrangement meant serving two masters, the insurance company by day and the agency all the time. Will was replacing Bernie Hassam. Until briefed, that was about all he knew.

The First Republic office was on the sixth floor of the Bernardo O'Higgins Tower, a plain ten-story concrete and glass building off an angular sunken plaza on the busy Alameda. When Will arrived in the tiny reception area the next morning, a small-boned woman in her thirties with dark curly hair and a scattering of freckles across pale cheeks greeted him.

"Welcome. You must be Señor Allen," she said in rapid-fire Spanish. She wasn't pretty but commanded an attractive bustling energy. Glossy red lipstick accentuated the curve of a mouth too large for the face. Eyebrows plucked into thin arches expressed the same hint of insolence as her smile. "I'm Leti."

Will smiled at her firm, efficient handshake.

"Mr. Hassam is expecting you."

She led him down a corridor past several vacant offices.

"I've put you in the office next to Mr. Hassam," she said as they approached a large corner office at the end of the hall.

Bernie Hassam rose from a cluttered desk. He wore a charcoal gray suit, a gold and black striped bow tie and a Chicago Cubs baseball cap cocked at a jaunty angle.

"Well, well, well...whatta we got here?" He stepped into the hallway with the friendly aggressiveness of a terrier sniffing a stranger. Small round glasses in gold metal frames pinched a beaked nose. His sharp, dark face already bore a five-o'clock shadow. Mid-thirties, Will guessed, of Mediterranean or Middle Eastern descent.

"Rick Allen," Will said with practiced authenticity, extending his hand.

Bernie squeezed Will's hand and assessed him with eyes so dark they were nearly black.

"Hello Rick. Pleased to meet ya," He spoke with a broad Chicago accent. "Oh, sorry…" removing the cap and slicking back his hair. "Forgot I had it on. That's the way it is around here, kinda like playing for the Cubs—absolutely hopeless!" He smiled again. "So, welcome to our humble home."

Bernie moved behind his desk and picked up a yellowed baseball lying among the clutter.

"Have a seat. Thanks, Leti. Could you close the door and hold my calls, please?"

Bernie waited until they were alone then asked, "So, what the hell happened Tuesday?"

"Is it safe?"

"More or less. Just me and Leti here, but she doesn't know about our extracurricular activities."

"The guy I was supposed to hand the money to didn't show up for the flight." Will described how he came to be detained and worked his way around to telling Bernie about the money.

Bernie seemed amused by Will's plight. He tossed the ball into the air with practiced precision, coming within an inch of the ceiling. "Yeah, I got a telex from Lemantour. Said the turkey changed his plans. Got cold feet apparently. We probably shouldn'a pushed our luck but figured, hey, since you were coming down anyway…" He gripped the ball tightly, aligning his fingers with the stitches as if preparing to throw a fastball. "I suppose we gotta decide what to do about the dough though. You know, whether to claim it or not."

"It's forty grand!" For Will there wasn't any question.

Bernie shrugged. "Yeah, well, that's for Lipton to decide. How's old Lemantour doing anyway?"

"Fine. He was leaving for Houston the next day. Said his son was scheduled for some medical tests."

"Really! Did he tell you his son's a dwarf?"

Will shook his head, unsure from Bernie's slight smile if he was pulling his leg.

"Yeah, it's true. You married, Rick?"

The continued use of his alias made Will wonder if Bernie realized it was an alias (of course; no doubt "Bernie" was, too). For an anxious moment Will didn't know whether to respond with his cover story or as himself. Fortunately, the answer for both was the same—"No."

"You're lucky. Being single makes the work a lot easier. Me, I've got a wife and two boys—three and six—with another in the oven." He pointed to a family portrait on his credenza: Bernie and a mousy woman sitting on a camelback couch with two exuberant boys in matching plaid shirts. "Woulda been three already 'cept my wife miscarried last year. That's the main reason we're leaving. She refuses to have this next one here. Can't say I blame her."

Bernie made one last slow pitch, snatched the ball out of the air and sat up straight. "So, lots to cover. Let's go over our stuff. At lunch we can talk all you want about the insurance trade."

He dropped the ball into his desk drawer and wheeled his chair closer to the desk. "Did Lemantour have you sign the bank account?"

"He did. I'm now an authorized signatory for Distribuidores del Sur."

"Good. Then let me show you what we do." Bernie went over to a safe bolted to the closet floor and crouched to dial the combination. He returned with several files and a ledger.

"So, now you gotta go to the bank's affiliate here and establish yourself as signatory. We can do that mañana. Then, when you get one of Lemantour's purchase orders, you gin up an invoice like this documenting an inter-company transfer." He handed a multi-page document to Will. "The invoice can be denominated in escudos but should request payment in dollars.

Then you ship something to them. Oh, and be sure the shipping docs stipulate CIF—cost, insurance, freight."

Will looked up as if to ask why.

"We have the auditors to consider. It may be a crate of scrap metal, but everything has to appear legit and arms-length. Are you familiar with Servicios Transportes Austral?"

Will nodded. Another CIA-chartered company.

"Good. They'll handle the crating, bills of lading and such, and then discreetly lose the shipment. You with me?"

"I think so."

Bernie handed Will another paper. "This is the account number," he said, leaning across the desk to point with his pen to the numbers typed at the top. "And these are the routing instructions. The bank in Mexico will wire funds in dollars to its affiliate here with instructions to deposit them into Distribuidores del Sur's account. From there you're free and clear to draw on them. By the way, if further currency restrictions go into effect, these procedures may change."

"What about the difference in inventory?"

Bernie nodded. "Good question. For *his* audit purposes, Lemantour will report a loss. Theft, damage in transit…whatever makes sense. Then you'll file an insurance claim. That's why we send it CIF. First Republic will reimburse you and you'll reimburse Lemantour. That way, the receipts and inventory match up and everybody's happy. Any questions?"

Will shook his head.

It was money laundering, though technically laundering in reverse. Greenbacks of the finest U.S. Treasury pedigree going downstream into dirty dollars and untraceable foreign currencies. Shell companies in the States transferring money through cooperative banks and insurance companies to other shell companies and their offshore subsidiaries in Switzerland, Panama, and the Cayman Islands. On paper these companies did a brisk business among themselves purchasing goods and services, some real, some vapor, and moving money around until it was hard to determine from where and, most importantly, from whom it came.

Will mostly knew about the receiving end—how to avoid red flags with foreign tax authorities by transferring limited amounts of cash, and how to cover the trail with receipts and invoices for nonexistent goods and services. Or, in this particular case, how to receive payments on behalf of Distribuidores del Sur of Santiago, a desk-drawer subsidiary of Lemantour's Distribuidores Cuauhtémoc of Toluca, for fake shipments made through another front company, Servicios Transportes Austral of Valparaiso—all supplemented by insurance distributions from First Republic's Bermuda-chartered corporation, which in turn received reimbursement from the CIA, whose own budget lay beyond scrutiny in the deep obscurity of other executive agencies.

"Good! We'll do one together this week. You'll get the hang of it quick enough."

Over lunch in a formal restaurant down a bustling pedestrian alley behind the office, Bernie shifted gears and described the business environment for First Republic with as much zest as he had money laundering.

"When I arrived here three years ago there were five Americans and a local staff of twelve. We had over 50 clients. Now, we've got six. We were completely blindsided by Allende's election. I mean, this used to be a fairly profitable market, but the UP not only killed the goose, they smashed the eggs.

"Right after they expropriated the copper mines, they nationalized the banks and insurance companies. Basically told us to kiss our local clients goodbye. Shoulda seen the reaction that got in New York!"

Will knew most of this but let Bernie talk. Before leaving New York he spent four months establishing his cover at First Republic, where he learned the basics of insurance in a dull management-training program and read through the branch's correspondence.

"Trade restrictions came next, which triggered a whole bunch of defaults. Our clients' subsidiaries couldn't get the currency to pay their bills. Couldn't buy assembly components or replacement parts." Bernie grimaced and patted his chest as if he suffered from a peptic ulcer.

"Naturally, as things got worse, FRIG stopped replacing the expats and began laying off the locals, until it came down to Leti and me. There's fuck all to do now." He poked at a piece of overcooked beef on his plate and put his fork down. "Welcome to the funhouse."

With Leti's help, Will found an apartment. At first she steered him toward Las Condes, the affluent neighborhood where Bernie and most expatriate families lived in large new American-style houses. La gente decente, she called them, the decent people. Despite Will's indications otherwise, she insisted that he look outside the city center.

"Nothing south of Plaza Italia. Too many rotos," Leti said disdainfully.

"Rotos?"

"You know, these people you see on the street with nothing to do. They'll steal anything you have if you aren't careful, including the shoes off your feet."

It was Will's first exposure to Chile's pervasive social elitism.

The next day Leti spotted a listing for a semi-furnished sublet in Bellavista, a barrio of Providencia. She demurred to answer Will's questions about the barrio. "It was once a nice neighborhood," she said finally, "but it's in decline. If you insist on living in the city, other parts of Providencia are nicer."

They went to look anyway. The neighborhood's narrow, cobbled, one-way streets charmed Will. Students sat on steps selling used books and artists displayed paintings and handmade jewelry on blankets along the curb. Several peñas, the Chilean equivalent of Greenwich Village cafés, advertised upcoming performances of nueva canción on handbills plastered on lampposts.

The third-floor apartment faced Cerro San Cristóbal, with its ancient funicular and pathways climbing to the park on its crest, crowned with a giant white statue of the Virgin Mary. The sunlit apartment was more than Will needed, but the location felt right. Without negotiating, he told the landlady, a woman in her sixties with hair tinted the color of a Brillo pad, he'd take it.

Leti clutched the string of cultured pearls she wore and accepted the American's foolishness with a dismissive sigh.

"You could have got it for less," she said on the way back to the office.

Will's new landlady lived in the apartment below and kept her door ajar to monitor the comings and goings of the building's residents, whose footsteps were telegraphed on a wide central staircase. She seemed simultaneously anxious and pleased about having Will as a tenant. He was another foreigner after all (a Frenchman lived across the hall, she informed him), and young and single at that. Yet his presence in her quiet, family-oriented building offered one irresistible benefit—access to dollars.

To supplement the few pieces already in the apartment, Will purchased an odd assortment of furniture from an expatriate family in Las Condes that was leaving the country. For ten dollars more, the man threw in a portable stereo and a small black-and-white television set. "No use to us back home. Wrong voltage."

That same week Will's meager household goods arrived: a few cartons of books, records and extra clothing. Taking pity on his apparent poverty, his landlady offered him a set of electric blue curtains for the bedroom, which he came home from work the next day to find installed. And, seeing that he had done nothing to soften the tread of his footsteps directly above her head, she had placed a hideous green rug on the living room floor. Will laughed and made a mental note: his landlady felt no compunction about entering the apartment when he wasn't home.

* * *

On a warm spring evening in early November, Will put Dylan's *Highway 61 Revisited* on his tinny new stereo and, happy with his newfound domesticity, began unpacking. He was arranging books on a shelf in the living room when he heard a knock on the door. He turned down the music, presuming the landlady had come to complain. Instead, a short man with a mop of wavy silver hair looked up with doleful gray eyes.

"This is very embarrassing," he said in English with a thick accent. "Imagine a Frenchman without the means to open a bottle of wine!" He held out the bottle. "Have you a corkscrew?"

He gave Will a disarming, offhand smile.

"I was going to let it breathe and invite you over. I am your neighbor," pointing to the door across the hall. "Roland Fabré, at your service," while making a slight bow.

"Rick Allen," Will said, opening the door wider. "I was just unpacking. Won't you come in? A corkscrew. Let's see…"

He returned from the kitchen with two juice glasses and a corkscrew. The Frenchman remained standing in the middle of the living room, staring up at the plain plaster ceiling as if it were an object to admire. The jacket of his dark suit was too large and hung loosely from his compact frame. His white shirt looked as if it had not been ironed and there was a smudge of something crusty like egg yolk on the thin blue knit tie.

"Ah!" He took the corkscrew and gave Will a delighted smile as if he forgot he'd asked for it. He lifted the limp arms up and down in bafflement, then grunted.

"Here, allow me." Will opened the bottle under the Frenchman's curious gaze. "I don't have any wine glasses," he apologized, handing a tumbler to his guest.

Roland Fabré pursed his lips and shrugged, which appeared to be his reaction to most things. "The type of glass is unimportant," he said politely. "It will not harm a good wine and, sadly, cannot make a bad wine good. Santé." He sniffed the glass and his flaring eyebrows inched together as he frowned critically before taking a long, squelching sip.

"Won't you sit down, Monsieur Fabré?"

"Please, call me Roland. And may I call you Richard?" pronouncing it "Reeshard."

He turned and inspected the lumpy stuffed chair behind him before selecting a straight-backed wooden chair to his right. He looked around the room as if he were a critic in an art gallery. His eyes floated from one dissimilar piece of furniture to the next and finally settled on the hideous green rug.

"So…" His lips pressed together but the thought remained unspoken. Roland removed a pack of cigarettes from his jacket pocket. "Cigarette?"

"Thanks, I have my own," Will said, retrieving his Marlboros and lighter from the dining-room table. When he returned, the Frenchman was already enveloped in a blue cloud of smoke.

"So…"

Will smiled at the strange, inarticulate man. "How long have you lived in Chile?"

Roland cocked his head as if calculating the answer to Will's question to the precise minute. "One year, more or less. I am a statistician. I came here to study the traffic for two years. Urban planning, I believe you say."

"You work for the government?"

"The UN. Same difference. Our client is the Municipality of Santiago. And you?"

"Insurance," Will said.

"Yes, that is what our landlady said. Insurance. That is very statistical. Very American."

He finished his glass of wine and poured himself another.

"I drink too much," he confided with an impish grin as he topped off Will's glass.

"Do you have family here?"

"No. My wife lives in France. We are divorced."

"What's it like working for the government?"

"Which? The UN or the municipality?"

Will gestured to indicate either.

"Governments everywhere, they are the same, no? The government here doesn't know what it wants. That's why I was sent. They think they want a French subway system because they believe it will make them more like the French. But they are *wrong*!" Uttered with such vehemence, the last word echoed against the walls. "In truth, the Chileans are more like the English."

Will shook his head. "How so?"

Roland smiled evasively. "They prefer tea to coffee." He placed his glass on the table and rose slowly from the chair.

"It is nice to meet you, Richard. I will leave the rest of the bottle for you."

"No need to go so soon," Will said.

"No, no. I merely wanted to introduce myself. You see, sometimes I grow very tired of myself...my opinions, my idiosyncrasies, my bad habits." He leaned over the coffee table and stubbed out his cigarette in the ashtray with a violent grinding motion as if to obliterate it. "I hope you will join me for dinner on another occasion. Then we can talk and share more wine. But tonight I am feeling very old and must go to bed."

At the door he looked up at Will and said with a quicksilver gleam, "Bonsoir. Or, what is it you say... 'Don't let the bedbug bite.'" He winked and crossed the hallway.

Later that night, after finishing the wine, doubtful of the need but aware of the protocol, Will dutifully sat down at the dining room table to make notes on his first unsolicited contact with a third-country national.

3

"Skip today's staff meeting. Here's your get-outa-jail card," Bill Bradshaw said as he handed Lipton a file. "I told the ambassador you have a report to write instead. He understands, concurs, and commiserates."

Bill loomed over Lipton's desk, hands in pockets, jingling his change. "The big dogs been bayin' at the moon, Ed."

Lipton opened the "restricted-handling" file and lifted the cover sheet to a cable from Dave Phillips:

IMMEDIATE SANTIAGO (EYES ONLY) / CLASSIFIED / SECRET:

CHILE IS FIRST ITEM ON AGENDA OF NSC BRIEFING 0800 HOURS FRIDAY. (N.B.: K TO ATTEND.) NEED STATUS REPORT FOR DCI ON ALL ACTIVE OPERATIONS BY END OF BUSINESS TODAY. REPEAT EOB TODAY. BE SURE TO INCLUDE:

1) PROJECTIONS FOR MARCH ELECTIONS, WITH STATUS REPORT ON EACH CONTESTED SEAT IN BOTH CHAMBERS.

2) ASSESSMENT OF LIKELY REACTION FROM SENIOR MILITARY OFFICERS IF ELECTION OUTCOME IS UNFAVORABLE.

3) YTD SUMMARY OF DISTRIBUTIONS TO POLITICAL PARTIES, LABOR SYNDICATES AND UNIONS, WITH RATIONALE FOR EACH.

4) MEDIA EXPENDITURES, IN PARTICULAR PROJECTED SUBSIDIES TO KEY OPPOSITION NEWSPAPERS.

5) OTHER INITIATIVES AND ANTICIPATED EXPENDITURES TO ACHIEVE DESIRED OUTCOME.

CONTINUE WITH INITIATIVES ON ALL FRONTS. NO ABATEMENT IN TACTICS OR FUNDING ANTICIPATED.

"Christ, Bill. We just gave 'em the plan. What do they expect in two weeks? And how the hell do they expect us to get any real work done if they constantly ask us to hold their hands?"

"Just get me what you can by noon."

"What the hell does this mean, 'No abatement in funding anticipated'?"

"Just what it says, I suppose."

"Then why are they saying it? The fuckers better not be getting cold feet."

"Shall we say noon, my office?" Bill slipped out the door.

Lipton spent the morning in the air-conditioned communications room under the gaze of the young marine guard on duty and with the Teletype machine clacking intermittently in his ear. Thick binders of top-secret cables lay stacked beside him on the metal worktable.

After restating the Related Missions Directive, which in cautious language declared the Station's goal as the obstruction of the Marxist government until it was removed from power, he proceeded one by one through the long list of their clandestine destabilization operations.

The real challenge was to make words he didn't believe sound convincing. After a year on the job Lipton had concluded that a coup was the only way to defeat Salvador Allende. The economic sanctions, the hard-line diplomacy, the covert destabilization programs weren't enough. They hadn't worked before Allende took office and they weren't working now, even if Bill and the ambassador thought otherwise.

By noon the memo was good enough to show Bill.

He carried two copies of his draft upstairs. Behind a closed door that meant *no* interruptions, he and Bill worked through lunch, going over the memo sentence by sentence, sometimes arguing for minutes over a single word.

"I've been thinking," Lipton said.

"Always a bad idea." Bill tapped his pencil against his lips as he studied the redlined draft.

"About the funding thing."

Now Bill looked up.

"Seems to me every time we tell them a coup isn't going to happen they throw more money at us."

"Yeah?"

"So, what's the message there?"

"What?"

"Come on, Bill. It's pretty obvious, isn't it? They're telling us they want a coup. They aren't saying it outright because they can't. They have to cover their asses. But that's what they're saying. P and K—that's what they really want."

Bill smiled. "Reverse psychology, huh?" He shook his head and circled a word on the report. "Been down that path before, thank you very much."

Bill might have said, Fool me twice, shame on me. In 1970, acting expressly on the President's orders to stop Allende from taking office, CIA backed a retired general's harebrained scheme to kidnap Chile's commander-in-chief, General René Schneider, and take control of the army. The conspirators botched the kidnapping and ended up killing Schneider in a shootout. The debacle left the agency scrambling to cover its tracks and recover its credibility with a White House that was irate, not because they had colluded in the attempt, but because the American hand was nearly exposed.

"Trust me," Bill said, "every day I hear loud and clear what HQ wants. Not to mention the ambassador. All they're saying about funding is that the objective is important."

Lipton shook his head. "Then why are they asking about the military's reaction if the opposition loses? Come on, Bill, look at the cable. The second point. Read between the lines."

Bill laughed.

"What?" Lipton asked.

"You mean instead of reading these lines here that say focus on the elections?"

Bill reached into his pocket for a ChapStick and rubbed it across his lips, then smacked his lips with gusto.

"Did I ever tell you the one about old Korry?"

Before Lipton could respond, Bill launched into a story about the previous ambassador. "Right after Allende won the election, he was ordered back to Washington for a meeting with P and K. They wouldn't tell him what it was about. 'Just get your sorry ass up here,' they said.

"So, some twenty hours and three flights later, the poor guy lands at National and hustles over to the White House in the same smelly shirt and rumpled suit he traveled in. He waits outside the oval office. It's thirty, forty minutes past his appointment time and he's getting antsy. But of course he can't show it. Finally, P's secretary tells him, 'You may go in now, Mr. Ambassador.' He gets ready to make his grand entrance, and just as he opens the door he hears P yell to K, 'That sonofabitch…that sonofabitch! I want that bastard out!'

"Naturally old Korry thinks he's been called all the way home to be fired. 'Oh,' P says, seeing him standing dumbstruck in the doorway. 'Not you. That other bastard, Allende.'"

Bill chuckled. Lipton smiled even though he'd heard it before. "That true?"

Bill shrugged and tilted back his chair. "Sounds like him, don't it? The point is, don't go jumping to conclusions."

By two in the afternoon Bill was comfortable enough that he could defend the memo if challenged by Phillips or the DCI, he told his deputy he would take it from there.

Lipton looked at his wristwatch. "Yeah, I have to go anyway. I'm meeting the new kid at three."

Ed Lipton had requested a seasoned professional to replace Bernie Hassam. Instead, he got a fresh-faced MBA type who, judging from his profile, was as green as Kermit the Frog. The personnel file said it all.

On the fourth page, behind the bio, cover ID and finger-prints, was something called a Myers-Briggs profile:

"Will P is an INTJ (Introversion-Intuition-Thinking-Judgment). These are strong individualists who seek new angles and novel ways to look at things. They are insightful and mentally quick; however, this may not be outwardly apparent since they keep a great deal to themselves. They are determined individuals who trust their vision of the possibilities regardless of what others think. They are the most independent of the sixteen personality types."

Who the hell are Meyers and Briggs, Lipton wondered, and what the fuck is an INTJ? Psychologists had apparently seized control of the agency's hiring and promotion process.

He paid closer attention to the performance evaluation written by Young Will's training officer, a flat-topped ex-marine named Whip Polachek. Lipton had worked with Whip in the Dominican Republic in 1965. A few years later, in Lebanon, Whip was badly wounded by a car bomb. He still bore the shrapnel scars on his face and walked with a serious limp. Ineligible for overseas duty, the poor guy was assigned the thankless task of training new recruits.

"Will P demonstrated mental resilience throughout training. He can also be evasive. Until he gains field experience, independent thinking may pose management challenges. Strengths: self-confidence, diligence, resourcefulness. Weaknesses: lack of team-work, cockiness." Then, in a telling aside, Whip scrawled at the bottom of the assessment, "I always got the feeling Will was not taking feedback seriously, even when being corrected. I constantly needed to drill home the importance of *why* we do things certain ways."

Lipton arrived at the Hotel Rincón early. Curious to see if the new kid followed procedures, he crossed the street to a small Spanish restaurant that was dark and empty and smelled of seafood. The owner stood cooling himself in front of an oscillating fan near the open door.

"We've stopped serving lunch," he announced in a Castilian accent.

"Just a beer," Lipton said.

He seated himself at the bar, his back to the wall and a side view out the door. He could see part way down the block and the hotel's faded entrance on the corner.

He paid for the beer and picked up the newspaper off the counter—a two-day-old copy of *Última Hora*. "Prats: 'No reprisals,'" stated the bold headline. In the cabinet reshuffle, Allende appointed General Prats, the army's commander-in-chief, to serve as minister of the interior as well. Prats quickly negotiated an end to the strike. Despite his loyal support of the government, the opposition still trusted him. He was an honorable man getting in the way of the solution—at least that's how Lipton saw it.

A knife sharpener lumbered up on a tricycle with a jury-rigged workbench on the back. The squat, square-shouldered man wore thick leather sandals and frayed gray twill pants cut off at the calf. He peered into the restaurant. The owner shook his head, so the man remounted his tricycle and pedaled away.

Next a young housewife pushing a perambulator passed by. Beneath a blue scarf, her dark red-toned hair curled in a short bob. She was tall and thin and walked with a determined stride. Something about her reminded Lipton of Renata.

A year earlier he was enjoying the honeymoon period of a plum new assignment in Rio—golfing, attending embassy parties, trying new restaurants, learning Portuguese—when he was unexpectedly asked to relocate to Chile. The order was softened with a promotion to Deputy Station Chief, but he was still disappointed.

Divorced nine months from his second wife, he had recently met a willowy and energetic Carioca twelve years his junior: Renata—a twenty-seven-year-old typist in the embassy's secretarial pool with caramel skin and a long slender neck like a Latin Audrey Hepburn. Lipton was having so much fun with her, he considered turning down the new assignment, promotion and all.

But Bill Bradshaw had been persuasive, insinuating that if they succeeded in Chile Lipton might be considered for a regional job. "The big dogs are pissing all over this one, Ed. It's the proverbial opportunity of a lifetime." Bill knew just which bone to set before his protégé.

When Lipton broke the news to Renata, she pouted for several long, abstinent days. To cheer her up, he bought her an expensive gold necklace and promised she would visit him. Of course, once he arrived in Santiago, work swallowed him up.

Young Will came into view. At least he bet it was the kid: fresh-faced, fair-haired, needing a haircut. He couldn't look more American if he tried—Dobie Gillis in a Beach Boy haircut, navy blazer, white button-down shirt and bright red tie.

Lipton checked his watch—Will P was right on time. He strolled past the hotel's entrance as if he were looking for another address and turned into a doorway beneath a green cross. Good, he's going into the pharmacy to make sure no one followed him. A moment later, he came out with a small satchel in his hand. Good, he's doing his SDR.

Lipton downed the rest of his beer. He waited for Will to go into the hotel then gave him a few more minutes—enough time to climb the stairs, find his way along the dark, unfamiliar hallway and wait before knocking on the door of the room. The kid would wait another thirty seconds and, when there was no answer, head back downstairs, walk around the block and try again.

Only after the kid emerged on the street and walked nonchalantly past the pharmacy did Lipton stand up and cross the street. He glanced back to make sure he wasn't being observed and went into the hotel.

* * *

It must have been ninety degrees in the room—a stuffy, shabby crevice on the third floor with ochre-colored walls stained gray near the ceiling from a water leak. Lipton opened the faucet in the mildewed bathroom and raised the window. A moment later there was a knock on the door.

"Is the music too loud?" the kid asked.

It was the code they had agreed upon. "No, but my uncle plays the trombone," Lipton responded.

The kid entered and extended his hand. "Hi, I'm Will." Smiling like an insurance salesman.

Lipton locked the door. "Take a seat."

He sized up his new officer—not as young as he first appeared, although his cheeks were baby pink from the heat. Attentive blue eyes exuded sincerity.

Will opened his briefcase and took out a notepad.

"You won't be taking notes," Lipton said, "You can take your jacket off if you want." He stripped off his own. His underarms were drenched.

"Nice place," Will said.

Lipton noted the sarcasm. "It's owned by one of our service agents. It's safe, convenient. You getting settled in?"

Will nodded. "Already found a place in Bellavista."

"I meant with Bernie's operation."

"Oh, yeah."

"Good. Let's go over things then." He lowered his voice. "First, Bernie told me about your hassle at customs, that the money was confiscated."

The kid's cheeks turned pinker than they already were. He shook his head apologetically. "Yeah, they found the damn compartment in my briefcase."

"Think they were tipped off?"

"No. It was dumb luck."

Lipton considered. "I've told Bernie to file the appeal before he leaves town, but I don't want you involved. If we get it back, good. If not, so be it."

"But—"

"No buts. I don't want you risking your cover for forty grand."

"But then how do I account for it?"

"It was confiscated…or is there something you're not telling me?"

The kid shook his head. "No, I just—"

"One of the hazards of the trade. Now, I take it you read the RMD and the cable traffic before you left." Will nodded. "Okay. We still want Allende and the UP out. We did all we could to keep the strike going, thinking the army would step in, but Prats didn't budge. So things have changed a bit. Our new orders are to make sure an opposition victory happens in the March elections."

"How do we do that?" Will asked. "I mean it's not like we control the vote."

"Of course not. Until the UP gets its way, this is still a democracy. But that doesn't mean we can't pitch our support to certain members of congress or play the political parties off one another. That's where the money comes in. We're also feeding information to the opposition press and planting disinformation with the UP's rags. The more we disrupt business as usual, the more votes we gain for the opposition.

"Unidad Popular gained three more seats last election. We don't plan on that happening again in March. This is Allende's last chance for legitimacy. If the UP gains control of congress, things will get ugly fast. El Compañero Presidente won't just be inviting his old pal Fidel down for another month-long vacation. He'll be wining and dining the Soviets and Chinese like there's no tomorrow."

"Shouldn't someone inform him Nixon's beaten him to it?"

The kid's smart-aleck smile reminded Lipton of Whip Polachek's reservations. He breathed in deeply, considered his words then exhaled.

"There's a big fucking difference between détente and sleeping with the enemy. Allende's a wolf in sheep's clothing. He claims to be a constitutionalist but his favorite pastime—other than banging his mistress—is to issue executive orders that violate the law. Then he goes around making speeches about the 'will of the proletariat.' All from a guy without a fucking mandate."

"I was kidding," Will said.

"Funny—ha, ha." Lipton took another deep breath but his annoyance remained. "Anyway, since the strike failed, we're back to square one. We've got lots of money, so there'll be no excuses. For good reasons not even the ambassador is fully aware of what we're doing. You read me?"

Will nodded.

"Now, your job is to get the money where we need it when we need it. That doesn't mean you get to sit around the office counting cash all day. I want you working. We've got less than four months. I want to make damn sure the wind blows our way come March 4. And with your lofty position at First Republic—what the hell is your title over there anyway?"

"Business Development Officer."

The kid's earnestness was amusing but Lipton maintained a straight face. "Yeah, well, listen up, Mr. BFD. I've got six other case officers busting their chops here. I'm gonna measure you the same way I measure them—by what you deliver. I want you targeting business prospects. If you can't recruit assets, you don't cut it as a case officer in my book. The next few days and weeks are critical. I want you working two hundred percent. We'll meet here once a week until I tell you differently. Any questions?"

Sweat trickled down Lipton's temples. His collar chafed. He stared at Will's pink face. After the wise-ass comments and the fuckup at the airport, he decided to lay down the ground rules.

"I suppose you learned all the latest tradecraft at the Farm."

"Never got there. They kept us away from Langley, and the Farm. Trained us up in New York. Brooklyn mostly."

Lipton recalled his own training, before the Farm existed.

Fun times. Playing hide and seek in the shops and tenements of Brooklyn, making drops in Prospect Park and practicing surveillance detection runs on long blocks of brownstones.

"Well, here's what I think. Call it Lipton 101. Just so we see eye to eye." He paused to breathe. The beer had bloated his stomach. His mouth tasted stale. "I know all the big-shots up in headquarters are keen on this NOC program. But, frankly, I'm not. Maybe if you had ten years under your belt like Bernie, coming in as a NOC might be useful. Maybe. Having good people on the ground not associated with the USG, that's handy. For plausible denial and all that shit. Some things definitely work better. Recruiting. Seeing. Hearing. Odd jobs we can't trust to agents. Information without filters. Less risk of embarrassment. Sound about right?"

Will nodded. He seemed a pleasant enough kid.

"But some things are worse. You're limited by your role. Just look at it from the target's point of view. You lack clarity. For him, there's always the shadow of a doubt. Are you really who you say you are? Fact is, you're not certified USDA beef. You follow?"

Again, a nod of assent.

"But all that aside, here's the real problem: you *don't* have ten years under your belt. I don't give a shit what kind of training you've had. You're not fucking James Bond. You're a grunt, like the lowliest fucking private, and you'll do what I tell you, when I tell you. That clear?"

Young Will gave the firm, efficient nod of a private to his drill sergeant. Lipton wasn't sure if it was sincere or another touch of insolence, so he laid into the kid.

"You fuck up and I send you home. Clear?

"You wear your cover like it's your skin. Clear?

"You blow my cover or anyone else's and you're fucking done. Clear?

"If you get into trouble, you try to get out of it on your own, just like at the airport. Only when all else fails do you contact me, and then you contact me *before* anyone else—I mean *anyone* else. That clear?"

Again Will nodded. Lipton paused to inhale.

"You're a bright, college-educated kid. Ever heard the word 'fungible'?"

"Sure…" Will returned his steady stare. If they were playing poker Lipton would have called his bluff.

"Yeah, well, if you don't know what it means, look it up. Because in my book, Will P, until proven otherwise, that is exactly what you are. Clear?"

— 4 —

*F*ungible: Capable of being exchanged like a commodity. Will was perfectly clear. He'd resisted being fungible all his adult life.

In the fall of 1969, the same autumn that the *New York Times* broke the story of the My Lai Massacre and President Nixon appealed to the silent majority to support his Vietnam strategy, Will started his senior year at the University of Arizona in Tucson. He was working toward a double major in history and Spanish, and living with four roommates in a dilapidated, roach-infested bungalow a few blocks west of campus.

Though far removed from the antiwar protests erupting on other college campuses, Will, like most of his friends, considered himself a liberal and a dove. When he turned eighteen, he had dutifully registered for the draft with the understanding that enrollment in the university ensured deferment. But then, in his senior year, the Selective Service did away with student deferments and instituted a lottery: just because you could afford the university, the reasoning went, you weren't exempt from serving your country. Like thousands of males between the ages of 18 and 26, Will's life was suddenly tossed in the air.

As the lottery date neared, he and his roommates debated the legitimacy of the war and discussed what they would do if drafted. For Will, the war seemed wrong, but he knew little about it except what he saw on TV (Walter Cronkite reporting the numbers of dead and wounded each night) or heard from friends who were equally uninformed. Will wasn't deeply political but prided himself on his objectivity, and he could see merit in both sides of the debate: the need to defend democracy from the spreading threat of communism on one hand, and the questionable value of fighting a cruel, winless proxy war on the other.

"So what'll you do if you're drafted?" his best friend, Tim Albright, asked as the two young men shared a joint on the back porch one late November afternoon while Jethro Tull blared through the open door from the living room. "I mean, seriously, would you skip to Canada?"

"Too cold. Mexico's warmer, and closer," replied Will. They had spent the previous summer together at the University of Guadalajara in an exchange program.

"Man, you can't go to Mexico. They'll extradite you in a flash. Canada, Sweden, those are pretty much your choices. Or change your name and go underground."

But Will wasn't being serious. If push came to shove, he would accept his fate and hope for the best. He didn't object to a few years in the service. He just didn't like the idea of having to shoot at someone or being shot at. In his heart he hoped the war would end and the problem simply go away.

The lottery took place on national television on December 1. Although it was a Monday evening, the five roommates turned the occasion into a party. They chipped in for a case of beer and Tim brought out a lid of grass from his stash. Joanne, the lone female in the house, kept cold beers coming while her roommates clustered around the portable black-and-white TV.

After an announcement that "Mayberry RFD" would not be seen that night in order to bring a special report, the newscast began. A beribboned lieutenant general in charge of the Selective Service described how the lottery would work. Then he invited a congressman from the Armed Services Committee to reach into a goldfish bowl and extract the first plastic capsule.

An anxious moment ticked by as the congressman handed the capsule to another uniformed officer who opened it and handed the slip of paper inside to a rigid soldier standing in front of a large board with columns of numbers. "September 14," the officer said dryly as his colleague pasted the date to the board at the top of the first column. "Number 001 is September 14."

At that moment the camera cut to the newscaster sitting in the audience who explained in a hushed voice that all young men born on September 14 between the years 1944 and 1950 would be the first called up to serve.

Will and his roommates watched in tense silence as the first dozen names were drawn. But with more beer and pot they grew garrulous. Brian Seifert turned red-faced with anger when his birthday was drawn at 038. Alan Worley drew 109. A long wait followed until they called Tim Albright's birthday at 241. Tim thrust a defiant middle finger at the TV announcer then lit a fat joint and smoked it like a cigar. Will began to wonder if he'd missed his number.

"I'm tellin' ya, it was called way back—lucky 13," Brian said.

The others grew restless and rowdy and Will had to shush them for each new announcement. Finally, "Number 360 is June 20. Repeat, number 360 is June 20."

In the time it took to utter those few words, the weight of being drafted lifted. Will slapped his knees in disbelief. His own good luck only accentuated the growing gloom of Brian and Alan who, if they didn't volunteer first, would receive induction notices by the start of the year.

"You fucking lucky bastard," Tim said. "Bet I don't go either. Unless it escalates into a fucking nuclear war, and then nothing much matters, does it?"

Will's luck *had* come through. The lottery brought instant clarity and freedom. Suddenly, he could plan his future.

As worry about the draft faded and graduation loomed, Will's views about the war became more ambivalent and his concerns shifted. He wasn't a rebel. As he learned from his own private rebellion against his father at fifteen, he didn't have the stomach for defiance or the smoldering anger for radicalism. A good career and the opportunity to earn decent money became more meaningful than demonstrations against what was wrong with America. Will wanted to make a difference in the world. He wanted what most young males want: success, excitement, romance, sex and love. But without the draft hanging over his head, and with dim prospects for a decent job, these desires took a pragmatic turn—he applied to graduate school.

A year later, in the spring of 1971, Will began his final semester at the Thunderbird Graduate School of International Management. He was living with his new girlfriend Sarah, running low on savings, thousands of dollars in debt from student loans, and still interviewing for a job.

The Thunderbird campus occupied an old army airfield on the outskirts of Phoenix amid empty desert and irrigated cotton fields. It was an unlikely location for an international business school, yet its fast-track curriculum of business courses, international studies and foreign languages appealed to liberal-arts graduates like Will who sought a fast track to a career.

On Tuesdays and Thursdays from 3:30 to 5:00 p.m., Will and a dozen other students gathered in the modern, unadorned inter-denominational chapel to hear Dr. Karl Ernst lecture on politics in Latin America. Dr. Ernst, a retired military man, was not shy about telling his students that he still worked as a government consultant. Some believed he worked for the State Department since he once served as deputy chief of mission to Panama, others that he consulted to one of the more secretive agencies: the Defense Intelligence Agency, the National Security Agency or the CIA. Such speculation only heightened the students' respect for their professor, and they listened to his opinions and prognostications with a reverence reserved for the oracle.

Dr. Ernst liked to amble across the chancel of the chapel as he lectured. Behind him, the blazing Arizona sun illuminated the amorphous stained glass window in imperial hues of purple and gold. The students sat in bleached oak pews and improvised writing surfaces by bracing books on laps, scribbling away while their professor addressed them in a low, gravelly voice.

Will suspected Dr. Ernst wore dentures, for he barely opened his mouth when he spoke. His head bobbed to a secret rhythm as he paced, his sly green eyes studying the floor, his stage voice rising and falling with an odd, unpredictable inflection.

"In Brazil the pattern was set *long* ago. The people, the vast majority of whom were illiterate, would elect these leftist demagogues—incompetent populists mostly—who kowtowed to union bosses and promised more jobs and higher wages. (Who wouldn't vote for *that*, especially if you can barely read or write your name!) And, sure enough, once the fools were in office, they'd wreck the economy, running up huge deficits on *whatever* welfare programs they'd promised: food subsidies, the nationalization of strategic industries, import substitution, you name it. Inflation and currency devaluations were inevitable, and the economy always ended up a shambles.

"This pattern started with Getúlio Vargas who ran as a populist in '34 and made himself dictator in '39 on the Franco model. Now, Vargas was a cagey one. He couldn't decide if he was for Hitler or Roosevelt until it finally looked like the Germans were going to lose. After the war, he decided he was more of a socialist after all, and the army was *forced* to intervene.

"The military ran the country for a few years, fixed things, then handed the government back to the civilians. And what did the *people* do? They went and reelected Vargas! That was in '51. Things quickly went to hell again. So, one more time, the military prepared to force him out. But before they could *act*, Vargas saved them the trouble and shot himself…" Dr. Ernst stopped in his tracks and scratched his head in apparent wonder at the foolishness of the world.

"The presidents who followed weren't much better. In just *two* of their so-called five-year plans, they made a complete mess of things. Negative GDP growth. Expropriations. Restrictions on the repatriation of profits. So, once again, the military had to step in and send the nincompoops packing.

"I happened to be in Brazil the last time, in '64..."

And with a gap-toothed grin on his golf-tan face, Dr. Ernst launched into a tale of observing war games near Salvador and schmoozing with the wives of colonels and aides-de-camp at black-tie cocktail parties in Rio de Janeiro.

"Of course, the U.S. was criticized for being too *quick* to recognize the military junta. What people didn't realize was, we *knew* these guys. They were professional soldiers. ESG boys—that's the Escola Superior de Guerra—trained in counterinsurgency, emergency preparedness and national security. Our military attachés had spent countless hours on the ground with them. We'd *trained* them in Panama. We'd *pushed* through loans for new aircraft and tanks. We *trusted* their agenda."

Dr. Ernst checked his watch.

"Well, all right. For next week, read the chapter on the Arbenz debacle in Guatemala. Incidentally, that's where our Argentine fellow traveler Che Guevara got his start. Now, you tell *me* that Communism isn't exported!"

Will was collecting his books and papers when he heard his name bellowed over the shuffling of students leaving the room.

"Porter," Dr. Ernst repeated, waving him forward.

Will made his way to the front of the chapel. There was no altar like those in the Catholic churches he had attended as a boy— no religious symbols at all—just a step onto a wide, carpeted platform with a podium.

A Brazilian student had pushed forward and was challenging Dr. Ernst's interpretation of events. The military government shut down his father's newsmagazine in 1964. What about that?

Dr. Ernst nodded. "Sometimes the temporary suppression of

civil rights is a necessity. But, look, today the Brazilian press is vibrant, vocal and *free*."

"My father had to sell his business," the student persisted.

"I'm sorry to hear that, son, but that doesn't change the rather compelling fact that overheated government spending was destroying the economy. Just look at the World Bank reports."

"Not everything is driven by economics," the student retorted.

"And there I beg to differ."

Dr. Ernst slipped his notes into a battered calfskin briefcase, indicating that the debate was over. He turned to Will. His tan face intensified the brightness of his green eyes. He clutched Will's arm and ushered him down the aisle toward the door.

"I just wanted to say I thought your latest editorial was pretty good."

"Thanks," Will said, squinting at the bright sunlight as they stepped outside. That semester he had assumed the editorship of the student newspaper. In his opinion the editorial was his finest piece to date, a balanced assessment of Nixon's decision to bomb Laos.

"Everyone worries about respecting national boundaries, but you can bet the Viet Cong don't give a damn about Laotian sovereignty while they're running weapons down the Ho Chi Minh Trail. You got that," Dr. Ernst said, winking, "while damn few in the real press do. Tell me, what are you planning to do after graduation?"

Will had taken the editorial job for the money but discovered he liked the power of words and the celebrity that came with seeing his name in print. Though he'd had no luck with job interviews at the major newspapers or magazines, he imagined a future as a foreign correspondent assigned to Hong Kong or Berlin, London or Paris. Still, it remained a dream, so he kept his response intentionally vague.

"I'm thinking about journalism, or maybe advertising."

Dr. Ernst nodded. "Good choices. Ever thought about the CIA?"

The directness of the question startled him. Was this how the CIA recruited spooks? Before he could respond, Dr. Ernst continued, "I suppose like everybody else here, you want to work overseas."

"I think so. At least for a while."

"You should consider the agency then. I can put you in touch with some folks who'll give you a good idea of what they're looking for. Interested? It'd be a lot more fun than joining those sissies who write advertising slogans all day. A waste of your talent if you ask me."

Will walked with his eyes down, avoiding Dr. Ernst's question as much as the glare of the late afternoon sun. High up in the date palms mourning doves cooed like conspirators. He would never have considered the CIA if someone he respected hadn't approached him. The idea of being specially anointed by Dr. Ernst flattered and thrilled him.

"Can I think about it?" he asked, wondering what Sarah would think.

"Of course! But don't think too long, Will. Life's all about action."

In mid-April, Will arrived in Washington, D.C. for his first interview. The agency booked his room at a Holiday Inn in Rosslyn, near the Potomac River.

His contact, a woman who called herself Sharon, told him to call from a pay phone when he arrived and to use the alias she provided him. Will suspected these precautions were less about security and more about fueling the imaginations of job candidates. Still, as he settled into his hotel, the thought did cross his mind that the room might be bugged. He dismissed the notion as nervous paranoia and went out to call Sharon. She told him someone would come by the hotel at eight the next morning.

At eight sharp he received a call from the lobby.

"Hello, my name's McPhearson. I'll be right up."

Will opened the door to a tall bald man in his sixties. Dressed in a trench coat, he looked like a tired old cliché coming in from the cold.

McPhearson surveyed the room as he entered. Without removing his overcoat, he sat down at the small Formica-topped table by the window, unzipped a vinyl portfolio, peeked inside, then zipped the portfolio shut. Will sat on the end of the bed. The white glare of a new spring day coming through the sheer curtains obscured McPhearson's face.

"First, let's talk a bit," McPhearson said. "All this cloak and dagger stuff can be a little intimidating. You're not intimidated are you, Will?"

"No."

"Good! Ever taken a polygraph?"

"No."

"Well, it's nothing much. However, I need to advise you that you are talking to a federal agency. Although our job isn't law enforcement, if you *should* admit to a felony, we *do* have the obligation to report it to the proper authorities. Haven't killed anyone, have you, Will?"

"No."

"That's good. Any questions then?"

Still processing the information, Will shook his head.

"Good! Then follow me."

McPhearson stood up, tucked the portfolio under his arm and walked to the door.

"Do I need to bring anything?"

"Just your room key."

Will followed McPhearson's stooped figure down the dim hallway to the elevator. They waited silently for the elevator to arrive then rode up two floors. They walked down an identical hallway to another room. McPhearson knocked on the door and a younger man with short, curly red hair opened it.

"Will Porter, Mike O'Dea."

Will sized up O'Dea as they acknowledged each other. He was only a few years older, maybe thirty, but there was a cheerless impatience to his greeting.

McPhearson grabbed O'Dea's newspaper off the bed and told his colleague to call him when he was finished. Then he left.

"Have a seat," O'Dea said, pointing to a chair facing the wall. A suitcase-sized box of electronic equipment rested on another chair facing the bed. Will sat down and O'Dea began sorting wires attached to the machine.

"This measures skin moisture," he said as he taped a metal clip at the end of one wire to Will's right index finger. He attached another to Will's ring finger. Next, he wrapped a blood pressure sleeve over Will's left bicep. "You've seen one of these before, right?"

Finally, he cinched a wide elastic strap around Will's chest, making sure that the band was not tangled or pinched. "This measures heart rate."

He drew the curtains across the window to darken the room, turned on the overhead light in the foyer and sat down on the bed behind Will.

"I'd like you to sit up straight and look ahead. I'm going to start with some obvious questions: your name, where you were born, that kind of thing. This will establish a baseline of your respiratory rates and rhythms. Then we'll proceed to other questions. Breathe normally and answer with simple declaratory statements. Yes or no is usually best. Got it?"

"Yes," Will said, his mouth too dry to say more.

After Will responded to each question O'Dea paused. Will guessed he was watching the needles' seismic movements across the graph paper. At one point O'Dea came around to adjust the strap on Will's chest. As he walked away, Will noticed his scuffed penny loafers and the threadbare heels of his socks. Somehow this depressed him. So far, everything he'd seen about the CIA was dowdy and frayed. Polyester and synthetic blends. Gray men on government salaries. Did he really want to be one of them?

They finished with the background questions and O'Dea came around to face him again.

"Alright," he said. "Now I'm going to ask you some questions the agency needs to know in order to continue your interview. Ready?"

"Sure." Feeling his heart skip and the blood rush to his face nevertheless.

O'Dea returned to his place behind him and began.

"Have you ever been arrested?"

"No."

"Have you ever been fined or ticketed for a misdemeanor?"

"Yes."

O'Dea stopped and came around to face Will.

"What for?"

"Speeding."

"That it?"

"Maybe a parking ticket or two."

"Anything else?"

Will shook his head. "Not that I can think of."

"Okay."

As O'Dea took his place, Will recalled an Alfred Hitchcock episode about a murderer who beat a polygraph test by computing math problems as he answered the interrogator's questions. "Did you kill Mr. Smith?" *Two times two is five.* "No." He wondered if that really worked, but now was not the time to find out.

"Other than the occasional traffic ticket, have you ever been fined or ticketed for a misdemeanor?"

"No."

"Have you ever committed or conspired to commit a crime against the U.S. government?"

"No."

"Have you ever committed or conspired to commit a treasonous act against the United States of America?"

"No."

"Have you ever committed or conspired to commit an illegal act outside the U.S.?"

"No."

After an hour of repetitive questioning on the topics of espionage, trade secrets, classified information and contact with foreign nationals, O'Dea stopped.

"Okay. You can relax for a while." He turned on the bedside lamp and studied the long scroll of results. He made a grunt, tore off the paper and came around to look directly at Will.

"So what aren't you telling me?"

"What do you mean?" Will heard his voice falter.

O'Dea unfurled the graph paper and pointed to the waving and spiking lines in red and blue ink on the black grid.

"See these? They're the results for the baseline questions I asked you. And these," he pointed to a row of lines farther down the scroll, "These are the results of the last few questions. See how the spikes are higher and more jagged?"

Will nodded.

"So what aren't you telling me?"

Will wasn't sure he wanted to tell O'Dea. As he answered one of the questions, his mind flashed on the time he and his college roommates went to the Tucson airport to retrieve a trunk that Tim Albright had shipped from Mexico. The trunk contained two kilos of Acapulco Gold. No sooner had Joanne signed for it than the Feds charged out of the terminal and shoved them against the car. Will could still recall the terrifying feeling of a gun barrel pressed against the base of his skull. He and his friends feigned ignorance. We were just picking up the trunk for a friend, they said. Where's your friend, the police asked. We don't know, they answered. Fortunately, Tim had used a false name. Joanne spent the night in jail but the police had no case and released her the next day.

But, was that conspiring to commit a felony against the U.S.

government? If he told O'Dea about Tim's dealing, could Tim still be busted? Will had not committed the felony himself, but was he exempt from prosecution? He wished now he'd asked McPhearson for clarification. O'Dea looked like the type who enjoyed drilling down until he hit bottom. Will would not betray his friend for a job and determined to muscle his way through.

"I don't know," he managed to say through his cottonmouth. "I'm telling you what I know."

O'Dea stared him in the eyes.

"Okay. Let's try it again."

He asked Will more questions. Most were the same as before but phrased differently. Dissected, reordered. Will answered to the best of his ability through his pounding heart.

It was nearly lunchtime when O'Dea told him to relax. He studied the graphs under the table lamp then came over to Will's chair.

"Okay," he said. "I think we're done here." He started to undo the wires attached to Will's body.

Unable to interpret O'Dea's voice or expression, Will asked, "So, what's next?"

O'Dea shrugged. "Go back to your room and wait for McPherson, I guess."

Will waited. He felt drained and uncertain. His stomach growled with hunger but he was reluctant to leave his room in case McPhearson called. Around one-thirty, McPhearson knocked on the door.

"Did you get any lunch?" he asked as he sat down at the table by the window. The light had shifted and Will could see his long, jowly face better this time.

"No, but that's okay."

McPhearson smiled and made a comment about watching his weight. "Well," he said, rearranging himself on his seat and untangling the belt of his trench coat from the back of the chair. He coughed into his hand to clear his throat. "I've spoken to O'Dea.

I'm afraid we aren't going to continue with the interviews today. We won't be going to Langley."

"Why not?" Despite his misgivings, Will felt disappointed.

McPhearson frowned. "The results of your test weren't satis-factory."

"But I told him the truth. I don't know what happened. I just didn't feel comfortable. I was thinking about what you'd said, about felonies, and I started worrying about some things... Not about me, but, you know, some things I've been around, sort of."

Inexplicably, Will found himself pleading, treating McPhearson like a confessor. Why was he making such an effort? Since his arrival in Washington, even before he arrived—as he filled out the application, completed the psychological tests and wrote the required essay—he had felt less and less sure that the CIA was a good fit. With each step he felt less like himself. Now, he simply wanted to win, to have them want him so he could reject them.

McPhearson's pale blue eyes seemed to soften. Were they playing him, Will wondered. Was this rejection another psycho-logical test?

"Well, these polygraphs are pretty accurate," McPhearson be-gan. "On occasion we've made an exception and brought some-one back, but usually the outcome hasn't changed... You seem like a bright young man. You come with a good recommendation. You passed all of the preliminary psychological tests—at least our psychologists tell me you're not crazy," attempting to make the situation lighter. "And you did a fine job on the essay. I suppose I could check with my superiors and see if they'd give you another chance."

"I appreciate your willingness to try, Mr. McPhearson," Will said, surprising himself.

"You'd have to come back another time, in a few weeks. Would you be willing to do that?"

"Yes."

* * *

Will returned to Washington the second week of May. The cherry blossoms were spent and their rotting petals clogged storm drains. Back in Phoenix he'd talked briefly with Dr. Ernst about his first interview, explaining without going into detail his reluctance to confess certain things in his past. Dr. Ernst listened and then let out a pop of air that turned out to be a guffaw. "Hell, Will! They don't give a damn about your peccadilloes. They only want to make sure you haven't sold your soul to the Soviets. Just tell 'em the truth."

This time Washington was a city under siege. War protesters, mostly college students, had converged from all quarters of the country. Police and National Guard troops were out in force, patrolling the makeshift encampments on the malls, chasing down and arresting the violent fringe, smashing through illegal barricades spontaneously erected.

"Shoulda seen it last week," the cabbie said. "They had all the bridges blocked. Ya couldn' move! Half the fuckin' city shut down… Say, you're not one of 'em, are ya?"

"No."

Though, with a different birthday, he might have been. From Tim Albright he'd heard that Brian Seifert had dodged the draft with a medical discharge but Alan Worley was in the army and shipping out to Vietnam. Tim, now married to Joanne, was still hedging his bets in Tucson.

From the marble column at Dupont Circle a hand-painted banner hung beside a North Vietnamese flag: "Impeach Nixon!" Kids Will's age, mostly longhaired and wearing patched bell-bottoms, clustered in parks and near monuments. Posters bearing white doves plastered telephone poles: Give peace a chance!

"They arrested so many of the basta'ds yesterday, they had to hold 'em in the arena," the driver said.

The cab let him off at the same hotel as before. On the Arlington side of the Potomac life was more normal. Traffic moved along the parkways and no tents were in sight.

"Hello," McPhearson greeted him on the phone the next morning at eight on the dot. As before, he led Will to a room on another floor, only this time the polygrapher was a tall thin black man who McPhearson introduced as Mr. Cleveland.

With long slender hands as nimble as spiders, Cleveland attached the wires to Will's fingers, arm and chest. He spoke little until he asked if Will was ready to begin. Cleveland described the procedure, the same as O'Dea had done, and started with the same test questions. Will swallowed and moistened his mouth.

"Look, before we go on I want to explain some things."

"Go ahead."

He told Cleveland about the previous test and, taking Dr. Ernst's advice to heart, described the incidents that had caused him to hold back. The association with drugs in college. The smoking of an occasional joint. A little hashish. Without naming names, the episode at the Tucson airport. His voice trailed off. He felt humiliated by Cleveland's silence, like a child caught in a lie.

When it was clear he had finished, Cleveland summed up, "So, we like the ganja, eh?" It was impossible to tell from his deadpan expression if he was offended or considered Will's crimes so petty he was only expressing boredom.

Cleveland reshaped his question. "Other than consuming, buying and selling small amounts of marijuana and other illegal drugs, or being an accomplice or accessory to others' buying and selling of such drugs, have you ever committed a felony crime against the U.S.?"

"Good to go!" McPhearson said that afternoon. "Only we're not going to Langley after all."

"What now?" Will asked, thinking another hurdle had risen in his path.

"Not to worry," McPhearson said. "We're considering you for something else, something called the NOC program. That stands for non-official cover. You'll meet a few people here at the hotel instead. We don't want to compromise you until we can determine if you're right for it."

The next morning Will met Patty, a psychologist with salt-and-pepper hair and a smile that exposed her upper gum. The severe gray pinstripe suit and thin navy blue bow tie contrasted with the floppy collar of the silky cream-colored blouse she wore. Patty said she worked in the personnel department and was responsible for identifying candidates for the next phase. She gave Will another battery of tests and in the afternoon they sat down on opposite sides of the dinette table for a chat that he soon discovered was as structured as any test, the questions unlike any he'd been asked in any job interview before this.

"So, tell me about growing up in Arizona," she began, smiling.

"What do you want to know?" asked Will with a soft laugh, disarmed.

"Well, I see you went to a Catholic grade school. Is it true what they say about nuns being so cruel? Were you a good boy, Will?"

He sensed she didn't expect a sincere answer. "Not especially."

"No? Then tell me, how do you see yourself. Just who is Will Porter?"

Will considered for a moment. "I guess I'm someone who tries to be a decent person."

"What does that mean to you?"

He wasn't really sure. "Hardworking, honest. Someone who wants to do the right thing."

"Do you mean honorable? Virtuous?" It was the same tone of voice she'd used to ask if he'd been a good boy. Only this time he didn't think the question was asked lightly.

"I suppose. Whatever that means."

She waited for him to elaborate. When he didn't, she continued. "It says here that you ran away from home at fifteen. Why?"

"Problems with my dad," Will said carefully. "He has a temper."

"Do you have a temper?"

"I try to manage it."

"Did you tell anyone back home that you are interviewing with us?"

"Only my girlfriend. And Dr. Ernst."

"Not your parents?"

"No."

"Why not?"

The answer was too difficult to explain. Because he barely spoke to his parents. Because he couldn't trust them. Because he still wasn't convinced the CIA was a good idea. Because Sarah wasn't, either. Maybe even because he liked having a few secrets.

"I figure the fewer people who know, the better."

Patty nodded. From there she asked few questions he could answer with a simple yes or no. She asked him to describe situations and give specifics. Had he fought much as a boy? How did he feel about losing? How did he break up with his first girlfriend? What did he like best about his best friend? Did he ever squeal on another kid? What happened? What was his father's best advice? Why? Did he ever get caught stealing? How did it make him feel? Did he ever cheat on an exam? How did he do it? Had he ever hurt an animal? Explain. Had he ever imagined killing anyone? How? Who was someone he really disliked. Why?

Finally she brought up his polygraph results and asked direct questions about his drinking and drug habits.

"Look, I'm pretty much your ordinary college graduate," Will said. "There's hardly anyone I know who hasn't smoked a little pot."

Patty smiled and looked at her notes. "You mean, committed a felony," she said with flinty precision.

"Possession's usually treated as a misdemeanor in Arizona," he countered.

A hairline flexing of her mouth was her only acknowledgement as she continued to write on the pad. "Last time I checked, buying and selling and shipping across borders wasn't, though."

She placed the notepad on the table and with deliberation set the pen on top of the pad. The action reminded Will of an assistant principal about to mete out punishment.

"You know, if we were considering you for an analyst position in headquarters, this kind of behavior wouldn't be tolerated. We fire people who use illegal drugs." She looked at him levelly. "But in the field, in the line of duty, it's grayer. We need a certain risk-taking profile or nothing gets done. The ability to think on one's feet, to take *appropriate* risks, has its place. Are we clear about the distinction?"

He'd been clenching his stomach muscles ever since she asked what virtue meant, and now he had the sensation of being punched in the gut.

"We're clear," he said.

5

B y December Bernie had shifted most of his responsibilities to Will and was spending less and less time in the office. When there, he sat at his desk with his legs propped up, reading newspapers. He took special interest in what he referred to as President Allende's "world tour."

"Look—all of the world's great capitals: Mexico City, Havana, Moscow…"

When Allende addressed the United Nations in New York, Will joined Bernie to listen to the broadcast. Bernie tossed his baseball in the air and joked as Allende accused foreign elements and multinational companies of attempting to derail the socialist transformation of Chile. As the General Assembly launched into applause, Bernie switched off the radio and said, "Gotta give credit where credit's due. It was a pretty good speech."

The following week a truck from Servicios Transportes Austral collected his household goods and he moved his family into a hotel. "Home by Christmas, Rick old pal! I'll think of you sweating down here as I stroll the halls of Langley and trade gossip in the cafeteria." At his wife's insistence, Bernie was forfeiting his NOC status for a desk job in HQ. He claimed it was what he wanted, too, but Will wondered if it was true.

The day before his departure, Bernie handed him the combination to his office safe and said, "How about lunch today?" Will thought he meant just the two of them, for passing the baton, but it turned out he meant a luncheon at the year-end general meeting of the UN's Economic Commission for Latin America, based in Santiago.

"If you ever wondered where all the socialists, Marxists-Leninists, Maoists and conspiracy-theorists hang out, this will be a real eye-opener," Bernie said as they drove to the event. Noontime traffic congested the Alameda and Bernie inched the company's Ford Falcon forward through honking cars at a gridlocked intersection.

"These are the guys who decide what's going to be nationalized next. It's for members only. But I usually get the gist of what's happening by talking to a few friends at lunch. They may be Marxists but they aren't a bad bunch... Hey, a Marxist economist—isn't that like an oxymoron?"

They turned onto the Costanera Norte freeway and headed toward the airport hotel where the meeting was taking place.

"Look—another one on strike!" Bernie said, spotting a factory draped in red and black banners. Surrounded by a chain-link fence, the long brick building looked abandoned.

"So where are all the strikers?"

Bernie laughed. "At home. Or over at union headquarters getting ready to demonstrate. Between holy days and work stoppages, the workers barely have time to work. Then they wonder why things are so fucked up."

The hotel's stark lobby bustled with attendees. Will followed Bernie up an escalator to the second floor where voices spilled into the hallway from a large ballroom. Men in dark three-piece suits and others in pastel guayaberas crowded around two bars at the back of the room.

Bernie nudged Will. "Guess which ones are the Marxists. It's the latest fashion statement from Havana."

They squeezed past clusters of animated conversation. Sidling toward the bar, Bernie acknowledged several people, shaking hands, squeezing arms and introducing Will.

Bernie ordered a gin and tonic for himself and a beer for Will. "Salud!"

A stout, bearded man in a pinstripe suit approached Bernie from behind and patted him on the back. "Mr. Hassam!" he said in English.

Bernie turned.

"Señor Saavedra! Here for economic enlightenment?" The two men shook hands as if it were an endurance contest.

The stocky man grinned.

"A good businessman always keeps an ear to the ground about his competition."

"Oh? Competing with the government now?" asked Bernie.

Saavedra leaned closer and partially covered his mouth with his hand. "Who knows?" he said in mock whisper. "Is the government competing with me?"

Bernie tipped his drink in appreciation. "I'll miss you, don Carlos. I'm heading back to the States tomorrow. For good! This is Rick Allen. He's my replacement. Looking to learn the ropes. What better place than here, eh?"

"My pleasure," Saavedra said. He extended his hand with a formal bow. Will imitated Bernie's forceful handshake. "But Bernie," continued Saavedra, "don't tell me you're leaving before all the fun begins."

Bernie beamed with collegial affection. "Don't let him fool you, Rick. Señor Saavedra runs a very successful transportation company. He used to be a customer, so I guess we still have to be nice to him."

"So, you are with First Republic too, Mr. Allen?"

Will gave Saavedra a business card. "I'm responsible for risk assessment."

Saavedra shared an amused glance with Bernie, "Well, you have certainly come to the right place." He produced a silver case from his coat pocket and presented Will a card in return.

Someone across the room waved. "Excuse me," Bernie said.

For an awkward moment Will and Carlos Saavedra stood silently together. Will asked about his business and Saavedra described his fleet of trucks.

"Mainly we have contracts with the mines."

As he launched into a description of his efforts to hedge gasoline prices, Will noticed a very tall, very thin, very blond man in a light linen suit enter the room and make his way through the sea of dark suits and guayaberas.

Saavedra followed Will's gaze and made a soft clucking sound.

"Have you met the representative from the Soviet Trade Ministry yet?"

"That guy in the light suit?"

"Comrade Kazatsky. Rumor has it he has Salvador Allende's ear. It was he, not the Soviet ambassador, who arranged the president's trip to Moscow."

Will sipped his beer and felt his pulse quicken. He had never seen a Soviet official before. It was as if all of his training fixed on this moment, like a captain on the open seas who has sighted an enemy warship emerging from the fog. Naively, he had not expected such an encounter here. Cuban pirates, perhaps, but not someone sailing under the Soviet flag.

"Are there many Russians in Chile?" Will asked.

"More every day since they extended the government a line of credit. Dr. Allende's trip was not for nothing. No doubt Russian tractors will be plowing our fields next."

An acquaintance of Saavedra's interrupted. Saavedra introduced him as an economist with the Agricultural Reform Corporation. The anxious myopic man seemed less interested in meeting Will than in steering people toward the tables so that lunch could be served. Bernie rejoined them and they found seats near the back of the room. The Russian took direct aim for a table in front of the podium, herding a coterie of fawning Chileans with his long arms.

Lunch was served and the noise of conversations in multiple languages rose over the clatter of knives and forks, making it difficult for Will to follow all that was being said at his table.

"...the French court made the right decision. The payment never should have been frozen. Kennecott had no legal right..."

"...and my youngest son is studying economics, just like his old man, ha, ha, ha! He just won a scholarship to the University of Chicago..."

"Will, you must join me for lunch at my club some day and visit our operation," Saavedra said.

"I'd like that."

"Perhaps after you have settled in. I'd like to practice my English. You can tell me what Americans think of things here."

The speaker, an official from the government budget office, took the podium to explain the UP's strategies for achieving the current five-year plan if copper prices continued to fall.

After lunch, while Bernie said goodbye to Saavedra, Will went to the men's room. A gray-haired man in a pale yellow guayabera occupied the nearest urinal, so Will took the farthest one.

As Will turned to rinse his hands, he heard a heavily accented voice greet the bathroom attendant. The tall Russian entered, catching Will's eyes in the mirror. He ambled over to a basin, and, humming softly, combed his hair. The room buzzed with tempered silence. The Chilean in the guayabera, who was taking his time to dry his hands, gave a quick nod to the Russian and left. The Russian brushed the lapels of his suit, straightened his tie and, with the faintest hint of a smile at Will, also left, tossing a coin into the attendant's basket on the way out.

Will was certain his presence had interrupted an exchange between handler and agent. He recognized all of the signs.

Next morning at their weekly meeting, Ed Lipton seemed impatient to leave the stuffy room in the Hotel Rincón. He checked off the items on Will's to-do list then, almost as an afterthought, asked, "Anything else?"

It was a question Lipton asked often, sometimes several times in the same meeting, as if he expected omissions.

"Yeah, I went to the ECLA meeting with Bernie yesterday."

Lipton nodded.

"Met a guy named Carlos Saavedra. Former client of FRIG. Trucking business. Bernie knows him. Seems successful, business oriented, conservative. Anti-UP."

"I vaguely remember the name."

"He's just been elected treasurer of the truck owners association in Santiago."

Lipton's jaw tautened. "Really. Any chance of getting to know him better?"

Will shrugged. "I think so. Like I said, he used to be a client."

"Good."

"Oh, one other thing." Will had saved his best for last. "A Soviet trade commissioner was there. Kuznatsky. Kaznotsky. Something like that."

"Svyataslav Kazatsky," Lipton said.

"You know him?"

"Sure, he's KGB."

"You know that?"

"Was he wearing a linen suit, look kinda like the Man from Glad?"

"How'd you know?"

Lipton smiled as he scribbled on a pocket-sized notepad.

"Because I spoke to him last night at a reception. He mentioned he was there."

"Does he know who you are?"

Lipton laughed. "I suspect so."

"But I saw him try to tag an asset in the men's room."

Will saw Lipton suppress a smile at the awkward way it came out.

"Maybe he just needed to take a leak. Who was he meeting?"

"I don't know. A guy in a guayabera."

"Shit, Will. That doesn't do much good, does it?"

"But it's something, isn't it?"

"Gee, let me see. I better send HQ an urgent cable: 'KGB making contact with Chilean government personnel in hotel men's rooms.' Yeah, that should get us both promoted. Next time find out who it is."

Lipton put away his notepad. "Look, I've got to go. Let's meet next Wednesday at 3:00. In the meantime, start getting to know this Saavedra guy."

He started to stand. "Oh…" and opened his briefcase. "Santa Claus came early." He handed Will a heavy padded envelope bound with two thick rubber bands.

Will removed the bands and peered inside—a standard-requisition Smith and Wesson, the same compact .40-caliber model he learned to shoot in training, with a box of ammo. The metallic scent of gun oil permeated the envelope.

"Remember how to use it?"

Will smirked and carefully refolded the pouch. He placed the package in his briefcase. He hated the whole gun thing. He was required to have a weapon, but that aspect of the job seemed far removed from his reality. He wasn't smuggling agents across the border. He was a money manager, forging invoices and doling out cash.

6

*W*ill spent the sweltering days leading up to Christmas working long hours, moving money from Mexico to Santiago and delivering envelopes of cash to agents he only knew by codename. First Republic also required a reconciliation of the branch accounts for its fiscal close, and Leti had taken the week off to be with her family.

At the last minute, Will thought about going to Viña del Mar for the three-day weekend but was unable to find a hotel. If Chileans were struggling with the world's highest inflation, the hordes going to the beach didn't seem to notice. He ended up spending the weekend alone, listening to music, reading, watching television, and going for several long runs. On Christmas Day he tried calling home several times—he would have liked to wish his mother a merry Christmas—but all the circuits were busy.

The week after Christmas passed slowly amid endless news stories about a plane crash in the Andes and the survivors' grisly resort to cannibalism. Will was relieved when Three Kings brought a close to the holidays and an end to his forced isolation. The next day Roland Fabré invited him to Le Figaro, a favorite French restaurant on Avenida Portugal.

Since November, Will had spent several evenings over a bottle of wine with Roland Fabré. Despite the age difference, he enjoyed the company of his odd neighbor and was mildly disappointed when Fabré's background check came back clean. Secretly, he'd hoped he was being courted by a foreign intelligence service. But, according to Lipton, Roland Fabré was who he said he was. The Frenchman's eccentricities were real, not a cover. The only evidence on file of any political activity was his signature on a petition demanding the release of Jean-Paul Sartre after the Marxist philosopher's arrest in May 1968.

Will left work around six-thirty and walked to Roland's office in a three-story municipal building. Inside the central courtyard two workmen were dismantling a large crèche. He followed the signs to the Metropolitan Planning Department, an expansive room crowded with drafting tables. On the walls, enlarged street maps looked as if they were held in place by the clusters of colored pins dotting them, representing the numbers of people served by each proposed subway station.

Most of the workers were gone for the day, although a few draftsmen still hunched over elaborate engineering drawings taped to drafting boards. Will recognized Roland's wavy white head of hair in a glass-enclosed office at the far end of the room. When he knocked on the open door, Roland turned as if startled.

"Reeshard! Come in, come in. I did not realize the time." The conflicting patterns of his attire—blue hounds-tooth sport coat, red-striped shirt and paisley tie—had the jarring impact of an Escher print. A cigar jutted from the corner of his mouth.

"Am I too early?"

"Not at all. Please." Roland cleared a pile of papers off a chair by his desk and swatted away the ash that fell as he did so. His desk was a clutter of papers, books and dirty coffee cups. Scraps of paper, bits of hole-punch, paperclips, and spent matches littered the floor underneath his chair.

Roland's somnolent eyes appraised him. Sometimes Will felt as if the Frenchman saw through or, more accurately, inside him. The gaze was not threatening, rather it was how he wished his father could have looked at him—with acceptance and sincere concern.

"So, what do you think?" Roland asked.

Will laughed. "About what?"

Roland absently trimmed the ash from his cigar on the steel handle of the desk drawer, clearly a habit since the nap of the maroon carpet below had acquired a permanent ashen pallor. "I don't know. My office? Is it nicer than insurance?"

Will nodded cheerfully. "Much."

Roland placed his briefcase on top of the cluttered desk and began randomly tossing things inside: a copy of *L'Express*, a fountain pen, a pack of cigarettes. After a reflective pause, he took a box of cigars from the drawer. "I have begun to suspect that the custodian has a taste for fine Cuban cigars," he said with a wink. He turned around, patted down his jacket and then uncovered his reading glasses beneath some papers on the desk and threw them in as well. "Ça y est!"

The restaurant was around the corner on a busy commercial street. A row of double-parked cars had caused a traffic jam directly in front. Horns honked. A group of men in black windbreakers stood in the doorway creating another jam on the sidewalk. Roland maneuvered past the unyielding men and greeted the owner, who conversed in French as he led them to a table in the crowded dining room. Mirrors made the narrow room feel larger and even more crowded.

Sitting down, Roland leaned forward and said, "There's a government VIP in the back room. That's why all the bodyguards. A big deal, apparently, but Georges won't say who."

No sooner had he spoken than the doors to the back room opened and a parade of men marched through the main room. Diners stopped what they were doing to watch. First, three muscular men went outside and whistled to the drivers. Four men in business suits followed. Finally, two more muscular men in suits filed out with the VIP, dwarfed by their size, walking between them. It was President Allende. The lenses of Allende's thick black-framed glasses flashed as he nodded to patrons, apologizing to several in passing for the disruption. A customer at the back of the room hissed and the woman he was with angrily flapped her napkin to shush him. In seconds Allende was out the door into a waiting car.

Will had seen countless pictures of El Compañero Presidente, read his speeches, heard his voice on the radio, but this was the nearest he was ever likely to come to the man. He had seen the energy in the room shift as Allende breezed through.

"I don't believe it!" he said.

Roland smothered his delight with his napkin. "VIP indeed! Georges will raise prices now!"

"Did you recognize any of the men with him?" Will asked, shifting from initial surprise to the sobriety of his intelligence duties. This *was* something to report to Lipton.

Roland shook his head. He tore into a hard roll and smeared butter on it then took a ravenous bite. "Georges may be able to tell us. Shall we start with an apéritif?"

Roland recommended the salmon but ordered the sole meunière for himself, so Will followed suit. Roland ordered everything in French. When Georges brought over the bottle of wine for Roland's inspection, Will could tell from the conversation's tone that Roland was teasing the owner about his discretion.

"Did he know who the others were?" Will asked again.

Roland shrugged.

"Remarkable, no? What do you think charisma is, Richard? Why is Doctor Allende able to stir the hearts of so many? Good or bad, you saw how people responded. I've seen many great men come and go…General de Gaulle, your President Kennedy, Mr. Churchill, even Mr. Hitler, who was more charismatic than any of them. What draws people to these men? After all, their ideas can be quite idiotic."

Roland chewed vigorously. "I think the good doctor is a sincere man who wants to do good for people. Isn't that why one becomes a doctor? Perhaps he believes politics must be more like medicine. Diagnose the illness, prescribe the cure. What do you think?"

Will was conscious that despite speaking English, others could overhear, and even if they didn't understand what was being said, they would know that the conversation was about their president.

"Then I think he should be sued for malpractice," he said softly.

Roland laughed. "I have a theory on leadership." He popped another piece of bread in his mouth. Will waited for him to finish chewing.

"You have heard of received ideas? Flaubert made a dictionary of them. The stupidities and clichés people spout in order not to think. You see, I believe people really don't want to think. Perhaps you think I am 'misanthrope'? You know this term?" Will smiled at the preposterous notion of Roland Fabré's misanthropy. "Most people prefer to go through life sleeping—in their work, in their lovemaking, in their marriages, in their conversations. And so they choose leaders who do not challenge them, ones who speak the same dull language.

"But the charismatic, he is different. He recognizes the power of language. His genius is with words. He is a visionary, a poet who mobilizes new metaphors. He knows that the old metaphors have literalized—you say this in English? The charismatic, on the other hand, conveys his ideas in words that sound familiar, but he turns them on end, uses them in new ways. This is why people become so excited when one of these persons comes along. He tickles them awake. His words are like a feather under the nose, and the people either awaken laughing or very angry. That is all this Vía Chilena of Doctor Allende's is."

"A feather tickling the nose?"

Roland waved his hand through the air as if to recant everything he just said. "This is only my theory. Doctor Allende's genius is to take these tired old words—Marxism, the proletariat, the homeland—and give them new meaning."

"You make it sound so harmless. How do you know they aren't the same stale ideas as before? Demagoguery, oppression, dictatorship, tyranny."

"Richard, you surprise me! You are much too young to view the world this way. As if you look through someone else's glasses. With frames more black than President Allende's!"

"Earlier this week I saw the Soviet attaché schmoozing at an economic meeting."

Roland puckered his lips and shrugged. A gesture to say, so what?

"The Cold War is a dying metaphor based on fear. That is precisely what President Allende is saying. Why can't there be another way? A Chilean Way. Marxism without totalitarianism. Communism with democracy."

"I didn't realize you were such a supporter."

"You see! I am an optimist after all! But seriously, what hope is there in defending what was? That is arrogant and it usually involves a lie. The world is not ours, Richard. Change is inevitable. Each generation must create its own vocabulary, shape its own metaphors, revolt from the past. Your Thomas Jefferson said that. We French know as well as you Americans, a revolution starts not with new ideas but with new words. In your case it was life, liberty and the pursuit of happiness. In ours, liberté, égalité, fraternité. Here, why not something else?"

Recalling Lipton's tidbit about the petition Roland had signed for Jean-Paul Sartre, Will decided to bait his host. "How about being and nothingness?" But the Frenchman didn't pick up on the allusion.

They ate a selection of cheeses for dessert, then drank coffee—real, rich black coffee, something Will had not tasted in weeks—and ordered cognac. Roland lit one of his Cuban cigars and Will smoked a cigarette. Georges came over to apologize:

they were out of cognac. They had been unable to obtain any for a month. Would the messieurs be interested in a local brandy? Roland shook his head dismissively and ordered whisky instead.

Over drinks, Will asked his host if he had fought in the resistance during the war. Roland rolled the cigar from one side of his mouth to the other and laughed.

"Why do people assume that everyone in France was either a Nazi sympathizer or a resistance fighter? You see! That too is a received idea. Of course, I forgive you because you are too young to know better. But, no, like most French people, I was neither. During the four years that the Germans occupied Paris I studied mathematics at university. When the liberation came, I continued my studies. The only difference, I specialized in statistics."

But Will wasn't satisfied. He'd seen *The Sorrow and the Pity* with its depictions of reprisal—the shaving of women's heads, the execution of collaborators. "Yes, but, after the war, did you witness any of the retributions?"

Roland gave Will a vague smile. He seemed uncomfortable with the subject. "You must think the world back then was black and white, like the movies, like *Casablanca.*

"Of course there were some who embraced Fascism, but most people simply did what they had to do to survive. In my opinion, those who took retribution were as cruel as the ones they accused. In the end, they were no different. I did *not* take part in those things. Yet I wonder—those who did participate, did they feel tremendous shame afterward, or did they bury it? It is not something people talk about now. As I said, people don't like to think, especially about their own cruel acts."

He looked at his watch, sighed, and wiped his mouth with the napkin. "You are a bad influence, Richard. I have enjoyed our conversation but have indulged too much. I will sleep badly tonight. Shall we go?"

7

*I*n ordinary times Will might have waited months before taking on such an important asset as Emilio Girardi. But, as Lipton kept saying, these were no ordinary times.

"The elections are a month away. P and K are screaming for results. And we're damn well going to deliver. Clear?"

It was the end of January—the dog days of summer—and although Lipton spoke softly, his voice rumbled like distant thunder across the stifling room in the Hotel Rincón. To someone listening from the other side of the door, he might have sounded like a scolding priest in a confessional.

"Because if K screams, the DCI screams. And if the DCI screams, I hear Teletype chattering in my sleep. That makes me scream. And if I scream…well, you get my point—shit flows downhill."

Lipton's thin lips flexed in a pitiless smile. Will attributed his boss's bullying to lack of sleep or too much caffeine.

He knew little about his boss. For security reasons that was how Lipton wanted it. Will didn't mind. His distaste for the man grew with each encounter. Lipton's muscular arms and tightly sprung stride exuded physical toughness. The short haircut and gruff manner of speech betrayed military training. Will suspected the Marines from the way Lipton always pushed to excel. He'd seen plenty of ex-soldiers during training: fearless, unreflective, duty-bound chain-of-command career men who jumped at superiors' orders and barked reflexively at subordinates. Pressure cookers of nervous energy who tried to intimidate others by conveying a mystique of latent deadly force. It was difficult to tell how much was bluster and how much real. But Lipton was different. The cool gray eyes squinting at Will conveyed a streetsmart cunning.

"What are you smirking at?"

Will blurted the first thing that came to mind. "When do I get to scream?"

Lipton chewed his lower lip then released the soft, chapped flesh. His jaw muscles relaxed and he laughed—at least that's how Will interpreted the faint exhalation. Maybe he wasn't a complete asshole.

"Scream all you want, bucko. Just do what I've told you to do. We need Girardi to crank up the heat. He's primed to go."

"Okay, but I don't get it. I thought the opposition was working together now. Isn't that the whole point of CODE?" Will asked, referring to the coalition of opposition parties formed to defeat Allende's coalition. In the troubled and confusing multiparty world of Chilean politics, the people's choice for the next election was reduced to Right or Left. "I mean, if the Christian Democrat has a better chance of winning, why are we funding a guy on the extreme right? Why aren't we backing the CD candidate?"

"Girardi's candidate is a crackpot fascist named Davíd Dávila who doesn't stand a snowball's chance in hell. His entire campaign is built on private property rights. He's calling for the army to storm the fincas taken over by the MIR and evict them so the land can be returned to its rightful owners. Talk about starting a fucking war!"

The Movimiento de la Izquierda Revolucionaria, or MIR, were extremist apostles of Marxist revolution. Taking advantage of the chaos created by the October general strike, they had seized businesses that supported the strikers and occupied the estates of absentee landlords. Mindful of their incendiary power within the left wing of his coalition, President Allende had allowed the illegal seizures to go unchallenged.

"But the fear factor plays to our advantage," continued Lipton. "When the UP sees how nuts this guy is, their own nuts will start brandishing their sickles and hammers, and the sane people, the majority of voters sitting on the fence, they'll move to the center. Call it Lipton's Law of Extreme Avoidance."

The logic didn't make much sense but Lipton wasn't interested in debating strategy. He gave Will a week to close the deal.

"What if he doesn't accept?"

"Then we move on," Lipton said. "Fuck him."

The meeting was over. Lipton got up to go.

"Oh, and here's your mail," tossing an inter-office envelope into Will's lap.

The envelope contained a half dozen letters with Will's government FPO address neatly written in his mother's hand.

"My mom worries a lot. She's never been out of the country, except to Nogales," said Will, embarrassed by the quantity.

"That's what moms are for," Lipton said with a look of forbearance. "I'll leave first."

Once alone, Will went into the bathroom and turned off the roaring faucet in the rust-stained tub. In the stillness he sifted through the letters, opened one, started to read, then tucked it back in the envelope. He had to tell his parents something when the FBI conducted his security clearance. They believed he traveled the continent working as a government contractor.

He waited five minutes, set the lock on the door and left. As he crossed the hallway to the stairwell he heard an adjacent door open and quickly close.

That Friday, Will drove to Concepción, the port city five-hundred kilometers south of Santiago, to meet Emilio Girardi. It was an overnight trip, eleven hours down depending on road conditions. He scheduled a late-afternoon appointment with Girardi and told Lipton he would be back in Santiago Saturday night. Will placed $10,000 in a manila envelope inside the hidden compartment of his briefcase then packed a clean shirt, a pair of underpants, socks and his toilet kit in the main compartment.

He arranged with Leti to take the company car, a powder blue 1962 Ford Falcon that had seen better days. Will checked the trunk for a spare tire and swirled the gas can: half full. He placed his briefcase in the passenger footwell and with the map on the seat beside him set out at four-thirty in the morning. After only one wrong turn, he headed south on the Pan-American Highway.

He drove with the windows down, relishing the fresh breeze blowing from the coast. The sun had not yet emerged over the peaks of the Andes and the cordillera stretched as far as the eye could see, like a massive cresting wave, a granite tsunami about to engulf the known world. He tuned the radio to a perky salsa.

Working-class barrios gave way to unpaved shantytowns where mangy dogs wandered between hovels made of discarded wood scraps and corrugated iron. Even at this early twilit hour, crowded buses played chicken crossing the highway to disgorge passengers in front of factories with grimy skylights.

An hour later the morning sun illuminated apple orchards, vineyards with neat rows of trellised grape vines and groves of gray-green olive trees. Near Rancagua, Will came to a turnoff for the road to El Teniente copper mine. A slow-moving long-bed truck with a heavy load of rebar chugged toward the mine, and he wondered if it was one of Carlos Saavedra's.

According to Lipton's background information, Emilio Girardi was a naturalized Chilean, an Italian immigrant who arrived shortly after the war. He had built a chain of newspapers in the southern half of the country, beginning in Concepción with *La Aurora de Concepción* and eventually establishing businesses as far south as Puerto Montt (*La Aurora de Llanquihue*) and as far north as Talca (*La Aurora de Talca*). Next, he set about buying radio stations with the same regional ambition.

Married to the daughter of a wealthy landowner in Concepción, Girardi had four children—three sons and a daughter. The eldest son now ran the newspapers and the second managed the radio stations. This freed el patrón to devote his time and energy to politics. In the last five years Girardi was transformed from a casual supporter of the conservative Partido Nacional to a fervent financial contributor to Patria y Libertad, the ultra-right-wing paramilitary formed to contest Salvador Allende's ascension to the presidency in 1970.

Girardi was doing his part for the extreme right by using his media to attack government policies. Despite strong nationalist tendencies, he was an astute enough businessman to recognize that financial underwriting of his political initiatives was not to be spurned, even if that underwriting came from foreign sources.

Through weeks of clandestine meetings and telephone exchanges, Lipton had worked out the general terms of a deal with Girardi. Will's job was to iron out where, when and how to apply the subsidies.

For their meeting Girardi suggested a seafood restaurant in the port of Talcahuano at five in the afternoon. The restaurant, a slouching wooden shack with café tables under blue umbrellas, was nearly deserted when Will arrived. The smell of brine and frying oil permeated the air, and scavenging seagulls on the seawall eyed the tables for leftovers.

Will selected a table away from the few other patrons. A middle-aged waiter strolled out with a menu. When Will only ordered a beer, the waiter, his face a blank of disinterest bordering on contempt, disappeared into the shack and didn't come back. Will turned his chair to survey the busy harbor. Fishing boats bobbed at their moorings amid oil slicks and flotsam. A man in yellow rubber overalls sitting on the gunwale of a trawler adjusted the floats on a large green net draped over his lap. Across the harbor, near an industrial area with conveyors jutting over gigantic mounds of coal and sulfur, a tugboat struggled to maneuver a coal-laden barge into deep water.

At five sharp a green Mercedes sedan pulled up in front of the restaurant. A silver-haired man in a charcoal gray suit threw open the rear door and climbed stiffly from the back seat. A uniformed driver hurried around to assist, but the man brushed him aside. A younger man in a camel blazer got out from the front passenger side, surveyed the street and stood by the curb. The silver-haired man approached the restaurant with a forceful stride, took one look at Will and came directly to his table.

"You must be my American insurance agent," he said in heavily accented English. He was ruggedly handsome, in his sixties, with sprightly gray-green eyes and a generous smile of white teeth.

Will stood up. "Ricardo Allen. A pleasure to meet you." Emilio Girardi gave his hand a firm shake. There was a resolution to his motions, a blend of determination and charm, that Will found captivating.

"Shall we?" he said, motioning Will to sit down. "Have you eaten yet?" he asked, shifting to Spanish. "The eel here is delicious. Also the lobster."

Will noticed as he sat down that the man in the camel blazer remained standing by the entrance. Then it dawned on him: he was the bodyguard.

The waiter came quickly to attention beside Emilio Girardi, greeting him as a regular. Girardi waved the menu away and without asking Will's preference ordered langostas and a bottle of white wine. The waiter gave a snap of the head and marched back to the kitchen, returning seconds later with bread, silverware and freshly ironed napkins.

Girardi devoted the first course to ask numerous personal

questions: how old Will was, where he had grown up, if he was married, if he had brothers and sisters. He seemed delighted with the responses even if he suspected that Will was not who he said he was, or that the answers to his questions were fabrications.

In training Will had learned how easy it was to steer a conversation toward information. Like many successful entrepreneurs, Girardi was enthralled with his own experience and voice. His question to Will about how long he had been in Chile led to a story about his arrival on a merchant vessel in 1947 with twenty dollars in his pocket. Will's description of his drive from Santiago led to a story about importing his car from Germany and how difficult it was now to find parts for it. Finally, he said, he gave up and imported a second one just for the parts. He spoke proudly of his sons, even the youngest who, he said with mock disapproval, was only interested in girls and auto racing. Girardi's solution: send him to Rome without a car to start a heavy course in civil engineering. He barely mentioned his wife or daughter except in passing.

After the meal was cleared and replaced with two glasses of brandy, they began to talk elliptically of business. Throughout the meal Will drank slowly. Still, he felt the alcohol infuse his thoughts and muddle his Spanish. In contrast Girardi's tone and focus became more precise as he tapped the table with his forefinger to emphasize his points.

"Did you know that the cost of newsprint has tripled in the last year alone? Tripled! And why? Because of government takeovers and incompetence. Yet they refuse to let us raise prices. Bad for inflation, they say. Meanwhile, who do you think is subsidizing these Marxist rags? Well, I'm not one to roll over. I left Italy because of the Communists and I'll be damned if I'm going to watch this country go to those dogs!"

A dark rage flashed across the rugged face. Now it was Will's job to charm.

"Yes, well, that's what we're here to discuss, isn't it? How to fend off the dogs together. I can offer advertising and public relations support, provided certain stipulations are met."

Girardi returned to his pleasant self. "Yes, and what would those be?"

"My company believes the people should hear the truth about this government's intentions. You can go down the list: expropriations of foreign companies, defaults on public debt, legal disputes with the international banks. People need to understand the consequences of the government's policies. You mentioned inflation, but it's potentially much more, isn't it? Just look at Cuba…an embargo, containment, isolation.

"Nevertheless, aggressive nationalism isn't the answer either. That only leads to protectionism, nepotism, social inequality, even intimidation… I think you know the concerns."

"Listen, my friend, sometimes a father needs to be strict with his children."

Will was certain Lipton had been over this ground before and suspected that Girardi was testing him for consistency, seeing if there was an opening he could turn to his advantage.

"Perhaps. But we believe moderation is best. If you want to advocate something more extreme, we can't—rather, my company can't support you despite sharing your concerns. Do we have agreement on this?"

"What kind of support are you proposing, young man?"

"Ten thousand dollars a month for the next three months, with a possibility to renew. The caveat is that we request the opportunity to provide you with some material…news, editorial information, that sort of thing. Also, in advance of the elections, we'd like to preview any political commentary you plan to publish on your editorial pages. Not to censor your ideas, simply to ensure that my company's interests are not compromised."

"And if you don't like what's written?"

"We might make suggestions, but ultimately the decision is yours, recognizing of course that your actions will be the basis of our evaluation for contract renewal."

Girardi gave Will a cagey smile. "I was under the impression there might also be a contribution to Patria y Libertad. We don't have the resources to offset the organized activities of the UP in this region. Much can be done to promote 'moderation,' as you call it, with very moderate resources."

Will grinned at Girardi's word play. "We would need an assurance that the contributions are not being used for something else, something more extreme. After what happened to ITT, my company is naturally very concerned about negative publicity."

Even Emilio Girardi must acknowledge the incident Will alluded to. Only a year earlier Jack Anderson had revealed in his newspaper column that the American multinational corporation ITT had schemed to overthrow Allende, ostensibly with CIA blessing. Allende made much of it in his UN speech, admonishing ITT, Anaconda Copper and Kennecott for attempting to disrupt the democratic process in Chile.

"What kind of proof?"

Will shook his head. "That's open for discussion. My company's intentions are clear: To support opposition parties and media until the current administration's efforts to suppress them change. If that means helping with administrative and operating expenses, it seems to me you could demonstrate those expenses fairly easily."

Girardi smiled. "I hope, young man, that you and your company are prepared to stay the course. It's going to get worse before it gets better here. As I said, I went down this road in Italy."

Sensing another story coming on, Will intervened by taking a piece of paper from his inside coat pocket. It was a copy of a cancelled check for $15,000 made out to Danilo Puente, the UP's candidate in Ñuble province for the same senate seat being contested by Girardi's crackpot, Davíd Dávila. The check was from the American Association of Federated Workers, a union organization fronted by the CIA, and had been deposited in a Swiss bank account. As far as Will knew it was real and someone had done a damn good job of convincing the candidate that no one would ever know about the payment. Leaking it now would destroy his campaign.

"This is the kind of information my company thinks the public should know," he said, handing the paper to Girardi. "If we are in agreement on terms, then you can demonstrate your good faith by publishing it."

Girardi took a pair of thin silver-framed reading glasses from his pocket and put them on. He studied the paper and his face bloomed with amusement.

"Can this be documented?" he asked, eyes gleaming over the top of the glasses.

"We believe it can. Unfortunately, the source must remain confidential."

"You realize, don Ricardo, that the accused gentleman will claim it's an inflammatory lie, if not slander. Anyone publishing this would be putting himself at considerable risk."

"Consider the risk of not publishing it," Will countered.

That night Will stayed in a cheap hotel near the university. He was pleased with how the meeting went. He'd handled the Italian well. Girardi accepted the $10,000 advance and was now on their payroll. While the meeting was still fresh, Will wrote his report, recalling the slightest details of their conversation, anything that might add to Girardi's dossier.

He sealed his notes in an envelope and placed the envelope in the hidden compartment of his briefcase. Then he opened his paperback copy of *Deliverance* and read about a canoe trip down a threatened river in the backwoods of Georgia.

Late in the evening a couple entered the room next to his. Their voices projected through the airshaft into his bathroom window—whispers followed by loud lovemaking on a creaking bed. The woman's voice rose in climax and was suddenly stifled, as if the man had covered her mouth with his hand. More whispering, then a shower running for several minutes, then subdued laughter. The outer door closed and all was quiet again.

Will found the tryst distracting and disquieting. Was it a young couple escaping their families, or some middle-aged professor and his mistress sneaking off together on a Friday night, or the hotel maid and her boyfriend? The possibilities made him feel very alone, and lonely. He had not had sex in over a year. Not for the first time since his assignment began, he thought of Sarah. He tried to imagine her long, leggy body, but the fact that she'd dumped him kept getting in the way.

Will left Concepción the following day. He stopped for gas but a flatbed truck blocked the station's entrance. At the next station, three men stood at a barricade of wooden sawhorses turning away cars that didn't have ration cards. Angry drivers jeered and honked horns. Each gas station Will came to was closed due to a work stoppage by the local truckers.

Will crossed a bridge over the gravel banks of the snaking Bío-Bío River. He checked the gas gauge and figured he could make it to the Pan-American Highway. The nearer he got to Santiago the better his chances would be to find gas. He should have filled the gas can before leaving Santiago.

He switched on the radio. The announcer and someone he addressed as "maestro" talked so rapidly and with such clipped accents, it was difficult for Will to follow. The maestro sounded Cuban. He talked about the need for a national literacy campaign, for teachers to go out to rural areas and into the poblaciones, and kept referring to "we." To Will's mounting annoyance, the interviewer didn't object. We who? We Chileans? We Latin Americans? We Communists? No one seemed to notice the insertion of that insidious pronoun into conversation. All of Emilio Girardi's anger and energy was focused on it. "We are blue, they are red. We believe in free trade, they believe in central economies." If there was a "we," it inevitably followed there must be a "they," or more often, "those bastards."

Will pressed lightly on the gas to conserve and coasted downhill. Most restaurants and shops on the highway were closed, and few cars came from the opposite direction. Near Chillán, he stopped at a mechanic's shop with its garage door open and asked if the owner had any gasoline or knew of a place nearby that did. The mechanic—his mouth a smear of grease on a dark, blank face—listened to Will's foreign accent and slowly wiped his hands on a filthy rag. He shook his head as if to say, even if he had gas, he wouldn't sell it to Will.

Will emptied the gas can into the tank. The needle on the gauge barely budged. Enough to get to Chillán, but if he couldn't find gas there, he'd have to spend the night and look for gas in the morning.

Chillán, as he came to it, reminded him of the slow-paced agricultural towns along California's Highway 101—Paso Robles or San Luis Obispo. He followed street signs to the plaza de armas and found himself engulfed by a demonstration. A crowd of women waved white handkerchiefs and banged pots and pans: "La única solución, que se tome el avión…" Will listened to several repetitions before he understood: "The only solution is that he gets on a plane…" They were chanting about Allende.

The streets were crowded with onlookers, cars honked. Traffic had slowed. Will pulled over and parked. On foot, he weaved through the crowd toward the plaza. He found a restaurant on the corner and from a table by the window watched the demonstration while he ate a sandwich. When he asked the waiter if he knew where he could get some gas, the waiter laughed. "Sure. Siphon it from Allende's car."

PART TWO

The Mannings

February – September 1973

The young homosexuals and the amorous girls,
and the drawn widows who suffer delirious insomnia,
and the young wives thirty hours pregnant,
and the hoarse cats that cross my garden in darkness,
like a necklace of sexually throbbing oysters
they surround my solitary residence,
like the sworn enemies of my soul,
like conspirators in dressing gowns
who exchange long deep kisses as countersign.

—Pablo Neruda, from "Caballero Solo"

8

*I*n the agricultural town of Chillán, an unmarried woman of twenty-three warranted almost as much speculation as the political crisis. Gabriela Manning saw the concern in the eyes of her mother, her aunt, her cousin, even her best friends: Why isn't this girl married? She's pretty, capable, well educated. What are we doing wrong?

Whenever she left the room she knew what the conversation would turn to, and upon her return braced for the well-meant but prying questions.

"Are you seeing anyone, dear?" Aunt María Elena might ask over Sunday lunch.

"Isn't that new reporter at the paper single?" cousin Julia would carefully inquire as they shopped together.

"Don't frown, Gabi. It will put a crease in your brow," her mother would warn. "And then what will you do?"

Gabriela tried to disregard these coded hints and admonitions. Had her father still been alive she was certain he would have supported her career aspirations, and there were many times when she dearly missed his reassuring hugs.

Señora Ema de Manning worried that her daughter's situation reflected a change in their social standing since her husband's sudden death.

"Is some sort of rumor going around town?" she asked her sister while Gabriela set the dining room table and pretended not to hear.

María Elena, who sat on the high-backed Victorian sofa that Dr. Manning's grandfather shipped from England in 1885, shook her head but continued to leaf through the latest issue of *Paula*.

"Hardly. These days, people simply don't know what good society is. All they care about is whether you have access to black-market cigarettes." She stood up and with a sibling's familiarity rearranged the flowers in the alabaster vase on the side table. "No, I just think Gabi is too focused on work. You know how men are—too self-absorbed to notice anything unless you put it right in front of them." And the two sisters laughed as one.

Only Gabriela's brother, Ernesto, seemed to understand her point of view. Or perhaps he only sought a partner in rebellion. He had sulked all summer, keeping to his room, lying on his bed smoking cigarettes and reading novels or listening to music, or climbing onto the roof late at night to smoke a joint alone. So, while mother and aunt worried about her, Gabriela worried about Ernesto.

That's why she was so pleased when Ernesto, as he dropped her off at work on this Saturday morning, suggested going to the stables with her in the afternoon. It was early February, still the height of summer. School didn't start for another month, but Ernesto claimed he needed to return to Santiago to begin his thesis. This outing would be a last chance to spend time together, just the two of them like in the carefree days before their father died.

Was Ernesto feeling the same pull of nostalgia?

She ran up the concrete stairs to the second-story office of *La Aurora*, which overlooked the plaza de armas. Large sycamores dappled with summer's fine white dust stood in the view of the corner office where Roberto "Beto" Bulnes, the newspaper's editor, worked. He looked up through a cigarette haze as Gabriela crossed the deserted editorial room to her desk.

"Hello, my love," he mumbled, cigarette hanging from his lip.

"Good morning, Beto." But his focus had already returned to the ash-strewn piles of invoices and accounts on his desk.

She slung her purse over the arm of her chair and picked up the broadside galleys of the society pages that the typesetter Armando had left for her review.

"No, no, no!" she muttered, finding a typo in the very first photo caption. The name of Chillán's most prominent lawyer transposed so that "Lic. Juan José Velasco Gómez" read "Lic. José Juan Gómez Velasco."

Sometimes she wondered if Armando did it on purpose. Only the week before she had discovered an errant paragraph of waxed type crookedly slapped across the engagement photo of her good friend, Ana María Lopez Holst. It would have spelled disaster if she had not checked.

She highlighted the transposed names with a blue pencil and wrote the correction on the edge of the board.

It was hardly the kind of journalism she had dreamed of when she graduated from university, but the job allowed her to stay in Chillán, and there was always the possibility, as Beto assured her, that some day she would receive more newsworthy assignments. "Unless, of course, you get married," he teased, adding with a wink, "And you know, love, I will propose myself if we can keep it a secret from my wife."

She worked diligently for the next two hours. Absorbed in her proofing, she only became conscious of the noise outside as it surged like a wave crashing onto the plaza—cheers, shouts, whistling, and honking horns.

She went to Beto's office to see what the commotion was.

Beto was already at the window. "Look! The starving women of Chillán," he said with a cynical roll of the eyes.

A crowd had gathered. Banners daubed with hand-painted slogans protested rising prices for flour and cornmeal. "Mothers against Allende," read one banner. "Female Power" another. Women armed with pots and pans and wooden spoons had formed a line that snaked around the square. Those without pots waved white handkerchiefs above their heads.

"La única solución, que se tome el avión..." they chanted.

Pedestrians paused to watch. Traffic slowed around the square.

"Shouldn't someone be covering this?"

Beto laughed, his sallow cheek creasing at the jowl as he tilted his head. "Why? They'll bang their pots for half an hour then go home to a lunch prepared by their maids. I can report on that from here. Hey, isn't that my wife?" He grinned and drew one last breath from a spent cigarette then stubbed the butt into an ashtray resting on the sill.

"Beto! It's still news."

"Trust me, by Monday they'll be more concerned with the pictures in your society pages. Finished?"

Gabriela nodded.

"Good, I'll let Armando know when he comes in."

At that moment another group, union men in hard hats and women in navy blue work smocks, appeared on the far side of the plaza in front of the cathedral. Waving pro-Allende signs, they shouted a competing slogan: "Allende, Allende, el pueblo te defiende..." Allende, Allende the people defend you.

In defiance, the banging and chanting of the women grew louder and more unified: "La única solución, que se tome el avión..."

"Okay, now it's getting interesting," admitted Beto.

Just then the flared fenders and bug-eyed headlamps of the little white Citroneta turned the corner with Ernesto at the wheel.

"Oh, I have to go..." Leaving Beto at the window.

She gathered her things and ran to the bathroom to change. A moment later, dressed in straw-colored breeches and white knee socks, she hurried past Beto's office, laughing. "My boots are in the car. See you Monday."

"Goodbye, my love." Despite his declared nonchalance, she noticed that he had taken a pad of paper and, with one elbow propped on the windowsill, was jotting notes.

Her brother waited at the curb. Passing cars honked, whether for or against the demonstration it was impossible to tell. Laughing at the chaos, Gabriela padded across the sidewalk and hopped into the car.

"Let's get the hell out of here," her brother said.

He tried going around the plaza but a noisy file of women crossing to the market blocked the way. "La única solución, que se tome el avión…"

Ernesto honked in rhythm. Gabriela recognized several neighbors and acquaintances, including her red-haired cousin who waved as she and a girlfriend passed by arm in arm.

Across the plaza the chant of the opposing faction grew more insistent: "Allende, Allende, el pueblo te defiende."

"Beto doesn't think this means anything," Gabriela said. "I think he's wrong."

"That's because he hates confrontation. He's a socialist at heart, even if he does work for the damned *Aurora*."

"No, he's just soft-hearted."

"Same thing… That's why I like him."

The parade finally dissipated and they proceeded away from the congestion of the square. Ernesto drove like a formula-one racer, revving the whining three-cylinder engine and shifting only when it sounded as if it were going to explode. Townscape gradually transformed into countryside.

"Slow down, Ernesto. It isn't a race."

She wished she could slow everything down—Ernesto's departure, the end of summer, the busy weeks measured edition by edition. She wanted to soak up the land's familiar beauty on this lovely afternoon and take time to admire these orchards, where apples hung heavy on limbs braced with makeshift wooden crutches, and the fields of tall corn ready for harvesting. In the distance, beyond windbreaks of delicate pines, the gentle snow-capped slopes of the Chillán volcanoes, cool and somber, stood out among the ragged peaks of the cordillera. She never tired of this landscape.

At a dusty pasture bordered by a weathered fence, three horses trotted alongside as the little car jogged up the rutted drive to the stable.

Ernesto parked in front of the barn. Gabriela pulled on her boots before going inside the cool tack room. The pleasant smell of oiled leather and saddle soap greeted them. Ernesto lifted Gabriela's saddle from the rack while she took the bridle from its post.

"Hello, Alonso," Gabriela said to a brown-skinned Mapuche brushing her horse in the aisle. Ernesto placed the saddle on the stall door and went outside for a smoke.

"How's my Rayo today?" She patted the tall black gelding on the neck.

"Fat," the groom responded as he bent down to clean the horse's hooves.

"No!"

Alonso leaned against the rear haunch to make the animal shift its weight, then gripped the horse's shank and made a clicking sound. The horse obligingly lifted its leg.

Gabriela's hand traced the horse's strong confirmation from the hard ridge of the withers to the smooth firm rump. She inspected the legs and walked around until she faced the white blaze on the horse's nose.

"Alonso, do you really think he's too fat?" she asked.

Alonso smiled but never made eye contact as he saddled the horse and loosely cinched the girth. The collar of Alonso's cotton shirt was frayed, she noticed, and the front of his brown twill pants had a greasy sheen as if they could repel water.

Gabriela placed the bit in Rayo's mouth and slipped the bridle over his ears before unfastening the halter. She led the horse to the ring. Ernesto leaned against the railing and smoked while she tightened the girth, mounted and made several warm-up loops at a trot. She took Rayo over three low jumps in the center of the ring. Each time she passed Ernesto, he made clucking noises, but the rest of the time her brother's handsome face was blank, his gaze abstracted as if he was barely there.

After an extended workout she dismounted and led Rayo to the side of the barn to bathe him. Ernesto sponged water over the horse's sweaty flanks, while she scraped it off. They played like children, laughing and joking and threatening each other with water. Then they led Rayo by the halter around the gravel drive to cool and dry.

"So, are you ever going to tell me what's going on?" she asked finally.

"Nothing's going on."

She gave him a challenging look.

"I just miss my friends," Ernesto said, laughing. "I hate being stuck here. I want to be back in Santiago. I hate this place and its narrow-minded people. You should, too. Honestly, I don't know how you stand it."

She walked on for a moment, fidgeting with the end of the rope lead. She suspected Ernesto's moodiness came from something else but she wasn't sure what. Maybe even he didn't know. "So, which is more true?" she asked, giving his arm a gentle squeeze. "Your love for your friends or your love for me?"

The question, with its echoes of childhood, made Ernesto laugh. One Christmas, with the extended family at a long dining table on the patio, and after much wine and conversation, their father proudly pronounced that he loved his children more than anything else in the world. Ernesto, who was five at the time, challenged him.

"But it's true!" his father insisted, "I love Gabi and I love you."

"Yes, but which is more true?" Ernesto demanded, to his father's delight.

Thereby a family game started that evolved into a kind of ritual, a shared code that often united the Mannings in laughter and left others bewildered.

"I love you equally," Ernesto said now.

"Liar!"

He laughed and she squeezed his hand as they walked one more loop.

It was nearly six when they handed Rayo back to Alonso. A golden light illuminated the walls of the weathered barn. Long shadows stretched from fence posts. Gabriela sighed. She felt gritty and hot but savored the scent of horses, the salty perspiration, even the dust in her hair. Sometimes she worried that days like these were a thing of the past, of girlhood.

"Can you drive?" Ernesto asked.

"Why?"

"Just drive, okay."

He tossed her the keys. She stowed her boots and riding hat in the trunk and drove cautiously down the uneven dirt road. Ernesto closed the hinged glass flap of the passenger window, took a packet of rolling papers and foil pouch from his pocket and started to roll a joint.

"*That's* what you had to do?"

Ernesto laughed. "I was planning to share."

It wasn't what Gabriela had expected, but it didn't matter. Ernesto was in a lighter mood, chatting about getting back to Santiago, laughing and criticizing her driving as he steadied himself in the pitching car.

He licked and pressed the edge of the paper to seal the joint and twisted the ends. A sweet cloud of marijuana smoke filled the car. Once he was certain it burned evenly, he pushed open the lower half of the hinged window. Fresh air washed through the car again. He offered the joint to Gabriela but she declined.

"Julia is coming over tonight to help Mami sew a dress," he said, holding the smoke in his lungs. "We should go out."

"And do what?"

Ernesto shrugged and exhaled.

"Well, I need to go home first. I can't go anywhere like this."

"Why not?" Ernesto laughed and took another long toke. When Gabriela refused a second time, he knocked off the ash, moistened his fingertips to snuff the joint and put the remains back in the foil pack.

The old Citroneta vibrated on the washboard road. Rows of almond trees whirred past. The car slipped in and out of cool shadows as the road dipped and twisted. On the western horizon the coastal range etched a dark line against a gold and aqua sky. Gabriela blocked the sun with her hand.

"Oh, I forgot," said Ernesto. "I bought you a gift." He turned for something on the opposite side of the back seat and cursed as the car lurched in a rut.

"What?" She glanced over her shoulder.

Only as she turned back did she see the car pulled to the side of the road and the young man holding up a red gas can. She swerved and the man turned sideways, stepping back from the Citroneta's fender like a toreador avoiding an enraged bull. In her panic she forgot to release the clutch as she slammed on the brake. The motor lugged. Ernesto swore and fell back into his seat. The car lurched to a stop.

"What the—" Ernesto righted himself and looked back. "Back up," he said, giggling, "I'll bet that guy just saw his whole life flash before his eyes." With shaking hands, Gabriela restarted the engine and reversed slowly toward the man. Ernesto extended his arm out the window in greeting.

"Sorry, friend," he said as the car came alongside. "We didn't see you."

"My mistake," the young man said. "I should have been more careful." He seemed unfazed by the near miss. His accent was foreign, faintly Mexican.

"Norteamericano?" Ernesto asked.

"Yes." The pale blue button-down shirt intensified the blue of his eyes.

"Out here? What, CIA? Spying on our sheep?"

The man laughed and held up the empty gas can.

"I was looking for a gas station. I'm headed for Santiago."

"Ah," Ernesto said.

Still embarrassed, Gabriela leaned forward to get a better look at the fair-haired stranger. "Can we give you a lift to town?"

"You won't find any gas tonight," Ernesto added. "It's these damned shortages."

"I know," the man said. He shifted his gaze to Gabriela. "Thank you. I'll get my things."

He put down the gas can and trotted back to the blue Ford Falcon.

"Let's hope he didn't shit in his pants," Ernesto muttered as he got out to open the trunk. The man returned with a briefcase and a corduroy sport coat.

"I really appreciate this," the man said to Gabriela as he climbed into the back seat. He cleared a space among the strewn magazines and books. "My name's Ricardo."

"I'm Gabriela, and my brother, Ernesto. We must stink of horses," she said. "We were just coming from the stable."

Ernesto pushed the passenger seat into place and hopped in. Gabriela pulled onto the road. In the rearview mirror she saw the man look back at his car.

"It will be okay," she said, wondering what an American was doing on an empty country road outside Chillán.

"Yes, our sheep don't drive," added Ernesto. "At least not very well." He was still high from the joint or the rush of the near miss or both. "How did you land out here?"

"I was in Concepción on business," the man explained. "I live in Santiago. Drove down yesterday for a meeting. When I tried to buy gas this morning the stations—at least the ones that were open—were only accepting ration cards."

Gabriela stole glimpses in the mirror of the friendly, sun-burned, Anglo-Saxon face. About her age or a little older. His Spanish was quite good but the American accent was amusing.

"I thought the situation would be better here. But it wasn't. At the last place the attendant told me there was a station out this way that had gas."

"Out here?" asked Ernesto.

"Think he was pulling my leg? Anyway, I ended up where you found me."

"How long were you waiting?"

"Not too long. But I was beginning to think I'd have to walk to town."

"Lucky my sister almost killed you."

Gabriela started to object but Ernesto and the American both laughed.

"There's a mechanic in town who might have gas," Ernesto said. He gave Gabriela instructions and they drove to a garage on Avenida Argentina. While Ernesto went to inquire, Gabriela and the American waited in the car. She suddenly grew self-conscious. He leaned against the passenger seat and she could hear his steady breathing. The day was still warm and the back of her blouse clung to the vinyl seat. She glanced at herself in the mirror and discreetly wiped a smudge of dirt from her brow.

Ernesto returned to the car. "No gas. And he doesn't know when he's going to get any."

"That's all right," the American said. "I appreciate everything you've done. Could you give me a ride to the plaza? I'll find a hotel."

Ernesto glanced at Gabriela but before she could decipher his look he said, "Sorry. We can't do that."

"Ah." The American sounded disappointed. "Well, it's not too far to walk from here, is it?"

"No, no. I mean you must come home with us."

The American protested but Ernesto refused to listen. "Look, my sister nearly took your life. It's the least we can do."

Gabriela looked at her brother as if he were crazy but didn't want to cause a fuss in front of the stranger. She started the car and headed for home.

9

When Will climbed into the boxy little car he noticed several things. First, the girl was strikingly pretty. Her long black hair was tied in a ponytail but several strands had escaped her barrette. Dressed in a white cotton blouse and pale yellow breeches with knee socks, the odd thing was, she wore no shoes.

Second, the odor of horses only partially masked the smell of pot, and he suspected the guy, Ernesto, was high.

Third, the magazines and newspapers he pushed aside on the back seat included *Punto Final*, the Communist weekly from Santiago. The few issues Will had seen extolled a Cuban-style revolution over Allende's more transitional Vía Chilena. Underneath the magazine were the yellowing pages of *La Tribuna*, a left-leaning newspaper also from the capital. But scattered on the floorboard, as if in contradiction, lay several issues of Girardi's right-wing *Aurora de Ñuble*, along with paperback translations of *Narcissus and Goldmund* and *Lord Jim*.

"Is one of you a student?" he asked, holding up the books.

Will caught Gabriela's glance in the rearview mirror: lively hazel eyes beneath bold straight eyebrows.

"Only before exams," Ernesto said. "Oh, would you hand me that?" He took the Hesse from Will. "*This* was what I was looking for," showing his sister. "I think you'll like it."

Gabriela said something lost to Will in the engine noise and air buffeting the windows. Ernesto giggled again, a scratchy laugh that caught in his throat. Brother and sister possessed similar features but in the feminine form they were refined, softened.

Their house was on the corner of a quiet tree-lined street of large houses behind high walls. Gabriela stopped at the curb while Ernesto hopped out to open a heavy wooden gate. Then she pulled into a paved courtyard and parked beside an ancient red Peugeot.

The courtyard was whitewashed and still bright in the fading light. Concrete pillars supported a clay-tiled ramada along the back wall. Magenta bougainvillea climbed one column and ran along the roofline. A spaniel came out of the shadows and sniffed Will's leg as he stepped from the car.

"Fidel," Ernesto said sternly, his voice echoing in the enclosure. "Scram!"

The dog ignored him. Gabriela called to the dog, which eagerly followed her down a passageway. Will took his briefcase from Ernesto and followed him. Halfway down the passage Ernesto stopped at a screen door.

"Mami?" he shouted.

A short middle-aged woman in a blue cotton dress chopped onions on a solid worktable in the middle of a tidy kitchen. Fresh greens were soaking in a large white enamel sink. Copper pots hung on a steel ring above the stove.

"Claudia, have you seen Mami?"

The maid wiped her eyes against her wrist. Seeing Will, her expression changed. "She went to church for a meeting," she said deferentially.

"Claudia, this is Ricardo Allen. We found him lying in the road."

"Aye, Neto!" She smiled and turned to Will, "At your service, Señor."

"He will be staying with us tonight. Can you make the other bed in my room?"

"Certainly. In just a moment," indicating the onions with a tilt of the head and returning to her chopping.

"This way," said Ernesto.

They crossed an inner patio with a long picnic table and large potted plants. Stacked firewood lay beneath a parrilla built into one wall. To the right of French doors into the house, a spiral staircase led to a second story. Will followed Ernesto up the wrought-iron steps to a rooftop terrace edged with pots of sun-scorched geraniums. They entered a low-ceilinged room with terracotta floor tiles and bead-board walls whitewashed like the patio.

"Jim Morrison!" Will said, pointing to one of several posters and photographs tacked above the twin beds. Books lay in stacks on a small desk and the lower drawer of a dresser was pulled out, exposing a pile of clothes. "You know the Doors?"

"Come on, baby, light my fire!" Ernesto pronounced in thickly accented English. Then reverting to Spanish, "Do you know Pablo Neruda, our Nobel laureate?" He pointed to a black-and-white photograph of a beak-nosed man in a beret with a dark-haired woman in shadow behind him. "He was born nearby, in Parral."

Che Guevara in his iconic beret stared from another poster.

"And are you a believer in the revolution?" Will asked.

"What?" Then seeing what Will referred to, he smiled. "No. But he had an interesting face, wouldn't you agree? Those eyes know something. A strong face, but also cruel."

Several personal photographs rounded out the montage. Gabriela holding up a langosta, lips puckered as if she were going to kiss it. A much younger Ernesto at a soccer match, standing beside a long-faced man with a small mouth and thin David Niven mustache.

"Who's that?"

"My father," Ernesto said. "He died last year."

"I'm sorry."

Ernesto shrugged. "He was a doctor. But he smoked too much and died of a heart attack. Cigarette?" offering one to Will from a pack lying on the desk, then lighting one for himself.

* * *

"A glass of wine, don Ricardo?" asked Ema de Manning as they settled in the living room. "No, come sit by me," patting the cushion beside her as Will was about to sit in a chair facing the gingerbread couch. "It's more comfortable." She was an attractive woman in her fifties with neatly coiffed hair.

Ernesto handed Will a full glass of wine, then presented smaller glasses to his mother and a full-figured woman with red hair who was introduced as his cousin Julia. Ernesto topped off his own glass and leaned against a breakfront at the other end of the room as though he didn't want to be there.

"So what brings you to Chile?" Señora Ema angled her head slightly as if aware that her straight, elegant nose and prominent cheekbones showed better that way.

"My company. Insurance."

"To Santiago?"

"Yes."

"How interesting! And where do you live?"

"In Bellavista."

"Ah, that's a nice neighborhood. At least it used to be. I lived not far from there before I married Dr. Manning. And is business good in the current situation?"

Will smiled, cautious not to say anything that might reflect a political perspective. From the way the family lived, the polite way they spoke, the affluence of the house, he suspected he already knew Señora de Manning's views on the government. But appearances could be deceiving. Allende himself came from a well-to-do family.

"It could be better."

"Ah, thanks to our president's initiatives," Julia said.

"Are you married, Ricardo?"

"Mami!" said Ernesto from across the room. "Don't be so personal."

"What?" exclaimed his mother.

"I don't mind," Will said. "I'm often asked. People wonder what a single person is doing here. Well, I'm not."

"Single?" Señora Ema's thin penciled eyebrows arched.

"No, married."

She flashed a wide, flirtatious smile. She must have been stunning in her youth, thought Will, which led him to wonder where Gabriela was.

Claudia entered the room. "Dinner is ready, Señora."

They were moving to the dining room when Gabriela finally appeared. She had washed her hair and changed into a sundress of the palest lavender. She gave her mother and Julia each a kiss on the cheek and greeted Will again, but she and Ernesto barely acknowledged the other's presence. There was none of the banter traded in the car.

"So, Julia, did you put him on a plane?" Ernesto asked as he passed the bowl of vegetables to Will.

"Did you see all those goons who came to the plaza? Thank goodness we were headed to the market or there might have been trouble."

"Julia participated in a protest march this afternoon," Gabriela said for Will's benefit.

"I saw it." And thinking about his report for Lipton, Will inquired, "Are anti-Allende demonstrations common here?"

"No. It's because of the elections," Ernesto said, gulping his wine.

"That was the first time they confronted us, though," said Julia.

"Who?" Will asked.

"The rotos," Julia said softly.

"So tell me, Julia, is it better to be a mummy than a roto?" Ernesto teased. Mummy, Will knew now, was slang for reactionary.

Julia squinted at her cousin's attack. "Don't be snide."

"Julia," Ernesto persisted, "what did the roto say to the mummy? 'My, what nice clothes you have! Can I have some like them?' And what did the mummy reply?... 'Only over my dead body!'"

Gabriela brought her napkin to her mouth, glanced at Will and then at her mother.

"Must we talk about politics at the dinner table?" Señora Ema intervened. She gave Will an anxious smile.

"No, let's talk about something more important," Ernesto said. "How is Mami's new dress coming along, Julia?"

Gabriela smothered a laugh and smiled into her plate. Señora Ema ignored the remark and Julia began to describe their sewing project as if the question had been devoid of sarcasm.

For the rest of the dinner, Ernesto remained silent, refilling his glass under his mother's disapproving glare. When Claudia came to clear the plates, Ernesto asked for another bottle of wine. His mother countermanded him and received a smoldering look in return.

"Ricardo, tomorrow we are attending ten o'clock mass," Señora Ema said. "You are welcome to join us. There's also a Protestant church in Chillán, but I'm not sure when the services are."

"No, I was raised Catholic," Will said to the Señora's obvious pleasure. What he didn't say was that he had stopped attending church when he was sixteen.

"Then you must join us."

"Unfortunately I don't have any clothes except what I'm wearing," hoping this might excuse him.

"You are fine dressed as you are. After all, you are a pilgrim of sorts. Ernesto, surely you have a tie you can lend don Ricardo."

In the morning, Claudia served tea and toast but conscientiously removed the tray an hour before mass. They could not all fit in one car so Ernesto and Gabriela took Will in the Citroneta while their mother, Julia and Claudia went in the Peugeot.

The cathedral was a striking modern building on a corner of the plaza where Will had watched the demonstration the day before. It rose in a series of steep concrete arches that looked as if they could be collapsed like a telescope.

"It looks like an armadillo's shell," he said as they approached. Ernesto and Gabriela laughed.

"Wait until you're in its belly."

"The old church was destroyed in the earthquake of 1939," said Gabriela. "This one's supposed to be earthquake-proof. I like it. It's simple. The way a church should be."

They joined the churchgoers hurrying from all directions across the square. Bells pealed from the belfry atop a massive concrete cross erected like a self-standing steeple. Gabriela paused on the steps to pin a black lace scarf on her head and as they entered she dipped her finger in the holy water font. Ernesto skipped his finger over the water and made the sign of the cross. Will imitated him.

Inside, Will was struck by how the concrete arches soared in concentric repetition to draw the eye toward a plain wooden crucifix above a stark rectangular altar. Narrow windows traced the vertical curve of the arches, diffusing a white glow against muted gray walls. It was like being inside the alabaster walls of a chambered nautilus.

The church was nearly full. Señora Ema sat with Claudia and Julia in a pew two-thirds of the way up the aisle. She moved toward the center of the pew to make room. Gabriela genuflected and squeezed past two older parishioners who refused to budge. Ernesto and Will slipped into the pew behind. Señora Ema leaned over and whispered something to Gabriela who adjusted the lace on her head. From his vantage point Will got to admire Gabriela's profile, the curve of her cheekbone, the dimple near her mouth and the fine straight nose shaped like her mother's.

Two altar boys in black cassocks and white surplices made a slow march up the center aisle, hands pressed together with thumbs crossed and fingertips pointed toward heaven, followed by the priest, in a white chasuble with a long green and gold satin stole draped over his shoulders. After placing his chalice on the altar and turning the pages of his missal, the priest cleared his throat and began. Will had never attended a mass in Spanish before, but he recognized the words—the contrition, the credo and the recitations of the congregation. The words reminded him of the Latin phrases he had memorized as an altar boy.

The priest's homily went on and on and Ernesto began to tap his foot. "You must care for the poor and the sick," the priest said, "but recognize that good deeds do no good if in the process you become poor or sick yourself. There is no reward or greater good if you forsake the goodness in yourself. A sickness of the soul is more dangerous than one of the body, a poverty of faith far worse than material poverty.

"Communism is nothing new. Christ, in his way, was a communist."

Heads lifted out of lethargy and eyebrows arched in surprise.

"But godlessness," the priest asserted in a louder voice, "is a sin. Communism without communion, without the moral force of religion, without faith in Christ, is a false creed. You may have doubts at times about the way the world is, doubts about injustice and suffering. You question if such wrongs are made by God or man. You may even feel anger at the cruelty you see in the world. But to renounce Jesus is the worst sin of all. Marxism is a sin, the sin of godless pride punishable with damnation!"

Ernesto clucked, louder than he intended judging from his own startled reaction. His mother turned and gave him a sharp glance that reminded Will of glares received from the nuns for misbehaving. Gabriela looked straight ahead, but the dimple deepened as she suppressed a smile.

At communion, the women filed up to the altar rail to receive the host. Ernesto stayed seated with Will.

"I need a cigarette," Ernesto said in a loud, impatient whisper. He started to stand. "Coming?"

Will worried how it would look to Señora de Manning, but

slipped from the pew. He followed Ernesto down the side aisle and out into bright sunshine, inhaling air free of incense and the musty lime of concrete. Ernesto lit a cigarette and offered one to Will. Then he extinguished the match with a shake and tossed it onto the step.

"I can't stand people who tell you who's damned and who isn't," he said. He held the cigarette between his thumb and two fingers like a joint. "Chile is full of arrogant assholes who tell you how to live. Priests. Politicians. As if they know better. It makes me sick."

"But you said you're not a Communist."

"I'm not!" Ernesto shook his head as if it were a ridiculous notion. "But apparently I'm no Catholic, either. At least, not according to that asshole."

The doors opened and the congregation streamed out—children running ahead, parents smiling and talking in subdued voices. They squinted at the brightness and gathered in familial clusters. Ernesto's mother, Julia, Claudia, and Gabriela emerged.

"Ernesto!" Señora Ema said as she approached. Her voice contained an exasperated edge. "Must you embarrass me so?"

Ernesto dropped his cigarette and crushed it under his toe.

"I was thinking Gabi and I could show Ricardo around town," he said. "Do you mind, Mami?"

"Well, don't be gone all afternoon. María Elena is coming by to pick up Julia and lunch is at two. Gabriela, make sure you bring don Ricardo back in time. I don't trust your brother." She laughed for Will's sake.

Gabriela looped her arm in Ernesto's. "That makes two of us, Mamá. Don't worry."

They gave him a quick walking tour of the downtown. There isn't much to see, they admitted. They pointed out the building on the plaza where Gabriela worked.

"You work for the *Aurora de Ñuble*?" Understanding now why the copies of Girardi's newspaper were in the back of the car.

"Yes," Gabriela said.

"Does the newspaper have a political position?" he asked, curious to see how they would portray it.

Ernesto sneered. "It's motto should be 'La Patria, preserved, pickled and mummified.' "

"Ernesto, it isn't that bad!"

"Isn't it?"

They passed the covered market, which was closed. Gabriela said it was famous for handicrafts.

"And sausages," Ernesto added, "Lots of sausages."

Next they walked to a statue of Bernardo O'Higgins, Chile's liberator hero and Chillán native, who either lost an important battle there against royalist defenders or avoided the blame for it. Will didn't quite follow the story because his tour guides kept interrupting each other with laughter and contradictions.

After the tour neither Gabriela nor Ernesto seemed anxious to return home. They drove to a boulder-strewn spot on the Ñuble River and parked near a grove of aspen-like trees with white bark and delicate trembling leaves. A gentle breeze stirred the yellow leaves carpeting the ground. Sunlight flickered in their eyes as they followed a footpath through the trees toward the sound of the river. Ernesto and Gabriela walked a few paces ahead of Will, holding hands until they came to the river.

Ernesto lit a cigarette and stared into the water. Gabriela leaned against a large smooth rock, closed her eyes and let out a relaxed sigh. She had removed the black lace from her head but still looked like a Catholic schoolgirl in her skirt and blouse.

Will dipped his hand into the cold clear water. He began to worry about getting back to Santiago and finishing his report for Lipton—it was already past two—and stood up. His action rousted Ernesto and Gabriela.

On the way back to the car Ernesto tossed the keys to Gabriela. "You drive." She gave him a suspicious look.

"Let's play a game," Ernesto proposed on the way home. "It's called 'More True.'"

Will leaned forward and rested his arms on the front seat.

"You start with two true statements, and the other person has to decide which is truer. So, if I said—" Ernesto glanced out the window for inspiration. "If I said the sun is shining, and Ricardo's shirt is blue, you have to decide which is more true."

"But they're both true," Will said.

"Of course, but one is clearly more true."

"Is it?"

"Of course, and you have to guess which. Gabi, let's show him."

"Okay," Gabriela said, keeping her attention on the road. "Which is more true: Ricardo's car is out of gas, or—"

"Or...?" Ernesto asked impatiently.

"Or, my brother is an idiot."

"That's too easy!" Ernesto turned to explain. "It's supposed to be something that isn't so obvious."

"Yes, I see what you mean," Will teased.

"Okay, I have a better one," Gabriela said. She had tethered her hair with the barrette but a loose strand at her temple kept blowing into her face. Now she brushed it aside. "Which is more true: Mamá is anxious to make a good impression on Ricardo, or, she was really relieved to learn that he's a Catholic?"

Ernesto giggled. "Good one! Let's see... I'd say, Mami is anxious to make a good impression."

Gabriela smiled. "Did you see it, too?"

"She's a sucker for gringos."

"Okay, your turn," said Gabriela.

Ernesto barely hesitated. "Which is more true: Ricardo thinks Gabriela is very sexy in her church clothes, especially that little lacey thing she puts on her head—" Gabriela objected, raising her hand toward her brother's mouth but Ernesto deflected it, "Or," he swallowed his laughter, "or, Gabriela thinks that by acting shy and proper around him, Ricardo will find her more attractive?"

"Oh! You pig!" Gabriela swatted her brother's arm. The car swerved and she recovered with a jerk of the wheel. "Sorry!" she said into the rearview mirror. Now Will understood how they had nearly hit him the day before.

The silence grew awkward. Neither Will nor Gabriela was ready to answer. Ernesto began to giggle at having created the awkwardness, and for a split second—before hers darted away—Will's eyes caught Gabriela's in the mirror.

"I know," he said, to save her from further discomfort. "The first is more true."

"Wrong! But you lie with honor!"

Gabriela remained silent, suddenly focusing intently on her driving.

"My sister is the—" for some reason Ernesto switched to English, "black duck—no, how do you say?"

"Sheep?" suggested Will.

"Yes, that's it!" Ernesto gave them a mischievous smile and reverted to Spanish. "Gabi is the black sheep of our family. As you may have already noticed."

But Gabriela refused to take the bait. They were approaching home. The gate was open. She turned into the courtyard and lurched to an abrupt stop beside her mother's car. It was close to three.

"I see you both need watches for Christmas." Señora Ema was seated at the patio table with Julia and another woman with a clear family resemblance. They had already finished the main course. Señora Ema introduced her sister, María Elena. Claudia came and went with trays of fruit and plates. "I stopped at the gas station on the way home. They don't expect a delivery until Wednesday at the earliest. It's becoming impossible to live in this country! The next thing you know, there will be no electricity except on Tuesdays and Thursdays."

"I'm taking the train to Santiago tomorrow," Ernesto said. "You could go with me."

"But my car…"

"Pick it up next weekend. It's not going to go anywhere."

Señora Ema and María Elena agreed with Ernesto's plan. "If you leave the keys with us, we can collect it once the gas arrives and have it waiting for you here. Gabriela, you and Julia could do that, couldn't you?"

"Of course, Mamá."

"Very well then. And Ricardo, please stay the weekend if you can," Señora Ema said. "Gabriela could take you riding."

"Mamá! Perhaps he doesn't ride."

"Actually, I like to ride," Will said. "I grew up riding horses. Even played polo occasionally."

"Polo!" Señora Ema said. "You see, darling. You judge people too quickly."

Gabriela looked down and bit her lip.

To the family, then, it was settled. "You've been much too kind," Will said. Ernesto laughed, a sound like a cat choking on a hairball, but he was unwilling to share whatever it was he found so amusing.

10

*C*haos erupted the next morning as Ernesto prepared for departure.

Will sat at the dining room table with a cup of Earl Grey tea and a piece of toast, while Señora Ema made casual conversation and leafed through the *Aurora de Ñuble*. Each time Ernesto yelled from the top of the spiral staircase to ask Claudia where something was—a favorite shirt, a book, his wristwatch—his mother lifted her eyes and reproached him for having left his packing to the last minute.

Gabriela, looking fresh in a mint green sleeveless dress, swept through the dining room on her way to the kitchen. Hair pushed behind her ear, she was attaching a gold earring as she breathlessly greeted her mother and Will. A moment later she returned with a piece of toast in her mouth. She leaned over her mother and separated the society pages from the rest of the newspaper.

"Gabriela, please don't eat standing up," her mother objected and glanced apologetically at Will.

Gabriela ignored the comment, scanned the pages with a critical eye and handed them back to her mother. "Ernesto, please!" she yelled from the doorway, "I can't be late for work." Then she disappeared down the hallway.

Señora Ema shook her head. "It's always like this with these two. In the summer when we used to go to our cottage in the cordillera, my husband Javier would hide in his study until everyone was waiting for him by the car. He said there was no point trying to make them go any faster."

Though she maintained a calm demeanor, her voice wavered as she implored Ernesto to come downstairs and eat breakfast.

Ernesto shuffled down the spiral staircase with a heavy suitcase and announced it was time to go. He would get something to eat at the station. Will thanked Señora Ema and Claudia.

After the whirlwind came the calm. Ernesto knelt beside his mother's chair. Señora Ema laid her hand on her son's head, closed her eyes and whispered a benediction. Then Ernesto stood and kissed his mother on both cheeks. It was a touching and surprising moment of intimacy. Will felt like an intruder. Ernesto gave Claudia a kiss on the cheek. Gabriela urged him to hurry and the chaotic winds began to swirl again. He couldn't remember where he put his knapsack. Claudia hurried to the back of the house to search for it. The dog began to bark. The knapsack was found on a chair in the hallway.

Finally they were off.

At the station, Gabriela and Ernesto hugged and exchanged pecks on the cheek, a far more casual goodbye than the previous departure. Gabriela shook Will's hand and told him not to worry about his car. She waved as she pulled away in the Citroneta.

The ticket agent said the train was late, so they went into the restaurant. Ernesto ordered scrambled eggs and shoveled them into his mouth at the counter. They bought cans of pear juice for the journey.

"Looks like this gas shortage is hitting everybody," Ernesto remarked. A large number of passengers occupied the platform.

They maneuvered past a ranch hand in a round brimmed hat with a finely tooled saddle propped on his shoulder, and skirted a priest in a white collar and black cassock. Two salesmen with black sample cases and newspapers tucked under arm, leaned against a pillar chatting. Farther down, a group of teenagers in hunter green school uniforms chattered near a drinking fountain.

When the crowded train pulled into the station Ernesto and Will had to walk through several cars before finding two facing seats. Ernesto took the seat next to a wizened woman in a black dress doing needlepoint. Will sat next to a man with his head tilted back, mouth open, snoring lightly.

As the train rolled north, on one side of the carriage Will could see the Central Valley stretching toward the gentle coastal range. On the other, the gray-blue foothills and imposing wall of the Andes.

Ernesto opened *Lord Jim* and slouched in his seat, holding the book in one hand while bracing his neck with the other. Will tried to read the book of Neruda's poetry Ernesto had lent him but was distracted by the stale fruity smell that permeated the carriage. Pistachio shells littered the sticky floor. The man beside Will woke with a snort, sat up and, excusing himself, stepped to the aisle and staggered toward the door.

"Ernesto, has your family always lived in Chillán?" Will asked over the noise of the train.

"My mother, yes. My father was born in Santiago," Ernesto answered without lifting his eyes from the book.

"I thought your mother said she lived in Santiago."

Now he looked up and yawned. "She went to school there. That's where they met."

Ernesto closed his book and slipped into the seat beside Will, politely acknowledging the watchful old woman as he shifted places.

"What do you think of Neruda?" he asked. "*Residencia en la Tierra* is his best but his odes are pretty good, too."

"Everything seems to be a poem to him: asparagus, salt, laziness."

Ernesto laughed. "Maybe so."

"Don't you find it hard to justify his privileged life as a diplomat with such romantic Stalinism?"

"That's his politics, not his poetry."

"How do you separate them?" Will asked, but Ernesto disregarded the question. "So, your mom and dad were at university together?"

Ernesto laid his head against the seat. "My father was in medical school. My mother attended a colegio for women... learning how to be a good upper-class wife. Speaking of privilege."

Will smiled at the cynical jab. "Is that where Gabriela went?" He hoped he was not being too obvious. He wanted the information both for himself and for the report he must file.

Ernesto shook his head. "No, she went to the Catholic University."

"Then why did you decide to go to the University of Chile?"

"It has a good law school."

"You're studying law?"

"No. It's what my father wanted me to study. When he died I switched to literature."

Ernesto looked out the window. Will saw a freight yard full of idle boxcars zip by. Stacked boxes of apples on the platform baked in the sun.

"So, do you have a girlfriend?" he asked.

Ernesto giggled his endearing hairball laugh and leaned toward Will. "What if I asked you so many questions, Ricardo? You've told us very little about yourself, yet for some reason we all like you. Isn't that enough?"

It was true. They had received him into their house. Accepted him at face value.

"Now, you tell me, which is more true?" Ernesto smiled slyly.

Expecting to be grilled, Will prepared his cover story.

"A) I can trust you as a friend because you *aren't* from here, or..." Ernesto hesitated. "Or B) as a foreigner you only say what you think people want to hear?"

He didn't think Ernesto intended to be mean, yet the comment stung.

"A," replied Will.

"Yes? Good." Ernesto leaned closer so he could ask the next question softly and still be heard over the racket of the train. "Then, which is more true: A) I lost my virginity when I was sixteen, or, B) You felt some tension between my mother and me?"

If he wanted to retain Ernesto's trust he had to answer honestly: "B."

Ernesto nudged his arm, a kind of encouragement.

"Exactly! So, to restate the evidence," sounding like a lawyer even if he was no longer studying to be one, "we've established Ricardo's trust, and that there is a strain between my mother and me. We can also assume, based on the rules of "More True," that I lost my virginity when I was sixteen. Correct?"

Ernesto seemed to weigh his next words. He glanced over at the old woman, ensuring that she still concentrated on her needlepoint.

"Then, which is more true: A) When Gabriela and Ernesto saw Ricardo in the road, it was Ernesto who wanted to stop, or B) A man can lose his virginity more than one way?"

Will felt the intensity of Ernesto's stare as he deciphered his meaning. It was all beginning to make sense—the moody detachment, the cynical humor, the rebellious flight from church. How does a homosexual survive in a conservative Catholic country like Chile?

Ernesto's eyes anxiously searched his. "Do you understand?"

"Does Gabriela know?"

"Of course! I trust her with everything."

"And your mother?"

Ernesto laughed and shook his head. "Intuitively, perhaps. But we've never spoken about it. Maybe that's part of the problem between us."

Will considered himself part of a tolerant new generation that could accept homosexuality without feeling threatened, but his guard came up. He felt the automatic fear of predation kick in. He had never known a homosexual, at least not one who admitted it.

"So, which is more true," Ernesto asked after the pause grew awkward. "A) Ricardo is able to accept his new friend as he is, or B) Ricardo doesn't know what to do with this information?"

Will wanted to tell him it didn't matter, but somehow it did. Homosexuality was much easier to accept in the abstract, from a distance, than face to face. A vague disappointment gripped him, as if Ernesto's information had destroyed his hopes for a real friendship. "Both," he responded with a forced smile.

"Ah, but that breaks the rules." A look of disappointment flashed across Ernesto's face. "That's the beauty of this game. One statement must always be truer than the other."

"Ernesto, it's okay," Will replied, wondering if Ernesto saw through the lie.

Ernesto smiled with apparent relief. "Thank you, Ricardo. It wasn't easy for me to tell you. But, if we are going to be friends, we must be honest with each other, no?"

"Yes," Will said, fully aware of the irony. While Ernesto had bravely eliminated the possibility of misleading him, he was like the homosexual compelled to conceal who he was.

The man returned to reclaim his seat and Ernesto moved across from Will. For the next several hours they rode in silence, reading.

On the outskirts of Santiago the train slowed to a runner's jog. Gray buildings crowded the tracks. They passed through parts of the city Will never saw in his commutes. Hovels scarcely better than lean-tos, crumbling warehouses, grimy Victorian-looking factories with yards full of rusting iron fenced by walls topped with glass shards or coiled barbed wire. Unpaved streets of numbing bleakness intersected the tracks for miles.

As the train lugged into Mapocho Station, restless passengers grabbed belongings from the overhead racks, collected children, donned hats and jackets and crowded the doorways at the ends of the car. Despite the station's light-filled, lacey wrought-iron structure, Will only noticed the dingy waiting rooms and restaurants in dimly lit alcoves with dirty floors and streaked windows. His mood had changed. It had been a long, exhausting weekend. He thought of Lipton and reports to write.

"Want to share a taxi?" Ernesto asked.

"Thanks, but I need to get to the office." It wasn't true but he was reluctant to let Ernesto know where he lived until Lipton had run a background check. From the wry expression that twisted his mouth, Ernesto must have thought Will's response was due to his revelation. "Here, let me give you my phone number," Will said to reassure him.

They agreed to talk later in the week. Then, in the Latin fashion, they embraced to say goodbye.

11

"And how is our Italian friend?" Lipton asked Will at their meeting two days later.

The jarring rattle of a jackhammer in the street below the hotel room eliminated the need for supplemental noise to mask the conversation. They huddled to hear each other's words.

"He loved the smut we gave him on Danilo Puente, who by the way has campaign posters plastered all around the university. He's clearly targeting the youth vote. Girardi's convinced that with more money his man Dávila can win."

Fucking Girardi. Lipton suspected he would divert a hefty percentage of every dollar they gave him to the coffers of Patria y Libertad. How much would actually go to Dávila's campaign was impossible to tell.

"He also says the Christian Democratic candidate doesn't stand a chance," Will continued. "He predicts the left wing of the PDC will drift to Puente and the right to Dávila."

"I'll bet. Did you explain that we don't want the PN and the PDC fighting each other just so they can both lose to the UP?"

Young Will nodded but he seemed unusually reserved, not a good sign. Either he was withholding information or something was bothering him.

"Okay," Lipton said. "Give him another thousand. But tell him it's for campaigning. And tell him to hire some of those PyL goons to deface Puente's posters. Have 'em paint a red star on 'em or something. Make it look like the MIR's work."

The jackhammer stopped suddenly, startling Lipton with the clarity of his own voice. "What else?" he asked more softly.

"I had to leave the car in Chillán. Ran out of gas. Had to take the train back."

"Good! That's one of the challenges in our line of work. We feel the pain of our success same as everyone else. Maybe these shortages will wake people up to the realities of Marxist life. In fact, that's an angle Girardi could use in one of his editorials."

"I'll have to go back for it. I left the keys with a family I met there."

"That'll have to wait. Too many other priorities right now."

The jackhammer started again, cleaving his brain with its percussion, which may be why it took him a second to register what Will had just said. He waited until it stopped.

"A family?" he asked, open-ended the way a shrink would.

"Yeah. A brother and sister gave me a ride to town. They promised to look after the car for me. Nice people really."

"Nice?"

"Yeah."

"Do these nice people have a name?"

The question pried a grin from Will. "Manning. But their father's dead. Ema Hernández de Manning, that's the mother."

"American father?"

"No, Chilean. An English grandfather, I think. It's all in my report."

Lipton wrote the name on his notepad anyway, and that simple action prompted Will to volunteer more.

"They seem like a decent family. Moderate, non-political. I rode back on the train with the son. He's a student at the University of Chile."

"Name?"

"Ernesto." Lipton jotted it down.

"What's he studying?"

"Literature."

"Politically active?"

"I don't think so…"

"What then?"

Will hesitated. "I think he's gay."

Lipton smiled. "A queer, eh?" He starred the name on the pad. "I'll bet he's a left-leaning queer then."

"I don't know. I didn't get a sense of any political affiliation, unless you consider the Doors one." Lipton looked up to see if Will was being sarcastic. "He had a poster on the wall is all."

Lipton closed his notepad. Now he was beginning to see.

"Will, you're not queer, are you?" momentarily withholding the smile that would tell him he was joking. Will smirked. "So, you stayed with this nice family?"

"I did. Isn't HQ always harping about more human intelligence?"

"Not quite what they mean, but good. Let's get to know the son better. Maybe he can help stir up trouble at the university."

Will looked bothered by the suggestion.

"Relax. It's not like I'm not asking you to take it up the ass or something." Now the grimace on Will's face did make him laugh. "Just gain his confidence. Be his pal."

"I told you, I don't think he's political."

"Maybe not. But his friends might be. What about blackmail?"

"What about it?"

"A macho country like this, it isn't good to be known as a fairy."

Will frowned.

"Just a thought. I'll do some checking and see if there's anything on the guy. Meantime, find out who his friends are. We need to make our opportunities, Will."

He didn't seem convinced, so Lipton added, "Headquarters is

on our case. We'll all be taking it up the ass if we don't show some progress pretty soon."

He thought the joke was pretty good but Will didn't react.

"Anything else?"

Will shook his head.

"Okay then."

Lipton stood up and slipped the notepad into the pocket of his suit coat. "Cheer up, Will. You seem depressed. Maybe you need to get laid. An army friend of mine told me of a place. Lots of pretty ladies. Safe. Clean. Let me know if you're interested."

Will reacted the way he expected, with a look of denial. Something was troubling him. Maybe it was simply the process of initiation. All those qualms of conscience. The new recruits marched out of training thinking they were masters of duplicity, super-spies. Then the inevitable disillusionment set in. Some were better equipped to handle the ambiguities than others. Maybe Young Will wasn't cut out to be a spy.

Lipton made a mental note: spend more time with his rookie.

That evening Lipton drove to the home of Flora Sanchez, the mistress of Major Felipe Covarrubias. Clouds had blown in from the coast, splitting the light from the setting sun into angled shafts that illuminated the crowns of trees and reflected off second-story windows. Down the street, a gang of children played soccer in the lengthening shadows.

One of a dozen identical row houses with faux half-timbered gables on a bare street in an unfinished development, Lipton knew Flora's by the stone statue beneath the bay window, a bare-breasted huntress aiming her bow and arrow toward the sky.

He was fifteen minutes early so he parked the Valiant and verified that the list his secretary had typed up included the names Will gave him that morning:

—Dr. Javier Manning (deceased), Chillán, Ñuble.

—Ma. Ema Hernández Alarcón de Manning (wife), Chillán, Ñuble

—Ernesto Manning Hernández (son), student, University of Chile.

Hadn't Will mentioned a girl, too? He didn't see her name on the list and couldn't find it on his notepad, either. It didn't matter. It would turn up in the investigation. He folded the sheet and placed it inside his breast pocket.

He glanced at his watch again and tapped a drumbeat on the steering wheel. His thoughts drifted to sex. Not the act itself but the way everything revolved around it, even espionage. Especially espionage. He didn't know what had triggered this thought. Maybe the fact that they paid Flora's rent as part of the major's monthly stipend. Or maybe it was the priceless recollection of Will's startled expression when he suggested spending more time with his new queer friend.

Lipton was pretty sure others thought about sex as much as he did, they just didn't admit it. So what about fags? Do they think about having sex with every man they meet? Fucking disgusting, yet he bet it was true…

It had been a long day and his mind really was wandering. Tired of waiting, he grabbed the paper bag from the seat beside him and got out.

A loud commercial jet banked low overhead as he unlatched the wooden gate, climbed the porch steps and knocked on the door.

Flora's thin dour face peered around the edge of the door before she opened it.

"Good evening, Eduardo. Felipe is out on the patio."

She escorted Lipton through the narrow living room, skirt swishing as she passed through the hallway. She wasn't Lipton's type but she had a nice ass.

Major Covarrubias, lean and trim in his blue-gray uniform, sat across from Flora's two boys at a picnic table covered in oilcloth.

Black dominoes stretched across the table in geometric spider legs. Major Covarrubias beamed as he placed his last two pieces. "Game!" The boys groaned and the major looked up and smiled.

"Eduardo, how nice to see you!" He rose and extended his hand.

"Hello, Felipe."

"Boys, we'll pick up later where we left off. Be sure to add your last points and keep track of who starts the next round."

Major Covarrubias led Lipton by the arm toward the house. "Let's talk inside."

"Don Eduardo, would you like something to drink?" Flora asked as she trailed a few paces behind them.

"Of course he would," Major Covarrubias said. "Bring us each a glass of sherry."

The two men sat down in the dining room. The major's gaunt face looked cadaverous in the muted light of a glass-bead chandelier that was too large and formal for the narrow room. Cropped silver hair circled his polished scalp. He sat with the erect posture of a career soldier.

Flora brought in a tray with two glasses and a decanter. The major waited for her to finish serving and leave the room before he lifted his glass, "Salud!"

"I brought you a little something," Lipton said, handing him the paper sack.

"Ah, thank you for remembering!" Delighted, the major peered inside. "It may seem like a silly hobby, but Flora's children adore them." He took several matchboxes from the bag and shuffled through them with intense curiosity. "All these places they've never been. It's my way of teaching them geography."

Somewhere in an apartment near the Santiago garrison, Major Covarrubias had a wife and teenage daughter. Since divorce was not an option in Chile, the major, like many others, had established a new existence outside a dead marriage. With two divorces behind him, Lipton could sympathize. In the major's shoes he'd do the same thing. He also admired the major's obvious affection for Flora's boys.

"Well, they won't learn much from these. Most are from places near Washington, D.C. Bill just got back."

"Thank you, Eduardo. And please thank Bill."

"So, how's life?" Lipton asked. "Been spending much time in Valparaíso?"

Major Covarrubias put down the bag. His eyes sparkled. "Haven't you heard? I've been reassigned to the Directorate of Intelligence. General Pinochet is keeping me much too busy with contingency planning to allow junkets to Valpo. Unfortunately I missed the latest round of coordination meetings. But you must know that! I ran into Captain Nolan last week at the Ministry of Defense. He had just returned from there."

Lipton raised his chin a fraction of an inch, a motion that neither confirmed nor denied. Of course he knew. Earlier in the week he'd run into Pete Nolan coming out of Bill Bradshaw's office. The naval attaché had mentioned the major's reassignment. Pete also told him the directorate was in the process of revising its "Internal Security War Game," the emergency plan General Pinochet had drafted the year before.

"Oh? How's old Pete doing?" he asked, not wanting to preempt the major's own interpretation of events.

"Fine. He had a bunch of Brazilian naval brass in tow. They wanted to discuss trilateral exercises for next fall."

"And what's keeping General Pinochet awake at night that he has you burning the midnight oil? The MIR? Students manning the barricades?"

The major's face remained grave. He took one of the matchboxes from the paper bag, slid open the cover and picked out a match.

"Extremists we can handle. It's the general population we worry about. You are an astute observer, Eduardo. In these elections, what should we be more afraid of, Unidad Popular gaining more seats or the opposition winning a majority?"

Lipton laughed. It was the same question they were assessing for Langley. If the UP won, Allende would press harder for his Vía Chilena, his euphemism for the gradual slide toward a Marxist state, and Patria y Libertad would likely start a civil war. If the opposition won, the workers' unions would uncover their weapons caches hidden in the industrial cordones and march into the streets claiming fraud. Which was worse?

"Good question. What does your boss think?" he asked.

Major Covarrubias struck the wooden match and held it up to his eyes. "Let's just say that our contingency plans cover both eventualities." He blew out the match.

Lipton smiled at the overt symbolism. The major was full of himself tonight.

"Tell me, do you believe President Allende's latest threat? Will he call on the workers to resist with arms if anyone tries to obstruct the elections? Or was that just a warning shot across the bow?"

"Without a doubt, without a doubt. He is merely describing what would be a certainty beyond his control."

"But you think the election is still too close to call?"

"I am a soldier, Eduardo, not a pollster. Our duty is to uphold the constitution."

"You sound just like General Prats," Lipton said. "Is that your boss's view as well?"

"Of course. General Prats is his commander in chief as well as mine."

"So, even if the UP gains more seats and your comrade president pushes for a Soviet-style unicameral congress, your boss will simply go along?"

"Eduardo, we've known each other for some time now, no? You should know better than to ask me to speculate on what someone might do if something happens based on what someone else might do after something else might happen."

Lipton lifted his glass, "Touché!" and downed the cheap sherry. He stood up. "I've kept you too long from your dominoes game. Please thank Flora for her hospitality."

"My pleasure. Let's find time for a game of tennis one of these days."

"Maybe after the elections," he said, smiling. "Oh, I nearly forgot—" He handed the major the list of names from his inside pocket. "The usual background check. Police records, that sort of thing... Much appreciated."

Major Covarrubias scanned the list, refolded the paper and tucked it in the pocket of his uniform.

"As long as Prats is in charge, the army won't do anything," Lipton warned Bill Bradshaw the next morning. "Especially if the elections go to the UP. At least that's the sense I get. No cojones. Which means we have to make damn sure these elections favor the opposition. Castrate the UP that way."

Bill nodded but was not fully listening. He leaned back and his padded leather desk chair creaked under his massive weight. Behind him, photos taken at different stages of his career with politicians and heads of state served as a montage of post-war Latin American history.

"You sound disappointed," Bill said. "Isn't that why we got all this money? So use it."

Lipton frowned and shook his head. "I'm not sure more money is the answer. It would be great if we could get the syndicates to shut down the whole damn country like they did last October, but people seem to be waiting to see what happens in these elections. The provocateurs refuse to provoke."

"Speaking of provocations, did you see this?" Bill tossed a folded copy of the *Times* across the desk:

Ex-CIA Chief Defends Agency Actions at Home and Abroad
Washington, Feb 7—Former director of Central Intelligence Richard Helms, ambassador-designate to Iran, testifying in a closed

meeting before the Senate Foreign Relations Committee today, defended the CIA's training of domestic police forces. He also denied any foreknowledge of the Watergate break-in, for which four former agency officers were indicted in January...

"You can bet they'll rake him over the coals before he gets any ambassadorship," Bill said. "Let's just hope they don't shine the spotlight too closely on us."

Lipton dropped the paper onto the desk. Clearly Bill's mind was elsewhere. "How's the new regime?" he asked, referring to Helms' replacement as DCI, James Schlesinger.

Bill smirked. "Supposedly the first thing out of his mouth was, 'I'm here to see that you fellas don't screw Mr. Richard M. Nixon.' Great start, huh? Makes our little problems pale in comparison, don't it?"

"Maybe, but how does that affect us?"

Bill shook his head. "That's what I'm trying to figure out. Phillips assures me it doesn't change anything..." Bill leaned back. "But don't you start worrying, Ed. I'll run interference. You just keep making good things happen. We'll make you big chief of regional ops yet." Bill raised his palm in mock Chippewa salute. The conversation was over.

Lipton returned to his office. Dave Phillips had been stationed in Rio when he headed regional ops. Why not Rio for him, too? For a split second he considered calling Renata. He had not talked to her in over a year. He pictured her tear-streaked face in the taxi on the day he left. How would she react if he did call? Instead, he dialed a friend in the Rio commercial section and made a discreet inquiry.

"Hey, Mike, how's things?"

"Ed Lipton! What a surprise. Did you hear? They just announced the embassy's moving to bloody Brasilia."

Lipton hadn't heard—so much for Rio—but it made a convenient ruse for his call. "That's why I was calling. Kinda sucks, huh? Not that it's a big surprise. You going?"

"Of course. But I may keep the family here and commute for a while. There's fuck all in Brasilia."

"What about all the locals?"

"Hasn't been decided yet. I guess some will be offered relocation. The rest will be replaced."

"Hey, is Renata still working there?"

"Renata? Sure."

"How's she doing?"

"Looking hotter than ever. Last I heard she's dating some air force captain assigned here. But *she* won't be going to Brasilia. We can hire typists there."

"No, I suppose not. Hey, does she still wear that gold necklace I bought her?"

His friend laughed. "You old scoundrel. Always. Should I say hello to her for you?"

"No… No, better not. Well, good catching up, Mike. Good luck with the move. Hope it works out for you."

Lipton hung up. Sooner or later the air force captain would be reassigned. Then, if he wanted, he could make his move. But first he had an election to win.

12

The sour mood that engulfed Will at Mapocho Station lingered like a hangover. He grew impatient and angered quickly at little things—missing the bus or having someone walking in front of him spit without looking. In the beginning, everything about his assignment was new and exciting. The job left him little time to think about himself, although sometimes, late at night or on weekends, the hollow silence became enormous. Usually the feeling was easily reversed by action or alcohol. But the weekend with the Mannings had exposed the root of his dissatisfaction—except for Roland Fabré, he had no friends.

That was why Ernesto's revelation had disappointed him so. It wasn't homophobia, at least not entirely. He liked the guy. He enjoyed the Chilean's sarcastic sense of humor and admired his honesty. Although he still worried that Ernesto might mistake his interest for something else and hit on him, a friendship seemed possible. No, what really bothered him was the idea of befriending Ernesto at Lipton's insistence. He had met the Mannings through a chance encounter. Yet now, duty intruded into even this small compartment of his private life. He could disregard Lipton's order and not get to know Ernesto better, but he didn't want to. For behind Ernesto was Gabriela.

With mixed feelings, Will telephoned Ernesto a few days after returning to Santiago to ask about the car.

"I haven't heard anything yet," Ernesto said. "But I should

know something by the end of the week. Want to get together Friday? Do you know the Café Super? It's across from the university bookstore. At seven?"

Will was happy to accept.

The Café Super was an American-style coffee shop—a bustling student hangout decorated with fake wood paneling, Formica-topped tables and bright orange padded-vinyl booths. Will was surprised when he arrived there to find four young men seated with Ernesto in a horseshoe-shaped booth near the door. He had expected to meet him alone.

As the group squeezed in to make room, Will's anxiety of being mistaken for a homosexual resurfaced and he fought off a momentary rush of paranoia, as if all eyes were fixed on the pack of sissies and he was one of them.

From the crest of the horseshoe, Ernesto introduced his fellow students.

"That's Miguel," pointing to the plump man beside Will who murmured hello. "Watch his hands," Ernesto joked and placed his own hand on the shoulder of a floppy-haired man with round over-sized glasses to his immediate left. "This is Juan-Ramón, the puppy of our group. And Lalo. And last but not least, Víctor. Smile, my love." He winked at the tall dour man opposite Will whose most striking feature was a long scar down his right cheek.

Ernesto was clearly the comedian of the bunch, the one whose jokes and infectious laughter bonded them. Will soon realized the main purpose of the gathering was to scrutinize him, and perhaps to test the limits of his tolerance. At least, that's how it felt as Víctor began to question him.

"How long have you been in Chile, Ricardo?" Víctor asked across the expanse of plates and cups, books and ashtrays. The scar was shiny, almost translucent, and Will was tempted to ask how he got it.

"Since November." From Víctor's mild reaction, Will sensed Ernesto had already told him all about the gringo, Ricardo Allen.

"And what do you think so far?" Wiry brown hair, tied in a

ponytail, and long sideburns framed the lines of Víctor's severe face. His wide-set eyes probed Will's.

"About what?"

A young waitress interrupted. Will ordered a Nescafé and Miguel asked for an apple pastry.

Víctor smiled. "About the Vía Chilena, our experiment in socialism."

"Is that what you call it—an experiment?"

Víctor smiled again, full lips exposing stained teeth.

"For an American it must be very frightening. Like homosexuality. Maricones and Marxists at your doorstep."

"Is it?" Will asked. "Are they?" He was being challenged, but he wasn't sure if his heterosexuality or citizenship was under fire.

Víctor stubbed out his cigarette. "You don't have to rant and pound your fist like Fidel Castro to be a revolutionary."

"Or be a queen to be queer," Ernesto said over the coffeeshop clatter. "Don't get him started, Ricardo. He'll have us all marching to La Moneda tonight."

The others laughed as if privy to an inside joke.

Víctor ignored the comment. "Castro's just another usurper. A better one than Batista, but he's shoving his revolution down people's throats all the same. Allende was elected."

"Yes. But unfortunately not by a majority."

"Neither was your President Lincoln."

Will's surprise must have registered on his face. If he had ever known that fact, he had forgotten it.

"Yes, it's true," Víctor persisted, sensing an advantage. "I think he had about the same popular vote as Doctor Allende. Did that make him any less of a president?"

"No, but look where it took us. Is civil war what you want here?"

Víctor frowned dismissively. "Is economic slavery any better than racial? That's what we have here. Chile is a cruel country, Ricardo, full of disparities and intolerance. We fear—no—we *hate* any difference, yet deep down we envy anyone who isn't one of us—strangers, foreigners. That's why we say nasty things about you behind your back."

Miguel looked up from the apple tart. "We do that to our friends, too, Víctor. Especially you!"

"No," countered Ernesto, "with friends we insult them to their faces!"

More laughter and things said so fast Will had a hard time keeping up. Suddenly Juan-Ramon and Lalo were prodding Víctor to let them out. They were going to a movie, they said, and tossed several wadded bills onto the table to cover their share of the tab. Soon Miguel left, too, leaving Ernesto, Víctor and Will alone together in the large booth.

Víctor sipped his coffee. Ernesto stretched out, languidly extending an arm across the top of the booth while smoking a cigarette with insouciant flourishes.

"Who said, 'I cruelly hate cruelty?'" Víctor asked. "Was it Montaigne?"

Wary from his misstep about Lincoln, Will shook his head. Ernesto rolled his eyes as if he'd heard the question before.

"Well, whoever said it was right," continued Víctor. "Allende hates the cruelty created by a society of haves and have-nots. Is it too much to ask for a daily liter of milk for every child? That's why the people voted for him. Right now he's trying to please everyone, but just wait. Either the Right or the Left will grab the power from him, and when they do, someone will pay. There's always a victim."

"Oh please, Víctor." Ernesto reached over and patted his friend's arm. "Enough gloom already!" He turned to Will. "Speaking of victims... Ricardo, when are you going to visit my mother? I spoke to Gabi today. She and Julia recovered your car."

From the coffee shop the three men shared a colectivo, one of the inexpensive taxis that run a regular route, to Providencia, where they disembarked at Avenida Pedro de Valdivia. Will was saying goodbye when Ernesto suggested that they buy some pisco and go to his place to listen to music.

It was one thing to spend time with Ernesto and his friends in a coffee shop, but going to his apartment, with his boyfriend? Was there some misunderstanding? Will dismissed his hesitance as more foolish paranoia. "Sure," he said, "but I can only stay for a while."

They walked down Avenida Ricardo Lyon and purchased the pisco in a small grocery store. On the corner of the next block, at a tall modern apartment building protected by a high wrought-iron fence, Ernesto unlocked the gate and opened the door to a stark marble-tiled lobby.

"Pretty nice place," Will said as the slow, cramped elevator carried them to the seventh floor. "When I was in school, I lived in dumps."

Ernesto laughed. "My father bought it as an investment when Gabi started university." He unlocked the apartment door.

The apartment was spare and furnished inexpensively. Books and records filled makeshift shelves of boards and concrete blocks. A modest, narrow kitchen opened onto the living room, and a sliding glass door led to a small balcony with a good western view toward the downtown.

Ernesto uncorked the bottle of pisco and poured healthy shots into three glasses. The warm Coca-Cola foamed from the bottle onto the counter. He giggled and brushed the mess into the sink then stirred Coke into the pisco.

"We call this piscola," he said, handing Will the first glass. "It's supposed to have a lime in it but I forgot to buy one. Salud!"

It tasted like a rum and Coke.

Víctor seemed more relaxed behind the apartment door. He dropped onto the couch and put his feet up on the glass and chrome coffee table. Will sat on the other end of the couch, while Ernesto, an unlit cigarette hanging from his lips, put a record on the portable hi-fi. On a scratchy, overplayed disc the Doors began, "People are strange when you're a stranger, faces look ugly when you're alone…"

Plopping into a beanbag chair, Ernesto joined Jim Morrison in the refrain, "When you're strange, no one remembers your name, when you're strange, when you're strange, when you're stra-a-a-a-nge…"

Will smiled. "So when did you discover the Doors?"

"A couple of years ago. I heard Jim Morrison sing "Light My Fire" on the radio in New York. I was hooked."

"New York! What were you doing there?"

"My father went on business and took me along. To educate his son… Little did he know that while he was attending his medical conference I was trying to find out where the queers hung out. Hell, I was seventeen and curious! I thought I was in a more tolerant country. But shit, I've *never* forgotten the looks people gave me as I came out of the little bookshops I found on the West Side. I mean, what did it matter to them? I was just a horny Chilean kid who barely spoke English looking for a blowjob."

If Ernesto hoped to shock Will, it didn't work.

Víctor seemed more bothered. "And you think the reaction would be any different here?" he asked sullenly.

"Do you think Allende can change people's attitudes?" Will asked Víctor, curious to find out just where this intense, angry man stood.

"About what? Tolerance for homosexuals?" Víctor placed his glass on the coffee table and flicked his cigarette over a large abalone-shell ashtray. "Why should they?" His expression assumed a fierce intolerance of its own. The scar running down his cheek stood out like a white-hot weld. "No, this will remain a closed, fucked-up society."

"Speaking of closed societies, I've developed a new theory for my thesis," Ernesto said, lighting his cigarette.

"Another?" Víctor asked indulgently.

Ernesto exhaled. "Here's my idea. Most of the world's great

sea literature deals with homosexuality, implicitly of course. Take *Lord Jim*. In my thesis I'm going to argue that it's an implicit appeal for homosexual tolerance, and that Marlow is a latent homosexual. Maybe Jim, too. I haven't decided about him yet. "

Will nearly choked on his drink.

"Joseph Conrad's *Lord Jim*?"

"Maybe Conrad was, too, come to think of it."

Will couldn't tell if Ernesto was serious.

"On what evidence do you base your hypothesis?" Víctor asked.

"Well, Marlow spends a lot of time talking about how handsome Jim is. 'One of us,' he keeps saying. Like Narcissus captivated by his own image. Let's face it, he's in love with Jim. Who can blame him? Jim's blond and hot."

"It's been a long, long time since I've read it, but wasn't Marlow talking about Jim as an English sailor?" asked Will.

"Sure, but such statements are open to interpretation. Isn't that what literature is all about?"

"I haven't read it, so I'm at a disadvantage. But your evidence seems inconclusive." Víctor sounded like a lawyer conducting a deposition. "The character is handsome. So what? You can't condemn a man for that. What else?"

"Well, Marlow is obsessed with Jim's character. And he's always hanging around other men—"

"He's a sailor!" Will insisted. "A Victorian sailor!"

Ernesto laughed and wagged his finger. "Yes, but heterosexual sailors don't hang around other men all the time. That's my point. When they're in port they're whoring in the brothels."

"That's gross stereotyping," Víctor said.

"I agree," said Will. But he was starting to feel a resurgence of the paranoia he had experienced earlier that night. "I'm straight and look, I'm here with you two."

Ernesto raised an eyebrow. "Yes, and I'd worry about your intentions, except I saw how you checked out my sister."

Will smiled and felt his cheeks flush, more embarrassed that he'd been so obvious than for being exposed, but Ernesto was too worked up to notice.

"Okay, then take Jim's fateful jump. Against his better instincts, he abandons ship with the rest of the crew and leaves all of the passengers aboard to fend for themselves. A desperate act of cowardice, right? But it's symbolic, too. Of what? Of breaking the unwritten moral code! And what does *that* remind you of?

"Then, for the rest of the book, he punishes himself and tries to disprove his bad behavior, like a maricón trying to be straight. I rest my case."

Both Ernesto and Víctor were laughing. Will no longer knew if any of the discussion had been serious. He suddenly felt like a third wheel.

"Actually, I'm fed up with implicit homosexuality in books," Ernesto continued. "And I'm tired of gay men being portrayed as cross-dressing fags. Maybe I'll write the first openly queer book in Latin America—the homoerotic adventures of a poor Chilean boy who comes to the big city and discovers true love. What do you think, Víctor?"

Ernesto had gone around the back of the couch to embrace Víctor in a playful headlock. Will didn't know where to look.

Víctor, too, seemed uncomfortable with this open display of affection. "Poor!" he scoffed. "So it will be fiction."

Will finished his piscola and stood up. "Well, I should go."

Before going to bed that night, under the buzz of caffeine and alcohol, Will wrote his report on Ernesto's friends, concentrating on Víctor. Imagining Lipton's gruff voice in his ear, he answered the questions he knew his boss would ask:

"I do not discern a specific political alignment, although Víctor Maragall clearly leans to the left. He was once active in the MIR's student organization but became disillusioned with the group's extremism. Although sympathetic to Allende's initiatives, he is skeptical of Allende's ability to keep the more extreme factions of Unidad Popular (the MIR, the MLN, even the Christian Radicals) in line. He believes that whoever wields power will become abusive toward the opposition, especially any dissenters within the UP. He claims he is no longer aligned with any political party.

"With the right inducement, Maragall might be recruited to inform on past associates and campus activities. It is difficult to tell if money, blackmail (given his sexual predilection), or an offer of protection from a contrived threat of blackmail would be the best inducement. The subject's motivations need to be better understood."

Sitting in his underwear, Will leaned back in his chair and reflected on MICE, the mnemonic for the motives that convert targets into agents: money, ideology, coercion, ego. Usually one predominates, his psych-ops instructor said. Which was Víctor's?

And what about love? Why wasn't it on the list?

"I did some checking on your new friends," Lipton said at their weekly meeting in the Hotel Rincón the following Wednesday afternoon. It was Valentine's Day.

"Turns out Dr. Manning was chief administrator at the Chillán Clinic. From an old family with a lot of dough. Graduated from Catholic University. Did his residency at St. Bart's in London. Solid Christian Democrat."

"Where'd you learn all that?" Will asked, impressed.

Lipton smiled. "Mom's more conservative. Opus Dei. Pillar of the church. The kid, Ernesto, is a lightweight. Much to Dad's consternation. Probably what killed him." Lipton cocked his wrist to emphasize his point. "Sent him to the Deutsche Schule hoping its Prussian traditions might knock some discipline into him. Apparently it only made matters worse. There's also a daughter. Did you meet her?"

"I told you I did."

"Did you?"

"Gabriela. What did you learn about her?" Will hoped this time his cheeks didn't betray him.

"Not much," Lipton said. "Went to Catholic University like her old man. Was engaged to the son of the Santiago industrialist Castillo Bernal."

"Engaged?"

Lipton's cool gray eyes lifted from his notes. "What? You got the hots for her? And here I thought that was your professional curiosity showing. But no, it's just your prick."

Fuck you, thought Will, but he pretended to laugh. Lipton's crude humor was irritating and tiresome.

"So what's up with the son?" Lipton asked, returning to business.

"We've met once and talked a couple times." Thinking of Ernesto, he added protectively, "Like you said, he's a lightweight. I don't think there's anything to be gained there."

"What about his boyfriend?"

Will shrugged and looked away. He pictured Víctor as he'd seen him last, dressed in his blue work shirt and khaki twill pants. "He's a possibility."

"Leftie? Commie? Anarchist? What?"

"I'm not sure exactly. None of the above. A law student from the wrong side of the tracks who quotes Montaigne."

"Who?"

Will dismissed his own comment with a condescending shake of the head. Lipton's ignorance of Montaigne didn't surprise him. "Nothing. A 16th Century French aristocrat who wrote essays."

"Fucking Chileans! No wonder this place is so screwed up. Didn't you say he was tied to the MIR?"

"The student chapter. He attended a few meetings, but he said all they did was sit around talking about how great Cuba was. Once he realized they were just a bunch of talkers, he stopped going."

"Meaning what? He wants more action? Fighting in the streets? Kidnappings? Bank holdups? Beheadings?"

"No. Nothing like that. I'm not sure really."

"Well, find out, Will. Don't be fooled by appearances. Let's see if we can put him into play and get some real dope on the MIR. Those fuckers are armed and dangerous. I know for a fact their leaders received guerilla training in Cuba. And they're building a paramilitary here. We've had reports of arms caches in the cordones, training camps in the mountains. Let's keep pressing. These lousy elections aren't gonna change anything. And when they're over, we'll need to refocus. Do a target study on this Maragall guy ASAP."

13

*L*eti kept pestering Will about the car. When was he going to retrieve it? Should she hire someone to drive it back?

Will sidestepped the issue, too busy to go for it himself but refusing to delegate.

Lipton had him running errands. With only three weeks until the elections, efforts to sabotage the UP were climaxing in a frenzy of payments. In his encoded ledger Will recorded disbursement after disbursement to an alphabet soup of political parties: Partido Nacional (PN), Partido Demócrata Cristiano (PDC), La Democracia Radical (DR), Partido de Izquierda Radical (PIR), and Partido Democrático Nacional (PADENA).

There were also unions, business associations and labor organizations with names like DIRINCO, CUPROCH, FRENAP and SOFOFA. Besides ongoing subsidies to opposition radio stations and newspapers, including Girardi's, the ledger contained many more payments to individuals who may or may not have been part of the opposition, people whose affiliations it was better not to know—insiders in Allende's Socialist Party, disgruntled organizers in the Central Union of Workers, informants within the Communist Party. As far as Will could tell, the only ones not on the take were the revolutionary cells of the MIR, which had given up on the democratic process and robbed banks instead.

Then, abruptly, two weeks before the elections, the errands fell off. Apparently those who could influence the vote, or claimed they could, had been paid. Will found himself with time on his hands.

On the third Monday of February, he toured Carlos Saavedra's truck depot in the Cordón de Los Cerillos, the sprawling industrial zone south of Santiago, a bastion of Marxist ideology in practice where workers attempted to run expropriated companies and union bosses organized vigilantes to guard against right-wing sabotage. Only in January, Allende had vowed that if civil war came to Chile he would defend the constitution from behind the barricades of Los Cerillos—and here those barricades were, manned by surly militants watching as Will drove through informal checkpoints.

Despite his soft-spoken demeanor, Carlos Saavedra responded to the surging militancy of the cordón like a besieged warlord. Four guards stood at the gated entrance to his walled depot. A chain-link fence topped with razor wire protected the diesel pumps in his yard. The steel door to his office stayed locked at all times, and inside he proudly showed Will a cache of handguns in his safe. "No one is going to take over this establishment without a fight and a few dead Marxists first," he vowed.

On Tuesday evening Will dined at Le Figaro with Roland Fabré. The restaurant was only half full and Georges, the owner, expressed frustration with the scarcity of ingredients. Toward the end of the dinner Roland confided to Will that he was dating a "mature" woman from his office.

"Why didn't you bring her along?" Will asked.

"Next time perhaps," said Roland, sounding pleased. "I did not want to presume."

Twice that week Will met Lipton. On Wednesday afternoon, at the Hotel Rincón, Lipton finally authorized Will's trip to Chillán. "But stop in Concepción and check up on Girardi." On Thursday evening he telephoned Will's apartment. He sounded drunk. "Meet me at the Hotel Carrera in an hour. I've got something for you," he said.

Will had not returned to the Hotel Carrera since his first week in country. As he passed through the revolving door and climbed the broad red-carpeted stairway to the atrium bar overlooking the plaza, he realized how much his impressions had changed in three months. Now, the fluted marble columns and inlaid copper murals, the etched-glass chandeliers and attentive, white-gloved waiter who greeted him at the entrance to the bar felt stuffy and elitist. The waiter escorted him to a low round table where Lipton sat in a barrel chair.

"Another pisco sour," Lipton said to the waiter as he drained the white foamy residue from his glass. "Best in Santiago, Dicky boy. Try one!"

"Urgent business to discuss," Lipton said after the waiter left. Will looked around the bar. Businessmen occupied most tables. Two or three parties included elegantly dressed wives. There was no way they could discuss any serious business here. Will's irritation grew when Lipton asked if he'd heard Nixon's latest speech about Vietnam. Will said he hadn't. He didn't feel like talking politics, particularly Vietnam, with Ed Lipton.

The waiter delivered their drinks and a bowl of peanuts to replace the one Lipton had emptied.

"I mean, 'peace with honor'…what the hell's that? Sounds like politico-speak for retreat. Let the dogs fight over the scraps. Adios amigos… How'd you like to be in stinking Saigon when the gooks start swarming down from the north? Gonna be a bloodbath."

"At least it won't be Americans getting killed."

Lipton briefly considered Will's comment. "I really don't get the people at home—" An elderly couple with Australian accents sat down at the next table. Lipton lowered his voice. "They want the good life but refuse to acknowledge the price. Don't have a clue about the things we have to do. Like people who order their steaks rare but won't go near a slaughterhouse. They should see the meat hanging in the markets here. Keeps perspective." Lipton finished his drink and flagged the waiter.

"Been to any meat markets here, Dicky? And I'm not talking about carne now." He gave Will a louche smile. "Which reminds me…"

He took a business card from his pocket, leaned over and slipped it into Will's jacket pocket. "A sleeping encyclopedia, my friend," tapping Will on the knee emphatically, "best way to get the lay of the land. So to speak."

Will looked at the card. On the front was a seahorse logo with the name of a restaurant. On the back, scrawled in pencil, "Salon de Violetas" and an address.

"As promised. Just tell 'em you're a friend of Major C. They'll take good care of you." Lipton squinted at his wristwatch. "Well, I have to go, but I'm glad we've had a chance to chat. Good to get to know each other a little better, don't you think?" He paid the bill and stood up. "Safe travels."

Puzzled and annoyed at this waste of time, Will watched his boss descend the broad marble staircase. He finished his drink (it was a good pisco sour) and allowed Lipton enough time to catch a cab before he got up to leave.

From the hotel he walked to the Alameda and took a colectivo to the north end of Parque Bustamante where dozens of teenage couples huddled on benches or lay on the grass, kissing and petting as if they were invisible to others. *Been to any meat markets, Dicky?* Lipton was clueless about what Will wanted. Thinking about Gabriela, Will took the business card from his pocket and tossed it into the river as he headed over the bridge.

The corner grocery store was still open. Badinia, the owner's daughter, sat on a stool at the counter, reading a fotonovela. She looked up and greeted Will with a broad smile.

"Hola lola," he said playfully. "I need a gift for a family—two women really. Any ideas?" He scanned the half-empty shelves behind her.

Badinia put her magazine down and slipped around the counter. Her gangly adolescent frame in the plain cotton shift and toothpick legs in white knee socks made Will smile. What was he doing asking a fifteen-year-old girl how to solve a question of etiquette?

"Cigarettes?" she asked, tapping her finger against her set lips as she walked down the aisle. "Or brandy perhaps?"

Will frowned. "What's customary?"

"Ah, I know!" She hurried behind the counter and disappeared into the curtained backroom. A minute later she returned with a gold box tied with a red ribbon. "My father just received these. Belgian chocolates!" She looked at the price written on the bottom and grimaced. "Oh..."

"How much?"

"A thousand escudos!"

Will winced. Over twenty dollars at the official exchange rate.

"What if I paid in dollars?"

Badinia looked perplexed. "Papá," she called through the curtain. An unshaven man emerged a moment later, sleeves rolled up, still chewing his dinner. Badinia rattled off an explanation. Her father wiped his mouth on the back of his hand, took a pen from the counter and made a quick calculation on the back of an old receipt. He mumbled the number to Badinia as if he couldn't tell Will directly.

"Five dollars," she said brightly. Will converted to escudos. The price had dropped three-quarters but the exchange rate was worse than he received elsewhere. Badinia's father was driving a hard bargain. Will decided not to haggle. He searched for a five-dollar bill in his wallet and handed it to Badinia. She immediately passed the note to her father who slipped it into his pocket.

Will had not seen Ernesto Manning for two weeks—since the night at the coffee shop—but spoke to him several times by telephone. As soon as he got Lipton's approval, he called to let Ernesto know he was going back to Chillán and asked if there was anything he could bring back for him.

"No, just give them a hug." Un abrazo, Ernesto said. Will wasn't sure it meant the same in Spanish as in English, but he promised he would.

On Friday morning he hurried to Mapocho Station only to learn that the southbound train was delayed. The ticket agent said the engine had broken down but another train was to depart from a different track. A fellow passenger warned Will that the original train had been derailed. "More sabotage," the man said in an angry whisper. The nationalized railroads, a symbol of socialism, were a frequent target of Patria y Libertad extremists. At least, that's what the government's media claimed. The opposition media blamed the MIR. "One of these days they're going to kill somebody—innocent people, kids, families," the man said in disgust. "To hell with all of them!"

The train left an hour late. After several scheduled stops and unexplained delays in the middle of nowhere, it arrived in Chillán. The bells of the cathedral chimed seven as Will gave the taxi driver the Mannings' address. When the cab turned onto the familiar street, Will saw the Falcon parked in front of the house.

He rang the bell. The dog barked. Claudia answered the door and ushered him into the living room. The tabletops gleamed and the room smelled of furniture polish as if they had prepared for his arrival.

"Please be seated, don Ricardo. I'll let the Señora know you are here. May I put your bag in Ernesto's room?"

A short while later he heard the clicking heels of Ema de Manning. Her recently permed hair looked a shade darker with a reddish tint that complemented her green-flecked tweed suit. She offered Will a powdered cheek.

"Thank you for letting me stay with you again," Will said. "These are for you," handing her the box of chocolates.

She seemed delighted by the courtesy. "We'll save them for dessert tonight." Sitting down, she smoothed her skirt. "Sit, sit," she said, patting the couch beside her. "Let's have a glass of wine. Gabriela is still out running errands."

She asked about his journey and if he had seen Ernesto before he left. Before Will could respond she assured him that his car was safe and filled with gas.

"Yes, I saw it. Thank you."

"So, Ricardo—" she left her sentence unfinished as Claudia returned.

Claudia presented Will with a glass of white wine and handed another to the Señora then bustled from the room. "So, tell me," resumed Señora Ema, "what are these horrible rotos in Santiago up to these days? We read such terrible things in the newspaper. It's hard to believe."

It was his first clear indication of Ema de Manning's political stance. The fact that she waited for Claudia to leave the room and still nearly whispered the word "roto," told Will everything. Here, he bet, was one vote for Girardi's crackpot reactionary, Davíd Dávila. Carefully choosing his words, he described how the train was delayed before his departure.

Señora Ema sipped her wine and delicately wiped her lips with a linen napkin. "You must think we're all barbarians here," she said.

"We have plenty of issues to divide us in the U.S., too. Vietnam, civil rights, abortion."

Señora Ema grimaced. "Yes, but here—well, my Jorge used to say, the only way we can put Chile back on track is to stop being nice to these people who cause all the trouble. Jorge and his colleagues stopped treating patients after they tried to take over the hospital. Only temporarily, but it was to make a point, 'You want to run this clinic? Fine. Then *you* treat the patients.'"

"What happened?"

"Ernesto scoffs at this. 'So much for the Hippocratic oath,' he says. But some sicknesses can't be cured. Marxism is one of them."

Her words reminded Will of the priest's homily that had angered Ernesto so. As if reading his mind she continued in a more worried tone, "Ernesto can be so hotheaded at times—well, he's young. What else would he be, I suppose?" She searched Will's face for a sign, as if she had uttered her bona fides and was waiting for the countersign.

Just then Gabriela entered the room, looking sporty in a red and white striped knit top and blue jeans. Her face was flushed as if she had been running. She dropped her purse on a side chair and greeted Will with a smile. He stood up and she offered her right cheek for a kiss. Will spent a dizzy second inhaling the faint citrus of her perfume as his lips brushed her cheek. Then he gave her a light hug. "That's from Ernesto."

She stepped back with a startled smile. "I don't believe you! He would never be so considerate," she said, laughing. "Hello Mamá." She leaned over to kiss her mother.

"Gabi, I hope you're going to change into something a little more proper for supper."

Gabriela gave Will an embarrassed, good-humored smile.

"Of course, Mamá. I wouldn't want to appear improper." There was a trace of Ernesto's sarcasm in her tone as she emphasized the last word.

"Not on my account, please. You look great," Will said.

"Thank you," Gabriela said.

"Then, for me, darling, please go change into a skirt," Señora Ema insisted.

In Will's honor, they grilled a large fillet of beef on the parrilla. Rather, Claudia tended the fire while Will, Señora de Manning and Gabriela, who had changed into a navy blue gabardine skirt and white sweater, relaxed on the patio. As adroit as Will was at steering the conversation away from himself, Señora Ema was equally adept at turning it back to the life story of Richard Henry Allen. Without Ernesto there to deflect her, she was persistent. With her bold, inquisitive nature, she would have made an excellent spy, thought Will. In the course of the evening he embellished his cover story as he answered her questions.

"I grew up in Wisconsin, on the shores of Lake Michigan," he said, channeling a summer spent with his cousins. Although Ema de Manning directed the conversation, he noticed that Gabriela listened attentively, and as much of Will's energy went into intriguing her as informing her mother. "It's a huge lake. It's so wide you can't see the other side. With a good wind it takes twelve hours to sail across, and it's as long as the distance between Santiago and Chillán. And does it get rough! I've been caught in storms that nearly ripped the sails from the masts even when reefed."

"Good heavens! And your mother and father still live there?"

"Yes. In a small municipality adjacent to Milwaukee, like Providencia is to Santiago."

"And how many siblings do you have?"

"I'm an only child." —At least that much was true.

"It must be hard for your parents to have you so far away."

"They know my work is important to me. I visit them whenever I can."

After dinner Señora Ema made a prominent display of unwrapping the chocolates Will had brought. As she lifted the lid her disappointment was visible although she made a valiant effort to conceal it. At some point in their travels the chocolates had melted then re-solidified and bloomed with a sugary white residue like mildew.

"I'm so sorry," Will said, equally embarrassed and irritated. He had taken good care of them on his travels and suspected they had come from the shop that way.

Señora Ema extracted one from its wrapper and took a small bite.

"They are still delicious," she said.

The next morning, after breakfast, Will met Gabriela in the courtyard to go riding. She was dressed in straw-colored breeches and the tall black riding boots he'd seen in the trunk of the car on their first meeting. The supple boots, now cleaned and polished, accentuated the curve of her calves.

Gabriela sized up Will's attire—sneakers, blue jeans, red polo shirt—with a skeptical lift of eyebrows.

"We should find some boots," she said.

"I'm all right. Unless I need spurs."

Gabriela cocked her head as she considered and the dimples at the corners of her mouth puckered. "I know," she said, and motioned for Will to wait. She hurried down the corridor to the section of the house he had never seen and came back with a pair of supple, worn boots. "Try these. They were my father's."

The boots pinched in the toes but he was able to squeeze into them.

"How are they?"

"Okay... if you carry me to the car."

She laughed and gathered her riding helmet and crop. Will hobbled behind her to the Citroneta. They drove east through town. After crossing a bridge, the paving ended. Will recognized the spot where his car had died. Soon they were driving past fenced orchards and stretches of open land. Far to the east, the gentle glaciated slopes of twin volcanoes, shaped like two breasts, dominated the skyline.

Gabriela turned onto a private road and the little car vibrated over washboard ruts. She steered toward a weathered barn with a corrugated steel roof.

Gabriela introduced Will to the groom, Alonso, whose features appeared flattened on a long, beardless face. Alonso greeted Gabriela in the same deferential tone Claudia used with Señora de Manning.

It was Alonso's birthday and Gabriela had brought him a gift—a plaid shirt. She held it up to his shoulders to verify it was the right size. Alonso thanked her softly without looking at her. He carefully folded the shirt and went to put it away.

"Alonso is Mapuche," Gabriela explained.

"Ah." Will had read about the tribe of Indians who resisted conquest for 300 years.

Alonso returned leading Gabriela's horse, a tall black gelding with a white star on his forehead.

"How's my Rayo?" she exclaimed.

Alonso held the reins close to the bit and patted the horse's neck while she mounted. Next he led out a wide bay mare for Will. Gabriela's horse was beautiful and alert and fitted with a martingale and double-reined bridle with a pelham bit. Will's mare wore a simple snaffle.

He laughed. "You're giving me the old workhorse of the barn, aren't you?"

Gabriela smiled. "She's a sweetie with a gentle gait. Her name is Imelda. She played polo in her younger days. I thought you'd like her." Her own horse snorted loudly.

Will swung up into the saddle, adjusted his stirrups and felt instantly at home—

Not the Marana home outside Tucson that included his mother's bitter regret for a bygone affluence sacrificed for marriage, and certainly not the one containing his father's alcohol-fueled dreams of renewal that always ended in toxic anger. Will preferred the fantasy home of his cover, embellished with Ivy League schools, polo and sailing—the one he had invented from a life glimpsed when he ran away at fifteen and spent a year in his aunt and uncle's large house in River Hills outside Milwaukee.

To help earn his keep, he had found a summer job at the polo grounds on Good Hope Road. He couldn't ride worth a damn when he started but he convinced the brogue-tongued stable boss to hire him anyway. He mucked stalls and cleaned tack and learned to swear in Spanish from the Mexican and Argentine grooms who traveled each season with the ponies between Milwaukee and Boca Raton. While his cousins attended Sunday polo matches with their Burberry blankets, picnic lunches and pastel girlfriends, Will worked at the far end of the field washing and cooling the spent ponies. By the end of summer he was skilled enough to canter one horse around the exercise field while leading two others.

Imelda responded well to neck-rein commands but Will noticed that Gabriela used the English two-handed technique.

"Let's go into the ring first," she said.

They trotted around the ring. Will posted awkwardly under Gabriela's critical eye. Then he put Imelda into a canter, making a figure eight and switching leads as he leaned the mare into the crossovers. He checked Imelda beside Gabriela, who smiled in surprise.

"You didn't think I could ride, did you?" he said.

Beneath the brim of the black riding cap her eyes narrowed and her dimples deepened. "Well, you never know," she laughed. "All Chilean men *claim* they can ride." And she bit her lip as if she had said something she shouldn't have. "There are some wonderful trails nearby. Let's go along the river."

She led him across the field and into the woods. Will became entranced by the sway of her hips in the tight yellow breeches as she moved with the rhythm of her horse's long gait. He was barely able to mind as she warned of branches and pointed out landmarks. He felt his emotional world shifting. For three months he had been absorbed in learning his job, uncertain of the romantic customs of the country and warned in training to avoid local attachments. But Gabriela was smart, kind, good-natured and beautiful. She not only aroused his desire but a yearning for a different world than the one he knew. He felt light and happy around her.

They came to a wide trail that followed the river. She turned in the saddle to see how he was doing.

"This is a good place to gallop. Soft sand, in case you fall off!"

Will laughed. "I have a hunch Imelda hasn't galloped in a very long time."

Gabriela spurred her horse and Rayo launched into a controlled canter. She let out the reins and the horse extended his neck, stretching into a gallop with the next stride. Will dug his heels into Imelda's sides. The startled horse farted and broke into a canter. He kicked again and used the excess rein like a crop on her neck. Imelda shifted into a gallop that was as smooth as any he had experienced. Soon he was racing alongside Gabriela.

As they neared the end of the clearing, Gabriela pulled on her reins and checked her horse. Like a barrel racer, the gelding came to a quick stop, rear haunches bracing as hooves skidded underneath. Will brought Imelda to a more gradual stop.

"This old girl shifts like my Ford!" he said, patting the horse's neck.

"I told you," Gabriela said. Her voice was breathless and happy.

He could tell he was being evaluated in a new light, as if his riding skills had transformed him. They walked for a while to let the horses cool. Gabriela turned up a narrow trail that forded a small stream and led to a eucalyptus grove. In the light breeze, the leaves shivered with a delicate dry rattle and the scent of eucalyptus rose from the crushed leaves underfoot. Gabriela dismounted and led her horse by the reins. Will followed her lead. They walked into a grassy clearing full of sunlight and birdsong. "This is one of my favorite places," she said.

The grass was too much temptation for the horses. They lunged to graze. Gabriela's horse jerked her backward as he dipped for a mouthful and she cried out. She recovered her balance, only to have her horse lift his head and snort a mouthful of green slobber toward her. Will laughed. She wiped her cheek. "Wait," he said, using his finger to remove a fleck she had missed. He wanted to lean under the brim of her cap and kiss her but she stepped back and wiped her face with her sleeve. "How terribly, terribly disgusting," she said in precise English.

She resumed walking.

"Where did you learn English?" he asked in English, hoping

to draw her out.

"At school," she said, reverting to Spanish. "I used to speak it better. In high school I dreamed of spending a year in North America. I even applied to a foreign exchange program with McGill University, in Montreal. It has an excellent journalism school. But at the last minute I decided not to go."

She glanced at Will but did not explain. She adjusted her grip on the bridle and continued walking.

Her father supported her desires for a career, she said, but her mother was anxious for her to settle down and marry. "I'm turning twenty-four in April," she acknowledged, "and in Chile that means it's time for a woman to marry if she doesn't want to risk becoming an old maid."

"Hardly," he said, laughing at the notion.

"I don't care what people think." Though she looked perplexed. "Sure, I want a husband and children someday, but I like what I'm doing at the newspaper, too. Even if the society page is trivial, I like the people I work with."

"Lots of women in the U.S. struggle with the same issue."

"And what conclusion have they come to?"

Recalling Sarah's unbending career drive, Will shrugged.

"That there's no right answer. Some have decided marriage will have to wait..."

"And what about love?"

Her lips compressed with stoic resolution. Was this an invitation to kiss her? It was such an intimate question.

"Ah, love!" he said, laughing. "That's the great destroyer, isn't it? The ruin of best-laid plans."

"Do you see it that way, Ricardo?" She stopped and pulled on her horse's reins. Will stopped, too, and turned toward her. There was a trace of puckish surprise on her face. "As a destroyer?"

He laughed nervously. "Of men's wills, yes."

"I see. And is that so bad?"

"No. In our hearts we want it. Who wants to think all the

time? Love allows us not to think…"

He didn't know what he was saying. He was stumbling into unknown territory and guessed that she sensed it.

"And have you ever been in love, Ricardo?"

"Two, maybe three times," he exaggerated.

But aside from the usual high-school infatuations and several college romances that started vaguely and ended more vaguely, Will had only been in love once, with Sarah. They had met in Spanish class at Thunderbird and three months later were living together. They circled around the question of marriage but launching their careers took precedence. Then Dr. Ernst and the CIA came along. As Will began the interview process, Sarah said she was okay with it, but as the interviews progressed, she started to pull away. "I'm not sure I could live my life that way, Will. What would I do? I couldn't work." A month later she moved out.

"And you?" Will asked, recalling Lipton's intelligence about an engagement.

Gabriela smiled. It was her turn to demur. "Once," she said, and a tingle of jealousy ran down his spine. "Ernesto couldn't stand him. He was a few years older than me. We met at the university and got engaged… He was the reason I didn't go to Canada. Then I found out from my girlfriend that he was seeing another woman. He lied about it. Even when I confronted him, he was unable to admit it. What kind of coward is that? And what kind of relationship is that? So, I broke up with him. Then my father died… I never realized how hard life could be."

Will took her hand and squeezed it. He was glad he had not tried to kiss her. It would have been too much too soon, overwhelming her at the wrong time. He wasn't sure what to say. He wanted to tell her the truth about himself but couldn't. He would need to clear it with Lipton first, and Lipton would say no. And yet, how would she react if he told her?

14

*S*unday, March 4, 1973 was Election Day. Lipton spent the morning in the office with the cathedral bells tolling loudly each quarter hour. Around noon he strolled up the Alameda toward the park. Sound trucks cruised by blaring party jingles. Cars packed with waving, cheering activists paraded up and down the avenue honking horns at placard-bearing supporters of the UP and CODE standing on opposite corners. In the park, last-ditch rallies enticed the milling crowds with the aroma of sausages cooking on charcoal braziers. Onlookers fanned themselves with political flyers or used them as impromptu shades from the late summer sun. Musicians sang patriotic songs and costumed performers danced the cueca.

That afternoon Bill Bradshaw hosted a barbecue at his house in Las Condes, followed by a low-stakes poker game for a few regulars. Lipton arrived late. The other guests already sat under an umbrella at a table near the pool, eating hamburgers.

The men adjourned to the family room for their game. Arnie Matlock, the Station's reports officer, went over to the hi-fi and turned on the radio. Two broadcasters jabbered about likely victories and defeats.

"No one's gonna know squat until tomorrow, least of all these blowhards," Bill said, switching off the radio. "Forget it for a while. Let's drink and be merry."

As Lipton shuffled the deck, Paul Gregorio, a junior officer reporting to Arnie, asked, "So if the opposition wins today, isn't this like the perfect op?"

A last-minute stand-in for the naval attaché Pete Nolan, Gregorio didn't know that they didn't talk shop at their poker games. The others sidestepped the indiscretion, but Arnie came to his protégé's aid.

"Depends how you define a perfect operation."

Lipton placed the deck in front of Stuart Hall, the barrel-chested army attaché. Hall cut the deck and Lipton started to deal. "Five card stud," he called.

"So how would you?" Gregorio persisted.

Outside, the swimming pool's blue water glinted. Bill's twin teenage daughters, wearing modest two-piece bathing suits, lay on chaises wagging their feet to pop music from a transistor radio. They looked like the Doublemint twins.

"Let's see, the perfect operation," began Arnie.

This oughta be good, thought Lipton as he arranged his hand, a reports guy spouting off on ops. He placed his cards face down on the table and picked up the deck.

"How many," he asked Gregorio.

The grinning analyst blinked at Lipton without comprehending. The bright eyes behind oversized glasses looked slightly crossed. He seemed nervous to be included in their game, with a twitchy result like a child overindulged on sugar.

"Two." Gregorio stifled an exuberant laugh as he picked up his cards.

"Two for me, too," Arnie said, then tried again, "The perfect operation is when—"

Again he was cut off. This time Joan Bradshaw, looking trim and very much the model Junior League hostess in red slacks and crisp white cotton blouse, cracked open the sliding glass door. "Anyone need another beer?" The men all grumbled assent and Joan stepped back outside.

"The perfect operation is the one you never knew existed,"

Bill said, cutting Arnie off before he said something stupid. Bill pulled three cards from his hand and tossed them to Lipton. "The one that a hundred years from now no one knows about. Not even the bosses. Imagine the history books blissfully describing a milestone event and no mention is made of how it really happened. Not a trace, not even a suspicion… That'd be the perfect operation."

"Think there's ever been one?" Gregorio asked.

"Well, if there was, you wouldn't know, would you?" Bill said patiently.

Stuart Hall smiled and asked for a card.

"And the rest?" Gregorio asked.

Lipton had nothing and replaced three of his own cards.

"The rest," Bill said, arranging his hand, "the rest are all fuckups."

"Case in point," Lipton said, folding. He stood up to open the patio door for Joan who had returned with a tray of beers.

The next day, in the ambassador's expansive ninth-floor conference room with its gleaming hardwood table and flags on stanchions behind the podium, a dozen people listened to the political consul Jim Sweets interpret the election results.

Lipton sat next to Bill Bradshaw who sat to the right of the ambassador. On the opposite side of the table were key officers from the economic, commercial and consular departments, as well as two of Sweets' number crunchers there to support their boss. Pete Nolan, the naval attaché, sporting a dark tan, and Stuart Hall, who won big at the poker game, sat directly across from Lipton.

Lipton glanced at his watch. Jim Sweets had been speaking for fifteen minutes. The faces around the table were a mix of grim, bored, and self-important. During one moment of statistical exegesis Lipton caught Pete Nolan's eye. The slightest smile of collusion flickered across the naval attaché's face.

"To answer your question, Mr. Ambassador, yes," Sweets said. "The UP gained two senate seats and six in the house, but overall the opposition did pretty well." He clutched a large green and white striped computer printout to which he referred whenever he lost his train of thought. On the chalkboard behind him he had scrawled the electoral results for the UP and CODE by region. "As a percentage of the overall electorate, the opposition gained votes compared to the last municipal elections. Unfortunately, these votes weren't concentrated in the most closely contested districts to beat the UP."

"But what's interesting," interjected a Sweets deputy, "is when you compare the results to the 1970 presidential election. The UP actually *increased* its overall percentage of the vote. That's why they've been so quick to claim a victory. It's all how you slice it."

The ambassador gave the underling a cool glare and returned his attention to the podium.

"So you see this as a victory for the opposition, Jim? Is that what we are to advise Washington? That progress was made?"

Sweets pursed his lips and pulled on the whiskers of his coppery beard. He looked like a doctoral candidate struggling to defend his thesis to a hardened dissertation panel. "Maybe not a victory, but a standoff. They held their ground. The UP still lacks a majority and the opposition, if they stay united, can still block any legislation the UP tries to pass," he said. "Wasn't that our bottom line?"

"Any fraud reported?" the ambassador inquired.

Sweets shook his head. "Nothing extraordinary. As far as we can tell, it was a fairly clean election."

The ambassador pressed his hands together before his mouth as if he were about to say grace.

"Is this how you see it, Bill?" he asked, shifting slightly to his right.

Bill Bradshaw, who was doodling on a legal pad, chuckled.

"Well, sir, if the UP is claiming a victory, and if the opposition is claiming a victory, I don't see why we can't, too." Half smiles appeared around the table.

"Are you speaking now as our Minister of Optimism?" the ambassador asked.

Bill laughed. He put down his pen, rubbed his chapped lips and leaned on his elbows.

"Ever heard the one about the Polish sanitation union? Told all its members they were gonna strike if management didn't concede to their demands by midnight. 'Check the morning paper,' they told 'em. Next morning the headline says, 'Negotiators reach impasse'—so all the workers went back to work."

Groans around the table, to Bill's apparent delight.

"Seems to me that's what we got here," he continued. "An impasse. Nobody knows what that means so things are gonna continue same as before."

After the meeting, Lipton hurried to catch up with Pete Nolan as he left the room. "You look like you just stepped off a yacht," he said. "Where you been?"

"Keeping the world safe," Nolan said, pressing the elevator button.

"I thought that was the air force's job. No, seriously. Were you in Valpo?"

Pete Nolan smiled, white teeth on the handsome tan face. "Maybe. But if I told you, you'd use it against me. Who won at poker?"

"Not me." The elevator arrived.

"Catch you later," Nolan said, stepping into the elevator.

Bill came slowly out of the conference room where he'd stayed to have a sidebar with the ambassador.

"That guy's too damn good looking to take seriously," Lipton said as he followed Bill into his office and closed the door.

"Who? The ambassador?"

"No. Nolan. But speaking of the ambassador, you don't really believe all that, do you?"

"All what?"

"What you said in the meeting."

Bill chuckled and picked up the mail from his inbox.

"Which part?"

Lipton contained his growing impatience with his boss' coyness. "About things staying the same."

"Of course not," Bill said, sorting through cables and memos. "But it's clear that's the message the ambassador's gonna deliver to his boss."

"And what are you going to tell yours?"

"That it's time to break the impasse. That's your job. Remember?"

15

"Okay, who performed 'Sea of Joy.' "

"Blind Faith."

"Who were?"

"Winwood, Clapton, Baker and—uh—Grinch."

"Who?"

"Fred Grinch."

"I don't think so."

"Something like that. Gresh, Grolsh."

They both laughed. Ernesto handed Will the joint.

Will took a deep toke then continued with the quiz. "Okay, who wrote 'Waterloo Sunset'?"

"Easy. The Kinks, 1967."

"Too easy, though technically Ray Davies wrote it."

"Same difference."

"Okay, name a song by Moby Grape."

"Who?"

"No, forget that. They sucked anyway. Name a song by Savoy Brown."

" 'I'm Tired.' "

"Damn! I'm impressed."

"I told you, huevón. I know my music."

"Then name three of the Bluesbreakers' guitarists."

"Let's see…Mayall and Clapton of course, and Peter Green."

"Not bad for a Chilean, but Mayall plays the harmonica."

"Hey, don't start insulting my nationality or I'll quiz you on Chile."

Will laughed and handed the joint back to Ernesto.

"So who are Los Blops?" asked Ernesto.

"You're making that up."

"No, they're super. We should go hear them sometime."

"I'll believe you when I see them."

"Very reasonable. You know Chile's motto?"

"What?"

"By Reason or by Fucking Force."

"That true?"

"More true."

They were still giggling when Víctor opened the door.

"Víctor!" Ernesto got up from the couch and gave him a hug. "Ricardo was just testing my knowledge of rock and roll."

Later, after drinking a few beers, they got into an argument about politics. When Will was alone with Ernesto the subject rarely came up, but with Víctor it was always just below the surface. Tonight Víctor was already furious about the emerging allegations against ITT as a U.S. Senate subcommittee scrutinized the company's underhanded dealings against Allende. The fact that the former head of the CIA, John McCone, was a director of the corporation didn't help matters. Every paper in Chile was following the story.

The discussion started calmly enough about a book Víctor was reading by a Uruguayan journalist, *The Open Veins of Latin America*. As Víctor peppered his description with anti-American undertones, Will made an outrageous comment to vent his own frustration. "Chile's problem is the same one that plagues the rest of Latin America. It's not economic dependence. It's intellectual dependence. The real problem is you haven't had an original thinker with an original idea in 500 years. First you blame the Spaniards, then the English, and now the Americans. Meanwhile you imitate everything we do. Colonialism! Imperialism! Marxism!

My ass! As if any of those ideas—all imported, by the way—applies here now. The trouble is, you're constantly running behind, struggling to catch up. Why don't you think for yourselves for a change and stop playing the victim?"

"And what makes you such an authority on Chile all of a sudden?" From Víctor's tone Will could tell he'd struck a nerve.

"I can see the situation more objectively than you."

"You believe that?"

"There's no such thing as objectivity," Ernesto said. "We're all hostages of our time and place."

"Bullshit. I've got no history or investment in what happens here. I'm an outsider looking in."

"But that too is a distortion," said Víctor, coming to Ernesto's defense. "How can you have an informed opinion without being part of the process?"

"That's stupid."

"Is it?" Ernesto glanced up from the joint he was rolling.

"Sure. I've seen similar things happen in the U.S., enough to have an opinion."

"I rest my case."

"What's that supposed to mean?"

"You aren't objective. You're tainted by your experience."

Will found the argument sophomoric and maddening.

"You're as much a victim of your upbringing as I am," Ernesto insisted. "Your upbringing is your identity and your identity shapes your opinions. Even if you tried to be somebody else, you couldn't, any more than Víctor or I could. You would simply be reacting to who you are."

"Bullshit. An objective opinion is one without bias. When I have no bias I have an objective opinion."

"That's circular reasoning," Víctor said.

Ernesto laughed. "Here, man, lighten up," offering the fresh joint to Will. "Stop trying to be the solution and become part of the problem."

* * *

At their next weekly meeting in the Hotel Rincón, Lipton handed Will a typewritten, one-page synopsis and asked him to review it for accuracy.

Víctor Maragall. Age 22. Born in Temuco. Grew up in Santiago from age seven. Mother deceased (suicide). Father, alcoholic, mostly unemployed. Víctor lives with his father in La Cisterna. He is the youngest of four siblings: Marta (30), Luís (29), and René (26). He won a scholarship to Colegio San Bartólomo, and subsequently to the University of Chile, paid for by the Centro de Simón Bólivar (funding expires this year). Studying philosophy and law. Has one more year before graduation. Member of law review. Works part-time at the university bookstore. Joined the student activist group, MUI, a sub-cell of the MIR, in 1971. Stopped attending meetings in June 1972. Homosexual, currently involved with another student, Ernesto Manning Hernández. Arrested for shoplifting (age 12), otherwise no police record.

Will handed the sheet back to Lipton.

"That about cover it?" Lipton asked.

"Looks good." A single page summarizing a six-week investigation and a file full of notes. That, thought Will, is what intelligence boils down to. They agreed that money, cash now and perhaps the lure of a scholarship later, would be the best inducement for Víctor.

"Good. Then I'll forward it to Washington for approval. As soon as we get it, let's reel him in."

That night Will woke from a dream that stayed with him all the next day and filled him with sadness. He was at home in Tucson, walking up the wash near his parents' house. The leaves on the branches of the mesquite trees and the delicate tips of the palo verde trees dripped from a sudden storm, like after a July monsoon. Will was explaining to Tim Albright, whom he couldn't see but whose presence he felt, how everything had changed from what they had aspired to in college. Their situations were different, he told him. He was happy that Tim was married and teaching high school. He was glad that Tim knew what he wanted to do with his life. But for him it wasn't so easy. As Will said goodbye without looking back at Tim, his voice choked with loss and yearning. Then Tim was gone and he was walking up the wash alone, his eyes drawn to the glistening bits of mica in the sand, his ears tuned to the crunch of the sand beneath his feet.

Within a week Lipton received the green light to approach Víctor. Will waited until they were alone and would have enough time to talk without being interrupted. The opportunity came on a Friday evening in April while he and Víctor waited for Ernesto to come home. They were supposed to go see *Goodbye, Mr. Chips* together, but Ernesto phoned to say he was going to be late.

"I told you," Víctor said into the receiver. After he hung up he explained to Will what had happened: A demonstration had blocked the streets around the university. The Carabineros refused to let people pass; cabs and busses were detoured. Ernesto was walking home.

Víctor flopped onto the couch and opened a magazine while Inti-Illimani played on the stereo.

"Poor Ernesto," Will said. "He was really looking forward to watching all those beautiful English schoolboys—his words not mine! These demonstrations are a real pain in the ass," working his way gently into the issue.

Víctor uttered vague agreement without looking up from the magazine. Inti-Illimani's somber rendition of "Run Run Se Fue Pa'l Norte" seemed to match his sullen mood.

"Has there been much more violence at the university?" Will asked. It was like fly fishing, numerous casts until one landed just right.

"A few fights. Some vandalism. What you'd expect," Víctor said. "Even at the university you have people of every stripe. Nazis and fascists. Marxists and Maoists. And everything in between." Víctor looked up. "It's like going to the zoo."

"My company keeps asking me what to expect. How am I supposed to know?"

Víctor dropped the magazine onto the couch.

"We very rarely talk about you, Ricardo, do we?"

"I lead a boring life. Half my job is assessing the investment climate here."

Víctor lit a cigarette and tossed the dying match into the abalone shell ashtray on the coffee table.

"And what do you tell them?"

"That things are broken and need to change."

Víctor blew smoke through a partial smile. "Spoken like an arrogant capitalist. And what's the rest?"

"Of what?"

"You said assessment was half of your job."

"Oh. The other half is making contacts. Doing business."

Víctor stared at Will. The pale scar down his cheek added to the intensity of his gaze. His face suddenly relaxed and he yawned. Will decided to take another cast.

"You know, I've been meaning to talk to you. You could help me."

"Yes? How?"

"With your involvement at the university, you must know what's going on, right? You know the leaders of these groups. What they think, how they react. If someone were going to make trouble, you'd know, wouldn't you? All of that is of interest to my associates." Will decided to jerk the line and see what happened. "I'll bet I could even get authorization to pay you something for that kind of information."

Víctor's thick eyebrows lifted. "Your company thinks that much of what students think and do?"

Will returned Víctor's stare. "It's more data. Bits of information to help assess the overall climate."

"The climate?" Víctor scoffed. "It's almost winter, Ricardo. It's going to be cold and gray. What more do you need to know?"

Will smiled.

"How much?" Víctor asked.

Will threw out a number that he thought an attractive incentive, even a little generous, but not enough to raise a red flag with Lipton. "Of course, this would have to be between us. Otherwise, Ernesto will want to know why he hasn't been offered something. Unfortunately I can't use a treatise on Lord Jim's latent homosexual tendencies."

Víctor laughed. "That's what I love about Ernesto. He's an innocent *and* a whore. Some of our friends think he's naïve. But he isn't really. He has simply chosen not to participate in things others worry about. Sometimes I get angry when he refuses to see what's going on politically. But I don't think he cares. If it doesn't affect him directly, he doesn't worry. 'But this *does* affect you,' I tell him. And he laughs... If he ran out of grass, he'd worry. If he couldn't read his books or listen to his music, he'd worry. But if Allende's in power, or Tomic, or Alessandri, it's all the same to him. I don't understand it really. Yet he's much happier than I am. He's like the birds."

"The birds?"

"You know, the birds of the field. They don't worry about anything. Neither does Ernesto."

"It helps to have money," Will said, trying to bring the conversation back on point. But Víctor followed his own course.

"Yes, but I wonder if there isn't a price, too. In his own way, Ernesto is an artist, creating his life as he goes. That carefree demeanor of his requires a special vision. But I worry that he's unrealistic. That he could be hurt. I'm the realist. With me around he has balance, but without me... I don't know...maybe somehow I encourage his behavior."

Víctor picked up the magazine and began to read again. Inti-Illimani were playing a brighter piece with intertwining harps and flutes. For now the conversation was over. Will felt fairly certain Víctor understood what he was asking for. At least he didn't say, "Go fuck yourself."

Will's hunch was confirmed several days later when Leti came into his office and in a suspicious tone announced that he had a visitor. He followed her back to the reception area and instantly recognized Víctor in his bulky sweater and ink-stained khakis. He looked thoroughly uncomfortable in the office setting, the first time Will had seen Víctor's composure challenged.

"What a surprise," Will said, shaking his hand. Víctor's eyes set upon him as if he were seeing Will in a new light.

"I was passing by and thought I might see what the company looks like that so desperately wants my weather reports."

Will glanced at Leti whose curiosity at the appearance of this long-haired, ill-dressed student was obvious. She fed a piece of paper into the typewriter and pretended not to listen.

Will would never have met an asset at the First Republic office, but it was too late now. He would need to come up with an explanation. In the meantime, he hastened Víctor from the reception area to his office and closed the door. He didn't want Víctor feeling more uncomfortable than he already must, for fear that he might turn and bolt. His presence there confirmed that Will had accomplished his goal. Now, gradually, discreetly, he would need to train him in the basic arts of tradecraft.

Will sat down behind his desk. Víctor remained standing, his hands in the deep pockets of the bulky Peruvian sweater. Normally so sure of himself, he looked around with nervous curiosity. The office, Will realized as he followed Víctor's eyes, was devoid of family photos or personal items. Just piles of paper and bound reports, a few files and binders, and a pile of old magazines and newspapers stacked on the credenza.

"I should have called first," Víctor apologized.

"That's all right. I'm glad you came by. So, does this mean you're willing to help?"

"Is the offer still good?"

Will nodded. He recognized Víctor's aggressive tone of voice. It was the same hungry tone Will had acquired as he competed for academic grants and scholarships—the pragmatic opportunism that comes from impoverishment and disadvantage. Víctor could be bought because there was nothing but advantage from being bought.

Except for the pieces of information gleaned from Ernesto, the few tidbits Víctor had revealed in casual conversation and what Lipton had uncovered in his background search, Will knew little about Víctor Maragall. He lived in a house that, Will guessed, was not much better than the shacks in the campamentos, those illegal shantytowns that were springing up like mushrooms around Santiago. He wasn't even sure if Víctor's house had indoor plumbing or if his father held title to the property. Víctor never spoke of home. If Ernesto had not introduced him to Will and if Will had not regularly encountered him in Providencia, he might easily have dismissed Víctor as a menial laborer, one of the many who survived on meager wages earned on the streets by day and who disappeared into the squalid, shadowy poblaciones at night. A roto, to use Leti's and Ema de Manning's demeaning term.

"You do know the information isn't for me specifically." It was the closest Will had ever come to admitting who and what he was.

Víctor gave him a slow deliberate nod. "When do I get paid?"

"I can put you on a retainer today. And as soon as you provide some information that I can forward to my company, there will be more."

"What kind of information exactly?"

"That political organization you belonged to, what's it called again?" he asked coyly.

"The MUI?"

"Yeah. Maybe you could start attending their meetings again. Any information on planned strikes or protests or acts of civil disobedience—that would be good to know. Names of its leaders, information about them. Even the smallest stuff—what they like to eat, where they shop, who their girlfriends are—it doesn't matter. It's all good."

Will paused to light a cigarette, allowing Víctor time to absorb the significance of what he was asking for.

"Is that all?" Víctor asked sarcastically.

"It's plenty. Don't do anything risky, Víctor. Just be alert and absorb what you hear."

"My respect for you has grown, Ricardo. You're not an ignorant American after all. But, it's strange, I think I like you less."

Will faced down the assault. He understood Víctor's anger; he'd felt it his whole life. He went over to the safe, took out a hundred dollars and handed the money to Víctor.

"In the future we'll meet somewhere else, at a park or a coffee shop or the library, okay? Not here. And, Víctor, let's keep this between ourselves. Not a word to anyone, especially Ernesto. Any compromise of confidentiality and the deal's off. Clear?"

After Víctor left, Will made a point of chatting with Leti. In the conversation he let drop that Víctor was a student he had met at the last American-Chile Chamber of Commerce meeting who was seeking a reference to his alma mater, Georgetown.

When he returned to his office he closed the door and leaned back in his chair. He should have felt pleased. Lipton would be off his case about penetrating the MIR's student cell. The cash would be good for Víctor, yet he wasn't asking him to do anything risky or illegal for it. Above all, he had managed to keep Ernesto and Gabriela outside the sphere of deception.

16

Will walked from his apartment to the base of the Cerro San Cristóbal funicular. Ten minutes early for his meeting, he sat on a bench and watched families stroll through the park. It was a Sunday afternoon in early June. A few yellow leaves fell in the mild breeze, a sign of winter's imminent arrival.

CHAPLIN (the cryptonym Lipton assigned to Víctor) entered the park through the main gate right on time. He wore his usual rumpled khakis, the bulky Peruvian cardigan that substituted for a coat and thick-soled work shoes. Víctor spotted Will on the bench (if Will was standing, he was not to approach) and clomped toward him with a steady, determined stride. From his body language, Will sensed he disliked being there.

In the two months since his recruitment, Víctor had proven invaluable. He identified the MIR's three student leaders, warned of campus demonstrations and handed over detailed notes of a secret meeting with Joaquín Peña, head of the Communist Party's paramilitary. The most important information Víctor revealed was the location of the group's meetings in the back of a Marxist bookshop on Calle Serrano. With the help of a technical team from Langley, Lipton managed to pick the lock one night and install an electronic bug in a light fixture. From this, they learned of a large weapons cache in a furniture factory in Maipú. Mysteriously, the factory caught fire a few days later and everything inside was destroyed. On May Day, Will opened *El Mercurio* to a full exposé, including photos of the charred weapons. Lipton was delighted.

Will stood up as Víctor approached. Without a word they walked to the funicular and purchased tickets. Most of the people waiting to ascend had crowded into the lower cars. The two men climbed the stairs to an empty upper car. Will surveyed the crowd for any sign of surveillance.

During the funicular's creaky ascent they had a stunning view of the city. Disembarking beneath the giant statue of the Virgin Mary, they walked to the lookout. Sulfurous smog obliterated the lower half of the Andes, but the peaks, fresh with an early snow, shimmered like an illusion in the hot air currents. It was as if they were floating on an island above the gritty tumult of the city. Even the roar of traffic on the Costanera Norte was muted at this peaceful height.

"We should meet up here more often," Will said to put Víctor at ease.

Víctor propped one foot against the low wall of the promontory and peered at the garbage that littered the vertiginous slope below. "I used to come up here as a kid to go swimming. There's a public pool over there," he said, pointing toward the eastern ridge. "We'd take the bus to the base, then walk up. The pool was about the only way to cool off in the summer."

"Who's we?" Will asked, turning to admire the Virgin, whose eyes and arms were lifted in supplication to the blue sky. "My mother, when she wasn't working. My brothers and I. Before my mother killed herself."

Ernesto had told Will about the suicide. It happened when Víctor was ten. Will recognized the reluctance in Víctor's voice, the wariness that prevented him from sharing personal information freely. The confusion of shame and pride. Though their stories were different, he was familiar with the emotions.

"Where'd you live back then?"

Víctor pointed to the west of the city center. "Over there. But then we moved in with my uncle for a while."

"Let's walk down," Will said, indicating the switchback path. The Cerro had a reputation for pickpockets and drug dealers and, according to Víctor, as a pickup place for gay men. No one was on the path and Will could safely steer the conversation toward business.

"So what happened at the latest meeting?" Will asked, as bees buzzed in the flowering acacia along the path.

"They handed out guns. A test of our commitment."

As Will mulled this, Víctor produced a flysheet from his back pocket and handed it to him: a call to strike with the Central Workers Confederation on June 20.

"What it doesn't say is that the organizers plan to lead the demonstration right through the striking miners in Plaza de la Constitución."

"Man! They're just asking for it, aren't they?"

"That's why they handed out pistols."

In the early days of their new relationship Will wondered if Víctor felt qualms about selling information. He never displayed a sign of conflict or remorse, never asked who was receiving it, and over time Will abandoned his concern. Still, he worried about Víctor's safety.

"Are you going?"

Víctor shook his head. "Of course not."

"Good. Because some heads are sure to be cracked that day."

He handed Víctor an envelope containing forty thousand escudos.

"My company liked your work so much, you got a raise."

Víctor tucked the envelope into his shirt pocket beneath the heavy cardigan sweater. Beads of sweat trickled down his forehead despite the fact they were walking downhill. "Good," he said.

"Incidentally, my company has a scholarship program for exceptional foreign students. It covers tuition and board at an American university. With your background in law, you'd make an excellent candidate. Would you be interested?"

Money and ego, thought Will. These were Víctor's motivators. But which, to borrow Ernesto's line, was more true?

"I'm too old for all this back and forth, crammed into those goddamn seats."

It was nearly 8:00 p.m. when Bill Bradshaw, coat on, suitcase in hand, dropped his suitcase and eased himself into the armchair in front of Lipton's desk. He looked haggard from his trip to Washington. His face was paler than usual, almost gray, his shoulders hunched. "Got any elixir in that cupboard of yours?"

Lipton brought out a bottle of Jack Daniels from his credenza and poured a healthy measure into two stained coffee mugs. He handed one to Bill. "Salud!"

"That's better," Bill said, smacking his lips after the first sip. "So, what's new?"

"You mean, besides the state of emergency Allende declared? Not much. The miners aren't going to give in. What's the latest up north?" The smoky fire of the whisky slipped down his throat. Good old Jack Daniels.

"Dave Phillips has had it rough. His daughter was killed in an auto accident. Out on a date and bam! Seventeen. Shit. That'd wipe you out for a while. But not old Dave. He's soldiering on… I keep thinking about my two. I tell Joanie all the time, boys will be the next big challenge."

Lipton sipped his whisky and pictured the lanky twins in two-pieces tanning themselves by the pool. Bill was probably too late.

"This whole Watergate thing has taken over Washington. It's all anybody talks about. The TV, the papers are filled with it. Meanwhile, P and K have Colby running defense. No trust anymore as far as I can tell. Not that there ever was much…" He dipped his finger into the mug and daubed his chapped lips with whisky. "Nope, I reckon it's about time to hop on my horse and ride into the sunset. Leave all this glamorous world travel and international intrigue to you young bucks. Go back to my spread in Virginia, become a gentleman farmer. Sounds pretty good, don't it?"

Lipton tapped his pen against the edge of the desk. He sensed the conversation was building to something. Down the hall, a mop clanked in the janitor's bucket.

"There's a cable coming. Phillips gave me a heads-up."

Instinctively, Lipton reached over and turned on the radio—Henry Mancini's "Charade" played. Technicians had recently scoured the office for bugs, but you never knew.

"Bottom line: they want us to back off."

Lipton felt the blood pound at his temples. "Fuck! I knew it. What now?"

Bill motioned for him to calm down.

"Not everything. They just want us to keep our distance from anyone who might actually be talking about a coup."

"Christ, Bill! Do they want a change here or not?"

"I asked Phillips that same question. No change in overall strategy."

"That's not what I meant."

"I know. I suppose this is for our own good. They don't want us associated with another failure. No smoking gun this time."

"For fuck sake!" Lipton downed the rest of the whisky.

"Yeah, but you weren't here for the firestorm after those idiots bungled the Schneider deal," Bill said. "I'm starting to think we'll never live that down. Not with this administration, at least."

"So, who do these new restrictions include? MILINTEL?" Lipton was supposed to meet Major Covarrubias later that evening for their weekly information exchange.

"Naw, that's routine. I think they mean any of the key players on the general staff.

"Is this across the board? Are Nolan and Hall being told to stand down too?"

"Don't know. But they'd hardly be the ones to take the heat if things went badly, would they? Let's face it, we're always the scapegoats. In people's minds, I mean. The bad boys, the ones to blame."

"This sucks."

"Well, we haven't received the cable yet, so keep calm. Remember, 'Our duty to defend...'" Bill said, paraphrasing the service oath. He placed the mug on the desk and carefully extracted himself from the chair. "Got any aspirin?" He winced as he straightened his back. Lipton shook his head. "Oh, by the way, I have a few more matchboxes for the Major. Drop by my office before you go."

17

*W*ill turned twenty-five on Wednesday, June 20, not that he could tell anyone. His passport gave his birthday as October 6. He woke up before the alarm went off and, feeling energetic, went for a run along the riverfront. The morning was cold and foggy, and the milky brown water of the Mapocho River foamed in eddies created by the discarded tires and garbage dumped on its gravel banks.

A quarter of a century! As birthdays went, this wasn't a bad one. He remembered far worse: on his fourteenth, his father put away four or five old fashioneds then taunted him until they nearly got into a fistfight.

After thirty minutes of running he bent over, gasping and coughing. His lungs burned and he knew he should quit smoking.

On the way back to his apartment he stopped in a bakery on Pio Nono and treated himself to a pastel de chocolate, taking it home to enjoy with his café con leche. After breakfast he showered and dressed quickly.

He needed to be in the office by nine. The day before, Leti handed him a phone message from a man named Gene Isaacson. When Will dialed the number, it turned out to be the Hotel Carrera. He asked for Isaacson.

A flat New Jersey accent issued from the other end, "Yeah, I'm here to do the audit."

"The audit?" Thinking he meant First Republic.

"What, Lipton didn't tell you?" Isaacson asked.

"Ah!" Mention of Lipton reframed the conversation. "Yes, the audit. He did mention it." Will laughed. "But I thought he meant at year end. You want to do it now?"

A cluck of the tongue. "Especially now."

"Okay, but the person I work with isn't aware of my extracurricular activities so we need to package this."

"They usually aren't. What if I'm a client or something?"

"How about a banker. From New York."

"Sure, whatever."

As soon as he got off the phone, Will called Lipton to confirm that the audit was legitimate.

"It is," Lipton said. "Give him what he needs but don't bend over backwards, either. I don't want bells ringing up in Langley just because we've overspent our budget or stretched a few accounting rules to get the job done. These guys don't get it that what we do isn't about having our i's dotted and t's crossed."

Isaacson arrived at the office promptly at nine. Will introduced him to Leti and then led him to his office.

Gene Isaacson was not who Will had expected from the strong, nasal voice on the phone. Tall, lanky, about the same age as Will, he wore a gray suit that hung from his bony shoulders like it was draped on a hanger. Deep inset eyes behind thick tortoiseshell glasses, a lopsided grin.

"Let's get the dirty work out of the way," Isaacson said after Will closed the office door. The gangly friendliness changed to accounting efficiency. "I'll run the audit first. Then we can do the tax forms. I need to see all the cash on hand."

Will went to the safe and came back with four bulging manila envelopes: nearly ninety thousand dollars in hundreds and fifties. There was another sixty thousand in escudos in the bank account of Distribuidores del Sur. As Lipton's money manager, he had been busy. In seven months, he had distributed over four hundred thousand dollars.

Isaacson set the envelopes down on Will's desk and started counting the contents. "I'll need receipts, too."

Will laughed. "It's not like we ask for receipts, you know."

Isaacson looked up from his tabulation and gave Will a loopy smile. "I mean whatever you use to reconcile the incoming cash…spending authorizations, that kind of thing."

Will went to the safe and came back with a file of bank authorizations, copies of invoices sent to Lemantour's Mexican operation, bills of lading, insurance claims. He also brought over his coded ledger.

"This is gonna take a while," Isaacson said.

Will nodded. "Would you like to use my adding machine?"

"No need." Isaacson reached into the open briefcase on the floor and proudly held up a black device the size of a transistor radio.

"Ever seen one of these pups?" Will shook his head. "It's an HP-80. Has financial formulas programmed right in. You wouldn't believe how much time it saves."

When Will didn't respond, Isaacson said, "If you want, you can do something else while I do this."

"That's okay. I'll just sit here and make some notes. No offense, but I like to keep what you're handling in eyesight. Smoke?"

Isaacson declined and started counting again. He placed the money in organized stacks on the desk, carefully tapping the keys of his calculator and annotating his findings in tiny handwriting on a legal pad.

"How do you keep track of where it goes?"

Will showed Isaacson the coded ledger. "Every penny's accounted for here." He explained how to decipher the ledger's columns of dates, amounts and codenames. "And these are Lipton's initials," he said, pointing to the authorizations beside each entry. Isaacson punched more numbers into his calculator.

"Looks like some of these clowns will have to get their meal tickets somewhere else from now on."

"What do you mean?"

"The new restrictions. Some of these are military, right?"

"So?"

Isaacson raised a pale eyebrow. "So, word came down last month. Opposition media and political parties only."

Will didn't know what Isaacson was talking about. But rather than put his foot in his mouth, he would ask Lipton for clarification.

The audit was completed by noon. Will suggested lunch at the Hotel Monte Carlo, but outside they were greeted by honking horns, standing traffic and a crowd of gawking pedestrians at the intersection. A cordon of Carabineros in riot gear blocked the side street. At the far end of the block a mass of students marched with banners in support of the miners' strike. This was the day Víctor had warned of a counter-demonstration.

"Let's go somewhere else," Will said.

They walked the other way to a café where Will sometimes bought a take-out sandwich. At the counter they ordered grilled pork sandwiches, which came smothered in avocado and onion.

"The miners have been on strike for two months over wages."

Isaacson took a large bite from his sandwich. "Yeah, I saw something in the paper this morning." He wiped avocado from the corner of his mouth.

"El Teniente is one of the country's largest copper mines and it's virtually shut down. No copper means no foreign exchange, and that means big trouble for Allende. You should see what it's doing to black-market prices." Hearing himself, Will smiled. He was reminded of Bernie Hassam's impressive knowledge the first time they met. After seven months on the job he was starting to sound like an old salt, too. "Now the students and professionals are backing the miners. Engineers, doctors, nurses...even accountants. People are pissed. Everyone's afraid the government will freeze their salaries next."

"They sure have some pretty women here," Isaacson said, hypnotized by the busty waitress as she brushed past. "Wish I spoke the lingo better."

Will laughed.

"Listen, it's my birthday today. Are you doing anything tonight? Feel like going out to dinner?"

Spending his birthday with an acquaintance, even one like Isaacson with his calculator and gawky looks, was better than spending it alone. Will had not taken a day off from being Richard Allen since arriving in Chile. At least with Isaacson he could relax to a certain extent.

"Sure."

"Good, I'll pick you up at seven-thirty. That way, if we feel like it, we'll have time to go to a nightclub afterwards. Who knows, maybe we'll run into a pretty woman who speaks *your* lingo."

After lunch Will helped Isaacson with the translation of the tax forms for Distribuidores del Sur, which they filled out together and Will signed. At four, Leti called a taxi and Isaacson went back to the hotel. At five, Leti stopped by the door to Will's office.

"Avoid the Alameda on your way home, Ricardo," she said, cinching the belt of her wool overcoat.

"Why?"

"I was just listening to the radio. The strikers got into a fight with some pro-Allende protesters, so the Carabineros intervened. Tear gas, even some shots fired. Apparently several people were wounded. I'd go home another way if I were you."

"Thanks. What about you?"

"My husband is coming to pick me up. I have to run. Ciao."

Will worked until seven then left for the Hotel Carrera. The plaza in front of La Moneda was littered with trash. The striking miners still maintained their position beside glowing bonfires in oil drums at the corner near the stock exchange. If Víctor's counter-demonstration got this far, the miners had clearly won. Carabineros patrolled the street and extra guards stood at the entrance to the presidential palace.

Will phoned Isaacson's room from the lobby, which was surprisingly empty of guests. Minutes later the accountant strode from the elevator looking like a scarecrow with both cuffs of his yellow shirt jutting from the sleeves of a gray suit cut for a shorter man. The concierge advised them that most of the restaurants in the area were closed due to the violence, so they took a cab to Providencia. On Avenida Providencia they found a popular seafood restaurant not only open for business but packed.

Isaacson scrutinized the prices and, doing the math out loud, converted to dollars to ensure that he did not exceed his per diem. He decided finally on the mussels. Will ordered the tuna and selected the wine.

"So do you travel much?" Will asked over the racket of voices bouncing off the tiled walls and floor.

"I'll say. Especially now."

"That's the second time you've said that. What so special about now?"

Isaacson gave him a lopsided grin. "Orders from the top. The new big cheese himself." He glanced around and leaned forward. "If you know who I mean. He's going through everything with a fine-tooth comb. Told us auditors not to come home until we've scoured the books everywhere. No stone unturned."

Did Isaacson mean William Colby? Will's knowledge of agency personnel and politics had always been limited, but after seven months in Chile he was even more in the dark. Lipton filtered organizational information, keeping it to the barest need-to-know essentials. Will had heard about Nixon replacing Richard Helms with James Schlesinger as DCI. Like every other employee in the agency, he had received Schlesinger's infamous May memo requesting information on any and all potentially illegal activities. Lipton had dutifully seen to it that Will initialed his copy as "received." Yet Will had to learn from the *New York Times* how much Schlesinger was despised at headquarters, and that he had just left for the Pentagon. William Colby was conditionally appointed as DCI, provided he followed through on Nixon's mandate to clean house. The agency was under siege from journalists, congressmen and the president himself. Every clandestine program was under review. Yet, here in Santiago, the politics all seemed very far away and irrelevant.

"Shit, and morale sucks!" Isaacson continued. "You field guys have always been suspicious of us, like we're the IRS or something. But getting people to cooperate now is almost impossible." He wrested a stubborn mussel from its shell with his fork and popped it into his mouth. "Meanwhile, people are quitting or getting fired." He chewed vigorously. "Leaving big holes in the organization. Big knowledge gaps. It ain't pretty."

"Uh-oh. Should I have been less cooperative with you?"

Isaacson grinned, licked his fingers and launched into a description of his recent travels. Will listened and drank and feigned interest, asking the occasional question to keep the conversation flowing. Isaacson was nice enough but dull and pedantic. Except for the wandering eye whenever an attractive woman went by, he seemed incurious about his surroundings. At least after this evening Will wouldn't have to write another damn report.

He ordered a brandy for each of them. "My treat," he said when Isaacson, concerned about his per diem, balked. Isaacson began to describe a book he had picked up in Heathrow airport.

"It's called *The Sovereign State*, by a guy named Sampson. The 'secret' history of ITT," he said, using his fingers to inflect the word. "I mean, I knew they got caught trying to pedal influence down here but I didn't realize how much clout they have. Did you know they own the hotel I'm staying in and seventy percent of the Chilean phone company?"

Will nodded and sipped his brandy.

"It's an interesting premise," continued Isaacson, "at least for a bean counter like me. Biased, sure—I mean the guy clearly has an ax to grind. But the argument that MNCs operate outside the legal jurisdiction of the countries they do business in is intriguing. Sovereign unto themselves, he argues. Kinda like the Company, huh?"

Even as he said it Isaacson must have realized his indiscretion. He looked down at the table. "Sorry," he said sheepishly.

"No problem," Will said, calmly finishing his drink. They were talking in English. It was unlikely anyone at the other tables had overhead or even understood what Isaacson had said in his thick New Jersey accent. "It's not like we're in Berlin or something. Why don't we get out of here? Feel like going to a club?"

Will flagged the waiter and paid the check. Isaacson watched the transaction closely.

"The tip's already included," he said as Will placed several hundred escudos on the tray.

"Thanks. I know. But it's common to round up."

Will found Isaacson's obliviousness amusing. Ambiance, customs, history, language—nothing but numbers and women was of much interest.

They were walking on the north side of Avenida Providencia, discussing where to go next, when they ran into Ernesto, Víctor and, to Will's enormous surprise, Gabriela, headed in the opposite direction.

"Don Ricardo!" Ernesto greeted him, raising his hand in mock salute.

"Cover time," Will managed to say to Isaacson as they stopped. He introduced the accountant as a colleague from New York. Gabriela was wearing a trim black leather jacket that looked great on her and Will caught Isaacson admiring her figure. Will gave her a kiss on the cheek.

"What about me?" Ernesto said.

"You don't deserve one," Will responded. "Why didn't you tell me Gabriela was here?"

Ernesto laughed. "We were just going home," he said, lifting a bottle of pisco from the pocket of his pea jacket. "The peñas are all closed. Police orders. But I hear there's a party at your place."

Will laughed. A chance to spend the evening with Gabriela suddenly took precedence over his duties as host. He turned to Isaacson to translate. "They say everything's closed. Are you up for going to my place instead? It's just across the river."

Ernesto designated himself DJ and flipped through Will's records, choosing the progression for the evening. Will and Gabriela went to the kitchen for glasses and something to mix with pisco. After rejecting canned tomato juice, they settled on ginger ale. Will also opened a bottle of red wine.

"It's so good to see you," he said, handing her a glass of wine. "What brings you to Santiago?"

"I drove the car up. Ernesto was too lazy to come down to fetch it… Actually, it's nice to get away once in a while."

"How's your mother? And Imelda?" In the living room "Suite: Judy Blue Eyes" rose to its harmonic crescendo.

Gabriela laughed. "Mamá keeps asking when you're coming down again. She insinuates that I said something mean to you. 'Whatever happened to that nice American?' Very subtle. Imelda is fat and happy."

Will smiled. Since their ride together Gabriela treated him differently. He felt a relaxed, unspoken connection.

"It's been very busy at work, otherwise I'd love to come down for a visit… I miss Imelda."

The dimples at the corners of her mouth deepened with her smile. She sipped her wine and surveyed the unadorned kitchen with a critical eye. "I see you and Ernesto share a similar sense of style." She peered down the darkened hallway that led to Will's bedroom then pivoted on her heels into the light of the kitchen. Her brow furrowed. "What do you call this? Camping Chic?"

They carried glasses and bottles into the living room. Víctor and Gene Isaacson sat on the couch attempting to communicate over the music. Ernesto knelt on the floor by the record player, flipping through Will's albums.

"Hey, Víctor… Víctor! Don't be so stingy!" he yelled, miming a cigarette.

Víctor stopped what he was saying in broken English and took a cellophane pack from his breast pocket and tossed it to Ernesto.

"No. The others." Throwing the pack back to Víctor.

Víctor smirked and tossed a second, half-crumpled cigarette pack to Ernesto. Ernesto carefully extracted a joint, moistened its seam with his tongue, twisted its ends and lit it. Soon the sweet fragrance of grass filled the apartment. Ernesto passed the joint to Gabriela who took a token puff and handed it to Will. Will glanced at Isaacson, wondering how he would react. He had been ignoring his guest to be with Gabriela, in part to let Isaacson know his boundaries. Will took a hit and offered the half-consumed joint to the accountant. Isaacson held it between his fingertips, away from his body, and passed it to Víctor. Ernesto giggled at the accountant's meticulous disdain.

"It won't hurt you, guapo," he said.

"Pardon?" Isaacson asked.

"Smoking a queer's joint don't make you queer," Ernesto said in English while exaggerating his mannerisms as if to test Isaacson's tolerance. Or perhaps he was testing Will's.

"No thanks," Isaacson said. "I'll stick to booze."

Víctor got off the couch and handed the joint back to Ernesto who held it up in offering to Isaacson. "First time for everything," he said.

"Knock it off, Ernesto," Will said in Spanish.

Ernesto giggled. "What?"

"You know damned well."

Isaacson smiled but looked uncomfortable not understanding what was being said. "Well, Rick, happy birthday. Many happy returns," he said, raising his glass to Will.

"Birthday? Is it you're birthday, Ricardo?" Ernesto asked. Gabriela, too, looked at him in surprise.

"Not until October," Will said. He gave Isaacson a look to deter him from saying something else. "Just a joke," he added.

"Too bad. Gabriela and I were ready to give you a birthday kiss. One on each cheek."

"Ernesto, you're drunk. Or high." Gabriela said.

"Or both!" Ernesto made a face at his sister. He went over to the stereo to turn up the volume.

A loud knock on the door cut through the music and, like children caught making mischief, everyone froze. As he went to the door, Will beckoned to Ernesto to snuff the joint. He expected to open it to his frowning landlady. Instead, Roland Fabré and a diminutive silver-haired woman in a fur coat stood in the hallway.

"Good evening, Reeshard. We heard the music. I thought you might like some company." Roland raised himself on his toes to peer past Will. "Ah! But I see we interrupt."

Will sighed with relief and welcomed them in.

"This is my lovely friend, Happy Sunshine." Roland's gray eyes gleamed as he introduced his girlfriend.

The woman's lips were colored bright red and her wide smile exposed fine white teeth. She laughed in denial as if the entire world knew that Roland Fabré was an outrageous mischief-maker. As the Frenchman helped her out of the luxurious coat to reveal a trim black dress with tiny rhinestones sewn on the collar, she offered a birdlike hand to Will and introduced herself as Felicidad del Sol.

Roland gallantly offered Felicidad his arm and led her into the smoke-filled living room. To each person in turn he introduced himself with a slight bow and proudly presented his girlfriend. Still holding the fur coat, Will stood in the hallway observing the scene in disbelief. His birthday was turning into something far more interesting than he ever could have imagined when he woke up that morning.

The next morning arrived much too brightly and much too soon. The apartment reeked of cigarette smoke. With a head in need of an aspirin and a cigarette in need of a match, Will picked up dirty glasses and ashtrays and deposited them in the kitchen sink. He noticed that his hand shook as he lit the cigarette on the burner of the stove. Pisco and pot were not a good combination.

He wondered how Gene Isaacson was doing. At two-thirty the accountant had left with the others, who promised to put him safely in a taxi back to the hotel. As he said goodbye, the drunken Isaacson mumbled that he was meeting Lipton at ten to go over the audit.

The thought of facing Lipton with a hangover made Will smile. He needed to get to work himself but dawdled, putting the records away first.

Like an archaeologist, he was able to reconstruct the party from the layers of records stacked in reverse chronological order beside the stereo: *Getz/Gilberto* on top—that album was played at Roland's request so that he and Felicidad could dance to "O Grande Amor" before finally saying goodnight. Underneath was *Santana*. Beneath that, the Rolling Stones' *Sympathy for the Devil*, which was playing around the time of the argument between Roland and Víctor. The record lay sitting outside its dust jacket on top of its white cover. Below that, Derek and the Dominos, with one of the discs carelessly stuffed between the two halves of the double album cover.

Will discerned a lead guitarist theme until he came to the

Moody Blues' *In Search of the Lost Chord*. He didn't even remember hearing that one and suspected that Ernesto took it out to play but never got around to it. Next, *Are You Experienced?* That, he remembered clearly, was the record playing when Roland knocked on the door. Underneath that, *Revolver*. And at the very bottom of the pile was *Crosby, Stills & Nash*. Yes, that's where the party began, with "Suite: Judy Blue Eyes," a song which would forever be associated with an image of Gabriela shuddering at the taste of pisco and tomato juice.

The argument had started over Víctor's assertion that the truth about the miners' strike would eventually come out. (What, Will wondered now, had he meant by that?) By that time they had smoked all of Víctor's joints and the conversation was laced with cryptic allusions.

"You make it sound like there's a truth with a capital T being withheld. That's nonsense. Truth is made not discovered," Roland responded.

"Bullshit," Víctor said. "It may be buried in lies but the truth is the truth."

Roland sipped his pisco and ginger ale then grimaced as if he had picked up someone else's drink by mistake. He placed it on the coffee table, pushing it away.

"The sun rises every morning," he said. "True? Since the dawn of man, hasn't it been absolutely true? Then what? Man goes up into space and sees that the sun doesn't rise at all. It is *not* true! Of course, in theory we have known this since Copernicus. But now, only now that a man has seen it differently, the statement becomes ridiculous. Why? The sun and earth have not changed. Our language has failed. Time for a new metaphor! The earth negotiates the sun, perhaps. No, that is not right…" Roland frowned. "This is why we need poets. As for the rest of us, perhaps we should stop insisting on absolute truths and start concentrating on agreement."

"That's stupid. Like denying the law of gravity?" Víctor asserted.

"Or one and one equals two?" Isaacson added, causing Víctor to nod appreciatively at his support.

For Isaacson's sake the argument was being conducted in a strange, awkward mix of English and Spanish. Ernesto had disappeared down the hallway to find the bathroom. Gabriela and Felicidad were having a separate conversation at the dining table. Will wanted to join them but felt compelled to stay with the men and translate this senseless debate for Isaacson.

"Socrates is a man. All men are mortal. Therefore, Socrates is mortal, no?" continued the Frenchman. "An irrefutable syllogism. The absolute truth! But the church tells us otherwise, doesn't it. We are all immortal, they say. So, which is true?"

"Please don't bring the church's foolishness into this," Víctor said.

"But you see? Without a vocabulary we agree upon, there can be no truth. True and false are contingent upon agreement. Change the meaning of the words, and the truth changes, too. If you believe red is white and I believe yellow is white, then there is no truth, no agreement on what is white. And on complex issues—what is moral, what is good, are the strikers right or wrong—agreement is even more difficult. Perhaps impossible."

Roland's claims momentarily stymied Víctor. He was about to say something but shook his head in speechless frustration. Isaacson, drunk on pisco, wore a lopsided grin as if he considered the Frenchman's statements absurd.

"That's relativistic crap!" Víctor finally stammered.

Roland raised his arms in a gesture of surrender then smiled with devilish delight. "So shoot me for disagreeing with you. Kill everyone who disagrees with you. Then you will have the whole truth. But not until then. Personally, I believe we would be much better off using our energy to distinguish *un*truths, those things we suspect to be lies. But, I may be wrong. I am a student of standard deviations, not a philosopher. And statistics tend to make one an ironist."

Víctor leaned forward, aggressively stubbing his cigarette butt into the ashtray. He was about to challenge Roland when Ernesto came back into the room, smiling impishly, and raised Will's gun over his head, pointed at the ceiling.

"Police! Freeze! You're all so busted!"

Ernesto burst out laughing and lowered the gun. No one else was laughing. Víctor glared at Will as if it were his fault Ernesto had the gun—the bastard must have gone through my dresser, thought Will—and Isaacson, mouth open, looked startled sober. Neither Roland Fabré nor the two women seemed to realize it was a real gun. Recovering from his initial shock, Will stood up.

"Ricardo," Ernesto said, gingerly surrendering the weapon to him, "what do you have this for?"

"More to the point, huevón, what are you doing with it?"

Ernesto gave Will his most endearing hairball laugh. "I was looking to see if you had any grass stashed away. Don't worry, I saw it wasn't loaded."

"Lucky for you, pendejo. Otherwise I'd be tempted to use it right about now." But it was hard to stay angry with Ernesto.

Ernesto giggled. "Seriously, what's it for?"

"My company makes us have one. For protection from idiots like you." It was true in a way. Will took the gun back to his bedroom and replaced it behind his socks, thankful he kept the ammunition separate, hidden under the kitchen sink.

18

*E*d Lipton pulled up to the red and white striped barricade in his Plymouth Valiant. One of four guards came to the driver's window and asked his purpose. It seemed pretty obvious. He was dressed in white shorts, a white polo shirt and a cable-knit tennis sweater with burgundy and navy blue stripes around the v-neck.

"I'm here to see Major Covarrubias," he said, lifting the tennis racquet in its wooden press from the seat beside him.

The guard nodded. Another soldier scanned the underside of the car with a round mirror attached to an aluminum pole.

After the all clear, the guard raised the barricade and waved Lipton through. The divided drive intersected another road encircling a vast parade ground. On the windswept field a company of soldiers in gray T-shirts was doing calisthenics. Low wooden barracks lined the far side of the field and administrative offices were to the right. On the left, between a cluster of two-story houses and the officers' club, two red clay tennis courts lay unused behind a chain-link fence.

Lipton parked his car in front of the club. Major Covarrubias, dressed in whites, came out carrying two racquets and a can of tennis balls.

"Good morning, Eduardo," he said, extending his hand. Out of uniform, he looked smaller but extremely fit. The white polo shirt revealed tufts of grizzled hair on his chest.

"Ready to be trounced?" Lipton asked.

Major Covarrubias laughed and gallantly swept his hand toward the courts. "After you."

Lipton had won a letter on his high school tennis team in Tacoma, but that was in 1951, and he played more golf than tennis now. They warmed up for five minutes then started a set. A young soldier dressed in green fatigues crouched by the net to perform the duties of ball boy. Lipton found his presence distracting.

Although more agile, Major Covarrubias had the disadvantage of being shorter and less able to put much speed on his serve. Lipton tried to serve and volley but found he wasn't quick enough coming to the net. He kept getting caught mid-court, out of position for the major's baseline shots and not close enough to the net for his drop shots. Lipton tended to overpower his own shots and the erratic wind didn't help his precision. He lost 6-4.

Between sets they rested on a bench while the soldier dragged a metal screen across the court and brushed off the tapelines with a broom. From the parade ground came rhythmic shouts of coordinated exercise. Major Covarrubias poured Lipton a glass of water from a pitcher on the table behind them.

"Your serve has improved," he said.

"Yeah, it's just the rest of my game that's gone to hell." Lipton wiped the stinging sweat from his eyes with a hand towel. He was more winded than he should be. "I see you still like to run me back and forth."

Covarrubias laughed. "Unfortunately, only one side can win. Shall we?"

Determined to beat his opponent in the next set, Lipton mixed up the pace and put more topspin on his returns. He stayed closer to the baseline and waited until Covarrubias approached the net, then he either went down the line or lobbed. The strategy worked. Major Covarrubias was showing a new level of frustration. He took fewer chances with his angles and muttered at his errors. At the critical moment of ad-out the major double faulted and Lipton broke serve to lead 5-4.

As Lipton prepared to serve for the set, he could see the major's determined concentration—the dark, focused eyes, the forward angle of the body, the taut legs ready to spring. Lipton was equally determined. Mostly, he wanted to win because he knew Major Covarrubias hated to lose.

They battled over each point, but Lipton kept the service advantage. At set point the obvious attack was to go for an ace in the backhand corner of the service box, so he aimed instead for the major's body. He tossed the ball high and put his shoulder into the serve, springing off his left leg as the racquet came down on the ball. He knew it was a good serve as soon as it left his racquet. The ball arced across the net, popped off the service line and kicked up high into Covarrubias' startled face. The major had no time to move around the shot. The ball ricocheted off his strings, struck the net tape and dropped on his side. Lipton gloated behind a straight face.

"Long!" Covarrubias shouted.

The call was not only suspect but late. As if reading Lipton's mind, Major Covarrubias trotted to the service box and tapped at a mark on the court.

"Long, yes?" he said, turning to the soldier for confirmation.

"Yes, sir!" the soldier said.

Bullshit. Anger renewed Lipton's energy. It was one thing to lose but another to be beaten by a cheater. Common sense said to serve a safe second serve. Instead, he smashed the ball as if it were his first. The ball skidded inside the right corner of the service box and zoomed flatly past Major Covarrubias' open racquet.

The major came reluctantly to the net to shake Lipton's hand. "Well done, Eduardo," he managed to say, though his truculent expression remained.

They sat on the bench again to drink water and cool down. The soldier dragged the court and when he was finished Major

Covarrubias dismissed him. The conversation came around to the miners' strike and the solidarity strikes that had followed.

"It's out of control," the major said tersely between breaths. "Increasingly, the only sane reaction to the current situation is disgust."

"Not censorship?" Lipton asked.

"Ah, you refer to *El Mercurio?*... I said 'sane' reaction."

The wind felt cool against Lipton's sweaty shirt. His right calf muscle was cramping. He stood up and put on his sweater.

Six days earlier, the government had shut down the country's largest newspaper, *El Mercurio*, for inciting subversion. Secretly subsidized by the CIA, the paper was the mainstay of the opposition, encouraging the strikers to continue their fight.

"What if I were to tell you," Covarrubias said with slow and precise annunciation, "that a number of officers feel another reaction would be entirely appropriate."

"Oh? You mean different than before?" Talking to coup plotters directly might violate orders but, as Bill assured him, talking about them with Major Covarrubias did not.

The major mopped the top of his head with a hand towel and wiped his cheeks. Exercise had made his face look gaunter than normal. His chest still heaved.

"Seriously. There have been rumors—all unconfirmed—that certain plans are under discussion."

"Any idea who's doing the discussing?"

Covarrubias smiled. "The cadre of commanders who believe the president has violated the constitution is larger than you think."

"And would they have support from the rank and file?"

Covarrubias raised his eyebrows. "Hard to say. That depends on who leads them, how many, and when."

"Surely not General Prats, though."

"No. I doubt it."

"And you, my friend, where do you stand?"

Major Covarrubias shook his head. "I've heard nothing to

convince me that these are anything more than rumors. I act on facts. Rumors are for women and journalists."

The rumors ended on the morning of June 29 when Lt. Colonel Roberto Souper, who was about to be relieved of his command for suspicions of disloyalty, led his Second Armored Regiment of light tanks, armored cars and some 100 troops on an assault of the presidential palace.

Major Covarrubias' innuendos were the only warning Lipton received of the Tancazo, as the media later dubbed it. Like most people, he learned of the revolt from the radio as he was driving to work that morning. The rebels blocked the main thoroughfares into the city but, failing to rouse the rest of the armed forces, they surrendered to General Prats. By 11:30 the incident was over.

Lipton was greatly relieved that the CIA had played no part in the fiasco. The failed putsch received the full finger-pointing scorn of the UP and became the butt of jokes. Editors gibed that the coup attempt was so poorly planned, one tank had to stop for fuel at a gas station on the way to La Moneda. It was laughable, except for the twenty-two civilians killed in the crossfire.

Major Covarrubias was far less critical of the failure when Lipton met him at Flora Sanchez's house for their weekly information exchange the next day. Lipton expected the major to be embarrassed by this blow to the army's prestige, but Covarrubias was in a jovial mood.

"It was a foolish effort by a foolish officer who was too arrogant to see his own foolish pride," he acknowledged. "But for the rest of us, it's the same lesson I tell Flora's boys: learn from your mistakes."

Lipton was intrigued. "And what did you take away from this, Major?"

"Not I, Eduardo, the general staff."

"Yes?"

"First, the armed forces must stand united, like the Three

Musketeers. Second, speaking as one who has planned for civil unrest, I can say that the top brass saw clearly how the workers' unions will react in a crisis. They were totally unprepared. Third, and most importantly, no foreign government, including your ambassador, protested the revolt."

Lipton weighed the major's remark.

"But I think you're being disingenuous with me, Eduardo," Covarrubias continued. "Surely you know all this from Pete Nolan. Or have his meetings in Valpo prevented you two from getting together for your regular poker games?"

As Lipton headed home from Flora's house, he reflected on the major's final comment. Pete Nolan had not mentioned any meetings in Valparaiso. But the swarthy, yacht-tan SOB hadn't been around much lately, either. Lipton saw all classified mail coming to the embassy. There was nothing to indicate that bilateral meetings were taking place—no minutes, no cables, not a single report or memorandum. So, what was Covarrubias talking about?

The question nagged him as he waited for a long red light, but his attention was abruptly distracted by a news bulletin on the radio: "The National Confederation of Truck Owners' Unions has called another nationwide strike. Effective tomorrow, July 1, the union has called on all 50,000 of its members to suspend shipments in protest of the latest rate restrictions and new tariffs on spare parts."

19

Gabriela felt awful and the steady rain made her feel even worse. On the plaza the tree branches sagged, the drenched leaves hung curled and limp. Although it was midday the office lights were on and a winter chill permeated the editorial room. She had made a bad mistake and Beto was receiving a lashing from the senior Girardi, el patrón, who called from Concepción to complain. She couldn't blame Armando this time. It was her fault.

She had confused the photo of a senator from the Partido Nacional, a good friend of Señor Girardi's, with one of a small-time Unidad Popular politician who was on trial for corruption. They looked virtually the same—late fifties, double-chinned, bushy mustached, with crooked grins and recessed eyes.

Poor Beto! He held the phone away from his ear while Girardi yelled, but he refused to name or blame Gabriela. His stolid defense only made her feel worse.

She looked up with a start when Ricardo opened the stairwell door. He looked around the editorial room, saw her and smiled. Gabriela straightened her slumped shoulders. All eyes fell on the blond stranger as he crossed the room toward her desk.

"Ricardo!" she said, standing up. "What are you doing here?"

Beto in his office was saying, "Yes, sir. Yes, sir. Absolutely. Will do."

Ricardo leaned to kiss her. His nose and lips were cold and damp against her cheek. He smelled of cigarettes. His corduroy sport coat was rain spattered. "I was passing through and thought I'd buy you lunch. Are you free?"

"Ernesto's gone. He went back to Santiago last week."

"I know. I saw him last weekend."

"Hmm!" She was still angry with her brother. After spending only a week of the winter break at home, he'd made excuses and left as quickly as he could, leaving her once again without the car.

She glanced at the clock: twenty to noon. She could leave a few minutes early. "Give me five minutes?"

She went into Beto's office. He was off the phone but his face remained agitated.

"Do I still have a job?"

Beto smiled. "You might, but I'm not sure I do."

"I'm so sorry, Beto. You should tell him it was my fault."

"Don't worry, my love. Señor Girardi isn't going to fire anyone. He just needed to vent. I told him we will print a correction. So, who's the good-looking gringo?" he asked with a sly nod toward Ricardo.

Gabriela smiled. "Just a friend."

"I see," he said, with a puckish smile.

"Can I leave for lunch now?"

"I don't know. If I say yes, am I going to lose you forever? Of course! Go!"

Gabriela went to the ladies' room and inspected herself in the mirror. She wished she'd worn something nicer than these old wool slacks and bulky sweater, but she had dressed for warmth.

Ricardo was chatting with Armando about the production process when she returned. He looked at her from the corner of his eye and smiled. Armando continued to talk but Ricardo interrupted to thank him and shook Armando's hand.

"All set?"

He helped her into her raincoat and escorted her to the door. She could feel the stealthy stares and almost hear the wisecracks that would follow their departure. At the base of the stairs, they stopped to discuss where to go. She suggested the sandwich shop a few doors down but he proposed the Hotel Isabel Riquelme. "Do you have time?" She nodded.

The hotel windows were steamed with condensation and the restaurant was nearly empty. He removed her coat and hung it on a hook by the entrance then wiped the rain from his brow, smoothed his hair and brushed the lapels of his coat. They settled at a table near a window and watched the slow drizzle. Cars splashed water over the curb as they passed.

"So what brings you here?" she asked again.

"I was in Concepción on business." He smiled and looked away; she noticed how his irises changed from pale to deep blue with the shift of light. "Very dull stuff. I'm heading back today."

"It's too bad you can't stay longer. If it ever clears up we could go riding."

"Work has been really busy. I have to get back. I wanted to see you, though."

"Do you have time to see mamá?"

"No. I really just wanted to see you."

The directness of the statement and the intense focus of his eyes made her feel warm and exposed simultaneously. The more time she spent with Ricardo, the more she saw the qualities Ernesto admired—the calm confidence and polite attentiveness. Ricardo actually listened, maybe because he straddled two worlds and two languages.

She told him what a terrible day she was having, and he laughed.

"I was once the editor of my school newspaper," he said. "An outside company typeset and printed it for us. One time before exams I was really, really busy and didn't have time to proof everything. I approved the printing not knowing that the typesetter, who wasn't very educated, had decided to change a few words in my editorial about Cuba. She thought I'd spelled them incorrectly, so she changed guerrillas to gorillas, and grisly to grizzly—you know, like the bear. In English they're almost the same. When the issue came out everyone thought I'd lost it, writing about gorillas hiding in the Sierra Maestra and grizzly attacks on poor cane farmers."

Ricardo laughed and Gabriela felt the anguish over her error lift. Ricardo's laughter grew fuller as she laughed, until they were exchanging looks that prompted more laughter.

Ricardo ordered a bottle of wine and, despite the work she needed to do that afternoon, she drank two glasses. The conversation was a tonic. She was laughing the way she did with Ernesto, and suddenly her thoughts were not about her job or her life in Chillán but something else, something new and exciting.

She asked if he planned to return to the United States once his assignment was up. Ricardo looked out the window and then gave her a half smile with another flash of his eyes. He seemed to be searching for words. "I don't know," he said finally. "I like it here. There's a lot to keep me here. But it's hard to see that far down the road. What about you? Do you ever think of leaving Chillán?"

She nodded and for the first time in a long time the possibility seemed real. She peeked at her wristwatch. "I better get back," she said. "I wish I could stay but I must tell Beto about the gorillas in the cordillera."

At the stairwell to the newspaper, she turned and brushed the rain from his coat lapel. "Don't you have a raincoat? Shall I find you an umbrella?" A few people walked by, trying to stay underneath the portico.

"It wasn't raining yesterday. Don't worry. I'm parked just around the corner."

"Thank you for lunch. And thank you for making me feel better," she said.

As he came closer, she thought he was going to give her a hug, but he placed his hand under her chin to raise it and kissed her, not on the cheek but on the lips. "When can you come up to Santiago again?" he asked, not quite breaking the embrace.

Lost in the moment, it was as if she didn't understand his words. Her mind drew a blank. "I don't know. My idiot brother has the car. But I'd like to. When will you be coming back?"

He shook his head. "Hard to say."

Armando came down the stairs. "Con permiso, excuse me," he said, stepping around them and dashing through the rain toward the sandwich shop.

"Call me if you do. Or even if you don't," she said. Then, she kissed him on the cheek. "Thank you again," she said with a happy laugh. "Stay dry." She turned and ran up the stairs.

On the long drive home to Santiago, Will tried to think about work: Girardi's angry words for the army's inaction during the Tancazo—"Someone ought to shoot Prats!"; the next few days' assignments; his Friday meeting with Víctor; the things he didn't manage to confide to Gabriela at lunch. But his brain kept skipping to a Doors song—damn Ernesto for playing them so often! "Before you drift into unconsciousness, I'd like to have another kiss, another flashing chance at bliss, another kiss, another kiss…"

20

*B*ill Bradshaw slipped in without making a noise but Ed Lipton noticed a shadow like a rain cloud cross his desk and looked up.

"Gotcha!" Bill said.

"What's up?" Lipton asked. He'd been deep in a detailed report on the truckers' strike, his focus still on the math. It was now August 24, fifty-four days into the strike. Thirty thousand truckers at roughly five dollars a week for eight weeks—over a million bucks! The truckers' syndicate had to be broke, even with CIA's subsidies. The 40 Committee's approval of another million dollars for opposition funding had come just in time. Now, with General Prats' humiliating resignation as commander in chief and General Pinochet's appointment, things were looking up.

Bill closed the office door and plopped into a metal armchair opposite Lipton. He rocked the chair back on two legs.

"Who said, 'The sign of a first-rate intelligence is the ability to hold two contradictory ideas at the same time and still be able to act'?"

"Never heard it before," Lipton said, wondering if the metal legs of the chair would hold the big man's weight.

"Hmm." Bill rubbed his chin. "Well, someone said it. Or something like it. For some reason it's always stuck with me. Seems like a pretty good description of what we do."

Lipton recognized one of Bill's roundabout openers to something sensitive. He put down the strike report.

"I've been on the phone for over an hour," Bill continued.

"Yeah?"

Lipton waited. A gust of gritty wind scratched at the window. Bill's continued silence meant it was something significant. Lipton reached around to his credenza and turned on the radio. A catchy commercial jingle for propane played, covering the conversation.

"I got a cable this morning that I wanted some clarification on."

"Yeah?" Con gas, con gas, la vida es mejor con gas!

"Yeah. About funding."

"Uh-huh." La vida es mejor con gas!

"Another change of plans."

Lipton squinted.

"Orders down from the top."

"I knew it! I could feel it in my bones. When Phillips told us to back off, I sensed something was up. And?"

"No more funding the private sector. Cease and desist."

"Christ, Bill!"

Bill raised his hands in surrender. "I know."

"Why don't they just shut us down and send us home? What the fuck are they thinking? Why now? Prats is out. We can beat these bastards, I know it."

Bill shook his head. "I know. I said the same thing."

"Well, why, for Christ's sake?"

"Other forces at work apparently. State Department, I suspect. Anyway, that million the 40 Committee approved has a big caveat attached. No funding the private sector without the ambassador's consent. Political parties, the media...all still okay. But...no truckers, no truck syndicates, no truck companies."

"But that changes everything. The strikers can't last."

Bill nodded.

"I don't get it. Is something going on we're not aware of?"

"Not that I know of."

"Then, with all due respect, the fucking 40 Committee ought to take their heads out of their asses. Let's go explain the situation to the ambassador."

Bill shook his head. "I've just come from there. No go. Said he didn't want an embarrassment if word leaked out. I told him we could do it securely—have been doing it—but he was adamant: 'Be creative, but stay within the limits of your guidance.'"

"What the hell's that supposed to mean?"

Bill rocked and frowned. Lipton searched his boss's face for the telltale signs of information being withheld but saw none. Which would be worse: if Bill knew more than he was saying, or if he didn't know what was happening? If the 40 Committee wanted a coup, restrictions on black ops made no sense. And if they didn't want a coup, then what the hell were they doing any of this for?

"If I didn't know better I'd say we were being set up," Lipton said.

"Set up? For what?"

Lipton shook his head. "I have no idea. For blame if things go badly. For denial. For one of your so-called perfect operations. Is it too paranoid to think that P and K could go around us? Around the 40 Committee even?

Bill laughed.

"Why would they do that?"

"How should I know? Hell, why did Watergate happen?" From the bemused, skeptical expression on Bill's face he realized that he did sound paranoid. Not a good thing.

"Okay, I need to think about this," he said, meaning the new restrictions.

"Atta boy!" Bill said, lowering his feet to the ground. He lifted himself out of the chair, opened the door and turned. "Be creative. Damn the torpedoes, full speed ahead!"

* * *

The solution came to Lipton that afternoon. He was reading the conclusions of the strike report ("more money needed to sustain momentum") when the nervous Paul Gregorio, curly hair still wet from showering after his noontime basketball game, knocked on the door.

"There's a walk-in downstairs who insists on speaking to someone from CIA." He gripped the door handle and grinned.

Though his real job was to monitor the media and write reports for Arne Matlock, Gregorio's cover was consular officer. He sometimes got stuck interviewing visa applicants and often had funny anecdotes about applicants' lies and omissions.

"And did you tell him there isn't anyone from CIA here?" Suspecting it was some crazy off his medications who saw secret code written in the clouds.

"Yeah. But he wasn't satisfied. Bill said you should handle it."

"Bill? What does the guy want?"

"Did I mention he works at the Cuban embassy?" said Gregorio with a gleeful grin.

"Smart-ass. Why the fuck didn't you say so?"

Lipton followed Gregorio downstairs to a small windowless conference room on the seventh floor barely larger than the table and four chairs it contained. A scrawny man with a long straight nose and a pencil-thin mustache, who reminded Lipton of a rat, attempted to stand but his chair hit the back wall. He wore a bulky wool jacket with large Inca motifs.

"I'm Ed Lipton, deputy political attaché. How can I help you?"

The man extended his hand. "My name is Javier López Valdívia. May I speak to you in confidence, Señor Lipton?" He glanced at Paul Gregorio who had squeezed into the chair beside him.

"You understand, we don't have CIA officers in diplomatic missions in friendly nations."

Javier Lopez lifted his head as if to take aim at Lipton down the barrel of his nose and started to laugh.

"Yes, and my boss is only agricultural advisor for milk production."

"Who would that be?" Lipton asked, cocking his head and squinting at the Chilean.

"Mario Sándoval."

Lipton knew the name. Supposedly the second in command of the Cuban intelligence service in Chile, possibly Lipton's direct counterpart, but no one had been able to confirm it.

"And what do you do for the Agricultural Assistance Mission, Mr. López? You're Chilean?"

"Of course! Someone needs to milk the cows, and if the boss doesn't like to get his hands dirty…" he said coyly.

That's when the idea came to Lipton. It was so simple. They needed a cutout like this López, who did the dirty work for Cuban Intelligence. If headquarters was going to prohibit funding the truckers directly, there was another way to get money into their hands. Contributions to a political party still met the scrutiny of the DCI and the 40 Committee. What they needed was someone they could trust to pass the money discreetly to the truckers' association. And he had the perfect candidates: Emilio Girardi and Carlos Saavedra.

Lo and behold, Young Will was the key to the kingdom!

That evening Will received his new top priority from Lipton. The next morning he called Carlos Saavedra and requested a meeting. Saavedra sounded relieved to have a diversion from the idleness created by the strike and suggested lunch at his club.

"They still manage to obtain decent produce on the black market," Saavedra said. "How it is delivered is anyone's guess."

"I'll pick you up at noon."

The club's ground-floor dining room was crowded with patrons as if no shortages existed and noisy with clanking utensils. Will and Saavedra followed their meal with a glass of port upstairs in a wood-paneled library that simulated an English men's club. The two sat in deep comfortable wing chairs upholstered in slightly worn burgundy brocade. A waiter in a starched white jacket and white gloves brought the port on a silver tray and placed the glasses on coasters on the mahogany table between them. Carlos Saavedra dismissed the waiter, then leaned forward and took two cigars from his suit pocket and offered one to Will.

"No thanks."

"No?" His small black eyes drilled into Will's. "Nasty habit, I suppose. You don't mind...?"

"Not at all." Will lit a cigarette.

"Cohibas and Havana Club are the only good things to come from Cuba," Saavedra said as he cut the end and lit his cigar. He smiled behind a billowing cloud of blue smoke like a gleeful gnome in a three-piece suit.

"You Americans are much more concerned about your health than we Chileans are. Our attitude is tainted by our heritage. The Spanish sense of fate. We lack your optimism." Saavedra clamped down on the cigar. "But I too am feeling optimistic, Ricardo."

"Yes? Why?"

"I was glad you called this morning. So many foreign businessmen have abandoned Chile and gone home. I thought that perhaps you had proven to be one of those."

"No. My company still hopes for a bright future here." Will was tired of small talk and wished they could get down to business. But he knew there was a formal dance, a ritual, that required patience...the drinks and light conversation, the long lunch, and eventually, away from the club, the real business. He sipped his port and listened for tidbits to add to his intelligence report, clues that might corroborate Saavedra's honesty or the unspoken motives behind his words.

"You know, when I was young I wanted to go to the United States to study civil engineering. That was in 1956. You were probably still a toddler—"

"Not quite…third grade."

"Yes? Well, my parents couldn't afford to send me. So, I stayed in Santiago and attended the university here. Then I went to work in my father's business—trucks!" he said with a wistful smile. "I dreamed of building bridges. Instead, I repaired trucks. Together, my father and I, we built the business up. Those were good days for business. You knew what to expect and if you worked hard, you succeeded. It didn't take brains so much as energy and contacts. And capital, of course. But with sufficient energy you made contacts and with contacts you found capital.

"Now, they want to take that opportunity away. Land for the landless, factories for the workers…and nothing for the men who create these things with their own hands. It can't go on, of course. Without free enterprise, without the drive to make something of yourself, a nation dies."

After lunch, Will drove Saavedra back to his depot in Los Cerillos and broached the subject of the strike.

"It can't continue for much longer," Saavedra confided. "Spirits are strong but money is running out. These men are losing money every day and they have families to feed, mortgages to pay. It will be hard to sustain much longer. They are drained. Most don't have the extra padding I do for the long haul," he said, patting his stomach. "We've done our part. Now this army of ours needs to find its balls. No more tanks stopping for red lights on the way to the palace."

Will smiled but let Saavedra continue.

"I'm very serious. If Allende won't resign, then someone needs to make him go. Quietly or not."

"How much are we talking about? To continue the strike, that is."

Saavedra shrugged. "A lot. The association is nearly broke. Thousands of dollars. Maybe a hundred thousand. It all depends."

"What about the opposition parties?"

"What about them?"

"Won't they support you?"

Saavedra laughed. "With what?"

"My company would support your cause. Unfortunately, our headquarters has said we can't. But I know someone, another client of ours, at a senior level in the Partido Nacional. He might be able to help. Would it be okay if I made an inquiry?"

They had arrived at Saavedra's depot. The yard was empty. His trucks, like those of his colleagues, were being guarded in an empty field miles away from the city where they were safe from expropriation and vandalism. Saavedra turned and faced Will.

"You see!" he said. "That's what I'm talking about, Ricardo. Ideas, contacts, relationships—that's what makes business. Not government decrees."

The next day Will barely made it to the Hotel Rincón in time for his three o'clock meeting with Lipton. From the bus station to La Moneda, protestors crowded the Alameda. Acrid plumes of black smoke rose from burning tires. A parade of packed busses and tractors towing flatbed trailers of Allende supporters passed by. Mostly union workers paid to come out, they shouted angrily for an end to the truckers' strike.

At the upper end of the Alameda, near Catholic University, Patria y Libertad was organizing a counter demonstration. Wearing armbands with a double diamond motif that resembled a geometric insect, hundreds of young men roared to the megaphoned encouragement of their leaders. Intimidated by the angry pulsing crowds, Will cut one street over and jogged the last ten blocks to the hotel.

Still catching his breath, he knocked and Lipton opened the door. Of course, Lipton only had to walk six blocks from the embassy, cutting through one of the pedestrian alleys, then across the Plaza de Armas.

"Shit, have you seen what's going on out there?" Will asked, wiping the sweat breaking on his forehead.

"Hard to miss."

"Who designed those PyL armbands, Goebbels?"

Lipton smiled. "So what have we got?"

Even from blocks away, the honking horns and chants could be heard with occasional crescendos of cheering.

"I asked Saavedra what it would take to keep things going. I got him down to seventy-five grand. At first he wanted a hundred."

Lipton tugged at his lower lip as he considered the amount. "How much time are we buying with that?"

"Maybe two weeks."

"Let's give him the hundred and tell him to make sure it's two weeks. Do we have that much?"

Will had already done his calculations at the office. "I've got a hundred and fifty available now and will have another fifty from Lemantour next week."

"Okay. Tell Girardi every damn dime of this goes to Saavedra. And remind him, we'll be checking on the other end."

Will nodded. At least a trip to Concepción to see Girardi meant another chance to stop in Chillán.

He debated whether to ask his next question.

"What?" asked Lipton.

"Nothing, just… Aren't you concerned how this looks on the books? I mean, such big amounts going to the Partido Nacional?"

"Nope. Just make sure that's exactly what the ledger shows."

21

*A*t 7:15 on Sunday evening, September 9, Lipton phoned Will at home. He didn't even bother to say who it was.

"Call me back from a pay phone."

Will went to the phone booth in the corner grocery shop and dialed the number Lipton gave him, a secure line at the embassy.

"Cancel your trip down to Girardi this week."

"Why?" Even though the truckers' strike had ended the week before, Will was counting on another trip to Concepción and a stop in Chillán on the way back, same as the week before. Now he'd have to tell Gabriela he wasn't coming.

"Listen, the shit's gonna hit the fan. Tomorrow or the day after. So get ready. And when it happens I want you to lay low until you hear from me. There's no telling how this is going to shake out. Nobody's going to stop and ask if you're an American before they shoot. You read me?"

"Yes. When do you want to meet next?"

"Not until I contact you. It may be a while. Keep this number and if there's an emergency, call me. I'd bring you into the embassy but I don't want to blow your cover. But if things get really bad—say you can't reach me and some goons are busting down your door—you know what to do, right? Get your ass over to the consulate or the embassy. No matter what. And keep your gun loaded and handy."

"Got it." A man with a toy poodle on a leash came into the store and peered into the phone booth. Will waited until he left before he asked the next question. "What about our assets?"

"What about 'em?"

"Shouldn't we give them a heads up?" It sounded stupid even as he asked.

"Fuck no!"

"But what if one of them contacts me?"

"They're on their own just like every other citizen." Lipton paused. "Keep calm and use your head, Will. Remember, this is what we're paid to do. And don't worry. I've got a good feeling about this one."

It was as much fatherly advice as Lipton had ever given him. The man actually sounded relaxed. Was Lipton one of those guys who become more clear-headed when the adrenaline kicks in? Will had heard of people in battles and accidents acting with complete calm. His own stomach fluttered with stage fright.

He remained in the booth after hanging up, listening to his heart palpitate as his thoughts turned to the people he knew. First and foremost, Gabriela in Chillán and Ernesto in Santiago.

Outside the booth Badinia sat at the counter reading a fotonovela. Here, too, was political intrigue brought to the personal level.

Realizing it might be days before stores opened again, he purchased a carton of oatmeal, milk, eggs, a large wedge of cheese, a bottle of red wine and two large bottles of beer. There was sugar but no bread, tea but no coffee, fruit but no yogurt. He bought what he could. Remarking on the unusual quantities, Badinia made a mistake and had to count his change twice. Normally he would have teased her about the error but he held out his hand without saying a word. She grew even more distracted by his odd silence and carefully placed the change in his hand. Will thanked her and, contrary to Lipton's precaution, said, "Listen, I heard there could be more trouble tomorrow. Take care, okay."

Monday morning he woke up and everything was normal. Had Lipton been wrong? He went to work at nine. Each time he saw Leti, he wanted to say something, give her some clue, but didn't dare. At 3:00 he told her to go home and left the office at 4:00.

That night he watched part of an old Cantinflas movie in which the comedian played a maid's boyfriend. When Cantinflas comes to her employers' house looking for a free meal, she tells him if he wants any of the chicken dinner she has prepared, he has to shoot a rabid dog wandering around first. He goes outside and fires off the gun, missing the dog but hoping the shots will convince his girlfriend that he has done the deed.

Will missed the next part of the movie while he cooked his own dinner, a pork chop and potatoes. When he returned, Cantinflas, who for some reason is now confused for a gangster, is accused of murdering another gangster named Bobby, a.k.a. "the fox terrier." In the trial the confusion allows Cantinflas to make a lot of rapid-fire jokes. "Of course I killed Bobby. He was a rabid cur."

Will didn't get much of the humor. He turned off the TV and tried to read. He took a bottle of scotch from the kitchen cupboard and poured himself a stiff drink. At two in the morning he started awake, still on the couch, and dragged himself to bed.

Tuesday morning, September 11, the alarm on his clock radio went off at seven. It was a clear, spring-like day. Will dressed quickly and turned on the TV: a soap opera on one channel, a cartoon on the other. Seeking news, he tuned the clock radio in his bedroom to Radio Agricultura and caught the tail end of an announcement. President Allende had just spoken from the presidential palace, warning of a naval uprising in Valparaíso. Armed personnel carriers were heading toward La Moneda. The president asked the nation's workers to stay calm and go to their factories.

Will plopped down on his bed. Radio Agricultura was aligned

with the conservatives. For all he knew this news was CIA propaganda. He searched for a UP-affiliated station, hoping to hear another perspective.

A few minutes after eight, President Allende came on the air again. His voice was forceful and calm. The head of the Carabineros was by his side, he said. He had ordered the palace guards to repel the insurgents and fully expected the armed forces to support the constitution they had sworn to defend. He would remain steadfast at La Moneda.

Was it another Tancazo? Will switched stations. A nervous announcer on the Communist Radio Magallanes reported that army troops had encircled La Moneda and gunfights were breaking out. UP militants, disregarding the president's call for calm, were sniping at the insurgents from rooftops near the palace.

Will ran to the TV in the living room. The cartoon was gone, replaced by a live broadcast of Allende's defense minister, Orlando Letelier, being arrested and taken away from the ministry in handcuffs. A moment later Will heard a loud swoosh overhead that rattled the windows and tingled down his spine. This was no Tancazo. If the army, navy and air force were involved, this was it. Allende would have to surrender.

Will ran to the window. The street was deserted. In the building opposite people stood at their windows, looking up. Another roar and he glimpsed a dull gray fighter jet swoop overhead, its growling backwash rending the sky. A series of rumbling percussions followed.

He raced to the bedroom, unplugged the clock radio and carried it into the living room so he could watch TV and listen to the radio simultaneously. Radio Agricultura was now playing the national anthem. He rolled the dial. Most stations had gone off the air, but Radio Corporación was still broadcasting. The announcer said troops and tanks had surrounded La Moneda, and jets had knocked out radio transmitters across the city. "We will continue to broadcast until they knock us off the air. The president, his bodyguards and a few loyal aides have locked themselves inside the palace. The situation is grave."

The TV suddenly cut to a live studio broadcast of a mustached general reading an ultimatum to President Allende and his bodyguards: Leave the palace by eleven or we will open fire. The network cut to a picture of the Chilean flag and played martial music.

Will switched back and forth between the radio stations still broadcasting. Remarkably, Radio Magallanes had a live phone connection to La Moneda. At nine-thirty, President Allende came on the air. He was unyielding. He refused to surrender to the lawbreakers, and in a steady, somber voice he spoke of the future as if he would not be there to see it.

"Workers of my country, I have faith in Chile and its destiny. Other men will overcome this dark and bitter moment when treason tries to impose itself."

Allende next said something about the avenues being open to free men again, but the urgent and anxious voices of colleagues in the background made his words difficult to decipher.

"Long live Chile! Long live the people! Long live the workers! These are my last words. I am certain that my sacrifice will not be in vain. I am certain that it will at least be a moral lesson that will chastise such treachery, cowardice and treason."

The broadcast ended abruptly with the popping of gunfire. In a choked voice the radio announcer reported that the army was firing on the palace.

At ten-thirty, Radio Magallanes suddenly went off the air. The next hour passed in slow, anxious minutes. The ultimatum hour passed. Near noon Will heard jets again, first the swoosh then the low percussive boom. A thundering explosion then silence. More explosions then a more intense silence.

The telephone rang, startling him. Thinking it was Lipton, he ran to the hall table and grabbed the receiver.

"I'm looking out my window at a black cloud rising above the presidential palace."

"Ernesto?" Will remembered that Ernesto's apartment had a

sweeping view of the downtown. "What else can you see?"

"Very little except smoke. There's an armored car full of soldiers on my corner. I think they bombed the radio towers earlier. Can you believe it? Here comes another plane... Shit! The bastards just fired another missile!"

A second later the thud rattled the windows of Will's apartment.

"Ernesto, where's Víctor?"

"At home I suppose."

"Good. Have you talked to your family?"

"Not yet."

"Call them if you can. Make sure they stay home. This is very bad. Then call me back, okay?"

There was another thud and Will wondered if Ernesto was still on the other end.

"Shit! Unbelievable!"

"Ernesto, we better get off the phone. Call home."

The early afternoon crawled by. Will kept trying the radio without luck. He ate some cheese and crackers and, suddenly thirsty, opened one of the big bottles of beer he'd bought. He wondered where Lipton was during all this. If he was at the embassy, he had a bird's-eye view of the battle.

By two, sunlight was slanting through the living room windows. The street outside was utterly quiet. The phone rang again.

"Did you hear?" It was Ernesto. "Allende shot himself."

"Shot himself!" Will put the phone down and switched channels on the television. He went back to the phone.

"Jesus, I can't believe this. This place is fucked."

"Did you reach your mom?"

"Yes, they're fine. Gabi went to work but they sent everyone home. Father Patricio sent over one of his henchmen as Mami's bodyguard."

"What for?"

Ernesto laughed cynically. "She was terrified the prisoners would be released from the jail and go on a rampage. Did you hear there's a curfew? The military junta—can you believe those fuckers actually call themselves that?—the fucking junta has declared that at five tonight anyone who's not home is free to go home, but at eight they shoot to kill."

"I hope Víctor's okay."

"He's a survivor. He'll be okay."

"What do you see out your window?"

"Just a lot of smoke. The palace must be on fire."

Will heard a commotion out in the hallway.

"I better go," he said. "Let's talk tomorrow."

Will hung up and opened his apartment door. Most of his neighbors had spontaneously convened in the hallway and on the staircase. Some looked dazed and frightened, their voices rising in outrage and grief. Others looked cautiously elated.

Roland Fabré waved and crossed the landing.

"Have you heard? It looks like they murdered our charismatic friend after all."

"I heard he shot himself."

"You don't really believe that, do you?"

Just then a man came crashing down the stairs from the floor above. He brushed past his neighbors without apology and nearly knocked the landlady over the banister as she tried to slow him down on the landing. Someone yelled after him, urging him to stay inside, but with a swat of his hands as if shooing a swarm of angry bees, he ran out into the street.

"That was Tulio," Roland said, shaking his head. "He is, was, a senior administrator in the Radical Party. He probably just realized they'll be coming after him and a lot of others in the next few hours. Or maybe he went to take his fight to the streets."

Roland's gray eyes were alive with excitement. "This should be good for business, no?"

"What do you mean?"

"Doesn't your company sell life insurances?"

Will frowned, not just at Roland's morbid sense of humor but at the growing sense that events were spiraling out of control. Though he was only a minor accomplice, Allende was dead.

"What about you?" he asked.

"Ah, I suspect the UN won't be welcome here shortly. Except as peacekeepers, perhaps.

PART THREE

Casualties

September – October 1973

Kill the bitch and you eliminate the litter.

—-General Augusto Pinochet Ugarte, Sept. 11, 1973

22

Roland Fabré's prognostications of civil war were nearly right. On the first night of curfew, Will woke to the sound of smashing glass in the street and the toy-like pop of a small-caliber handgun followed by frantic shouts, a burst of machine-gun fire, then deadly silence. On the second night the darkness reverberated with distant explosions as if people across the city were celebrating the New Year.

Two days went by without word from Lipton. Will's sense of isolation turned to restlessness. He tried several times to call Leti at home, only to get a busy signal. Curious, he dialed Ernesto then the office with the same result. No wonder he hadn't heard from Lipton, the phones weren't working.

On the third day the junta lifted the curfew for several hours. Will ventured into the neighborhood with Roland Fabré, hunting for an open grocery store. The shop where the skinny schoolgirl Badinia worked was shuttered. Except for more broken glass than usual, a few overturned garbage bins and the absence of street vendors and traffic, the streets of Bellavista looked no different than before the coup. Most startling was the burst of color, with houses festooned as for a national holiday. The red, white and blue of Chilean flags had blossomed in windows and fluttered from windowsills and rooftops.

"Por la razón o la fuerza," Will said, reciting the national motto. "I'm surprised at the show of support."

"How do you know it isn't a protest?" asked Roland. "After all, what does the flag represent if not the social contract?"

Will looked up at their building's façade where their landlady had planted a row of small flags in her windowsill flowerboxes. He suspected his own interpretation was the accurate one.

"See how preoccupied everyone looks," Roland remarked as a man in a hurry crossed their path. "As if wearing masks. That is fear, Richard. I saw it many times during the occupation."

It was true. Everyone coming toward them avoided eye contact.

Finding only a hardware store open, Will left Roland at their building and determined to walk to the office. As soon as he came to the river he realized what a refuge his neighborhood was. Blank-faced soldiers guarded the bridge and an acrid smell of burning rubber and diesel fuel hung in the air. On the other side of the river, charred remains of overturned cars lay in the middle of rubble-strewn intersections. Noxious black smoke rose from piles of smoldering tires erected as barricades the night before. An armored personnel carrier plowed through these impromptu obstacles as if they didn't exist. Near Catholic University, an army work detail under the supervision of a barking sergeant was busy tearing down banners and whitewashing walls. The soldiers worked methodically, obliterating graffiti and the posters of every political party, right or left, without discrimination.

It took an hour to walk to his office and he was sweating by the time he got there. The small plaza in front of the Bernardo O'Higgins Tower was deserted, the building locked. He pounded on the lobby door. The security guard poked his head from a utility room at the end of the corridor. When he recognized Will, he shuffled over to let him in.

The phone in Will's office still worked. He called Lipton, who picked up after one ring.

"It was nearly perfect," Lipton said, sounding tired but jubilant, like a hoarse football fan after a win. "These guys really know how to do things once they set their minds to it."

"Yeah, but Allende—" Will said.

"Shit, Will. You play with fire, you're gonna get burned."

"The people in my building think he was murdered."

Lipton scoffed. "Pinochet's got the cojones to do it, I'll say that much. But I have it on good authority that Allende shot himself. With his own AK47. A gift from Castro no less."

He said he had some work for Will to do and they agreed to meet the following afternoon at the Hotel Carrera.

On the walk home, a desperate man brushed past Will, chased by two baton-wielding Carabineros. The man cut in front of oncoming traffic on Avenida Bellavista and was struck by a car. His body twisted in the air, smacked against the windshield and slid to the ground. Will didn't stay to see what happened next. Worried about the impending curfew, he hurried home.

The next day, walking from his office to the hotel, Will stopped in Plaza de la Constitución to stare in disbelief at the ruins of La Moneda. Seeing the bombed and charred remains up close drove home the reality of September 11. Scores of people had come out to see the destruction firsthand, making the scene even stranger. Silently, they gathered beneath the building's shell to gawk at its gutted roof and the black stains where fire had scorched the stone scrollwork on the lintels. Bullet and shrapnel scars pockmarked the length of the façade.

Tense soldiers with machine guns at the ready guarded a perimeter established with metal barricades, and a tank loomed in the shadow of the Social Security building, its cannon ominously pointed at the Hotel Carrera.

The hotel was crowded with restless foreigners—journalists and Red Cross workers who had flown in after the coup, stranded tourists and businessmen with little interest in venturing outside. The bar buzzed in multiple languages. Will waited in the lobby and struck up a conversation with a Swedish Red Cross worker. He borrowed the man's day-old copy of the *Guardian* and read about mass arrests, thousands detained in the national stadium, and bullet-ridden bodies dumped along roadsides. He refolded the paper and handed it back.

"Thanks. You'd think the *Guardian* would check their facts before publishing something."

The Swede looked at Will with a quizzical expression. "Pardon me?"

"Come on! It's like the exaggerations they told at the start of World War One...bayoneted babies, raped nuns."

"Have you been outside?" the man asked, sounding offended. "My team has been trying to get inside the national stadium for two days. They refuse to let us in. We've heard they're lining up people in front of firing squads without a trial. And that, my friend, is *not* an exaggeration."

Will still didn't believe it. He'd seen too much propaganda issued by both sides before the coup. What the Swede didn't seem to understand was that a coup was inevitable. And yet, Will had to admit (to himself if not the Swede), he had not imagined such violent consequences: the bombed palace, the death of Allende. Could his imagination be failing him again? A neighbor had raced down the stairs in panic onto the street. Another man flung himself headlong into an oncoming car, and Will had simply watched. Was he becoming impervious to cruelty?

Lipton's appearance across the lobby arrested these disturbing thoughts. As he watched his boss approach, Will realized how much he had come to despise him. Lipton's light gray suit was wrinkled and grease-spotted. His face was florid, as if he'd been drinking. Will braced for another drunken encounter. Lipton coughed into his hand as he came up to Will then growled something about getting out of the hotel. Not drunk, Will realized. He was sick. The puffy red face and bloodshot eyes were the effects of fever.

"Where were you during it all?" Will asked after they cut across the street.

"Up there," Lipton said, pointing to the rooftop of the embassy building. "You shoulda seen our marines. They were scared shitless. Can't say I blame 'em. They expected a mob to storm the embassy. We were ready to shred documents if necesasry. It was pretty intense. Tanks on the plaza, snipers on the rooftops.

"You got to hand it to Allende, though," he continued feverishly. "He must have known his goose was cooked. Everyone thought he'd call the workers to arms, which woulda meant a real bloodbath, but he didn't."

They walked up Paseo Ahumada, past wary guards at the entrance to the Bank of Chile, toward the cathedral. It was another mild, sunny day, just like the day of the coup. Their shadows trailed them in the bright white light.

"Is it true what they're saying about the stadium?" Will asked.

"They have to hold people somewhere. Mostly a bunch of curfew breakers. You know, looters and hooligans. But they've arrested plenty of extremists, too. The Spanish and Mexican embassies are overflowing with terrified Commies. We've had our hands full, too, dealing with all the Americans trying to get out."

Four armed soldiers watched over the half-deserted Plaza de Armas from a jeep parked in the shade of the cathedral. Lipton steered Will around the outer edge of the littered square, empty of the usual crowds of shoppers and pickpockets. Benches lay broken and overturned. A detail of soldiers in green fatigues worked at one end, tossing tires and crushed steel drums, bricks and pieces of splintered lumber into the back of a truck. Lipton seemed not to notice the destruction. His nose had begun to run and he sniffled between bursts of speech.

"The ambassador has asked me—in my day job, that is—to go over to the stadium and make sure no Americans were rounded up accidentally. We've had reports a few were. While I'm there I want to make sure they don't shoot any of our guys by mistake."

"Then it's true?"

Lipton gave Will a sideways glance. "Get in touch with your

assets. Make sure they're okay. If you can't get ahold of some-body, I need to know pronto."

He must have been going full bore around the clock, doing his cover duties by day and his covert duties at night. No wonder he had a cold. His feverish urgency made the listless time Will had spent in his apartment seem frivolous and lazy.

"Got it," Will said. "Anything else I can do to help?"

Lipton stopped to take a crumpled handkerchief from his pocket and sneezed into it.

"Yeah," he said, wiping his nose. "Make sure our records are current and one-hundred-percent accurate. This coup is front-page news. I don't want some liberal congressman stateside call-ing us onto the carpet and telling us we were out of line. We fol-lowed orders and I want that clearly evidenced."

"You mean the payments to the truckers."

"We didn't pay the truckers, Will. That's the bloody point."

Lipton stopped again, raised his handkerchief to his nose as he grimaced and sneezed loudly.

Lipton knew he was coming down with a cold the day he called Will and the other NOCs to warn them of the coup. He couldn't sleep after his meeting with Bill Bradshaw and Pete Nolan, and then worked eighteen hours in a head-pounding funk.

Despite his bravura performance as an insider, he only learned of the coup preparations the night before he called Will. On Saturday evening he had just returned home from the hippo-drome where he'd spent the afternoon watching a series of races with a congressman from the PDC when Bill phoned and asked him to come into the office right away. When he arrived on the dark and deserted ninth floor around 9:00 p.m., he heard voices inside Bill's office but found the door locked. He knocked and Pete Nolan, wearing a white polo shirt and jeans, opened it.

"Ed," Pete said. Looking like he'd swallowed the canary.

Sitting behind his large desk with only the desk lamp on, Bill, despite the short-sleeved madras plaid shirt he wore, seemed unusually glum.

"Thanks for coming in, Ed. Have a seat."

The radio chattered in the background. Lipton braced himself.

Bill wiped his mouth with a big paw. "Pete's been briefing me on some things and I thought we should get you involved."

In the next thirty minutes, as Bill informed him of the ultra-secret, ultra-restricted meetings between special envoys from Washington and select leaders of the Chilean armed forces, Lipton saw his whole career being flushed down the toilet. He might as well have been working for the post office. True to his worst fears, the shit was going down and they had excluded the Station from the planning and, apparently, even from knowing about it until now. As if they couldn't be trusted or would screw it up. Was the reputation of the CIA that bad?

"You guys have been doing a great job," said Nolan patronizingly. "We knew we could count on you to maintain the pressure with your political and economic ops. The current situation, with the strikes and the congress at loggerheads, makes the execution of this plan a lot more palatable, and a lot more justifiable to the public. But the higher-ups decided, since it was a military op, it required military oversight exclusively."

"What, and now you're going to hand us our balls back?" Lipton said.

"Now Ed—" Bill interjected.

Nolan gave Lipton a flash of his movie-star smile, which right then Lipton wanted to smash. "Not even the ambassador knows what's about to happen, Ed. I'm giving you guys a heads-up so you can protect your assets and manage your ops accordingly, that's all. But stay clear of the fireworks. We all are. This is a Chilean deal and that's how it's going to play. If it doesn't work out, things may change. But these guys are taking all the risk."

"Do Phillips and Colby know?" Lipton asked.

"They've been advised," Nolan said. Lipton gave an incredulous snort.

"Right. Well, we're all on the same team. Let's hope this brings an end to our problem," Bill said. "Thanks, Pete." Then, turning to Lipton, "Let's get our folks off the streets and have 'em keep their heads down."

Lipton felt like saying, Fuck you, fuck this. I'm going home to get drunk.

But of course he didn't. He was a good soldier and would soldier on.

Will tracked down his agents one by one.

Carlos Saavedra had spent the entire week at his company's garage, sleeping in the cab of a truck with a loaded rifle in his lap, ready to shoot anyone who tried to break in.

"So how's the change affecting your business?" Will asked when they finally connected by telephone.

"The curfew is making it difficult for my drivers on the long hauls. But thank God for our military heroes, Ricardo."

"I heard Comrade Kazatsky was kicked out of the country. Escorted onto a plane the day after the coup." Lipton had shared that tidbit with Will. "Think his linen suits will be warm enough for Moscow?"

"Ha!" Saavedra said, relishing the news. "They should have lined him and the entire Soviet and Cuban missions up against a wall and shot them. To hell with diplomatic immunity!" Such vehemence from this seemingly mild-mannered man surprised Will and reminded him of Roland Fabré's comments about the retributions in France after the war.

Will did not need to contact Emilio Girardi. Girardi called him. He sounded exhilarated.

"So what happens to Patria y Libertad?" Will asked.

"Disbanded, of course. But there is still a need for vigilance. Unofficially, we are working with the police. The rats will attempt to flee, but not if we can trap them first."

Will confirmed that the payments would also come to an end.

"Naturally. And advertising is down to nothing, but at least now we can obtain newsprint at a reasonable price. My biggest concern, the junta has suspended our broadcasting license. They've tarred us with the same brush as the Communist stations. We are prohibited from transmitting. I expect it's only temporary. I'm lobbying for a different solution."

With his numerous contacts on the ultra-conservative right, Will had no doubt that Girardi would succeed in his efforts.

Only Víctor remained unaccounted for. Will had no way to reach him except through his job at the university bookstore, which was closed indefinitely, or through Ernesto, and Will had not spoken to him since their phone conversation during the coup. He called Ernesto, expecting to find them both at the apartment in Providencia. But Ernesto said he hadn't heard from Víctor since the day before coup.

"Aren't you worried?" Will asked, trying not to show his concern.

"Not really. Víctor knows how to get along."

"Can't you call him?"

"They don't have a phone," Ernesto said. "But he's not there anyway."

"How do you know that?"

"He told me, 'If there's ever a coup, I'll have to go into hiding.'"

"Shit, then how do you get in touch with each other?"

"He's got a key. He'll show up when it's safe."

In ten days, Santiago was already adapting to its new, post-coup sobriety. The long days passed by with a grim, nose-to-thegrindstone sameness. Mundane concerns became preoccupations. Curfew began at 8:00 p.m., so by seven-thirty cabs grew scarce and busses crowded as people scrambled to get home.

Stores reopened with restricted hours, and although there were fewer shortages, the challenge now was to find the items one needed in the limited hours of business. Price controls went into effect. The escudo stabilized and the black market collapsed (although Will's landlady continued to appreciate his rent in dollars). Those caught attempting to profit from scarcities were arrested. Businesses adjusted. Movie theaters showed more matinees. Restaurants, normally open until midnight, filled with customers in the afternoon. Still, a pervasive restraint guided conversations. Patrons' eyes anxiously roved across other tables as they whispered stories over lunch about detained friends and enemies, relatives and neighbors.

Soldiers regularly patrolled the neighborhood. At night unmarked white Ford Falcons raced down empty streets on mysterious missions. There was still the occasional disruption. Late one evening while reading in bed, Will heard the crack of splintering wood in the street below. He rushed to the window. Five or six soldiers were smashing in the door of a house across the street. Two jeeps blocked the sidewalk. The drivers, illuminated by the dim light from the hallway, waited while the others charged inside. Minutes later they hauled out a woman in her nightgown and a shirtless and shoeless man in handcuffs. They shoved them into the jeep and drove away.

Will spent his days at the office writing reports. His First Republic bosses in New York already wanted assessments of the post-coup business climate. Should they reenter the market? Was the junta receptive to foreign investment? Were regulations on foreign ownership likely to change? Will had no idea and neither did any of his contacts. The generals, he suspected, had other things on their minds. Still, he gleaned what he could from newspapers and business acquaintances. Leti, whose only comment about the general state of affairs was that it now took her twenty minutes longer to get to work on overcrowded busses, typed and dispatched his reports.

Each day Will called Ernesto to ask if he'd heard from Víctor, but there was no news. Then, twelve days after the coup, Ernesto called him.

"He's dead."

"Who?" Will's chest tightened, thinking he meant Víctor.

"Neruda."

Will laughed with relief. "I'm sorry. It's not funny."

He knew how much Ernesto revered the poet. He recalled the photograph on Ernesto's bedroom wall in Chillán and still had the poetry collection Ernesto had pressed upon him the first time they met.

"They are killing off our cultural patrimony one person at a time," Ernesto said gravely. "Allende, Jara, Neruda…anyone that was good—caput. And you laugh!"

"Ernesto! Everything isn't a conspiracy, you know. He had cancer. Sometimes people just die."

He was not to be consoled. "It doesn't matter. What's the fucking difference, right?"

"Have you heard from Víctor?"

"He's staying with his uncle."

Will felt an instantaneous release of anxiety. "Well, shit, you might have told me."

"Why?"

"Weren't you worried?"

"No. Who can you trust these days? Ricardo, we must attend the funeral, make a statement."

"Neruda's? I don't think that's a good idea."

"We must! It's exactly what is needed. Tuesday morning. I'm meeting Víctor first. We'll pick you up."

* * *

On Tuesday, Ernesto arrived at Will's apartment dressed in an outfit worthy of Oscar Wilde. He wore a black suit over a rumpled white shirt and a thin black tie. A pale white gardenia poked from the buttonhole on his lapel.

"Let's go," he said. "People are already lining up." He looked as if he hadn't eaten in weeks. His eyes were fever bright and his straight black hair had grown long enough to brush his shoulders.

"Where's Víctor?"

"He said he'll meet us there."

They hurried toward Neruda's house, La Chascona, which was not far from Will's apartment.

"I'm not sure about this," Will said.

But he was curious, too. The junta had downplayed Neruda's death and, to avoid a public demonstration, had tried to delay the funeral until after curfew. *El Mercurio* only noted the time and location in the small print of its obituary page.

"They say the army ransacked his house," Ernesto said. "The man's dying and they ransacked his house! Smashed up his collections, overturned his bookshelves, tossed his papers on the floor, trampled his personal belongings. What a disgrace! It was nothing but a brutal act of intimidation. They knew exactly what they were doing. 'If we can do this to the greatest voice of Chile, a Nobel laureate, just watch what we can do to you!' The bastards!"

"He was a Communist senator, too, don't forget."

Ernesto smirked. For one so seemingly oblivious to politics, he was taking Neruda's death personally. The violence had made him more of an Allende sympathizer than he had ever been before the coup. Will also detected a trace of fear in his friend's voice.

"You know," he said, walking briskly to keep up with Ernesto's dark figure, "maybe you should get away for a while. Why don't you go home? Take Víctor with you. Santiago is no place to be right now." And thinking of Gabriela, he added, "It would be fun. I could come down for a weekend and we could just hang out in Chillán or go to the beach."

They were approaching the crowded street where the funeral procession was to pass by. As if to emphasize what Will was saying, a man with a 35mm camera boldly snapped their picture.

"Fuck you, asshole!" Ernesto yelled at the photographer, who was clearly a plainclothes policeman. The man disregarded Ernesto and turned to take a picture of other mourners.

"Ironic, isn't it," Ernesto said after calming himself. "My own country has become safer for you than for me."

The funeral procession came around the corner and the heads of the waiting crowd turned to watch. A cortege of men and women dressed in dark suits and black dresses escorted a plain gray coffin draped in the flag with massive sprays of white camellias and red carnations. As the procession made its way slowly up the street, an astounding thing happened. The crowd, pressing along the curb to catch a glimpse, began to sing the Internationale. Doors and windows opened and people tossed flowers onto the coffin as it passed by. Ernesto suddenly began to cry and wiped his eyes. Will didn't know what to make of his friend's emotional display but suspected that Ernesto's tears were not only for the death of the poet.

Behind the procession came three unmarked cars filled with men who stared back at the crowd and snapped photographs.

"Maybe you're right," Ernesto said. "Maybe it's time to get out of here. School's fucked anyway. Half of my teachers are in jail." He lit a cigarette and inhaled deeply then coughed as if the smoke had caught in his throat.

"So where's Víctor? I thought he was going to be here."

"Hell if I know," Ernesto said through his coughing fit.

23

*E*arly Monday, the first of October, Roland Fabré knocked on Will's door as he was leaving for work. Roland looked perturbed, waves of silver hair flaring wildly from his head.

"Richard, I must ask you a favor," he said, stepping into Will's living room.

"Sure."

"Thank you, but allow me to explain before you agree. I have a mission that requires a car. I am hoping you might be willing to lend me yours. There is some risk."

"Mission? Roland, have you joined the resistance?" Will joked, but the Frenchman took the question seriously.

"I must deliver something to the French embassy tonight."

"Tonight? You mean, break the curfew?"

Roland tilted his head, as if to split hairs with Will's statement. "Perhaps. Yes, there is that risk."

"Roland! Do you even know how to drive a car?"

"Of course!" He seemed insulted. "Since long before you were born."

"What are you taking?"

Reluctant to reply, Roland took a cigarette from his pocket and rummaged for a match.

"This is what happens when you become entangled by the heart—you do foolish things." He lit the cigarette and blew smoke toward the ceiling. "It is Felicidad's son, Sergio. He is not very bright. A plumber's apprentice, and not a very good one. But he was active in the union and the union was very active in the Communist Party. Now he is afraid of arrest. He heard that his name is on a list because one of his colleagues was arrested and taken to the stadium. Sergio has been in hiding. I spoke with an acquaintance at the embassy. They are turning people away now, but if I can deliver him there tonight, he promised they will take him in and provide him with a visa."

From Roland's troubled expression Will knew it would be better not to get involved, but recalling the risky things he'd done to be with Gabriela, he understood and sympathized with his friend's predicament. "So where's the French embassy located?" he asked. Roland's face brightened. They agreed to meet that evening at seven.

On leaving the office, Will took the Falcon from the parking garage and drove home. Roland was waiting for him, the door to his cluttered apartment ajar. He poured a cognac for himself and offered one to Will. "For the nerves," he said.

"No thanks," said Will.

The plan was to pick up Felicidad who would take them to her son's hiding place, which turned out to be Sergio's grandmother's apartment. Plenty of cars were still on the streets, but army vehicles were already moving into position at major intersections and Carabineros patrolled in preparation for the eight o'clock curfew.

"Why are we doing this now instead of tomorrow morning?" Will asked.

"The embassies, at least the sympathetic ones, are now under surveillance. If the police can prevent people from getting inside, they remain fair game. My embassy friend says several cars have attempted to crash through the gate. They had to put up barricades. And the other night some poor man was climbing over the wall when he got caught. They pulled him back to the sidewalk and hauled him away. I'm doing as I was told. My friend believes the best time is just before the curfew comes into effect. During the changing of the guard, so to speak."

With Will at the wheel, Roland in the front seat and Felicidad in the back, they drove to the San Joaquín neighborhood, a barrio of shops and modest homes. The kiosks were closing, rolling down their shutters. Will looked at his watch: seven twenty-two.

"Down the block, on the right," Felicidad said, tapping Roland's shoulder. Will turned into the narrow driveway of a crumbling three-story apartment building. They drove behind the building into a weed-infested yard shielded by high cinderblock walls.

They parked beside several old cars in front of a large propane tank. They waited in silence, a precaution that reminded Will of the many surveillance detection runs he had practiced in training. The sky began to fade to a dusky gray. Dogs barked on the other side of the wall. No one appeared to be following them.

They watched a bamboo blind that covered the balcony of the top-floor apartment for the signal. Someone raised the bamboo shade to reveal wash drying on a clothesline and then lowered it again.

"Okay," Felicidad said.

Will started the engine and drove to the building's side entrance. While he kept the car running, Felicidad and Roland climbed the stairs to the third floor. A few minutes later, Roland hurried back and opened the rear door facing the building. Felicidad came down next carrying a blanket. On her heels a fat young man in a T-shirt ducked into the car. Sergio sprawled flat on the seat and Felicidad draped the blanket over him. It hardly seemed possible that the tiny, bird-like woman and this large man with the sweaty face and mop of dark hair could be related. Roland hopped into the front seat and waved his hand to go. As they had agreed beforehand, Felicidad stayed behind.

Once on Avenida Vicuña Mackenna Will drove at the speed limit but pushed the yellow lights and watched for army vehicles or flashing lights in the rearview mirror.

At 7:45 p.m. there were still plenty of cars on the street but most had yellow passes displayed in their windows.

"Think we'll make it?" Will asked as they neared Providencia.

"Here, Sergio," Roland said passing the bottle of cognac to the back. "Take a big drink and spill some on your shirt. If we are stopped, pretend to be passed out."

They had concocted a lame excuse but it was all they could come up with: We are foreigners. Our friend drank too much and we are taking him home. Curfew? We didn't realize that applied to us...

"What if they don't believe you?" Sergio asked.

Roland and Will glanced at each other but neither responded.

They drove in tense silence, and at first Will didn't know what to make of the noise he began to hear, a soft wavering moan. He glanced at Roland who returned a look of embarrassment. It was Sergio, whimpering uncontrollably beneath his blanket, a pitiful, hysterical blubbering and sniffling.

Roland gave directions as they neared the embassy. Will turned onto a quiet one-way residential street with cars parked on both sides. The French flag drooped from a pole behind a high wall. As Roland had warned, bollards now blocked the entrance to a driveway also secured by two tall iron gates.

They saw no army or police units. Roland glanced at his watch. "Pull up in front of the driveway. I'll ring the bell. Sergio, get ready."

The blubbering intensified then stopped entirely, as if Sergio really had passed out.

Will pulled over. Roland leapt to the curb. No sooner had he pressed the bell than the gate opened and a tall, thin man in a dark suit waved urgently.

Will scanned the street in front and checked his rearview mirror. He saw nothing to alarm him. "Okay, Sergio, run like the devil."

Panting, Sergio tossed off the blanket, pushed open the door and clambered out. Despite his girth he barreled across the sidewalk past Roland Fabré through the gate. Roland barely had time to nod to his friend before the gate shut.

After Roland climbed back in, Will pulled into the street and stepped on the accelerator. Curfew was only two minutes away.

"If they stop us now we should be able to wiggle out of it," he said. Roland replied with a vague grunt.

As they turned onto Pio Nono behind an occupied taxi, four soldiers in a jeep drove onto the sidewalk beside the bridge, but the soldiers did not react.

Five minutes later they arrived home. As they entered the building, Roland patted Will on the back and thanked him. "We all have our weaknesses," he said, "but cowardice is most unattractive, no? This is one reason why I never wanted children. What if they should grow up to disappoint us?"

24

Three weeks after the coup, on a soft evening in early October, Will arrived home from work to catch the sunset's reflection in the windowpanes of the building across the street. Hints of spring were in the warm air and lengthening days. The sky's luminous pinks had just faded to steely blue when the telephone rang.

"Ricardo?"

"Gabriela!" He knew without her saying. "Where are you?"

"Here, in Santiago. I can't find Ernesto. Have you seen him?"

"Isn't he in Chillán? The last time I saw him he was talking about going home. That was over a week ago."

"God, no. I don't know what to do—" Her voice collapsed into a worried silence.

"Where are you?"

"At the apartment. I tried calling you earlier. I've tried everyone I know."

Will looked at his watch: seven-ten. He calculated how long it would take to get to Ernesto's.

"I'll be right over."

He threw on a sweater and ran out to flag a cab. By the time he got to Avenida Providencia, the stores and restaurants were closing. The clubs and peñas he had visited with Ernesto looked permanently shuttered, their signs darkened.

At the intersection with Avenida Ricardo Lyon an army jeep

with a mounted .50-caliber machine gun pulled onto the traffic island in preparation for curfew. Ernesto's side street was ghostly still. Will paid the cabbie and didn't wait for change. He pressed the bell at the front gate. Gabriela's anxious voice greeted him through the intercom, and she buzzed him in. As the elevator lugged to the seventh floor he caught his reflection in the mirrored panels—in truth, he had no idea how to help Gabriela.

She was waiting for him at the apartment door. Even in distress she was beautiful.

"Ricardo, thank you for coming." She offered him a cheek to kiss. Once inside the narrow entrance to the apartment she gave him a fuller hug. He embraced the softness of the cashmere sweater and inhaled patchouli as he kissed her more fully. She broke his embrace. "I'm so frightened."

"Tell me what happened."

Everything in the apartment was as he had seen it last: the stereo, the records stacked against the wall, the books stuffed onto the makeshift shelves. On a shelf above the stereo was something new—a small shrine composed of a newspaper photo of Pablo Neruda, a bunch of desiccated flowers in a small vase and a half-burnt candle.

Gabriela paced the room before settling onto the couch. Will sat down beside her. She tugged a cigarette from a pack lying on the coffee table and lit it.

"I didn't know you smoke."

"There are lots of things you don't know about me," she said, exhaling and tossing the match into the abalone shell ashtray. "I usually hide my bad habits better," she said with a wan smile. Will took a cigarette and joined her. "It isn't like Ernesto to disappear without a word," she continued. "I haven't said anything to Mamá, but I'm really worried."

"I'm sure he's fine. Have you spoken to Víctor?"

"I can't reach him. I looked for him at the university, but no one has seen him." This corroborated Will's own recent attempts.

She swept a hand through her hair. "Where are my manners? Can I offer you a glass of Ernesto's wine?" For the first time she laughed lightly. It sounded just like something Ernesto would say.

"Let me." Will went to the kitchen. He searched in the drawers for a corkscrew and opened a bottle of table wine. "Maybe they went to Viña for a long weekend," he said.

Gabriela shook her head. "I tried to phone him three times last week. The neighbor says she hasn't seen him in ten days."

A blackened bunch of bananas, like a shriveled hand clawing the counter, confirmed what she said.

"Last time I saw him was at Neruda's funeral. He was pretty upset." Will returned with the wine. "I told him to get out of the city for a while and suggested going home. I told him I could let Víctor know if he decided to. That was the last I talked to him. I haven't been able to reach Víctor, either. Think they could be hiding somewhere?'

"Why?"

Will shrugged. He pictured Víctor being handed a gun at a secret MIR meeting. How to say what he couldn't say outright?

"Come on, Gabi. Víctor was outspoken and the police have been rounding people up. Besides, any deviation…"

She stubbed out the half-finished cigarette then leaned back, rubbed her temples and sighed. The cashmere sweater crept above her waist and she quickly pulled it back into place.

"I wish my father were still alive. He would know what to do. Everything's so fucked up right now." She laughed and covered her mouth as if surprised by her words.

"Can you help me, Ricardo? Would your embassy be able to help? I can't go to the police."

"Why not?"

"Impossible! It would raise suspicions, make him a target."

"Of what?"

"You can't trust them. People are disappearing for no reason."

"Gabi, those are just wild rumors. If people are being detained it's because of something they did."

"You are so naïve, Ricardo." The rebuke was given in the gentlest way.

"Well, we can't do anything about it tonight." Will glanced at his watch. Curfew began in fifteen minutes. Even now he ran the risk of arrest. "I have to go," he said, standing up.

Gabriela stood and took his hand.

"Ricardo—" The urgency of her voice stopped him. "Don't go."

It was the signal he'd been waiting for. As difficult as it was to admit, he had rushed to the apartment to be with her more than over any deep concern for Ernesto's welfare. Knowing Ernesto, he was bored and drinking too much in some miserable hiding place with Víctor. It crossed Will's mind that she might have come to the same conclusion even before she called him. Was this incident merely a pretense on both sides?

He reached over and raised her chin with his index finger. Their eyes met in unabashed frankness. He leaned closer and kissed her. Her lips parted and he felt the edge of her teeth on his tongue as he kissed her again more deeply.

"Stay with me tonight."

They fell back onto the couch. He kissed her neck and felt the whisper of her pulse on his lips. His mouth brushed her earlobe. He inhaled the sweet hint of patchouli at the base of her neck. He wanted to possess her, to feel the warmth of her breath in his ear. He had wanted her ever since he first saw her. He reached under her sweater and cupped a firm breast.

"Wait," she said, sitting up and reaching to unfasten her brassiere. She pulled the sweater over her head and he watched in awe as her breasts emerged, then her excited face amid a stream of wild hair crackling with static electricity. She smoothed her hair with her hand, exposing the sharp angles of her collarbone and shoulder blades. Her skin was the color of café con leche, her breasts smaller than he had imagined, her torso slender, each rib gently defined. She stood up and led him to the bedroom.

They made love in the tender, tentative way of initiates, and afterward Will lay in a languorous oblivion. Gradually, the unfamiliar sounds of the building penetrated his consciousness—the rattle of the balcony's glass door from a gust of wind, the hum of the refrigerator as its motor clicked on.

She was warm beside him. He raised himself on an elbow and caressed her hip, tracing the seductive curve he had first noticed on their ride together.

"Gabi, will you forgive me?" He took a strand of hair that had fallen across her face and gently tucked it behind her ear, then he caressed her cheek. "All those stupid things I said about love. I didn't know what I was saying. I've been in love with you ever since I first saw you. I wanted you then and I want you now, again!"

Gabriela laughed. He pulled her on top of him and they made love again. This time he watched the shimmering veil of her long dark hair obscure her face as she moved.

They fell asleep nestled together, Will holding her against him. Near midnight she woke with a start. He stroked her back to soothe her.

"I don't know if I can sleep," she said.

"Watch Ernesto walk in now," Will said.

"If only he would!"

She went into the bathroom and Will thought he heard her cry. She came back with a glass of water and offered him a drink. He turned on the bedside lamp and adjusted the shade to keep the glare from their eyes. They lay together.

"Are you okay?" he asked. He pressed his nose into the soft scent at the nape of her neck and stroked her forearm.

"I can't stop thinking about Ernesto. Thank you for staying with me tonight, Ricardo. It helps to have you here."

Each time she said his alias he felt a desperate urge to tell her the truth but quashed it. Now was not the time.

"Ricardo—" She turned to face him.

"Which is more true?" he interrupted.

He had not realized how the question would remind them both of Ernesto. Gabriela smiled but a ripple of worry crossed her face.

"Yes?" she asked, putting her hand to his cheek.

"A) I can't believe this is happening, or B) I've fallen in love."

Gabriela kissed him, a soft peck on the lips. "It must be B, Ricardo. It's true for me."

In the morning they made love again and afterward he fell into a deep sleep. When he awoke Gabriela was gone. He found a note on the kitchen counter saying she would be back in ten minutes. He turned on the water heater and showered. When he came out of the bathroom, she was back, working in the kitchen.

"There was nothing in the refrigerator except beer," she said.

He leaned against the kitchen counter while she prepared a spinach omelet. With a domestic energy he hadn't seen before, Gabriela solicited his desires about every detail of the breakfast until he assured her that he was fine with anything she cooked. He was starving. At the table they drank Nescafé sweetened with condensed milk and dipped thick slices of crusty bread into their cups.

She lived in the apartment when she was at the university, she said, and hated to give it up. Ernesto had offered to share it with her, but she knew she had no choice. She had to return to Chillán to be with her mother. "In Chile, a single woman doesn't live away from home," she explained.

Will listened with fascination. From their lovemaking he knew she was not a virgin. Not that he cared, but it surprised him after imagining, naively perhaps, the challenges of seducing a respectable Chilean woman. Sexual customs and mores were enough of a mystery to him in the United States, they were doubly so here in Chile. Will wondered who had been her first lover and how many she'd had. Was it in this apartment that she lost her virginity? He chased these jealous thoughts from his mind. She could tell him the story of her love life in her own way, in her own time.

"I know a few people at the embassy," he said. "I'll talk to them today. It may take a few days, but don't worry, I'll find out what I can."

Gabriela nodded and lifted the cup to her lips with both hands.

"Will I see you tonight?" he asked.

"I have to return to Chillán."

This news dashed Will's hopes and his face must have expressed his disappointment.

"I promised Beto that I'd be back in time to proof the paper. And Mamá will wonder if I stay too long."

"I understand. I was just hoping. When will we see each other next?"

"I'll come back if you hear anything."

He looked at his watch—he was already late for work—and stood up. "I've got to go," he said. She stood up and they embraced in a long kiss like newlyweds.

"You know, I had a premonition about you. The first time I saw you," she said.

"You did?"

"Yes. Standing in the road. I knew you had come into our lives for a reason. I didn't know why, but I felt it."

Will's overactive brain tried to grapple with the long string of lies since that day. Still, this was not the time to come clean.

"Uh-oh. And now?" As if someone else were asking the question for him.

"Definitely. Now I know." She smiled.

"What?" He cupped her chin in his hand, lightly caressing the dimple to the right of her mouth with his thumb, something he had longed to do ever since he first noticed it in the rearview mirror of the Citroneta.

"To be my guardian angel."

He kissed her again and felt a stirring in his groin. He pulled away. "Well, this guardian angel wants to do devilish things to you. I better go."

By the time he returned to his apartment, changed his clothes and found a cab downtown, it was nearly eleven. Leti looked up from her typing and gave him a careful second look. Did something show? Had the expression on his face changed? Were his cheeks still flushed? Inside he felt it, too. A spring in his step, a skip in his heart, joy in his eyes. He was in love. He could not stop thinking about Gabriela—her scent, the lively amber eyes beneath those serious eyebrows, the curve of her hip beneath the sheets, her warmth as she lay beside him, the sound of her soft, steady breathing as she slept facing him.

Will called Lipton on the secure line and his secretary answered. Mr. Lipton is out, she said. Will left a message for him to call as soon as he returned. Mid-afternoon Lipton finally called back and said he was on the way out the door for another appointment. They agreed to meet at the Hotel Rincón at five o'clock.

Will left the office at four. He stopped in a pharmacy to purchase a box of condoms. He had not thought to ask Gabriela if she was using any precautions. He detested the things but didn't want to get her into trouble—although, as he stood in line at the counter, the thought of having a child with her thrilled him. He imagined building a new life with her, leaving the CIA, working for First Republic, coming home to her at night. It would be a good life.

He used his errands to ensure that he wasn't being followed—the procedure seemed unnecessary in post-coup Chile—then took a cab and got out a block from the hotel. He waited while a white Falcon sped past before going inside. He headed up the stairs to the third floor. Lipton was already in the room and opened the door when Will knocked.

"So, what's up?" Lipton asked. He sat on the end of the single bed. Water ran in the bathroom faucet. The room smelled musty and unused.

Will sat down on a spindly chair by the dresser.

"Remember Ernesto Manning?"

"What about him?"

"His sister called me yesterday. She hasn't heard from him in two weeks."

Lipton shrugged. "Like a lot of people. That's what you called me here for?"

"She asked if I could help her locate him. She's afraid he's been detained."

"And what did you say?"

"I said I knew a few people at the embassy and would see what I could do."

"Why the fuck did you volunteer that?"

"Because it's true."

Lipton stared at him from across the room. "Are you fucking her?"

"No!" Will didn't know why he denied it, but it was done. He could feel the blood rush to his face. He dared not look away from Lipton's gray gaze.

"So tell her to go to the police."

"She's afraid to."

Lipton frowned.

"It isn't just Ernesto. Víctor's disappeared, too."

"Yeah? Smart guy. Probably gone underground. Maybe he and lover-boy have flown the coop along with the other bleeding half of Chile."

Will shook his head. "I haven't seen him since the coup. You said I should let you know if any of our assets was unaccounted for. Well, he's our guy, isn't he?"

Lipton started to say something, paused, then said, "I'll see what I can do."

"That's all I'm asking. I mean, if they did seek asylum in an embassy, surely there's a list of names somewhere. And if they are being detained, we should be getting them out. Right?"

"I said I'll see what I can do. You know, despite what you might think, we don't run this country. What else?"

For a split second Will debated whether to tell the truth about Gabriela but, angered by Lipton's surliness, he decided against it. He could come clean on his next polygraph.

25

*L*ipton saw the way Will dropped eye contact and flushed when he asked if he was sleeping with the girl. He had interrogated enough people to recognize the telltale signs of a lie. Not that he really cared what Will P did in his private life, as long as it didn't compromise his cover. But the lying pissed him off.

The girl, Gabriela Manning, had checked out. There was nothing in her background to concern him. His immediate concern was with Will. Based on what he had said and done, his judgment was clouded, his behavior risky and unprofessional.

Treat it as a performance issue in his next review, Bill Bradshaw would advise. In the meantime, maybe if Will got laid he'd get back to work.

Lipton telephoned Felipe Covarrubias when he returned to the embassy and congratulated him on his promotion to colonel.

"Thank you, Eduardo. You keep well informed, I see. Yes, General Contreras has asked me to join his new intelligence unit. No more of this rivalry between the armed forces trying to prove which branch is smarter. We report directly to General Pinochet. Needless to say, we are extremely busy. No time for tennis now." Lipton detected a boastful note in the lament. "So, what can I do for you?"

"Two persons of interest to the U.S. mission: one Víctor Maragall and an Ernesto Manning. If you have any information on their whereabouts, it would be greatly appreciated."

"Certainly. I'll have my adjutant, Major Olivares, look into it."

Lipton bristled. Maybe the newly minted colonel was merely concerned about appearances, but it sounded like Covarrubias was telling him *he* was now too important to supply information directly to American intelligence officers.

"If it isn't too much trouble," he said with icy clarity, while thinking: And good luck paying for your mistress on a colonel's salary, you prick.

The bag of matchbooks Bill Bradshaw had left for Covarrubias still lay on top of his file cabinet. After hanging up, Lipton tossed them into the wastebasket.

Will met Lipton in front of the American consulate at noon the next day. The walls of the consulate, a target of countless anti-American graffiti attacks before the coup, were freshly painted. The building's colonial façade looked dignified and tranquil. A bright new American flag waved gently on a staff above the portico.

They crossed to the park on the other side of the street. The gravel paths, recently raked, were virtually deserted and the two men strolled as if they had nothing else to do but feed the pigeons and admire the new flowerbeds on a sunny spring day.

Although he was grateful not to be inside the dank Hotel Rincón, Will was surprised at the openness of Lipton's choice of meeting place. Will had on his blue suit and already felt hot in the sun. Lipton, who wore a gray raincoat over his suit, must have been cooking.

"I was able to get some information," Lipton said, stopping to sit at a park bench. He unbuttoned the raincoat. "The good news is, our man's all right. Although he's finished as an asset."

"All right?" The steady roar of traffic on the avenue washed over their conversation.

"Shit, it's like fucking summer already..." Lipton loosened

the knot of his tie and unfastened the top button of his shirt. "Yeah. He and your friend were stopped by a military patrol on the highway outside Parral. I don't know what they were thinking. It was right before curfew. The patrol was setting up their checkpoint. You know, turning people around if they weren't already heading home."

Lipton paused and Will looked to see what had distracted him. A group of bouncing schoolgirls in bright blue jumpers had arrived at the corner on the opposite side of the busy street. Their teacher, a woman whose figure and long black hair reminded Will of Gabriela, corralled them at the curb. When the light turned green she stepped into the crosswalk and turned to face down the four lanes of cars with arms outstretched, as if she and not the red light were the force stopping them. She waved the girls forward and they joined hands to form a long human chain. Once they were successfully across the street Lipton began again.

"Anyway, the dumbfucks tried to run the checkpoint, so the grunts chased 'em down. Your pals claimed they didn't see the soldier waving them over, or some bullshit like that.

"The soldiers found a whole bunch of shit in the car: some pot, a pile of Communist newspapers and, of all things, a gun. When the soldiers asked what they were doing nobody seemed to have a good answer. I mean, fuck, a few old Commie rags, okay. But drugs? A gun? In this environment? How fucking stupid can you get?"

"So what happened?"

"What do you think? The patrol figured they'd caught a couple of MIR terrorists. They arrested 'em. Roughed 'em up, I suspect."

Will imagined the two men being handcuffed and wondered if Ernesto had kept his mouth shut.

"Shit."

"Hey, it's what they do," Lipton said matter-of-factly. "Took 'em back to their base for interrogation. Turned out, both were on the list—"

"What list?"

"Come on, Will. Víctor was active in a MIR cell. Think MIL-INTEL didn't already have a file on him? And as for your friend...well, they knew he was a fag, and the pot and gun were found in the fucker's car."

"But the gun was Víctor's."

Lipton spread open his coat and readjusted his seat on the bench.

"It doesn't matter whose it was, does it? Look, what I wanted to tell you... The unfortunate thing is, your friend Ernesto's dead."

The words, uttered so casually, didn't register. They went through Will as if he were a ghost, untouched by the world's agonies. "You're messing with me, right?"

Lipton gave him a surprised look. "I'm fucking serious."

Panic set in. "But you just said—"

"I said Víctor's okay. At least as far as I know."

Will couldn't breathe. He thought he was going to be sick. He felt paralyzed yet wanted to flee or curl up and cover his head with his hands the way he did as a boy when his father went on the rampage. He didn't dare show any sign of emotional collapse in front of Lipton. Surreptitiously, he clutched the edge of the bench with both hands.

"Fortunately, he was on the list of assets we gave them." Lipton's blunt voice pierced the fog in Will's brain. "They let him go. He's probably back in Santiago by now."

Nothing Lipton said made sense.

"This can't—I don't—" Panic swept over him. He turned to Lipton for help. But he had lied to him about Gabriela. Did Lipton know? Was the man cruel enough to play such a heartless game with him? "I don't believe it!" Will managed to say.

"Shit, Will. You think I joke about people's lives?" Lipton made a dry spitting sound as if a hair was stuck to his tongue. "It's shitty, I know. Thing is, you can't tell the sister about this. We—you—aren't supposed to know. Are we clear?"

Rage and loathing scalded Will's face. He shook from a sudden wave of intense paranoia. It was his fault Ernesto went to Chillán. He had suggested it.

"I've got to go," he said. He didn't know where but he needed to escape. His brain wasn't working. Lipton must be playing a vengeful joke on him. This isn't real, he assured himself. This isn't real. This can't be real.

He stood up. Bright sunlight and unwanted tears blinded his eyes as he recited his mantra. If Lipton said anything as Will walked away, he didn't hear.

He walked without a sense of time or direction. For a few frightening seconds at a busy intersection, he didn't know where he was or how he'd gotten there. He searched in panic for street signs—there, Avenida Rancagua and Vicuña Mackenna. Recovering his bearings, he turned back toward home.

If Ernesto was dead, it was his fault. Ernesto would be alive if he had never befriended him, or if he had not recruited Víctor and asked him to attend the MIR meetings, or if he had not encouraged Ernesto to leave Santiago.

Will struggled with something Lipton had said: *they knew he was a fag*. How did they know? And what did it matter? Had they killed him for being a homosexual? How much of Will's reports did Lipton share with Chilean intelligence? And why wasn't Ernesto also on Lipton's list?

Lipton. Will was no longer sure what Lipton knew or didn't know, or what he made of his sudden flight from the park.

By the time he arrived home he was overheated and breathless and his skin felt clammy. He rummaged in the kitchen and found half a bottle of Dewars. He went to the living room and collapsed onto the sofa. He swallowed two quick shots but they did little to soothe his nerves.

—Which is more true (and remember, huevón, one is always

more true than the other): A) Ernesto died because you lied to him, or B) He died because you lied to yourself?

It was as if he could hear Ernesto's unique inflection as he reproached himself.

—Which is more true: A) You would have risked anything to sleep with Gabriela, or B) You loved your lies more than Ernesto?

—Which is more true…

The telephone rang. Will didn't answer. If it was Lipton, he could go fuck himself. If it was Gabriela, he couldn't face her. What would he say? As the day went dark, he remained on the sofa. For the first time in his life he drank without pleasure. In punishing rounds of self-recrimination and shots of whisky, he grew belligerent, then tearful and self-pitying, then exhausted and numb. The phone rang twice more.

Will woke the next morning with a hangover and a parched mouth. But his mind was set with a new, hardened line of reasoning. What had happened was not his fault. Ernesto had openly declared his homosexuality. Ernesto had befriended Will as much as Will had befriended him. Will had tried to protect him from the political storm but Ernesto behaved as if he were immune to its ferocity. Ernesto knew Víctor's politics and affiliations. He had made his own choices.

Nor could Will change what had happened. Still, he felt sick to his stomach when he thought about it.

What to do about Gabriela was more difficult. He loved her and believed she loved him. She would understand. Not now, but some day.

She called that morning. Despite a breathless tightening in his chest that nearly swallowed his voice, he picked up the phone determined to reveal nothing.

"Hello, my love," she said. "Where have you been? I called three times last night. I became worried."

"I was at the office," he said, sensitive to the fact that he was still lying. "I needed to finish some work."

"Ricardo, the police found the car. It was on the side of the highway near Parral. They called Mamá. They told her it was abandoned. I had to tell her the truth, that I haven't been able to find Ernesto."

"Do the police know where he is?" Will suddenly clung to the fantastic hope that Lipton was wrong, though these new facts argued the contrary.

Gabriela responded with a cluck of contempt for the police. "Were you able to learn anything through your contacts?"

"Nothing yet."

"Can you come down? I'm really worried now." She paused and then whispered, "I need your help with something. I can't talk over the phone. Mamá is thinking the worst and saying terrible things."

"I'll leave first thing tomorrow." Friday was Columbus Day, a holiday. He wouldn't be missed if he left the day before, and he'd have three days to be with her in case the truth came out.

"Thank you, thank you, thank you! I love you so much."

"I love you, too…but Gabi…this isn't good news."

"I know."

After sharing several more endearments they hung up. Will felt awful. It was just one more deception, yet he no longer recognized himself. All he felt was disgust for Richard Henry Allen.

"I'm taking the car," Will told Leti on Thursday morning. The loaded pistol and a thousand dollars were already stowed inside the hidden compartment of his briefcase. He didn't say where he was going or when he was coming back, and the fierce way he announced his plans, Leti didn't dare ask.

Seven hours later he sped through Parral, keeping his eyes on the road, avoiding thoughts of Ernesto. Ninety minutes later he arrived at the Mannings and knocked on the door. The dog barked. Gabriela, dressed in blue jeans and a plain cotton blouse opened the door and rushed outside, giving him a hug and a passionate kiss. "You look tired, my love. Was it a long drive?" she asked, leading him into the living room.

"I need to talk to you before Mamá finds out you're here," she whispered. Her face was pale, her brow creased from unremitting worry. Seeing her, knowing what he knew, he felt compassion and self-loathing simultaneously.

The living room was dark. Gabriela turned on a table lamp and, tossing off her sandals, settled on the high-backed Victorian couch. Will sat down beside her.

She folded her legs underneath her and shifted sideways toward him. Will turned to face her. Her hand fluttered along the piping of a throw pillow she held in her lap. Her toenails gleamed with fresh red polish.

"I spoke to Alonso today." The steady tick of the grandfather clock in the hallway punctuated the pause as Will tried to comprehend.

"Who's Alonso?"

"The groom at the stables."

"Ah!" Will recalled the quiet Mapuche who had led Imelda from the barn on a golden day that seemed a millennium ago. Gabriela had given the groom a gift of a new plaid shirt for his birthday.

"He told me some scary things."

"What kind of things?"

"Well, Alonso has a brother, a half brother actually, named Pedro. He's younger than Alonso and lives in Parral. He works on a finca caring for horses, same as Alonso." Will nodded. "Only Pedro has always been a troublemaker. He used to work at our stable. But he drinks and chases after women. I remember when he lived with Alonso. You could see it in his eyes."

"What?"

Gabriela tilted her head. "Just something. You know, the way he stared at you. It always gave me the creeps."

Whatever Gabriela had to share, she was going to tell it her own way. And no matter what she had uncovered, he already knew the worst. Ernesto was dead. Looking into her serious face he saw stark reminders of her brother, and the anguish was like something stuck in his throat. He entwined his fingers in hers as much for himself as for her.

"Anyway, Pedro was arrested with some others for disorderly conduct. They were in a cantina, drinking, and got angry when the owner started to close early for curfew. A fight broke out. First the police arrived, then a truck full of soldiers. The soldiers shoved them to the ground. The owner said he only wanted to break up the fight, not press charges. But the captain in charge ordered them into the back of a truck.

"One of them resisted and a soldier rammed him in the groin with his gun. 'Any more questions?' the captain asked. The others helped the injured man into the truck then got in themselves."

"Including Pedro?" Will asked.

Gabriela nodded. "They couldn't see where they were going but Pedro knew they were heading away from town. The soldiers sat on benches over Pedro and his friends, who were jammed together on the floor. Pedro said the soldiers all looked really young and refused to make eye contact. That's when he started to get a bad feeling."

Will felt as if he were hearing the details Lipton had not provided. He pictured Ernesto and Víctor in this Pedro's place and imagined the fear they must have felt.

"Finally the truck stopped and they were told to get out. It was dark. Pedro didn't know where they were but he saw a group of low buildings, like storerooms or stables. There was a tall watchtower beyond the buildings, some oil drums. It didn't look like an army base, he said, and definitely wasn't a police station.

"Two soldiers dragged the injured guy away. The rest were led to one of the sheds and shoved into a cell. Like a stall, Pedro said, but with a concrete floor and walls. The soldiers turned out the lights, leaving them in complete darkness. That's when other prisoners started whispering through the vents. They wanted to know where the new men were from and why they were there. The old prisoners told them their names and pleaded for Pedro and the others to memorize them so that when they got out they could let their families know they were still alive. 'Where are we?' asked one of Pedro's friends. 'Colonia Dignidad,' said a man in the other cell."

Gabriela's eyes had grown wider as she told Will the story. She was leaning closer. Now she took a deep breath and, looking down, nervously fingered the cushion in her lap as if searching for any detail that she might have omitted.

"Ricardo, I know this place! It's between Chillán and Parral...a large finca run by a bunch of fanatics! My boss Beto once tried to write a story about them. They claim to be some kind of religious group but Beto says they're more like Nazis. They came from Germany after the war, at least the leaders did."

"Fine, but Gabi—"

"No, but here's the most important thing," she interrupted, lowering her voice to a whisper and clutching Will's hand. "One of the prisoners said there was a man in his cell who was unconscious. He'd been badly beaten the night before. This man said the unconscious man's name was Ernesto, from Chillán!"

Gabriela looked at Will. Her face was taut with certainty.

"Colonia Dignidad isn't far from where Ernesto's car was found. It *must* be him, locked up just like these men. Unconscious!"

For a brief moment Will wondered if it could be true, if Lipton could be wrong, but he shook his head. "Why? It could be anyone."

"Why not? For speeding. For being such a big mouth. How should I know?"

"But all you have is a flimsy story Alonso heard from this Pedro about some guy possibly named Ernesto."

"It's him, I feel certain! We have to go there."

"And do what?"

"Show them that we know. Demand his release."

"Gabi, don't you think you're being rash?"

"Ricardo, we're talking about my brother. We have to go there…as soon as possible."

Gabriela's passion filled him with sadness and desire. He wanted to believe she was right and Lipton was wrong. He should tell her everything now in order to put a stop to this impetuous notion. But where would he begin? The things he needed to say seemed overwhelmingly complex. And yet, one single truth led to every other: Gabi, My name isn't Richard Allen. It's Will Porter… I don't work for First Republic. I work for the CIA… I helped make the coup happen… And that can't be Ernesto because…

All the other deceptions seemed trivial compared to this one about Ernesto. But the thought of losing her after such an admission threw him into turmoil. Fear overcame him whenever he prepared to tell her. Wouldn't it be easier, wasn't it possible to maintain the lie?

Unable to conquer his fear, and unnerved by Gabriela's determination, Will nodded as if he agreed.

A moment later a door closed down the hallway and Gabriela's mother came into the room. Like teenagers caught necking, Will and Gabriela jumped up from the couch together. Ema de Manning seemed surprised to see him and wrapped her cardigan sweater more tightly around herself. Her face was drawn as if she had not slept in days.

"Don Ricardo, did you hear? My Ernesto's missing!"

Will nodded. Señora Ema looked absently around the room.

"I was looking for a cigarette," she said, lifting the lid of an enamel box on the table and closing it with frustration. Will offered her one of his. She already held a matchbook in her hand and lit the cigarette before he could draw his lighter.

"I just got off the phone with Father Patricio," she said to Gabriela. "He will ask the Monsignor to make some inquiries." She looked at Will. "Could the American embassy assist us? I don't know how, but…"

"I've already asked," Will said. He didn't know what else to say.

"Thank you," Señora Ema said, exhaling the smoke in a long sigh, too preoccupied to notice that Will was holding Gabriela's hand.

26

*G*abriela was too wound up to think straight. She wanted to drive to Parral that night until Will reminded her of the curfew. At the base of the wrought iron stairs leading to Ernesto's room, in the shadows of the interior patio, they kissed. The furtive embrace aroused him. "Come upstairs with me," he whispered.

Gabriela pulled away.

"I can't...not here, not now." Then, smiling sadly at Will's frustrated expression, she rewarded him with another kiss, this one light and swift. "My angel. I don't know what I would have done without you here." She placed her hand to his cheek. "Good night, my love."

Will watched her steal down the hallway, then he climbed the spiral stairs to the second story and entered Ernesto's room. Everything was in its place: the twin beds, the posters and photographs, the books, the ashtray on the desk, the clothes in the closet. He thought he'd steeled himself, but he wasn't prepared for the shock of seeing Ernesto's personal things. Though he didn't believe in ghosts, the room felt haunted. He undressed quickly, turned out the light and tried to go to sleep.

The next morning they told Gabriela's mother they were going riding. To carry out their ruse they put Gabriela's riding boots and helmet in the trunk of Will's car.

Gabriela sat next to him on the bench seat, navigating. Both dressed in blue jeans and sweaters, they might have been a young married couple out for a day of shopping or a holiday drive. He couldn't resist putting his arm around her. Gabriela attempted a smile, but her thoughts were clearly elsewhere. He took his arm away to make the turn onto the Pan-American Highway.

"We need to figure out what we're going to do," he said, anxious to know what she was thinking. Unable to sleep the night before, he had wrestled with his own ideas. The details of Lipton's account about Ernesto's arrest were too accurate to be a case of mistaken identity. But could Lipton have gotten part of the story wrong? Will dismissed the idea that Lipton had misled him intentionally, maliciously. But going back and forth over Gabriela's story, he had to admit there were some extraordinary coincidences. Could Ernesto still be alive? His head said no, but he would never forgive himself if it were true and he talked her out of going to her brother's aid. And if she was wrong? What then would this journey into the lion's den reveal? Ernesto's murder? His lies?

"If Ernesto is there, we have to find him and make sure he's all right," she replied.

"Yes, but how?" registering the clipped edge to his voice.

"I don't know."

They crossed over the Ñuble River and in half an hour were passing through the pueblo of San Carlos. After multiple trips from Santiago the way was now familiar. At the Perquilauquen River a road sign announced they were in Linares Province.

"Slow down. I think this is it," she said as they came to an unmarked intersection with a gravel road. "Yes, turn here." Her voice swelled with emotion.

A shiver ran down Will's spine as he steered toward the mountains. Determined for now to live with his deceptions, he risked jeopardizing everything to be with her on this fool's mission.

The road followed the river, which sluiced white over rapids and spread in multiple channels around gravelly sand bars. The mountains rose dramatically in front of them, layers of peaks crusted with snow. At higher elevations a spring snowstorm had dusted the evergreens, yet down in the valley the trees were bright green with new growth and the grass bent with seed.

Will had expected the colony to be closer to the highway. They drove for several miles toward the cordillera, and saw fewer and fewer signs of civilization. A dust plume eddied behind them, swallowing the road. No cars came from the other direction. It was as if they were alone in a beautiful desolate world.

Ten minutes later they saw a steel arch over the road with "Colonia Dignidad" in iron letters welded to it. A galvanized steel gate rested open, and the tires zinged over a cattle grate as they passed underneath the archway. A barbed wire fence ran along the edge of the property, extending uphill as far as the eye could see and downhill toward the banks of the river.

"Friendly looking place," he said. Past the gate they came to a fork in the road. A hand-painted sign nailed to a tree read: "Restaurante/Clínica" with an arrow pointing to the right, along the river.

Will slowed down and raised his hand in inquiry.

"Follow the sign, I guess," Gabriela said.

"People actually come out here to eat?"

Around the next curve the road opened into a wide pastoral valley with planted fields of corn and sorghum. A sparkling blue lake fringed with trees framed the distant end of the valley. They drove down an arrow-straight lane lined with plane tress whose branches canopied the road in pleasant dappled shade. The lane ended at a small town square dominated by a gabled building with a wide porch supported by rough-hewn timbers. Shutters carved with Bavarian motifs framed the upper windows, and flowerboxes overflowed with purple and white pansies.

Opposite the restaurant was a plain wooden building with "Clínica" inscribed on the lintel above the door. Several one-story buildings of indeterminate usage, an open structure covering farm equipment and stacked hay bales, and a white clapboard chapel filled out the square. The place reminded Will of the little towns tucked away in remote parts of Arizona, vestiges of long forgotten mining booms, that now barely survived on the needs of the local cattle ranches.

"Unbelievable," he said as he parked in front of the restaurant.

"I told you." Gabriela opened and closed her purse. If she was looking for something she didn't find it.

"What do we do now? I don't see a police station."

Gabriela ran her hand through her hair and contemplated the quiet front of the restaurant. A dun-colored mongrel slept soundly in a patch of sun on the porch, paws dangling off the edge. In one window they could see the silhouettes of two patrons. The front door was open but a screen door prevented them from seeing inside.

"What time is it?"

Will looked at his watch: "Almost eleven."

"Let's go in and order something. Maybe we can learn more there."

They went into the restaurant. The people in the window turned out to be the waiter and a female cook. Both appeared startled by the presence of customers. The waiter, wearing a loden green vest, stood up and guided them to a rustic wooden table with heavy benches instead of chairs. The cook quickly disappeared through saloon doors into the kitchen.

"The special of the day is pastel de choclo," the waiter said, handing them each a handwritten menu.

"This can't be the place," Will said after the waiter had gone into the kitchen. "Alonso or his brother must have been wrong. It doesn't make any sense."

"Appearances can be deceiving," Gabriela said, over the menu.

"Yes, they can," he acknowledged.

He ordered the special and was surprised how good it was, like a shepherd's pie topped with a corn meal crust instead of mashed potatoes and containing large pieces of chicken, olives, egg, carrots and peas.

"The taste reminds me of green corn tamales when they're in season," he said, then realized he'd let slip a detail from his real past, not the fictional one of his Wisconsin cover. Gabriela would never know it, and yet the slip gave him pause.

Gabriela took two bites of her pastel and left the rest. "I'm too nervous to eat," she said.

They saw nothing unusual from the restaurant. After lunch, they walked across the square and peered through the glass door of the clinic. A wizened nurse at the front desk looked up, startled to see two faces pressed against the glass. She came to the door. "May I help you?"

"Do you have a patient named Ernesto Manning?" Gabriela asked.

The nurse gave them a wary look and shook her head. "This is a day clinic."

They went back into the hot noon sun. The dusty square was deserted. A man in a loose blue shirt steered an old rust-colored tractor across a nearby field. His baggy shirt flapping like a flag, he drove up a curving dirt road over the ridge and disappeared. More buildings stood along the crest of the hill beside a wooden water tower. There was no sign of soldiers or prisoners. Gabriela sighed as if conceding defeat.

They got into the car and started back toward the highway. At the fork in the road Gabriela said, "Ricardo, stop! The water tower!" She looked up the other road that curved uphill to the northeast. It looked less used but appeared to lead toward the buildings they had seen on the ridge. "Up there!"

He thought he'd dissuaded her. Reluctantly, Will turned the car around. The side road was not as well graded as the one to the square. In several places spring rains had washed it out. The Falcon dipped and bounced over the rough patches. Will kept to the ruts and tall spring grass swished against the car's chassis. Around a curve they came to a chain across the road that prevented them from going any farther. They didn't notice the small guardhouse on the left in the shade of a large oak tree until the guard approached. Will started to back up.

The guard was young and dressed in green fatigues and sauntered toward the car. He wore no helmet or insignias to indicate that he was anything but a guard for the colony. His shirt was unbuttoned to the waist but Will noticed a pistol holstered at his right hip. Will flagged his attention.

"We were at the restaurant and saw the lake. We were hoping to reach it this way. Can you let us through?"

"This area is closed to the public. The lake is private property."

"Oh...too bad," Will said, smiling. "We just wanted to take a look and come right back. No chance of letting us through?"

The guard was neither amused nor interested in further conversation. He spun his finger in a circle to indicate that Will needed to turn around. Without waiting to see if Will obeyed, he returned to the shade of the tiny guardhouse and plopped down on an aluminum lawn chair.

As Will slowly backed up, Gabriela grew animated, turning sideways to face him. "Ricardo, this must be it," she whispered, her voice full of bottled energy. "What can we do?"

"Nothing, Gabi."

"But if Ernesto's here that must be where they are keeping him."

"That guy was not interested in debating the point. And by the way, he had a gun."

The Falcon shimmied as they crossed the last washout before reaching the fork in the road.

"But we can't do nothing. Please stop!" She opened the door.

Will braked. "Gabi, what are you doing?"

"I'm going to walk there."

"Gabi—no. It's too dangerous. If these guys are soldiers, they aren't messing around. You saw that kid. He looked about sixteen."

"I don't care." She stepped out of the car and knelt down to tie her shoelace. The more she resisted, the more he admired her determination.

"Wait!" Will said. He pulled the car off the road and got out. If there was ever a time to tell her the truth about Ernesto and, consequentially, about himself, it was now. "Wait, Gabi." Still he hesitated, hoping to dissuade her instead. "Listen, if we can get close enough to look around and still don't see anything, will you promise to give this up and come back to the car?"

She gave him a petulant look, the dark eyebrows drawn together. He had never seen her look quite so fierce or so beautiful. He couldn't tell if she was angry at him for trying to stop her or at not knowing the fate of her brother. Will reached for her hand and she started to cry. Her legs collapsed underneath her and she dropped cross-legged to the ground. She wiped away her tears and her chest heaved.

"You don't understand. I need to know that my brother is all right."

"I know," he said, helping her up and holding her. "I know," he repeated with tenderness. The top of her head smelled of fresh air and sunshine. "Look, what if we go up to the ridge and look around."

Still struggling to compose herself, she nodded.

A low cattle fence blocked their ascent. Will gingerly pressed down on the top strand of barbed wire and helped Gabriela climb over. They clambered up the slope, clutching at the branches of shrubs and the trunks of trees for support, careful to angle away from the road and the guardhouse.

"Gabi, I haven't wanted to say this," he said, panting from

the climb, "but it's not good that you haven't heard anything from Ernesto."

"Think I don't know that?"

"Yes, but—"

"Halt!"

Four soldiers dressed in green fatigues descended from the ridgeline, M14 rifles held at the ready. Will noticed corporal stripes on the sweat-stained sleeve of the one who had shouted the command. Like a Saturday matinee cowboy during a stickup, Will instinctively raised his hands to show he was unarmed. Gabriela defiantly brushed the hair from her face. Her canvas sneakers fought for traction on the rocky slope.

The four soldiers circled so closely that the two captives could neither step backward nor forward. The brim of the young corporal's pillbox cap came close to Will's face. Sunglasses obscured his eyes. Too late Will realized they should have prepared a story for this eventuality. He decided to make one up and trust Gabriela to follow his lead.

"Hi, we were looking for a secluded spot…you know…" He smiled and hoped his tone and raised eyebrows expressed sufficient lust that the young soldier would understand. But the corporal remained serious. No smile. The other soldiers stood silent as stone.

"You were told not to enter this area," the corporal said. "You are trespassing." The patrol must have watched from the ridge as the Falcon stopped at the guardhouse. "Your identification, please."

For a split second Will considered challenging the soldiers' authority but decided against it. His passport was in his briefcase in the trunk of the car so he slowly lowered one hand and reached for his wallet. He took out the Wisconsin driver's license. "I'm an American," he said. The guard studied the foreign license then turned to Gabriela.

"It's in my purse," she said. "In the car."

"Down to the car," the corporal ordered. Two soldiers led the way with Will and Gabriela, holding hands for balance, sliding behind them. The corporal and the third soldier brought up the rear.

At the car, the corporal ordered one of his men to retrieve Gabriela's purse from the front seat and told Will to open the trunk.

"What right do you have to search my car?"

Challenging the corporal's authority was the wrong thing to do. The corporal jutted his chin toward one of his men, who shoved Will against the car with his rifle. Will surrendered the keys.

The soldier searched the trunk, finding Gabriela's riding clothes on top of Will's knapsack and briefcase, and the red gas can with several dirty rags on top of the spare tire. He rifled through the knapsack and the corporal instructed him to open the briefcase.

"It's locked," Will said.

"Then unlock it," the corporal responded.

Will turned the combination.

"Now stand back," demanded the corporal. Will did as he was told. The soldier opened the case and sifted through its contents: a roadmap, an issue of *Time*, a spiral notebook. He tossed each item into the well of the trunk as he searched. Will's passport was tucked in the sleeve on the lid flap. The soldier removed it and closed the case.

The other soldier handed Gabriela's driver's license to the corporal.

"I demand to know if you are holding Ernesto Manning under arrest. He is my brother and I have a right to know."

So much for continuing the ruse about a romantic tryst in the woods. Gabriela's brash statement had laid bare Will's lie. If they weren't in trouble before, they were now.

The corporal unhooked a walkie-talkie from his bandolier. He pushed a button and spoke softly into the mouthpiece as if he were whispering into his lover's ear. Through crackling static a voice responded in disjointed words. The corporal requested a truck.

They didn't bother with handcuffs or restraints. Will and Gabriela were sandwiched between two soldiers in the back seat of the Yagán, a hard-topped jeep-like vehicle. The corporal sat beside the driver with Will's briefcase and Gabriela's purse at his feet. The fourth soldier balanced on the passenger-side running board, holding on for dear life.

Will gave Gabriela's hand a gentle squeeze, in part to reassure her but also to deter her from saying anything to make matters worse. He needed to come up with a plan, a story, but was drawing a blank. As the truck bounced up the road toward the low buildings he studied the faces of the soldiers. Could one of these kids have been responsible for Ernesto's death? There was nothing in their sleepy expressions to indicate such capacity for violence. One wore a teenager's faint attempt at a moustache. The other, full lipped and round-faced, had a smattering of acne on his cheeks.

The Yagán pulled up to the front of a long concrete blockhouse with a corrugated steel roof. The windowless building stood in sharp profile against the bright blue sky. Will squinted from the noonday glare as he climbed from the back seat. A soldier pointed toward the building.

Will entered ahead of Gabriela and his eyes took a moment to adjust. Slowly the room emerged, stark gray, with a rough concrete floor and block walls. The outer room led to another behind it. A wide wooden door on the back wall of the inner room was closed and padlocked. A wood stove stood in the corner, its sooty door ajar. There was a metal desk and chair in the middle of the first room and a wooden bench against the wall. Behind the desk stacked crates rose to the low ceiling.

A soldier pointed to the bench, told them to sit and stood facing them with his rifle at the ready. Outside, the other soldiers stood at ease, huddled in conversation. Suddenly, all stiffened to attention and saluted. An officer wearing a camouflage uniform entered with the corporal. The young soldier inside saluted. The officer ignored it, his attention drawn to Will and Gabriela.

He was a handsome man with a heavy beard and a head of thick dark hair closely cropped to the scalp. Lean and broad shouldered, he reminded Will of a varsity wrestler he'd known in high school whose name he couldn't now remember.

"Good day. I am Captain Salazar of the Military Police. The corporal informs me that you were found trespassing. This property is restricted to the army. Under the circumstances these are serious charges. Who are you and what are you doing here?"

He stood in front of them, arms akimbo, his right hand resting on top of the holster attached to a wide black leather belt. His gray-green eyes were intense and direct. The half-smile was neither friendly nor reassuring, more like a gesture of civility.

Before Will could respond, Gabriela was speaking with defiant anger. "We are looking for my brother, Ernesto Manning. We believe you are keeping him here illegally."

The captain's jaw clenched as he looked down at Gabriela with a bold gaze, almost of admiration.

"Don't tell me what I can or can't do, Señorita. What is your name?"

"You have my driver's license. Gabriela Manning Hernández."

The captain disregarded Gabriela's insolence. "And you?" looking at Will.

"Richard Allen. I'm her fiancé." He did not dare glance Gabriela's way to see how she reacted to this statement.

"Norteamericano?"

"Yes."

"Why won't you tell me if my brother's here?" Gabriela interrupted.

The captain turned his head very slowly and stared at Gabriela. "Private," he said to the soldier standing behind him. "Remove her."

The soldier forced Gabriela up by the arm.

"Ricardo—" she said, resisting as he shoved her out the door.

Will was too stunned to speak. Why had they taken her away? Where? What if she challenged them again? Would they hit her? Were they capable of worse?

"Listen, Gabriela is my fiancée, and if you do anything to harm her I will report you to the American embassy. I am an American citizen. I work for an American company and have every legal right to be in Chile."

"Perhaps, but you don't have the right to be on this property, Señor…" The captain circled around the desk and glanced at Will's passport, "Señor Allen. Now, are you going to tell me what you were doing here?" He sat down on the corner of the desk and exhaled loudly, telegraphing his impatience.

"We didn't know this was a restricted area. My fiancée is telling the truth. We were looking for her brother. We heard that he might have been detained here."

"Yes, her brother…" Captain Salazar pretended to search for the name, testing Will's corroboration of Gabriela's story.

"Ernesto Manning," Will said.

If the captain recognized the name, his face did not reveal it.

"And why would he be detained here? This is a military unit. We conduct training exercises."

Will assessed the captain's position. If Ernesto died in their custody, the captain surely knew. But he didn't know that Will knew.

"It's something she heard. Her brother was arrested near Parral."

"Is he a Communist?"

"No."

"Is your girlfriend a Communist?"

"No."

"Are you a Communist, Señor Allen?"

"Of course not."

"What is the name of your company?"

"First Republic Insurance Group. My business cards are in my briefcase."

Captain Salazar motioned to the corporal who called to one of the soldiers outside. A moment later the soldier brought in Will's briefcase and opened it on the desk. The false bottom had been torn apart.

"Yes, we found the gun and the money," Captain Salazar said, closing the lid. "Now, would you like to tell me what you are really doing here? If we don't get the truth from you, we can always ask your fiancée."

It was the slightest of threats spoken matter-of-factly. Panic gripped Will's heart. If he had been alone he might have continued to defend against their intimidation, but with Gabriela in the equation he decided without another moment's hesitation on a more certain course. He needed to act swiftly. They could be doing something horrible to Gabriela as they spoke.

"May I speak to you in private?"

The captain assessed the change in Will's tone. Sensing victory, he told the corporal to wait outside. After the corporal left he looked at Will expectantly.

"Captain, I need you to keep confidential what I'm about to tell you. At least until you verify it. But, will you promise me that Gabriela will not be harmed? Can I trust you?" He was hardly in a position to negotiate terms.

"Of course," Captain Salazar said, no doubt agreeing only to keep him talking. To tell more was a calculated risk, but Will inhaled and took it.

"I work for the U.S. government. For certain reasons," and here he glanced down at the dusty concrete floor, "I'm not attached to the embassy. But you can confirm what I'm telling you by contacting Mr. Ed Lipton at the embassy in Santiago."

"I see. And if you work for the embassy, what are you doing here?" Captain Salazar asked skeptically. Will had to ponder for a moment.

"Gabriela asked for my help. She heard about this place from someone else and would have come on her own. I wanted to prevent her from doing something foolish, to protect her. I love her very much." His face flushed and his heart was racing but he didn't care. He felt a great relief for having finally released the truth. By breaking cover he regained himself.

"I see. All for love, is that it?"

As Will had expected, Captain Salazar seemed more amused than convinced by the confession, so he added, "I also know what really happened to her brother and another man named Víctor Maragall." Captain Salazar blinked but there was no sign of recognition or acknowledgement of complicity. "Gabriela doesn't know any of what I have just told you. About my work, and especially about her brother."

The captain lifted his chin and smiled as if he had just solved a riddle. He stood up and went to the door. He spoke briefly to the corporal, who saluted and trotted away. The captain came back into the room. The toes of his heavy black boots were covered in fine white dust.

Joe Borgia—the name suddenly came to Will, the high-school wrestler of whom the captain reminded him.

"Please write down the name of this person who can confirm your story," the captain said. "It will take some time to verify what you have said. We don't have a telephone here. Only a radio."

The captain's collegial treatment more than the confession caused Will to shudder. As he printed "Ed Lipton, Political Officer, U.S. Embassy, Santiago" on the piece of paper he suddenly felt chilled and feverish.

"Now will you bring Gabriela back, please? I want to know she's all right."

Captain Salazar said, "As soon as we have confirmed your statement."

On Columbus Day, Ed Lipton was at home watching a televised football match. Colo-Colo's Snow Whites (the light jerseys) against the University of Chile's Blues (the dark jerseys). Colo-Colo was ahead 2-1 and Lipton was elated because he had a hundred bucks riding on the outcome: the Snow Whites by one goal. But there were still fifteen minutes of play.

It had been a long time since he'd spent an afternoon at home. Because of the holiday, the city was deathly quiet. People were at home or in the parks or at the beaches with their families. The free time left him feeling uneasy. Too much time to dwell on the way the top brass had treated them, to ponder the state of his career, to be tempted to call Renata. As long as the game was on he was fine, but as soon as it was over he would need to go somewhere, a hotel bar, a whorehouse, anywhere, or the stillness would get to him. But for now he was good, drinking a beer and enjoying the fresh breeze puffing out the drapes through the open balcony door. From the roars and cheers in his neighbor's apartment he could tell they were rooting for the Blues. If only politics were as simple.

The telephone rang. Annoyed at the timing, he put down his beer and got up to answer it. He assumed it was Bill Bradshaw, who had talked about having a barbecue that weekend, or that arrogant asshole Pete Nolan, who had the audacity to suggest a poker game after royally fucking them over. He was momentarily disadvantaged when the voice on the other end said in Spanish, "Hello Eduardo. I'm not disturbing you at a bad time, am I?" It took Lipton a second to recognize Colonel Covarrubias' voice.

"Felipe, is that you? To what do I owe the pleasure?"

"I'm afraid we have a matter that requires your attention."

"Oh?" The Blues' midfielder stole the ball from the Snow Whites' forward and was charging down the field.

"Yes, I was contacted by one of my captains today, in Linares." The midfielder passed the ball to his forward who was undefended in front of the goal.

"Yes?" The Colo-Colo goalkeeper dove to block the forward's kick, deflecting it out of bounds. It would be the Blues' ball.

"It seems they have detained an American who claims to work for you. A person by the name of Richard Allen."

At mention of the name Lipton turned away from the TV even though the two teams were setting up for the corner kick. He pressed his lips together and held his breath, counting to ten.

"He said to contact you," the colonel continued.

The idiot had blown his cover. Lipton felt his ears pop.

"Detained? What for? Linares, did you say?" What the hell was Will doing there?

"He was caught trespassing on one of our top-security bases. With a girl named...Gabriela Manning, from Chillán. I take it you know him."

Now Lipton understood completely: A hound dog chasing a bitch in heat. "Afraid I do."

"Yes, well...this is most unfortunate, as you know," said the colonel as a loud cheer rose from the neighbor's apartment. Lipton dared not look at the TV.

"Yes, I do." Neither he nor Colonel Covarrubias wanted to deal with this embarrassing situation. It was one thing to have embassy personnel doing intelligence work. The Chileans were willing to turn a blind eye to that. But uncovering a NOC was another story. Young Will was going home, or somewhere, but he wasn't staying in Chile. "I apologize that this problem has occurred, Felipe. And I sincerely appreciate the fact that you took the time to call me personally. What can we do to remedy the situation?"

Conceding authority was the right tactic even though it irked Lipton to suck up to the prick.

"Yes, yes, yes, of course," the colonel said, making noises of pacification. "Here's what I suggest then. We will release the young man. The girl, too, I suppose. But give me your word that he will be out of the country by the end of the month. It's unfortunate, but I have no choice in the matter. We can no more allow a foreign agent to operate within our borders than you could in the United States."

"That's very generous of you, Colonel."

"Then I take it we have a gentlemen's agreement?"

"We do."

"Very good, Eduardo. Let's put this matter behind us as quickly and as quietly as we can."

The match was over. The Blues had tied Colo-Colo with a penalty kick.

Lipton assessed the damage. He could put Will on a plane to Montevideo on Monday if necessary. From there they could transition his agents and shut down any compromised operations. As he thought through the consequences, Lipton's anger grew into a fury. There were bank accounts, financial ledgers and operating cash to consider. Not to mention the lost opportunities and being down one man. He'd have to notify Bill, and the ambassador. Hell, let Bill do that. But he'd have to notify Langley and Cal Jacobs, the Station Chief in Montevideo. The idiot better have a damn good explanation for fucking up like this or his career is finished.

And if he's fucked up *my* chances for getting out of here, Lipton concluded, I'll finish it for him.

27

*W*ill found the envelope as he entered his apartment late Sunday afternoon. Left blank, he knew who had slipped it under the door. Inside was a blunt note in an angry scrawl: *Call me immediately—L.*

On the long drive home from Chillán he had gone through cycles of elation and dread. Now, he simply felt exhausted and was suffering from a severe headache the likes of which he'd never experienced before. Is this a migraine? he wondered, feeling sick to his stomach. Although it was only four in the afternoon, he went to his bedroom, drew the curtains and tried to sleep through the piercing pain.

Captain Salazar had kept his word, more or less. After five anxious hours, he came back into the room where Will was being held and returned his briefcase, including the money and the gun.

"One more thing, Señor Allen," the captain said before escorting him outside, "The incident with your fiancée's brother was an unfortunate accident. The young man brought it on himself. Nevertheless, it was most unfortunate. Do you understand?"

Will thought he was going to be sick. The captain was confirming his worst fear, but he managed to breathe through his disgust and nod.

Outside, Gabriela was standing beside the car, loosely guarded by the soldier with the wispy mustache. Will felt dazed by the sunlight and his guilt. The corporal handed the car keys to the captain, who turned to face the two detainees.

"Since your police records are clean, we are letting you go. But understand this: If you are ever found trespassing on this property again or attempt to interfere with military operations in any way, you will face the severest penalties." He paused then addressed Gabriela directly, "I don't know what you heard about your brother, Señorita, but he is not being held here. I suggest you check with the Carabineros."

Will was sickened by the performance. The captain handed the keys to him with complicit silence.

"Corporal, escort them off the property."

The first wave of dread came as they headed back to Chillán. Gabriela's face glowed with excitement, as if the captain's statement had freed her from the immediate worry about Ernesto: hope cruelly springing from a lie.

"They didn't do anything to you, did they?" Will asked. "I was so afraid when they took you away."

"No. They took me to another room and locked the door. I just sat there and waited by myself. I was afraid for you. What did they do?"

"Nothing really. Asked a few questions. I told them I was an American and you were my fiancée and that I'd report them to the embassy if they harmed you in any way."

Gabriela smiled bashfully. Will wondered what he had said to cause her reaction then smiled, too. They drove silently for a while.

"I meant it, Gabi. I want to marry you. Being held there, I realized how much I love you."

Gabriela slipped closer on the seat and stroked the back of his head. "See, you are my guardian angel after all."

He took this as an acceptance and smiled. He asked her to light him a cigarette. She lit one of his Marlboros with the car lighter and placed it between his lips. She followed this with a light kiss on his cheek. The tobacco tasted sweet and lubricated his mouth. He was relishing the first hit of nicotine when the dread struck again, the complexity of the untold truth and the recognition that they had only been released because Lipton must have confirmed his statement. Fuck it, Will thought, too enraptured by his newfound happiness to dwell in shadows.

But the dread returned in full when Will called Lipton at home Sunday night.

"You better have a fucking good reason for this. Meet me at my office tomorrow at 9:00 a.m."

"You mean the Hotel Rincón?"

"Not much need for secrecy now, is there?" Lipton scoffed.

The next morning Will took the elevator to the seventh floor reception area of the embassy, a waiting room with rows of chairs already crowded with clients. Will showed his passport to the marine behind the plate glass window and asked for Ed Lipton. In the year since his arrival he had been to the embassy only once, when he registered his name and address as any other American living in country would.

"Someone will be down to get you, Mr. Allen," the guard said after speaking on the phone.

A few minutes later a middle-aged secretary in a green jumper and yellow short-sleeved blouse came for him.

She waved her security badge at the guard and took Will up the stairwell to the next floor. Will followed her brisk stride down a corridor past several secretaries' desks and a coffee station to a row of offices. Lipton's office was in the middle across from a room barred by a steel fire door and guarded by a sentry. The secretary poked her head into the office. "Mr. Allen is here."

Will entered and the woman closed the door behind him. Lipton was seated at his desk with an open file, a scowl on his face.

"Sit down." He didn't stand up. He closed the file then placed his elbows on the desk and cupped his hands in front of his mouth. Venetian blinds cut long diagonal shadows across the desk and Lipton's face. His eyes were slits.

"You lied to me. You've been banging this chick all along and you never admitted it." Will started to protest but Lipton didn't let him. "You've compromised yourself and a whole bunch of operations all for the sake of some pussy."

"I haven't compromised anything." Will had rehearsed what he was going to say, starting with an apology, but Lipton's attack changed everything. "The only person who knows is that captain I spoke to and whoever he spoke to."

"You think? Christ, Will, are you that fucking stupid?"

Will bit his tongue. It was like talking to his father after he'd had too much to drink. There was no reasoning, only violent spewing anger.

"So you think you can just carry on. 'Oh, so sorry to be spying on your country, Captain So-and-so. So sorry, Colonel Such-and-Such.' What the hell were you thinking? And what the hell were you doing?"

Will felt his face flush. All of the bottled anger over Ernesto's death poured out as rage.

"First of all, it's not what you think. The reason we were there was because Gabriela found out that's where her brother was taken. And now, you tell me, why was he taken there, Ed? And how did they know he was gay, Ed?" He was unable to hide his contempt for Lipton any longer. "I didn't lie to you any more than you lied to me by not telling me you were feeding my reports to your MILINTEL pals."

Attacking Lipton was the wrong approach, as Will quickly saw.

"Who the fuck are you to tell me what to do? You've violated your oath and jeopardized a whole shitload of operations."

"Yeah, like what? Handing out money to strikers against orders?"

Will thought he saw Lipton's gray eyes flinch at the accusation. But his boss responded with the cool command that comes with power.

"They've generously given you until the end of the month to leave the country. But right now I'm inclined to put you on a plane back to the States tonight."

The threat had its effect. Startled by the verdict, Will envisioned being sent home as persona non-grata before he could even explain to Gabriela what had happened. He exhaled and held up his hands in concession.

"Look, this isn't the way I meant to come in here. I'm sorry. I know you're just doing your job and that I screwed up." He pressed his thumbnail into the flesh of his index finger. "I haven't compromised anything except my own situation. And that really doesn't matter because I've already made a decision. I'm going to resign."

"Yeah? And do what?" Though less belligerent than a moment ago, Lipton's tone was hardly friendly.

"I'm not sure exactly." The last thing he was willing to do was admit to Lipton that he was in love with Gabriela. He would not subject his deepest emotions to this man's sneering cynicism. "I just know that I'm not cut out for this work…"

Will rubbed his lips. His mouth was dry. He could have used a cigarette. Was Lipton bluffing about having to leave the country?

He had planned to inform Lipton that he wanted to leave the agency and stay in Chile. If he couldn't continue to work for First Republic, there were other jobs, other contacts he'd made. Something would turn up. He would marry Gabriela and they would live in Santiago. He even hoped to keep his alias and cover documents. He wasn't sure how that worked but figured Lipton would know. Surely he wasn't the first person to leave the agency while under cover. He was going to create a new life.

"I thought I could do this job, but it turns out I can't." His heart pounded. "I need to start fresh, be something else. Find a new vocabulary…" He was confused. He sounded like Roland Fabré.

"A new vo-cab-u-lar-y?" Lipton said with derisive exaggeration. "Like what? Lemonade springs and the bluebird sings?"

Will regretted having said it. His eyes scanned the office. It was as impersonal as his own at First Republic. No photos, no trinkets. Humorless and hopeless. He did not want to become another Lipton.

"It's just that things made sense before and now they don't."

He had not meant to take the conversation into a critical or political direction but he had spoken before he could stop himself. Will smiled at Lipton's obvious confusion. "I didn't expect to feel so...I don't know, cold-blooded. Maybe I was naïve. But a lot of people got hurt here. And we did that."

Lipton's face brightened with comprehension.

"They would have gotten hurt anyway. Trust me. And maybe a whole lot more of 'em."

Not Ernesto, thought Will.

"Shit, Will, you can't bleed for every asshole who gets himself into trouble or you'll go nuts. It's a fucking cruel world."

"Maybe. But I never meant to make it worse."

Lipton smiled with apparent relish at the direction the conversation was headed: the political fight, the bleeding liberal fight, the generational fight.

"You saw what those Marxist bastards were up to. You've seen how quickly things get fucked up. We're at war, whether we like it or not."

Will was studying the scuffed wood grain on the front of Lipton's battered desk. He looked up but didn't respond.

"Don't tell me you'd rather stick your head in the sand? We've got to fight these assholes on all fronts because, believe it or not, they see us as a threat. Not because of ideology—that's just more bullshit—but because we are the richest, most powerful nation on earth. We could destroy them if we were so inclined and they know it. And they hate us for it. They want what we have. They want our power and they'll try to take us down to get it. It *is* that black and white, Will... A new vocabulary! Fuck yes! Let's call a spade a spade."

Will shook his head. "That's not what I'm talking about."

"Then what *are* you talking about?"

"Who I want to be. How I want to live. And it isn't the way I've been living."

Lipton regarded Will with a strange half-smile, a look of incredulity.

"Fuck, Will. I really don't know what you're talking about. Maybe you don't either. But if I were you, I wouldn't just quit. I can reassign you to Montevideo. Or go home if you like. You're due for some home leave anyway. Hell, take an analyst job at headquarters. But don't throw away your training and the experience you've gained here."

Will wondered if his quitting would somehow reflect negatively on Lipton. Why else did Lipton care if he quit? "I didn't come here to debate it. I've already made up my mind. Even if I have to leave the country, I'll come back as me."

Lipton stared at him for the longest time, chewing on the edge of a chapped lower lip.

"It's the girl, isn't it?"

Now Will grew defensive. He looked away from Lipton's firm gaze and refused to respond.

"Look, I'm the last person to chastise you for getting a little poontang," Lipton said, leaning forward in his rumpled gray suit and smiling with avuncular familiarity. "But you're making a big mistake if you're basing a career decision on it. I'm telling you."

It was so clear now. Will detested the man and everything he stood for—lies, cruelty, arrogance. "I don't see it that way," he managed to say.

"No, you wouldn't," Lipton said. "That's because you're thinking with your dick."

28

*I*t was hard for Gabriela not to look over her shoulder each time she left the house. Now that the army had her name, she felt as if she were under constant surveillance.

The Monday after her release, she asked Julia to go with her to Parral to recover the Citroneta. At the police station she inquired about Ernesto, but the officious sergeant who handed her the keys claimed to know nothing about the driver of the car, only where it had been found. This only increased her worry.

She decided to ask Beto if she could work part time, which meant telling him about Ernesto's disappearance. He told her to take whatever time off she needed. Then he confided that he was searching for a way under the new censorship restrictions to report on the disturbing tips coming from across the province— rumors of mutilated bodies floating in rivers, of mysterious flights over the ocean late at night, of screams from police cells, of morgues filled with unidentified bodies. Difficult to verify, little of this information was publishable even if the publisher allowed it, and Señor Girardi refused. Beto did what he could. He kept the reports in a special file locked in his desk drawer, hoping that some day he might connect the dots between the names of the missing and the rumors. He showed Gabriela his file and said he would include Ernesto's information.

"Why?" she asked, nearly in tears. "My brother isn't a Communist. He's never done anything to anyone."

On Wednesday, she arrived at work early and went through the unopened mail: more announcements of weddings, engagements, births, anniversaries, business events and grand openings, upcoming art exhibits, recitals and lectures. Ernesto had disappeared and the world was behaving as if nothing had happened.

She opened an envelope like the rest and was startled by its contents—a note carefully printed in pencil on a sheet of spiral notebook paper: "Call me. 02-235-7223. Víctor." Gabriela turned over the envelope. The letter was addressed to her, postmarked from Santiago, without a return address.

Certain Víctor would know where Ernesto was, she grew excited. She picked up the phone then returned it to its cradle. She looked around the office, suddenly conscious of how much could be overheard. Guillermo, the city reporter, was sitting across the room talking on the telephone. Mercedes, the typist, was clacking away on the ancient typewriter at the next desk. Armando was leaning over the production table doing something to the waxing machine.

Gabriela took the letter and went to Beto's office.

"Yes, my love?" Beto stood beside an open file drawer, preoccupied with his search. The pilled and ink-smudged cardigan sweater hung from his slouching shoulders.

Gabriela closed the door.

"Beto, look what I received this morning."

Beto shoved the file drawer shut and took the piece of paper from her.

"It's from a friend of my brother. He may have news."

"Have you called him?"

Gabriela shook her head. "Not yet. Do you think it's safe? Could it be a trap?"

Beto stubbed out his cigarette in a filthy ashtray and studied the letter. He scratched his sallow cheek, bristly with a two-day growth of beard.

"It's a Santiago number. Do you recognize it?"

Gabriela studied the number and shook her head.

"Call from here. They won't be able to trace it, except to the office."

Beto offered her his desk chair and slid the phone toward her. Gabriela dialed the number. The phone rang six or seven times. She was about to hang up when a man's soft voice answered.

"Víctor?"

"Who is calling?"

"Gabriela—" She was about to give her last name but Beto frantically waved his palm in front of her and shook his head.

"A friend," she said.

The man on the other end seemed to weigh the legitimacy of her claim.

"Just a minute." He put the phone down and Gabriela heard footsteps, hard heels on tile or concrete. A door banged and a moment later footsteps approached. Still no one came to the phone. "Hello?" Gabriela asked. More footsteps then the scraping sound of the receiver being lifted.

"Yes?"

"Víctor?"

"Gabriela?"

"I just got your letter. Where are you? Where's Ernesto?"

"I'm sorry but can you prove it's you? What is the name of your special game?"

"You mean, More True?"

Víctor became less guarded. "I'm sorry but you can't be too careful now. Are you alone?"

"Yes...no, not exactly. My boss is here. He's letting me use his office."

A pause as Víctor considered this. "Can you trust him?"

"Yes." Gabriela looked at Beto sitting on the other side of the desk, his soft brown eyes filled with glum curiosity. She smiled. "Yes, I do. But why all these precautions, Víctor? Where are you? Where's Ernesto?"

Gabriela heard Víctor shift the receiver then the scratchy click of a cigarette lighter.

"You don't know?" Another pause as he exhaled and her heart started to sink.

"Know what?"

"My God! Gabriela, Ernesto's dead."

She pressed her eyes shut as if to block out the words.

Víctor's voice wavered, which made it difficult to understand what he said next. "They killed him. It's my fault."

Gabriela fumbled with the receiver. Images of her brother and her mother flashed through her mind. She couldn't breathe. Like someone choking, she stared mutely at Beto, begging for help. He rushed around the desk and braced her shoulders just as her arms went limp. Beto picked up the receiver from the desk.

"This is Gabi's friend," he said. "We must call you back."

Gabriela tried to brush Beto's arm away and wildly grabbed for the receiver but he had already hung up. She buried her head in her arms, sobbing. Beto placed his hands on her shaking shoulders. Gabriela sat up, her face swollen with tears.

"Beto, he says my brother is dead." She could barely get the words out. She groaned and started to cry but the sounds came out as stammers. Beto held her by the shoulders. She felt dizzy and pushed the chair away from the desk. She needed to stand. She wiped her eyes on her sleeve. "I need to talk to him. My God, my God, what is Mamá going to do? My God, she'll die! Oh—" Her heart felt as if it were imploding. "I need to call him back."

"Are you sure? Shall I dial for you?"

She sniffled and nodded. Beto offered her his handkerchief. He dialed the number and handed her the phone. This time Víctor answered. He too had composed himself.

"Víctor, are you sure? You can't—"

Víctor spoke with deliberation.

"Gabriela, I was there. We were arrested in Parral. They took us to an army base in the middle of nowhere, tied us to chairs and beat the crap out of us. They said we were terrorists. They accused me of being MIR. 'We have a dossier on you,' they said." Víctor's voice faltered. It took him a few seconds to regain control of his breathing. "Ernesto started cursing them, saying they were full of shit. Then, four of them came in with hoods over their heads and threatened me with a tire iron. Ernesto went wild and wouldn't shut up. So they stripped him and beat him unconscious."

"But that doesn't mean he's dead."

Gabriela latched onto the glimmer of hope. Seeing brightness through the haze of her tears. The person lying unconscious in the cell next to Pedro's *must* be Ernesto. The captain must have lied.

Víctor's urgent whisper sliced through her fantasy. "Gabriela—I saw him!" He started to cry again.

Gabriela closed her eyes: Dear God, please let this be untrue.

"They made me watch. It was as if they knew who we were. As they beat him they called him 'queer' and 'fag.' And then, when he could no longer stand—I don't know how to tell you this—they…they sodomized him with a broom handle. He wasn't moving. They started hitting me again. I thought they were going to kill me, too. But an officer came in and stopped them. All of a sudden they were taking me to the infirmary and cleaning me up. They stitched and bandaged my cuts. As they were taking me back to the cell I—that's when I saw Ernesto's body on the floor. He was dead, Gabriela. I'm sure of it. I thought they were messing with me, playing sick games, and I prepared to be beaten again. I was ready to tell them anything, whatever they wanted to hear. I no longer cared. I expected to die. Instead that cunt of an officer came into the cell and said I was lucky. 'We found your name on a special list.'

"Lucky! They'd just made me watch them torture and kill the man I loved! The officer stuffed 500 escudos in my pocket and ordered his men to drop me at the bus station."

Gabriela's head was swimming. Nothing made sense. "What do you mean, a special list?"

"I don't know…" She could hear Víctor's panicked breathing. "I think it had something to do with Ricardo, the American."

"Ricardo?" Now she was utterly confused. She had not told a soul about Ricardo's proposal. She had kept it close to her heart, a tender new shoot of certainty for whenever the uncertainty of Ernesto's whereabouts became unbearable. "Why?"

"Because, I was working for him."

"What do you mean? Víctor, what are you saying?" A worm was gnawing at her heart. She could feel it nibbling at the edges of her nascent joy, the fragile green leaf being devoured slowly and completely. Everything she cherished—her brother, her lover, her hope.

Víctor's voice was barely audible. "It was me they wanted, not Ernesto. I'm certain of it…for what I'd been doing. They thought I was MIR."

"No, Víctor. I'm sorry, I can't—I have to go. I can't listen any more right now." She gave Beto a helpless look. Beto took the receiver from her, said something to Víctor, and hung up. He squeezed Gabriela's shoulder and said something in a kind tone but Gabriela was too devastated to comprehend.

By the end of their meeting Will and Lipton had come to an agreement. Lipton relented and gave him until the end of the month—a little more than two weeks—to wrap up his business. Will suspected it was in Lipton's best interest to make a smooth transfer of the operation. Will agreed to take his three-week home leave and while in the States meet with the personnel department in Langley. If he still wanted to resign after discussing his options with them, Lipton said, so be it.

Once the deal was settled, they spent the rest of the morning reviewing the status of Will's operations, almost like business as usual except Will felt a lightness of heart he had never experienced on the job before.

He had no intention of continuing to work for the agency, although he didn't tell Lipton this—one final deception to preserve a semblance of loyalty and mutual interest.

Will's only concern now was Gabriela. He'd have to tell her he was going away. He could blame his sudden departure on business. But not knowing when he would be back was more difficult to explain. And if he should have to return as Will Porter... He would cross that bridge when he came to it.

On Wednesday he received the sweetest letter from her, written the same day he'd left Chillán: "My Dearest Ricardo, You left only two hours ago and I miss you already! I can't believe what happened this weekend. You were so good to help me. I'm sorry I got you into trouble, and you were so brave trying to protect me. It makes me love you even more. By the way, I confess I took your blue shirt when I was getting my boots from the trunk of your car. Forgive me, but it smells like you and I will wear it to bed until I have you beside me again. Call me soon, my love."

He called that evening but Claudia answered. With unusual formality she said that Gabriela was out. He asked her to tell Gabriela he had called and that she could call him back any time that night. But she didn't.

The next day Will went to the office and told Leti that he was going home at the end of the month. He didn't mention that he might not return to the branch. There was no point in creating unnecessary concern over an unknown.

He spent the morning working on reconciliations in Lipton's ledger then hand-carried the safe's contents—ledgers, cash, documents and his gun—to the embassy and left them with Lipton. With the tools of his trade out of his hands he felt a sense of freedom and renewal. He returned to the office and called Roland Fabré, inviting him to lunch. The Frenchman might know someone who could give him a job if needed.

Le Figaro was still crowded when they met there at 2:00 p.m. Roland, looking relaxed and happy, was already seated at a table along the mirrored wall, sipping a kir cassis. Before Will could say anything, Roland announced that he had important news: his contract was ending and he was returning to France. Felicidad and he were set to leave before Christmas. Will expressed his heartfelt sadness, and then gave the Frenchman his own news.

"I'm engaged!"

"Splendid! Let's have some champagne to celebrate," Roland said.

The waiter, a young Chilean, brought a bottle of a local vintage to the table, explaining that they had no French champagne.

"Then, young man, you have no champagne," insisted Roland petulantly. "No matter," he said, indicating for the waiter to open the bottle. "Let's not allow one sour note to dampen an otherwise joyful occasion." They raised their glasses. "To Richard's new life of love."

"And to your safe journey home."

Too drunk to do much work for the rest of the afternoon, Will skimmed magazines looking for business opportunities. He read about Chile's improving debt service and growing dollar reserves. The IMF had already come to the aid of the junta and granted a loan. Economists predicted a bright future if the new government could control inflation. Exports showed the promise of returning to pre-1970 levels.

He left the office at six and rode down in a crowded elevator. As he pushed through the revolving door a wave of warm air scented with summer's promise hit his senses. He debated whether to walk or take the bus and decided it was a fine evening to walk. He would call Gabriela when he got home. On the way he would stop at the corner grocery store to buy dinner and tease Badinia about her boyfriends.

"Ricardo!"

He knew the voice instantly and turned.

Dressed in a gray windbreaker and his customary khaki pants, Víctor crossed the plaza toward him. Will smiled in disbelief. Instinctively he looked for Ernesto and felt again the terrible, implacable ache of remorse. He had so many questions for Víctor.

"I have something for you," Víctor said as he came near, his face unrevealing and the scar red as a fresh wound. He took his hand from his jacket pocket, raised a pistol and fired at point blank range.

29

*A*rnie Matlock, the Station's reports officer, liked to arrive at the embassy early and leave early. He delighted in being first to read the day's incoming cable traffic. On Friday morning Ed Lipton arrived at the embassy at seven-thirty. Arnie was waiting outside his office.

"You better see this." His tone was grim but his eyes betrayed excitement. Lipton took the handwritten telecon memo Arnie held in front of him.

At 11:30 the night before, the duty officer recorded a conversation with someone named Detective Morales from the Carabineros. Lipton skipped to the subject line: Amcit murdered in Santiago.

After reading the memo twice, the first thing he did was go into his office and start calling each of his six remaining case officers to alert them of a potential threat. Next, he called Bill Bradshaw at home.

"Shit. How'd it happen?" Bill asked.

"I don't know."

"Damn! Have you taken precautions?"

"Yes."

A long, heavy pause. "Christ, I never even met the kid... Any idea who did it?"

"No. We received a call from the Carabineros last night. I'll call this Detective Morales and find out what I can."

"Think blowing his cover had anything to do with it?"

"I'll let you know what I find out."

"Okay. You know the drill. It's a security breach until we learn otherwise. Let Langley know. I forget who runs Internal Investigations these days, but make sure you copy them."

"Right."

"Have you told the ambassador?"

"Not yet. I thought you…"

Bill heaved a heavy sigh. "Jiminy Cricket! Two weeks to go—just what he wants to hear." The ambassador's imminent departure had been announced on Monday, news that for Lipton was subsequently trumped by Bill's confidential advisement that he too was leaving. By Thanksgiving Bill planned to be back home taking his last polygraph in preparation for early retirement. Now he said, "Let me know if you need any help, Ed. And keep me informed. I should be in the office by ten."

"Will do."

"Oh, and Ed… This isn't a reflection on you."

"Right." But if it wasn't, why the hell did Bill have to say it?

Lipton introduced himself to Detective Morales as one of the embassy's consular staff. The detective was friendly and candid but sounded skeptical of resolving the case. They were treating the crime as a routine homicide. They had interviewed the witnesses, inspected the crime scene and scheduled an autopsy for that afternoon.

"Any sign of a political motive?"

"None that we know of."

"Since he was an American citizen, we'd like copies of your findings for our own report," Lipton said.

"Of course. We will be happy to cooperate. But please don't expect too much, Señor Lipton."

"What do you mean?"

The detective's voice was phlegmatic. "I currently have fifty-six, now fifty-seven, homicides that I am investigating personally, each with a family or a loved one or a person of influence asking me to expedite their particular case. Of course, I tell them I am doing just that. And of course, as a result of the workload, I am doing just the opposite... Fifty-seven cases, Señor Lipton! I simply want to be honest with you as one public servant to another. I will do what I can, but do not expect miracles."

Lipton's own investigation turned up little. On Monday he interviewed the office assistant at First Republic and Will's landlady, who mentioned Roland Fabré. The Frenchman was too upset to provide any useful information except that Will was engaged to Gabriela Manning.

Lipton reviewed Will's intelligence reports for clues then contacted Will's assets to reassure them. Girardi first, then Saavedra. He didn't know how to find Víctor Maragall.

Reluctantly, he called Colonel Covarrubias. The colonel had already been informed of the death. He expressed his condolences but sounded faintly relieved at the elimination of an unresolved problem. He, too, worried about a political motive and promised to apply pressure to the ongoing police investigation, in particular the ballistics analysis. "If it was extremists, we will both want to know. Wouldn't you agree, Eduardo?"

But Lipton was beginning to believe what Detective Morales suspected, that Will's murder was a random act of xenophobic violence.

However, to complete his investigation he still needed to interview Gabriela Manning. He telephoned and left her a message at home, but she didn't return his call. He wasn't surprised. In the space of two weeks the girl had been hit with her brother's disappearance and her fiancé's murder. Yet he needed to close the loop to finish his report for Langley. He decided to drive down to

Chillán. It meant an overnight trip, but it was worth it, if only to glimpse the girl who had seduced Will into breaking cover.

Lipton arrived in Chillán at four on Wednesday afternoon. He checked into the Hotel Isabel Riquelme across the street from the plaza de armas. The hotel was oversized with a worn and dated interior. The lobby's carpet felt tacky underfoot and the second-floor hallway smelled of cigarettes and cooking oil. From the hotel he telephoned the Mannings. The maid answered.

"This is Ed Lipton. I think I spoke to you earlier this week. I'm with the U.S. Embassy. Is Gabriela Manning available?"

"No, señor, she is at work."

"I see. What time does she usually return home?"

"Six or seven."

"Would you have her call me? I'm staying at the Hotel Isabel Riquelme."

"Here? In Chillán?"

"Yes. Room 216. Please tell her I'd like to speak to her about Richard Allen. It will only take a few minutes."

"I will give her your message. As soon as she returns."

Lipton went down to the empty bar. He heard voices behind a black padded door to the kitchen and waited, scanning the bottles lined up on glass shelves in front of a mirrored wall. He spied a new bottle of Jack Daniels on the second row then encountered his own tired face in the mirror and frowned.

The ambassador was leaving at the end of the month, then Bill... When would he get to leave this stinking country?

A dishwasher emerged from the kitchen carrying a stack of plates. "Oh, one moment," he said and retreated into the kitchen to shout to someone. A short, chinless man in a bulging white shirt and red vest strolled into the bar, wiping his hands on a dirty dishtowel.

"Jack Daniels, with ice."

The bartender moved slowly to fill the request. "Norteamericano?" he asked as he placed the drink on a cocktail napkin.

Lipton nodded. The bartender mused on this tidbit while he arranged glasses on a tray beneath the counter.

"Seems pretty quiet," Lipton said.

The bartender shrugged. "That's life in Chillán—practice for death."

Lipton acknowledged the witticism with a half-smile. He sucked on an ice cube. Was the remark a cynical commentary on the state of the country or simply a meaningless quip about small-town life? Given how indolent the bartender seemed and how dull the place, he decided on the latter. But the question made him wonder: Did this man vote for Allende? Does a bartender in Chillán care who's in power or if he even has a vote? And what did he think of the coup? Of the junta?

If asked, the bartender would surely give an evasive response. Politics had disappeared from the conversation in Chile. Resigned to not knowing the man's political views, and realizing he didn't really care, Lipton finished his drink. Good old Jack Daniels.

He did not hear back from Gabriela Manning, so at seven he decided to go to her house. He got directions from the front desk clerk and drove around the plaza past the modern cathedral onto a tree-lined residential street of large affluent homes. A few minutes later he found the house on the southwest corner of a quiet intersection and parked on the street. He approached the front door through a squeaky wrought-iron gate and rang the bell. A dog barked.

Eventually a woman in a maid's blue smock opened the door.

"I'm Ed Lipton." The woman's eyes widened in recognition of the name. "I was wondering if I might speak to Señorita Manning now."

She hesitated, then opened the door wider, nervously stepping aside to let him in.

"She has only just arrived. Let me see if she will see you.

Please—" she said, indicating a chair in the living room. "One moment."

The maid disappeared down a hallway. Lipton surveyed a formal room centered on an ugly old couch with polished mahogany end tables, gleaming knick-knacks and lace antimacassars carefully pinned to upholstered chairs. A clock ticked loudly in the hallway. He studied the geometric intricacies of the worn Oriental rug under his feet and listened.

There was a commotion down the hallway. The maid returned with two women, one young in a white cotton blouse and dark blue skirt, the second older wearing a somber gray dress. Lipton stood up. After escorting the women to the threshold, the maid hastened away.

He could tell instantly from the resemblance that he was meeting mother and daughter. Gabriela stood proudly erect as she shook his hand. She was pretty but her expression was fixed in a stern frown that Lipton construed as grief. The mother looked emotionally spent; her almond-shaped eyes shifted restlessly about the room.

"I'm sorry to come unannounced. I left a message. I'm with the American embassy and need to ask you a few questions about Richard Allen."

The mother perched on the edge of the stiff-backed Victorian sofa like a bird about to fly away. Gabriela took charge, indicating for Lipton to be seated. She folded her skirt tightly underneath her legs as she sat down beside her mother.

"What do you want to know?"

"First, let me express my condolences. I understand that you and Mr. Allen were engaged."

"No, we were not," she responded sharply.

"No? I was under the impression…" This was an interesting contradiction. Was she covering up in front of her mother?

"No."

"Then how would you describe your relationship?"

"We knew each other. He was a friend of my brother." The way she compressed her lips told him she was lying. He let it go.

"I see. Well, as a consular officer, it's one of my unfortunate duties to do things like this. When an American citizen is murdered, we must become involved. May I ask a few questions?"

Gabriela's arms pressed against her sides and her body barely moved as she consented.

He had prepared a set of questions that skirted the sensitive issue of Will's work but might provide an opportunity to glean information without her realizing it. He had the upper hand. She didn't know about her brother's death or that he knew about the foolhardy escapade at Colonia Dignidad. And, according to Will, she had no idea about his cover or the fact that he compromised it to win their release.

"Did Señor Allen ever indicate to you that his life was in danger? Had he ever been threatened by anyone or have cause to be alarmed for his safety?"

Gabriela shook her head. Her mother took her daughter's hand and held it.

"So you don't have any idea who might have shot him, or why?"

"No." Her voice was barely a whisper. "The police already asked me this."

The curt reply was one more indication of her reluctance to be questioned. "Yes, well, it helps me to hear your answers directly. Did Señor Allen mention any business dealings, or…" he pretended to search for the word even though he knew precisely what he wanted to ask, "or any personal activities that he was reluctant to discuss with you?"

Again she shook her head.

"When was the last time you communicated with him?"

"Last week. I wrote him a letter. He had stayed with us the weekend before. I don't even know if he received it before—"

She didn't know that her letter was found among Will's things at the morgue. Detective Morales must have been discreet for his own reasons.

"He stayed here? Did anything unusual happen that weekend? Did he behave oddly?" he asked, curious to see if she would mention Colonia Dignidad.

"No."

The lie was understandable given what had happened. But he wondered what else she was withholding and decided to raise the ante. "Could Señor Allen's murder be connected in any way to your brother's disappearance?"

"Please!" The mother clasped her long, thin hands in her lap and her eyes fixed on Lipton. "Do you know something about my son? Can you tell us anything?"

Mother and daughter seemed traumatized, the household locked in uncertainty, fear and grief. Mentioning the son had opened a door of fading hope.

He shook his head. "I'm sorry, Señora. I only heard this from the police."

The mother leaned back, collapsed nearly, against the couch. Gabriela turned and patted her mother's hand and whispered consolation. Señora de Manning wiped a tear from the corner of her eye. Then she stood up and excused herself. "I must find a tissue," she explained breathlessly. Lipton stood up as she left the room. Gabriela's fierce stare met his as he sat down again.

"She doesn't know that my brother is dead," she said after her mother was beyond hearing.

Lipton pretended not to understand. "Sorry?"

"Are you a spy, too?" she asked.

The question was uttered so softly he was unsure he'd heard it correctly.

"Pardon me?"

"Think I don't know?"

Lipton leaned forward, as if by bringing his body closer he might head off an unwanted outcome. Her comment opened up a whole new dimension to his inquiry. "Know what, Señorita?"

"Who Ricardo worked for."

"You mean First Republic?"

Gabriela's laugh was more like an incredulous gasp. Her bright eyes projected disgust, or contempt, or both. "I'm finished answering your questions. Please leave us alone."

Driving back to the hotel, Lipton's mind raced through the possibilities—an exciting process similar to when, finally called by his opponent in a poker game, he placed his cards on the table and waited to see his opponent's hand.

So she knew about Ernesto's death. Had Will told her? Had Will also told her about his double life and lied to him? How else could she have known? From something surreptitiously seen or overheard? Why did she withhold the information about going to Colonia Dignidad? Could she have been the source of a breach that led to Will's death?

And did she challenge him just now out of an angry desire to reveal that she knew the truth, or in an attempt to confirm her suspicions? If the latter, she had been disappointed. But was there a risk in her believing what she believed?

Lipton arrived at the hotel and his conclusions at the same time: She didn't know anything for sure. She didn't seem capable of causing harm to Will. And, most importantly, she could do no real harm to him or his remaining operatives.

The sun falling across Ed Lipton's desk on Halloween day held the intensity of summer, the promise of more sweltering heat coming to Santiago soon.

He looked up from the pile of mail on his desk to find a grinning Bill Bradshaw standing in front of him.

"Gotcha! God, I'm gonna miss seeing you try not to react." Bill was happy, counting the days until he was on his farm in Virginia. "Have you finished the report on Will P yet?"

"Which one? The Embassy report or HQ's?"

"The Embassy's. Hell, I thought you'd already written the other one."

Lipton shook his head. He hadn't written either.

Bill misinterpreted his frown. "Go easy on yourself, Ed. It wasn't your fault."

"When do you need it?"

"Today would be good. The ambassador's outa here tomorrow and I promised it. Let's put the matter to rest. Can do?"

"Can do."

By the time Lipton turned around from his credenza with the file, Bill was gone.

What Bill had said was true. He should have finished both reports by now. He opened the file: notes filling several pages on a legal pad with the paper-clipped documents he had received from the Carabineros, including two Polaroids of the pale corpse, one a grisly close-up of the wounds.

He fed a piece of letterhead into the typewriter and began to compose the consular report. Brevity was best since copies would be routed to Langley, the FBI and the State Department's central files.

CONFIDENTIAL

United States Government Memorandum
To: Deputy Chief of Mission
From: Ed Lipton – Political Officer
Date: October 31, 1973
Subject: Mr. Richard Henry Allen

Richard H. Allen, an American citizen living in Santiago and working as an employee of First Republic Insurance Group (New York), was murdered outside the company's offices at Avenida Bernardo O'Higgins, 600, on Thursday, October 18. Mr. Allen received a fatal gunshot wound to the chest at close range. The ballistics analysis indicates a 9mm caliber handgun was used in the assault. An autopsy revealed that one of the two bullets pierced the victim's aorta. Death was immediate.

Witnesses reported that the shooting occurred at approximately 6:15 p.m. as the subject left work. According to three witnesses, two men were waiting in a dark blue car parked in a loading zone in front of the building. When Mr. Allen appeared on the street, the passenger stepped from the car and approached. Witnesses describe the assailant as a man in his twenties or thirties of average height, wearing a light gray or blue windbreaker. The assailant shouted something, causing Mr. Allen to turn, at which point the assailant produced a handgun from his jacket and fired two shots at point-blank range. The gunman then ran to the car, which drove off in light traffic. The license number and make of car (Fiat according to two witnesses, Simca according to the third) were not clearly identified.

Police investigators have been unable to establish a motive for the crime. Evidence does not suggest an act of political terrorism or an attack directed against the USG. Moreover, no political faction or terrorist organization has claimed responsibility. Since witnesses indicate that Mr. Allen may have known his attacker, police suspect the crime was personal or business-related foul play. Attempted robbery has not been ruled out as a motive, although no valuables were taken. The police continue to investigate. The Embassy is cooperating with local authorities and has requested copies of all findings.

The Embassy notified the Department of State of the death on October 19. Following the autopsy, the body was released into Embassy custody. At the request of the victim's family, the body was returned to the United States via Braniff flight 1623 to Dallas on October 26.

Lipton read what he had written, initialed the page and proceeded to the second report, this one to be encrypted and cabled only to Langley:

CLASSIFIED / SECRET
To: CWHD
From: DCOS-Chile
Date: October 31, 1973
Subject: Death of Officer Will P
The Carabineros have been unable to determine a motive

for the murder of case officer William P, alias Richard Henry Allen. (See attached memorandum.) A reliable contact in the newly formed Directorate of National Intelligence (DINA), informs us that the act may have been an assassination coordinated and conducted by leftist extremists of the Movimiento de Izquierda Revolucionaria (MIR). Ballistics analysis indicates the weapon was of East German or Czechoslovakian origin, although neither DINA nor the Carabineros has been able to trace the weapon to any of the outlawed political factions believed to be operating inside Chile or externally. Significantly, no evidence suggests the involvement of a third-party government.

It is possible that Will P was the victim of an indiscriminate attack by an unknown criminal faction operating for non-political purposes. Given the unknown motive and identity of the perpetrators, every precaution has been taken with our active field operatives.

Despite the unclear circumstances surrounding his death, I recommend that Will P be considered a casualty of the covert operations implemented to oppose the previous Marxist Government of Chile, and that he receive posthumous recognition for his services in the line of duty, including any and all death benefits that may apply.

"Will, Will, Will," Lipton muttered as he walked the message to the communications room for encryption. The recommendation was a small token but there was little else he could do to help the devious bastard now.

POSTSCRIPT

Which Is More True?

A)

KISSINGER: The Chilean thing is getting consolidated and of course the newspapers are bleeding because a pro-Communist government has been overthrown.

NIXON: Isn't that something. Isn't that something.

KISSINGER: I mean instead of celebrating—in the Eisenhower period we would be heroes.

NIXON: Well, we didn't—as you know—our hand doesn't show on this one though.

KISSINGER: We didn't do it. I mean we helped them. [Garbled] created the conditions as great as possible.

NIXON: That is right. And that is the way it is going to be played.

—Telephone transcript, September 16, 1973, five days after the coup. Declassified and released, May 2004.

Or B)

Allende was overthrown eventually not because of anything that was done from the outside, but because his system didn't work in Chile and Chile decided to throw it out.

—Richard M. Nixon to David Frost in a television interview broadcast on May 25, 1977.

Acknowledgements

My interest in Chile began in the summer of 1973, when I met a girl from Chillán who has since become a dear friend. She was an AFS exchange student at the time. She told me how she arrived in the United States the year before with almost no money: foreign exchange restrictions prevented a 16-year-old traveling overseas alone to take with her more than $25. Shortly after we met the Tancazo took place, and only a few days later she returned home to a country that was about to change forever.

I am indebted to the following authors for their interpretations of the historical record: Peter Kornbluh, *The Pinochet File*; Nathaniel Davis, *The Last Two Years of Salvador Allende*; Robert Moss, *Chile's Marxist Experiment*; and Jonathan Haslam, *The Nixon Administration and the Death of Allende's Chile*. I am grateful to Mark Rudolph, Eugenia Toledo-Keyser, my sisters, Elizabeth and Leslie Gething, the Seattle Heights Writing Group, and Grupo Cervantes for their thoughtful comments on early drafts.

About the Author

Tom Gething studied English literature and creative writing at the University of Arizona. He spent a career in international business before pursuing fiction writing in earnest. *Under a False Flag* is his first novel. Though primarily based on historical research, it builds on his experience living, working and traveling in Latin America. He lives in the Seattle area. For more information, please go to: http://tomgething.wordpress.com

Made in the USA
Middletown, DE
07 May 2015